THE girl IN THE gatehouse

THE girl
IN THE
gatehouse

JULIE KLASSEN

BETHANY HOUSE PUBLISHERS

Minneapolis, Minnesota

Published by Bethany House Publishers
11400 Hampshire Avenue South
Bloomington, Minnesota 55438

Bethany House Publishers is a division of
Baker Publishing Group, Grand Rapids, Michigan.

Printed in the United States of America

Library of Congress Cataloging-in-Publication Data

Klassen, Julie.
    The girl in the gatehouse / Julie Klassen.
        p.   cm.
    ISBN   978-0-7642-0708-2 (pbk.)
    1. Women authors—Fiction. 2. England—Social life and customs—19th century—Fiction. I. Title.
    PS3611.L37G57   2010
    813'.6—dc22

                                               2010036779

To Brian,

who loves and forgives

And in loving memory of my mother and biggest fan

Loretta "Lori" Theisen

———————

June 1940 – August 2010

Mutual Forgiveness of each vice,

Such are the Gates of Paradise.

—William Blake

But small is the gate

and narrow the road that leads to life,

and only a few find it.

—Jesus Christ (NIV)

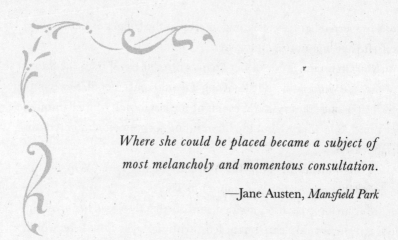

Where she could be placed became a subject of most melancholy and momentous consultation.

—Jane Austen, *Mansfield Park*

chapter 1

September 1813

The end of the only life I've known, thought Mariah Aubrey, looking back through the carriage window at the shrinking figures of her mother and sister. Nineteen-year-old Julia stood in the foreground, shoulders heaving as she wept. The sight seared Mariah's heart. Their mother stood behind, hand on Julia's arm, in consolation, in empathy— perhaps even in restraint. And there came their father, down the steps of Attwood Park. He had not come out to bid her farewell. He would not, he insisted, "sanction vice, nor seek to lessen its disgrace." But now he draped one arm around his wife and the other around his younger daughter, turning and shepherding them back inside, back into the only home Mariah had ever known. And might never see again.

Mariah turned back around. Miss Dixon, on the opposite bench, quickly averted her gaze, feigning interest in the fringes of her reticule, as if she had not noticed any tears.

Mariah bit the inside of her lip to control its trembling. She stared out the side window, despite knowing it would make her ill. She barely saw the passing countryside as events of the last month whirled through her mind. She winced, but the life-rending scenes neither altered nor disappeared.

"Long journey ahead, Miss Mariah," Dixon said. "Why not try to sleep? The miles shall pass more quickly."

Mariah forced a smile, nodded, and obediently closed her eyes. She doubted she would sleep, but at least with her eyes closed she would not see the pity on the face of her last ally in the world.

They traveled for two days, stopping at various coaching inns to change horses, stretch limbs, and take hurried meals. Late in the second day, Mariah fell into exhausted sleep at last, only to be jostled awake when the hired post-chaise careened, sending her slamming into its side.

"What happened?" she asked, righting herself.

Dixon straightened her hat atop blond hair threaded with silver. "I believe the driver swerved to avoid a lamb." She surveyed the pasture beyond the window. "We are definitely in sheep country."

Mariah rubbed her offended shoulder and looked out the windows on either side of the post-chaise. They were following a gentle, sparkling river on one side, and on the other, a rolling meadow dotted with white-faced sheep and nearly grown lambs. The river curved before them, and they crossed it on a stone bridge, passing a pair of red-brick mills on its bank. They entered a village of blond-stone cottages, with an inn, apothecary shop, stonemason's, and steepled parish church clustered around a triangular green.

"Is this Whitmore?" Mariah asked.

"I hope so." Dixon sighed. "My bones have had more than enough of these poorly sprung seats." Her former nanny was barely fifty, but she complained like a much older woman.

They left the small village behind, and only a few minutes later, the carriage made a sharp turn. Mariah looked up in time to see the imposing entrance to an estate—its high wall broken by an open columned gate.

Dixon leaned toward the window, like a potted plant seeking light. "Where is the gatehouse?"

"This must be the main entrance," Mariah said, explaining what she recalled from her aunt's letter. "The gatehouse is at a second entrance no longer in use."

Mariah could still barely grasp that she was now expected to live on her own, with only Miss Dixon as companion. Her father had insisted that even had there been no other young lady in his house to be endangered by Mariah's character, still he would not so insult the neighborhood by continuing to harbor her. How his words had cut, and cut still.

The carriage passed through the gate and followed a drive encircling acres of landscaped grounds—shaped hedges and a rose garden around a reflecting pond. At the apex of the curved drive stood impressive seventeenth-century Windrush Court. The manor house of golden blond stone stood two-and-a-half-stories high with dormer windows jutting from its slate roof. Banks of tall mullioned windows winked from both ground and first floors.

The carriage halted before the manor and lurched as the groom hopped down to lower the step. The front door of the house opened, and from between the columned archway stepped not her aunt but rather an odd figure. A man in his late fifties, in a plain dark suit of clothes, without the livery or regal bearing of either footman or butler. There was something unnatural about the way he held himself, as if one shoulder hitched slightly higher than the other.

The groom opened the carriage door, but the approaching man held up his palm to halt his progress. "Hold, there. One moment."

He gave Mariah a stiff bow. "Jeremiah Martin." He lifted his balding head, wreathed in silvery grey hair. "Are you Miss Aubrey?"

"Yes. Is my aunt not expecting me?"

"She is. But I am to direct you to the gatehouse."

"Thank you." Mariah hesitated. "May I quickly greet Mrs. Prin-Hallsey first?"

"No, madam. I am to take you to the gatehouse straightaway."

Her aunt had offered her a place to live but refused to receive her in person? Mariah glanced at Dixon to see how the opinionated woman would react, but Dixon was not looking at her. She was staring at the man, or rather at the hook that protruded where his left hand should be.

"I see." Mariah hoped her disappointment and embarrassment were concealed behind a stiff smile.

The man's blue eyes held hers a moment before flitting away. "I shall climb up and direct the coachman. Big place, Windrush Court."

A moment later, the carriage again lurched to life and rounded the other side of the curved drive.

Mariah glanced back at the house. The curtains on one of the first-floor windows parted and then closed. Then the carriage turned right, away from the manor house, and entered a copse of redwood and horse chestnut trees.

As they bounced along, Mariah swallowed back the hurt that her aunt had not at least greeted her. When the woman had been married to Mariah's uncle, "Aunt Fran" had shown an interest in her, even invited her to visit on several occasions. Though never an overly warm person, her aunt had been kind to Mariah in her youth, which only made this rejection more painful.

Impulsively, Mariah reached over and squeezed her companion's hand. "Thank you for coming with me."

Dixon pressed her hand in return, her blue eyes bright with unshed tears. "And what else would I have done?"

The carriage passed a gardener's cottage, with a wheelbarrow of potted autumn mums before it and a glass hothouse beside it. Then a carpenter's workshop, evidenced by long planks suspended between sawhorses. Over these hunched a thin middle-aged man who paused to tip his hat as they passed.

The trees thickened and the lane narrowed where grass and weeds had been allowed to breach a formerly well-maintained drive. Mariah craned her neck, looking through the trees for a glimpse of the gatehouse.

There it was.

Tall and narrow, built of caramel-colored Cotswold stone. *Not so bad*, Mariah thought. The gatehouse looked like a miniature two-story castle attached to an arched gate, with a turreted tower on either side of the gate, a story taller than the house itself. From the far turret and the opposite side of the gatehouse, the high wall that enclosed the entire estate curved away and disappeared within the wood.

The carriage halted, and the groom again hopped down and opened the door. This time, Mr. Martin did not protest their exit. In fact, descending from the equipage seemed to consume his full attention.

Mariah stepped down and regarded the large gate with ornamental filigrees atop sturdy iron bars. It had clearly been a major thoroughfare in and out of the estate at some point. Now it wore a thick chain and rusted padlock.

At closer inspection, the gatehouse itself appeared forlorn. The stone walls were cankered, the window glass cloudy, and several panes cracked. The small garden was overgrown and leggy. The adjacent pair of outbuildings—a small stable and woodshed—in a slumping state of disrepair. A rope swing hung from a tree, its wooden seat broken in two.

Mariah glanced at Dixon, but she was once again staring at Mr. Martin. The man paused near them to fish jingling keys from his pocket, and Dixon lifted a scented handkerchief to her nose without subtlety. The man did have a pungent odor. Not of uncleanliness,

Mariah surmised, but something else. Whatever it was, Dixon clearly disapproved.

He glanced over at Mariah and said sternly, "That gate is to remain locked, unless in case of fire or other dire emergency."

Curiosity pricked Mariah. "May I ask why?"

He lifted his normal right shoulder so that both were raised in a shrug. "Hasn't been used in years. Not since the road outside the main gate was widened into a turnpike."

His answer did not fully explain the locked gate, but Mariah did not press him.

Mr. Martin unlocked and pushed open the gatehouse door. He handed her the keys, and Mariah eagerly entered her new home.

The cloying odor of musty dampness and stale air met them inside a small kitchen. Dust covered the table and work counter. Dixon lifted an old basket upturned on the sideboard, only to discover a scattering of fennel-seed mouse droppings beneath. Her small nose wrinkled.

Mariah stepped from the kitchen into the drawing room at the front of the gatehouse. Something scurried out of sight as she entered. Dust-cloths shrouded a saggy settee and a wing chair. Water stains marked the wall beneath the front bow window, but at least the roof seemed sound. The moth-eaten draperies deserved to be burned and replaced, but perhaps they could wash and mend them instead. Mariah sighed. So very much to do, and such limited funds with which to do it.

Mr. Martin bade the coachman and groom to haul down their trunks and valises from the carriage boot and roof and carry them inside, but he departed without offering to help. Perhaps he could not, with a hook for a hand. Or perhaps he did not think this strange young woman, this distant relation of his mistress, worth the effort.

Dixon directed the transfer of two crates of foodstuffs and utensils into the dim kitchen, a crate of books and linens into the drawing room, and the trunks abovestairs.

Following the men, Dixon and Mariah climbed the narrow staircase to the first floor up, the banister shaking in their hands. There, they found one bedchamber on either end of a narrow passageway, with a small sitting room between them.

"Which would you like, Dixon?" Mariah asked, relieved to find the rooms habitable.

"You should have the larger, of course." Dixon hesitated at the window of the larger bedchamber, which overlooked the road and wood beyond. Above the treetops appeared the roof of a stark, boxlike building. Three black chimneys jutted from its ramparts, loosing coal smoke in triune columns of sooty grey.

"Not much of a view, I am afraid. If you'd prefer the other room, I don't mind."

"This is fine, Dixon. Thank you. What do you suppose that building is?"

"Don't know. But one strong wind and we'll be sweeping its soot from our floors." She turned. "Well, we had best get busy. This place won't scrub itself."

๑

For several days, Mariah and Dixon undertook the cleaning and airing of the gatehouse from ceiling to floorboard, from attic to cellar. They had to evict several creatures that had taken up residence in the chimneys and sweep up heaps of droppings. This was the only reason Dixon did not object when Mariah suggested adopting the cat that began shadowing their every move as they went in and out carrying filthy draperies to scald and refuse to burn.

On their fourth day there, Dixon called, "Miss Mariah! There's a carriage coming up the lane."

Mariah's heart lurched. A carriage from within the gated estate. Who could it be? She raced to the kitchen window and looked out at a grand coach pulled by a pair of matched bays. A liveried footman stepped down, opened its door, and offered his hand to the occupant.

There she was. Her aunt, the former Francesca Norris, now Mrs. Prin-Hallsey.

Her hair was different than Mariah remembered—rabbit-fur grey, curled and piled high in an elegant coif, with long corkscrew curls cascading over one shoulder. A wig, certainly. Aunt Norris had never had such thick hair, and what she'd had was reddish brown. Her aunt's face was powdered very light, but her brows and lashes were dark, making her brown eyes large and doelike. She wore a burgundy day dress with threads of silver and a high-necked lace collar. She held her head erect and walked regally toward the door. Mariah hurried to open it, but Dixon stayed her with a firm hand.

"Allow me, miss," she said in her most respectful voice, whipping the cap from Mariah's head. Mariah quickly untied her apron.

Dixon opened the door before Mariah could retreat into the drawing room. She was left standing there as her aunt strode into the humble kitchen as though she owned the place. And, in a sense, Mariah supposed she did.

"Aunt . . . That is, Mrs. Prin-Hallsey. How good to see you again." Mariah tossed the apron onto the table and curtsied.

"Is it?"

"Of course. Perhaps not . . . under such circumstances, but yes, I am happy to see you."

A smile compressed the woman's small, thin mouth. She dipped her head in graceful acknowledgement and followed Mariah into the drawing room.

She ignored Mariah's offer of a chair. "I shan't stay." Her large eyes studied her face. "How old are you now, Mariah? One and twenty?"

"Four and twenty."

The dark brows rose. "Really. Well. I shan't go on about how much older you are since last we met, for I don't wish you to return the favor. I will own you look well."

"Thank you. As do you."

Her aunt nodded. "And how are you settling in?"

"Very well, I think," Mariah said. "I appreciate your offer of lodgings."

Mrs. Prin-Hallsey waved her thanks away. "I am sorry I could not greet you upon your arrival. Hugh . . . That is, *I* was indisposed." She gestured through the open kitchen door to two footmen waiting outside. "I have brought a few things."

The liveried young men stepped inside, the first hefting an ornate square chest.

"This is a chest I brought with me to Windrush Court. It contains only a few personal belongings. I would feel more at ease if it were under your roof for now. My relationship with my late husband's son, Hugh, is difficult at best. You understand."

Mariah didn't understand but simply nodded.

With a delicate gloved hand, Mrs. Prin-Hallsey gestured the second footman forward.

"And here are a few things for you." Her aunt began lifting items from the basket the young man held. "This candle lamp was my grandmother's." She held up a twine-wrapped bundle of candles. "And a dozen tapers to go with it. And here is a tin of coffee and another of tea. Cook sent along a variety of baked goods as well." With a wave of her hand, she directed the footman to hand the basket to Mariah.

"I shall have the chest put in the attic, shall I?" Mrs. Prin-Hallsey said. "The turret has attic space as I remember?"

"Yes," Mariah answered, though the question had clearly been rhetorical. She wondered how her aunt knew about the attic, and couldn't imagine what might have possessed her to venture inside this long-abandoned gatehouse before now.

The young footman bearing the chest started for the stairs.

"Have you anything else you would like my men to carry up to the attic while we are here?"

Mariah thought quickly. "We have two trunks, now all but empty, in the first-floor passage."

"Very well." Mrs. Prin-Hallsey nodded toward the second footman, and he followed the first.

Mariah felt discomfited at strangers making free with what had so quickly become her home. Still, she smiled at Mrs. Prin-Hallsey. "Thank you, Aunt Fran." The old name slipped out before Mariah could think the better of it.

The woman's eyes widened. "That is an address I have not heard in years, nor missed either. You may call me—" she considered—"Aunt Francesca. Or Mrs. Prin-Hallsey, if you prefer."

"Of course. Forgive me." Mariah felt chastised, yet her aunt had not minded the name before. "And thank you again for the gifts."

Once more, the elegant nod of acknowledgement. "Think nothing of it."

A few minutes later, her aunt was gone, her entourage with her.

Mariah took herself back upstairs, glad to see how much space had been freed by the removal of the trunks. She found herself standing at the window, staring at the roof and chimneys visible above the autumn-gold trees.

The floorboard squeaked behind her, announcing Dixon's presence. "I asked one of those footmen about the building across the road."

"Oh?" Mariah glanced at Dixon over her shoulder. "And what did you find out?"

Gaze fixed on the window, her companion said quietly, "That's the parish poorhouse."

Mariah stared at the dark roof once more and shuddered. *Poorhouse* . . . Suddenly the gatehouse did not seem like such a bad fate.

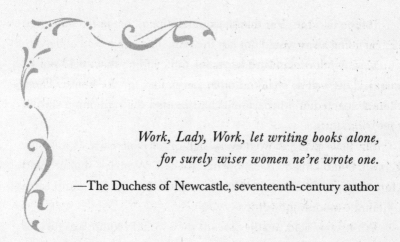

Work, Lady, Work, let writing books alone,
for surely wiser women ne're wrote one.

—The Duchess of Newcastle, seventeenth-century author

chapter 2

FIVE MONTHS LATER
FEBRUARY 1814

*L*ate autumn and winter had been cold, lonely, and disheartening. Mrs. Prin-Hallsey had not once returned, nor had she invited her niece to the great house. Mariah had heard from the estate carpenter, Jack Strong, that the mistress had been ill during much of December and January. Miss Dixon, too, had fallen ill. She suffered from the ague for several endless weeks during which Mariah had used the greater portion of her strength—as well as her funds—to keep Dixon's bedchamber warm and her every need met. Even so, how Dixon had shivered and wheezed. Mariah had walked to the village apothecary several times to purchase remedies as well as heavy wool socks and a muffler—made, she was told, by "inmates of Honora House," the poorhouse so near her own abode.

It soon became clear that the annual stipend her father had given her on going away would not last the year. They had been obliged to purchase window glass and fabric for the bedding that could not be salvaged, as well as coal and other necessities for the house. Then, the unexpected apothecary bills had eroded the remaining sum to precarious lows.

But now spring showed every sign of arriving early. It was only February, and already the snow had melted. Wrinkled rhubarb and clumps of purple crocus had begun to push through the damp earth to join the modest snowdrops.

While less frigid weather meant they would require less fuel for their fires, and could soon plant a vegetable garden, still their plight was desperate. Mariah pored over their household accounts and determined she would have to do something very soon. She recalled the words of Admiral Nelson, *"Desperate affairs require desperate measures,"* and knew it was time for her to take desperate measures as well.

She dipped a quill into the inkpot and began a letter to her brother Henry. A few years her senior, Henry Aubrey was a struggling junior solicitor in Oxford. She had not seen him since last summer but was certain their father had apprised him of the situation and forbidden him to harbor her. But her request, Mariah reasoned, was of a professional rather than a personal nature.

In her letter, Mariah described her "desperate" proposal and asked Henry to call at the Windrush gatehouse if he thought it feasible, or simply to write a reply in the negative if he thought it not. She hated to risk their father's wrath, or to drag Henry away from his work, if he judged her plan a futile one.

Dixon, much improved, posted the letter for her.

For the remainder of that week, Mariah spent a great deal of time pacing back and forth across the drawing room, while Dixon calmly attended to their mending.

"Do you think he will come?" Mariah asked for the twentieth time.

Dixon pulled a long thread through a torn shift. "Did you not write and ask him to come?"

"Yes, but perhaps he has spoken with Father. Thought the better of it."

"He will come," Dixon insisted. "You must trust your brother, and trust God."

Mariah did trust Henry. She was not as sure about God. Not anymore.

In the midst of her worry, the good-natured estate gardener, Albert Phelps, came over with a basket of flower bulbs. Both he and Jack Strong had proved helpful neighbors over the long fall and winter. Mr. Phelps was stout and had closely cropped salt-and-pepper hair and a clear glint in his eye whenever he looked at Dixon. This amused Mariah but seemed to make the older woman wary.

"They don't look like much now," Mr. Phelps said. "But before you know it, these gladioli and freesias will burst forth and brighten your back garden."

Dixon was stiff and silent, so Mariah thanked the man in her stead.

"I'd be happy to plant them for ya, if you like." He was looking at Dixon as he made his offer, so this time Mariah awaited her friend's reply.

Dixon lifted her chin and said coolly, "We are both grateful for your help, Mr. Phelps."

A broad smile lit his ruddy face. "And in a few weeks, I shall bring a crate of seedlings I started in the hothouse. Bit early yet. But just right for bulbs."

Mariah wondered if a man had ever brought flowers—even flower bulbs—to Miss Dixon. For a moment, Mariah set aside her worries and smiled.

It was about time.

On Saturday afternoon a knock sounded at the front door of the gatehouse—a rarity indeed—and Dixon rose to answer it. When Mariah saw Henry standing in the threshold, her heart and throat constricted. She longed to run to him and throw her arms around his neck, but she hesitated as she had never done before in his presence. Would he be cold toward her now? Distant? Disapproving?

"Mariah." His eyes lit with warmth and compassion, and he strode forward to greet her.

Her reserve fell away and she relished his embrace. "Oh, Henry, thank you for coming. I was afraid you would not. I would not have blamed you, but—"

"Of course I came, Rye. As soon as I could."

Mariah studied her brother as he kindly greeted Dixon. He appeared much the same as ever—still handsome, though perhaps his waistline had thickened a bit and his brown hair, the same shade as her own, had thinned.

After Dixon excused herself, Mariah looked up into Henry's hazel eyes, so like their mother's. "Do you think it a ridiculous idea? Please tell me if you do."

"I do not. I think it a marvelous notion. Perhaps a way to bring some good out of this muddle." He lowered himself onto the settee. "Which one, do you think?"

"I was thinking of *The Brambles of Bath*." She sat beside him. "Anonymously of course. I have revised and edited it over the winter. But *Daughters* is nearly finished as well, if you think that one better."

"I enjoyed them both. Julia did as well, I remember. Hmm . . ." He stroked his chin. "You may wish to change the titles, if you don't want Father to recognize them."

Their father loathed novels, denouncing them as a poor influence on impressionable young women. "Excellent point," she said. "No need to give Father more to disapprove of."

Henry's eyes turned plaintive. "Rye . . ."

But Mariah cut him off. She didn't want his pity or to discuss the past. "Do you think that publisher you know might be interested?"

He inhaled. "No idea. I can but ask."

"Are you sure you do not mind doing so? Should Father find out . . ."

"I think the chances of that happening are rather slim." He took her hand. "I am happy to do it. I wish there were more I could do, but—"

"Hush, Henry. I know. I am grateful you came at all. I would not take money from you even if you had it to give. This way you can honestly say you have not harbored me."

Henry crossed his arms over his chest and frowned. "I know they cannot have you at home with Julia, but not to provide for his own daughter . . ."

"Do not judge him harshly," Mariah soothed. "He no doubt thought the amount he gave me would last a full year. You know Mamma and Weston handle all the financial affairs and have done so for years."

"Could you not write and ask for more?"

She gave him a pointed look. "Would you?"

He shuddered. "Never."

"I no doubt could have managed more efficiently, but . . ."

Dixon came in carrying a tray of coffee and biscuits. "You do an amazing job, Miss Mariah. Never doubt it. Bricks without straw, I'd say."

Henry's brows rose. "Indeed?" He smiled at Mariah and squeezed her hand. "I am proud of you."

"Proud? I . . . Thank you, Henry." Tears stung her eyes.

He looked flustered at her reaction. "There now, don't go spoiling your complexion over me." He stood. "Thank you, Dixon, but I cannot stay. Now, where is this masterpiece?"

Mariah rose and stepped to the drawing room table. There, she rewrote the cover page with a revised title, *A Winter in Bath*, and wrapped the manuscript in brown paper and twine. Dixon, meanwhile, handed her brother a bundle of biscuits for the journey home.

Henry thanked her, and then turned expectant eyes toward Mariah.

She hesitated, cradling the thick rectangle in her arms. What if the publisher thought it awful? He very well might. Still, she had to try. She handed over the heavy parcel.

Henry weighed it in his hand. "I thought you said a novel, not a dictionary!" He winked.

Mariah tried to smile but failed. "Be careful with it, Henry. It is my only copy of the final draft."

"Never fear. I shall guard it as though it were your firstborn." He placed his free hand on Mariah's shoulder. "Now, take care, my dear, and go and finish the second!"

On a Friday morning in late February, Mariah took a respite from writing. She stood at her bedchamber window, watching as two boys from the poorhouse stretched a length of rope across the seldom-traveled road. Curiosity rising, she unlatched and pushed open her window.

"Good morning, boys," she called down. "What are you doing with that rope?"

"Hello, miss!" Stout eleven-year-old George waved his jaunty newsboy cap. "We're charging a toll for any girl what wants to cross."

Mariah felt her brows rise. "A toll on this road? How much?"

George and his chum Sam exchanged grins. "Just one."

Mariah cocked her head to the side. "One what?"

"One kiss."

Scrawny Sam broke out laughing and covered his mouth with a grimy hand. George looked at him as though he were an idiot.

"It is Kissing Friday, is it not?" George defended.

Is it? Mariah had completely forgotten. "I suppose it is. But I don't think you shall have much business there."

George shrugged. "We've already kissed every girl in the poorhouse."

Sam nodded vigorously.

George dug the toe of his boot into the dirt. "I don't suppose you have any need to cross this way, miss?"

Mariah smiled. "I am afraid not, George. Perhaps some other lucky lady will come along."

"Could be."

"And when she does," Sam shouted, "we'll be ready for her!"

Shaking her head, Mariah waved and shut the window. *Kissing Friday.* How long it had been since she'd thought of it. The one day schoolboys could buss any girl they chose without fear of retribution.

Mariah took herself downstairs to see what she might find to eat. She was feeling peckish, for she had eaten little at breakfast. Dixon had scorched the porridge again.

The kitchen was empty, but through the open window she heard voices outside in the back garden.

"Do you know what day it is, Miss Dixon?" the gardener asked, a grin on his ruddy face and a twinkle in his eye.

"Friday?"

"Not just any Friday. It's Kissing Friday—and you know what that means."

Dixon planted a fist on her hip. "Mr. Phelps. You are no schoolboy. I hope you are not thinking of stealing a kiss."

"Aww, Miss Dixon, don't make me pinch yer backside."

Outrage stretched Dixon's features. "My—! You would not dare."

He shrugged easily. "That is the traditional penalty."

"Albert Phelps, if you dare pinch my . . . anything, you shall find this trowel upside your head forthwith!"

"Miss Dixonnnn . . ." He pouted, looking very like an overgrown little boy. Like George or Sam, only less adorable.

Mariah bit back a grin at the man's antics. She had to admire his courage.

"Just a kiss on the cheek, then?" He pinched the air. "A small one?"

From the window, Mariah had a clear view of Dixon in her gardening gloves and apron, an old bonnet framing her thin face and prominent blue eyes. She looked irritated and . . . something else. What was it?

"Oh, very well," Dixon said in a longsuffering manner, tilting her head and offering her cheek like a patient preparing to be lanced. But Mr. Phelps did not swoop down. Instead, he leaned in carefully and pressed a slow, gentle kiss on Miss Dixon's cheek. For a moment, Dixon did not move, just stood there, face tilted, eyes . . . filling with tears.

"Th-thank you, Mr. Phelps," she murmured distractedly.

"Thank *you*, Miss Dixon." The gardener beamed, seemingly unaware of the sheen in her eyes. He slapped his hat against his leg, set it jauntily upon his head, and strode away.

He met the tall, thin carpenter, Jack Strong, coming up the lane.

"She thanked me for kissin' 'er!" he called, pleased as could be.

Mariah expected Dixon to shout some rejoinder or at least to grumble about lips that kiss and tell, but instead she peeled off her gloves and drifted, dazed, into the kitchen.

Concerned, Mariah asked, "Dixon, what is it?"

Tears again shimmered in Dixon's blue eyes. "Who would have guessed? To have my first kiss like that . . ."

Mariah pressed her friend's hand. "Plenty of girls have their first kiss on Kissing Friday. I know I did."

Dixon expelled a dry puff of air. "My first kiss, and no doubt my last."

Mariah grinned. "Not if Mr. Phelps has anything to say about it."

Dixon squeezed her eyes shut and slowly shook her head. "Old fool."

But whether referring to Mr. Phelps or herself, Mariah wasn't certain.

She stepped outside to thank Jack Strong for coming to repair the rope swing and to ask after his wife, who was housekeeper up at the great house. Then, taking a piece of cheese with her, Mariah went upstairs to continue revising *Daughters of Brighton*, a story of two cousins—one vivacious, the other timid and chaste—both in love with the same man. She paused once more at the window, nibbling her cheddar. George and Sam had given up or moved on, for the road was empty. Mariah thought dully that perhaps she ought to have obliged the boys with a kiss. It might have been her last as well.

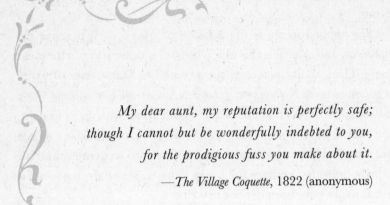

My dear aunt, my reputation is perfectly safe;
though I cannot but be wonderfully indebted to you,
for the prodigious fuss you make about it.

—*The Village Coquette*, 1822 (anonymous)

chapter 3

hen a knock shook the gatehouse the next morning, Mariah laid aside her quill, rose from the little writing table in the sitting room, and hurried downstairs, expecting to find Jack Strong or Mr. Phelps.

But neither man stood on her back doorstep. Instead it was Jeremiah Martin, her aunt's manservant.

Mariah shivered. Perhaps it was his icy blue eyes. The strange high shoulder. The hook. Or the sudden fear at what his unexpected call might bode. He had not come to the gatehouse since the day Mariah and Dixon arrived last autumn.

"Hello. Mr. Martin, is it?"

"Just Martin, if you please." He gave the barest bow, black suit straining. "The mistress bids you come to the great house."

Dread filled her. "Is Mrs. Prin-Hallsey unwell?"

"That is it exactly, miss. At the strike of eleven and not before."

He turned and walked away, his gait awkward as he swung the one hand but held the hook tightly to his side.

Dixon appeared at her elbow. "I am surprised a woman like your aunt can abide having that man about the place."

"It is surprising," Mariah agreed. She shook her head, lips pursed. "What can she want?"

At the appointed hour, Mariah walked over to the great house, dressed in one of her finer frocks of Clarence blue. She climbed the stairs and crossed the covered portico to the imposing front door. She had knocked only once when the door swung open. Martin, brushing past the footman, gestured her inside. "Two minutes late."

Mariah bristled. "The walk took longer than I expected."

With a dismissive wave, he led the way through an echoing entry hall adorned with a massive stone fireplace. Glancing up, Mariah saw a magnificent ceiling with carved and painted medallions of fruit, flowers, angels, and birds.

They reached the grand staircase. At the landing were displayed two large formal portraits lit by a glittering chandelier above. The first was of a man in middling years, with thick gray hair and long side-whiskers, his green eyes downturned and nearly sad. Beside it was a portrait of an arrogantly handsome young man, with black hair and dark eyes, and a jewel in his cravat. "Who are they, Martin?"

"The older gentleman is the mistress's late husband, Mr. Frederick Prin-Hallsey. And the younger man is his son, Master Hugh."

Mariah nodded and followed Martin up the remaining stairs and down an echoing corridor. At its end, he opened a paneled door and gestured her inside, closing the door behind her.

While the rooms Mariah had passed had struck her as being stark, this room was crowded with furnishings—paintings, clocks, candelabra, and statuary. At the center of it all, Francesca Prin-Hallsey sat upright in a neatly made canopied bed. She was fully dressed in black crepe and lace and her curled wig. A lap rug over her legs was the only concession to her invalid status.

"Mariah. Thank you for coming. Does black suit me? I think not, but Dr. Gaston assures me I shall go any day, so I wish to be prepared. You see Miss Jones here in black as well." She lifted a lace-wreathed hand toward a plain but kind-looking woman sitting on the far side of the bed. "She does not like it, but I say why wait for all the fuss and ceremony until after I am dead and buried and cannot enjoy it?"

Miss Jones shook her head, sharing a wry smile with Mariah. She wore an unadorned bombazine day dress and was sewing what appeared to be black funeral arm bands. Mariah hoped they would not be needed for a long while.

Mariah sat in a hard-backed chair near the bed. "You look well to me, Aunt."

"Do I? Dr. *Ghastly* will not like to hear it. Hugh either, I daresay."

Mariah did not know how to respond.

Mrs. Prin-Hallsey straightened her lace cuffs. "How is life in the gatehouse?"

"Fine. Quiet."

"You still have my chest?"

"Of course."

"Have you looked inside?"

Mariah hesitated. "I . . . no . . ."

Her aunt's eyes twinkled. "Aha. You tried, but found it locked, did you not?" She pulled at the chain around her neck, and from her bodice emerged an ornate old key.

"And nor shall you, until I am dead and buried." She tucked the key back into its hiding place. "After that, you may sift through my things all you like. You never know. You may find something valuable, or at least interesting."

Before Mariah could thank her, her aunt continued, "Whatever you do, do not tell Hugh. Some of my things have gone missing already, and I suspect he is selling whatever he can to pay down his gambling debts. Wicked boy."

Her aunt cocked her head to one side, and for a moment, Mariah feared the heavy wig would topple.

"I remember you as a child, my dear." She regarded Mariah levelly. "You and I have more in common than you might guess."

"How so?"

Mrs. Prin-Hallsey smiled cryptically and then leaned forward. "If Hugh throws you out after I die, take the chest with you. Promise me that."

Would he? Mariah swallowed. "I promise."

"Good. That is settled." Francesca Prin-Hallsey leaned back against her cushions and closed her eyes. Mariah realized she had been dismissed.

On her way down the portico stairs, Mariah saw a man striding toward the house from the stable. She recognized him from the portrait hanging inside. Hugh Prin-Hallsey, only son and heir of Frederick Prin-Hallsey, by his first wife. Both now deceased. Though still handsome—tall, with straight black hair, thick dark brows and side-whiskers—Hugh appeared a decade older than the portrait and was somewhere in his mid to late thirties. He wore a well-made riding coat and walked with an easy, long-legged stride and elegant bearing. As he neared, she noticed a few lines between his brows and alongside a smirking mouth.

His dark eyes lit with interest. "Hello there. How do you do? Hugh Prin-Hallsey." He bowed. "And you are?"

She hesitated, fearing his reaction when he learned who she was. "I am Miss Aubrey. And I know who you are."

"Do you indeed? Have we met? I should think I would remember such a lovely creature."

"We have not met. But I have seen your portrait in the house."

"Have you? And what do you think?" He puffed out his chest and lifted his chin. "Does it do me justice?"

She grinned at his comical swagger. "Whatever the artist was paid, the sum was too little."

He quirked one heavy black brow. "I think the lady replies in riddles."

She changed the subject. "I have just been to see Mrs. Prin-Hallsey, who is not in the best of health, as you know."

She noticed him wince, and wondered if the news distressed him as much as it appeared to.

He quickly righted this misapprehension. "How I dislike hearing that name used for anyone but my dear mamma—God rest her soul." He sighed.

"I am sorry." For his mother's death or for using her appellation, Mariah did not clarify.

His wince deepened into a grimace. "Do not tell me you are the supposed *niece*."

She smiled apologetically. "I am afraid so. I live in the gatehouse."

"So I have recently learned. Pity."

She wanted to ask which aspect of these circumstances inspired the word, but refrained.

He folded his arms behind his back. "You say your aunt is not in good health?"

"No. The physician told her it will not be long."

"Excellent. First good news I have had all month."

Mariah gaped. "Mr. Prin-Hallsey, that is unkind in you."

"No doubt. But I'll not feign a regret I do not feel. How she would scoff if I did. She is well aware of my opinion of her, and I daresay her opinion of me is little better."

Mariah could not contradict him. "Still, she looked well to me."

"That's too bad. Say—" He gave her a sharp look. "How much are you paying for the gatehouse?"

She stared at him, stunned at the bold question. The truth was she paid nothing. "I . . . That is, your . . . my aunt was very generous in allowing me—"

"Never mind—I shall speak with my steward on the matter. And now I must bid you good day, Miss . . . ?"

"Aubrey."

He frowned. "Aubrey . . . I have heard that name before. But you say we have not met?"

She shook her head.

"Well. It will come to me. Now, please excuse me. I must go in and make certain the old bat is not hoarding any more of my mother's things. Good day."

"Good day," she murmured, but he had already mounted the stairs.

Mariah watched him disappear into the house, not knowing which she feared more. What he might do when he learned of her free rent, or what he might remember about her.

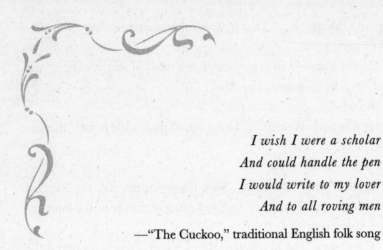

I wish I were a scholar
And could handle the pen
I would write to my lover
And to all roving men

—"The Cuckoo," traditional English folk song

chapter 4

ariah set her quill in its holder and rose.
Ting.

There was the sound again, at her window pane. She stepped to the window and peered down through the wavy glass. There below her, as she had anticipated, was the round, expectant face of George Barnes. While the other poorhouse children Mariah had seen were thin, George managed to remain stout. He had fair cheeks that blushed easily, small pale blue eyes, and light brown hair. He wore a snug tweed jacket and riding breeches, stained and worn thin at the knees.

She pried up the lever and pushed open the window. She could already hear Dixon at the front door below.

"You there. Cease and desist this instant. Do you mean to break the windows? Have you any idea the price of glass these days, young man?"

"Sorry, mum. I only meant to get 'er attention."

"Then why not knock at the door like a decent person?"

Mariah knew the answer to this but noticed with approval that the eleven-year-old was clever enough not to reply. He was no doubt afraid Miss Dixon would box his ears.

"Here I am, Mr. Barnes," Mariah called down. "Ball thrown over the gate again, was it?"

"That's it, miss. Sorry, miss."

"No trouble. I shall be down directly."

She met Dixon at the bottom of the narrow stairs. Her former nanny scowled. "You've spoilt him, Miss Mariah. He'll run you ragged if you let him."

"I don't mind. I have been sitting too long as it is." Mariah eyed Dixon's bonnet and shawl. "Where are you off to?"

A flicker of apology creased her friend's narrow face. "Mrs. Watford's. You know, for tea and whist."

"Of course. Have a nice time."

Since her recovery, Dixon had returned to visiting her new friends on the estate and in the village, while Mariah limited her own society to Dixon, her cat, Chaucer, and a few poorhouse children.

Dixon tilted her head. "Will you come, Miss Mariah? You would be most welcome." Her prominent, hooded blue eyes were gentle. And radiated pity.

"Thank you, no, Dixon. Do you need me to finish the jam?"

"If you would not mind. The pots are cooling now. And I have left a nice fish stew for your dinner."

Mariah forced a smile. "Thank you."

Dixon pulled on gloves and hooked a covered basket over her arm. Mariah wondered what offering Dixon was bearing to poor Mrs. Watford. Hopefully not fish stew.

After Dixon left, Mariah walked to the kitchen door. Outside, she crossed the damp grass and looked this way and that for the ball.

George Barnes stood on the other side of the gate, looking for all the world like a young convict behind bars, though she was the one inside.

"There it is." He pointed. "Under that shrub with the white flowers."

She bent and plucked the ball from beneath the blackthorn already blooming on this early March day. Noticing the torn seam and threadbare state of the old hide ball, she wished she had the money to buy him a new one.

"There you are, Mr. Barnes." She tossed the ball easily over the gate.

He caught it in one hand. "Good throw!" he said. "Thanks."

She ought to be a good throw. A good catch too. She had grown up with two older brothers, after all. Henry, as well as Richard, whom she had not seen since he and his wife sailed for India two years ago.

George turned and scampered across the yard to the poorhouse lane, where he rejoined a group of stringy boys awaiting him.

Mariah returned to the kitchen, wrinkling her nose at the smell of Dixon's fish stew. A loaf of bread which had failed to rise properly sat on the sideboard. Miss Dixon had many sterling qualities. She was loyal, intelligent, hardworking, and forthright. But the woman simply could not cook a palatable meal. Which, Mariah supposed, was not surprising, considering she'd been hired into the Aubrey household years ago as nursery-governess, and not a cook. She had been Nanny Dixon to Mariah and Julia when the girls were young. The thought brought pain. How Mariah missed her sister.

She sighed and dipped a modest serving of stew into a chipped bowl. With effort, she sawed off a shingle of bread, then sat alone at the kitchen table. Briefly bowing her head, she said quietly, "For your provision of food and shelter, and Dixon, I am truly thankful." She felt awkward and uncomfortable as she prayed, as if talking with an estranged friend—one she had wronged very badly.

Her six-fingered cat, Chaucer, came and curled around her ankles. The stray with the extra digit had earned his keep by catching many a gatehouse mouse over the fall and winter. But now that spring was in the air, he spent his time hunting out of doors and often left his small victims on her doorstep.

Mariah set her bowl, with the remaining morsels of stew, onto the floor at her feet. "There you are, you little beggar. Don't tell Dixon, or neither of us shall hear the end of it."

The silver and grey cat sniffed at the bowl, then walked away, leaving the scraps of fish and potato untouched.

Rising, Mariah donned her work apron and did the washing up. Then, not wanting any stray hairs to end up in the jam, she donned a white cap. She cut tissue, brushed oil and beaten egg whites onto each side of the thin paper, and then covered each pot with the oiled and egged papers.

Not everyone liked rhubarb, Mariah knew. It was viewed as primarily medicinal by many. Considering Dixon's recent malady, Mariah thought it wise to preserve all they could from the patch that had sprung up beside the stable. She preferred strawberry or raspberry jam herself, but those fruits would not be in season until June and July respectively. Last week, Dixon had gone to the village market and purchased at discount a basket of past-peak imported oranges. These, plus several exorbitantly priced lemons, they had boiled with sugar into marmalade, pots of which stood proudly on their larder shelves.

The last jar covered, Mariah glanced up through the kitchen window and noticed how dark it already was, although the March days were becoming longer. A storm was brewing. Had Dixon taken an umbrella?

A crack of thunder rent the air, and Mariah jumped. She wiped her hands on her apron and stared out at the roiling sky, feeling her emotions roil in tandem.

Perhaps it was the approaching storm that made her give in. Or the fact that Dixon was out for the evening, leaving her alone in the gatehouse. There was no one to witness her weakness.

Or perhaps it was because her mood had sunk as low as Venus in the morning sky, as it sometimes did when the past revisited her, each memory like a sharp hailstone pinging, pecking against her brain. *How could I have been so stupid? Foolish, foolish girl!* And doubts and despondency would rise like waves in the North Sea, threatening to crumble her stoic façade. Had she conjured up, imagined the whole affair? Surely not. Had he not given her every assurance of his love? Of their future together? Was he really as innocent of misleading her as he later insisted?

She needed, once more, to reassure herself their courtship had not been merely the fancy of a desperate young woman.

The proof was tucked away in the attic, at the bottom of her trunk, where Dixon was not apt to stumble upon it whilst tidying the rooms. Where Mariah would not be tempted to look too often, to while away her days, her life, on futile regrets. She had gone for months without venturing up the steep turret stairs and would have resisted longer had curiosity over her aunt's chest not gotten the better of her one gloomy midwinter afternoon. She had gone up and attempted to peek inside—to no avail. Even then she had not looked into her own trunk, or reread her own letters. Most days she was strong enough without them.

Not today. Not tonight in an empty house—an old ramshackle gatehouse—far from home, far from family, with the wind howling and the rain lashing the windowpanes and her soul heaving with loneliness and loss.

She lit her brightest candle lamp, the stout, heavy one her aunt had given her, and carried it upstairs.

The flame guttered and swayed, casting flickering shadows on the narrow staircase rising from the passage outside Dixon's bedchamber to the attic above. The old wooden stairs creaked beneath her slippered feet, and the attic door whined when she pushed it open. Inside, the wind shook the turret and whistled through the cracks around the solitary narrow window. Beyond it, lightning flashed, momentarily brightening the small musty room nearly filled by her and Dixon's trunks, her aunt's ornate chest, and a few odds and ends of broken furniture.

She pulled an old cloth from her apron pocket to wipe the floor, then sank to her knees before her own trunk and lifted the heavy lid. She slid aside a layer of crinkled paper and a tissue-wrapped parcel, which contained her grandmother's lace shawl—too delicate to wear, too dear to part with. Beneath this were two bandboxes, stacked. In the first was a hat, as one would expect of a bandbox, a confection of flowers and ribbons and springtime, as youthful and flirtatious as she had once been. If she but opened the lid and peeked inside, she would be transported back to that day. The last day she had worn it. And likely ever would.

She set this box aside and lifted forth the second hat box, leaning back and settling it on her legs. She raised its lid and placed it next to her, as well as a thin children's reader, which she'd kept as a reminder of happier days. And to disguise what lay beneath.

Her fingers no longer trembled as they once had when she lifted the ribbon-bound bundle of letters, but her heart still pounded. A sickly feeling descended upon her, as if she were a child having eaten too many sweets, and anticipating the stomachache and nausea ahead.

She slipped the first letter from the ribbon and unfolded it, emotions pumping. Would the reassurance she sought be there? Or had she tried too hard to read between the lines, to find the meaning she desired, when it simply wasn't there? She picked up the candle lamp in one hand, while the letter fluttered in the other.

My dear girl,

    How sorry I am to tell you that it is not within my power to return in time for the Westons' ball as I had hoped. My father insists my European tour shall not be complete without a fortnight in Rome. As he is paying for the trip, I feel duty bound to honor his wishes. But soon we shall be together, and neither duty nor distance shall keep us apart.

For now, the lock of your hair, and thoughts of you, bring both peace and torment to my lonely heart. . . .

A sharp pounding shook the gatehouse, loud enough to be heard over the wind and rain. Mariah's heart started. She dropped the letter, like a thief, caught. Who could be knocking? Dixon had the key.

She quickly folded the letter and stuck it with the rest of the bundle back inside the bandbox and, fingers belatedly trembling, returned everything into its hiding place and hurriedly shut the trunk.

Bang, bang, bang.

Her heart leapt to her throat.

Who in the world would be out in this? Whoever it was could not bear good tidings. *Lord, let Dixon be well. Please, not a relapse. And let nothing have happened to Henry. . . .*

Bang, bang, bang.

"All right! All right!"

Wiping her hands on her stained apron, Mariah huffed down the stairs and across the drawing room, carrying the candle lamp as she went. She hesitated before opening the front door. The Strongs and Mr. Phelps always came to the kitchen door. And Henry would not call so late. She hesitated all the more because she was alone and it was all but dark outside. Was it really wise to open her door to some unknown caller?

Another round of pounding roused her ire, and she unlocked and opened the door a few inches, saying as tartly as Dixon might, "You need not break the door."

She froze. Her pulse pounded in her ears as loudly as the knocking had been. Her mind shouted, *Danger!* A man stood in cocked hat and greatcoat. Tall, imposing, grim. A stranger. A strange man at her door at night? She fought the urge to slam and lock the door. How she wished Dixon would return.

She lifted the lamp higher to see his face. Saw a grimace of pain there . . . a gash on his cheek. She opened the door a few inches more.

"Yes?" she asked, her voice sounding too timid. She drew her shoulders back, determined not to show fear. He need not know she was alone.

He grimaced again, from pain and perhaps to clear the rain from his eyes. "Is your master at home?"

She hesitated as reactions—annoyance, offense, alarm—wrestled for preeminence. He presumed she was a servant. Casting a swift glance down at herself, she realized there was little else he could think. She was wearing a mobcap, a dingy puce frock she wore to help Dixon with messy chores, and a soiled apron besides.

But as much as she wanted to sharply retort that she had no master and wasn't a servant, she was too fearful of letting him know there was no man in the house, or anyone else for that matter.

"What do you need?" she asked instead.

"My horse has thrown me. He is running loose in the meadow beyond that copse there, and I cannot catch him. I am afraid he will injure himself."

Mariah nodded. A call for help. She had never been able to resist one.

"One moment."

She did not invite him inside to wait. Rather, she quickly closed the door and pulled on an oilcloth coat from the wall pegs beside it. She ran to the kitchen and stuffed several items into her pockets. Then, pausing to light a tin-and-glass lantern, she jogged back to the front door. She let herself out and brushed past him before he could voice the protest already forming on his frowning face. His hat, drawn down low against the rain, obscured his features. He appeared to be about thirty years old, but beyond that, she formed no distinct impression.

Lantern high, she hurried though the pouring rain toward the copse. How she wished she had her own horse with her. But even had her father allowed it, she could never have afforded the mare's upkeep.

Glancing over her shoulder, she noticed that the man hobbled after her with a jerky limp.

He muttered, "Heaven knows where he's got to by now."

He was right. A horse spooked by lightning could run headlong and be halfway across the county by now. Or could fall into some unseen burrow and break his leg. They needed to hurry.

"Do you live nearby?" she asked, wondering if the horse might have taken himself back to the warm security of his stable once divested of its rider. Just because the man was a stranger to *her* did not mean he did not live in the area. She rarely ventured beyond the walled estate and, except when Dixon was ill, avoided going into the village altogether.

"No. I was on my way to Bourton when the, er, mishap occurred."

Pushing through the narrow copse of trees, Mariah spotted the white horse at the edge of the meadow, one rein apparently ensnared by low branches or brambles. Before she could thank providence for their good fortune, thunder shot the sky. The spooked creature reared up, pulling the rein loose, and bolted across the open meadow, then stopped again a short distance away.

"Follow me," she said quietly. She crept forward, hand outstretched, palm up. The white horse swung its head toward them, hesitated, but did not flee. They were able to draw within twenty feet or so of the frightened animal.

"Call to him gently," she urged.

He hesitated. "What do I say?"

"Just call his name."

When he said nothing, she glanced at him. The man looked surprisingly nervous. Was he actually afraid of his own horse?

"I don't recall his name," he said, sheepish. "I have only just acquired him."

Sighing, Mariah handed him the lantern and approached the horse gingerly, reaching into her pocket as she walked.

He called after her in a loud whisper, "Have you brought a rope?"

"No, have you?" she shot back. It was his horse after all.

She had brought two things far better. Sugar cubes and a carrot. With slow steps, soothing words, and the lure of an extended carrot, the horse allowed her near. She deftly took hold of one loose rein while his whiskered muzzle shuddered and sniffed the carrot. She let him eat the tip before taking the second rein and allowing him to perceive he had been caught. If anything, the horse seemed relieved to be captive once more. Realizing it might be difficult for him to eat the whole carrot with his bit in place, she offered him a sugar cube as reward instead.

Thunder rumbled once more, and the horse shied, but Mariah kept hold of him, murmuring soothing words. "Shh . . . it is all right. You are safe now."

Beside her, the man said, "I have just recalled his name. It is Storm."

How fitting, Mariah thought.

Together they led the horse across the meadow and up the road to the gatehouse, the rain lessening as they went. How Mariah wished she might unlock the gate and usher the weary horse into the stable. But she doubted that this qualified as a "dire emergency."

"We should look him over by lamplight. Make certain he is not injured."

The man nodded.

She tied the horse to the gate, then held the lamp near as she ran ink-stained fingers over the horse's pure white legs and checked his hooves. Leaning over, she happened to see that the stranger's white pantaloons—beneath his coat and above his boots—were stained with mud and blood.

"He seems fine," Mariah said. "Which is more than I can say for you. How is the leg? Shall I ride in for the apothecary?"

"Don't trouble yourself. It is merely a scratch."

She doubted it but had no desire to go riding into the village at night. And certainly not astride a stranger's horse, soaked to the skin. She didn't want to add fodder to the gossip mill.

"The rain has let up," she pointed out. "Still, you might let him rest awhile before continuing on to Bourton."

The front door opened, and Dixon appeared in the threshold holding a candle, which guttered in the wet wind.

"There you are, miss. I was frantic to find the house empty. Oh." She paused, eyes widening. "Who is this, pray?"

Mariah followed Dixon's startled gaze to the tall man on the other side of the horse.

"Oh. This is . . . Actually, I have no idea."

"Forgive me." The man swept off his high, narrow hat, which she only now realized was the cocked hat of a naval officer, and gave a brief bow, wavy dark hair falling across his brow. "Captain Matthew Bryant. At your service. And in your debt."

Dixon's thin eyebrows rose.

Mariah explained, "I have merely helped Captain Bryant find his horse, which ran off in the storm."

She turned back to the man, noticing his handsome face, with a straight nose and defined cheekbones. "Would you care to come inside, Captain, and warm yourself by the fire? We haven't much to offer you by way of refreshment, I am afraid, but—"

Dixon frowned. "There is plenty of fish stew."

To Mariah's relief, he quickly declined. "Thank you, but I shan't trespass on your time any longer. I cannot imagine Bourton is too much farther?"

"No. Less than a mile down this road."

"Excellent. Again, thank you for your help. Perhaps I shall be able to return the kindness one day."

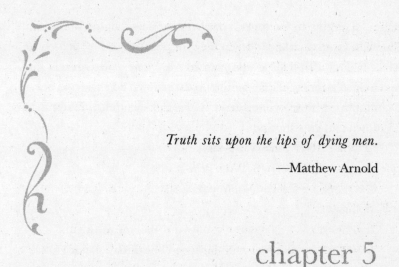

Truth sits upon the lips of dying men.

—Matthew Arnold

chapter 5

*W*hen another knock shook the gatehouse the next morning, Mariah's heart gave a little leap. Had Captain Bryant returned, to ask her name and thank her once again?

Foolish girl, she admonished herself. Laying aside her quill, she rose from the writing table in the sitting room and hurried downstairs with none of the trepidation of the night before.

But it was not the front door that rattled but the rear kitchen door. And it was not Captain Bryant standing on her doorstep. It was Martin, her aunt's hook-handed manservant.

His expression was grim indeed. "She has asked for you again, Miss Aubrey. We'd best not tarry."

Mariah wrapped a light shawl around her shoulders against the damp March breeze and followed him from the gatehouse. Though she was nearly as tall as he was, she had difficulty keeping up with his rapid pace up the drive.

When Mariah entered Mrs. Prin-Hallsey's crowded bedchamber, she was obliged to skirt a wheeled invalid chair she had not noticed before. Stepping to the foot of the bed, she saw that her aunt's skin was waxy thin and her eyes vaguely focused, until they lighted on Mariah. Mrs. Prin-Hallsey gestured to Miss Jones, who quickly rose and helped position her farther up on the pillows. The wig had at last been replaced by an ornamental cap. From beneath it, a few strands of brown and grey showed.

"Mariah." Her voice was weak.

Mariah stepped closer. "Mrs. Prin-Hallsey."

She shook her head. "Not that name."

"Francesca."

Another shake. "The name you used to call me. As a girl."

Tears bit Mariah's eyes and thickened her throat. "Aunt Fran."

The woman closed her eyes as though to relish the sound, and so Mariah repeated it, provoking a hint of a smile on her aunt's face.

Fran Prin-Hallsey accepted the drink Miss Jones brought to her lips, then allowed the maid to dab her mouth with a handkerchief before looking once more at Mariah. "Remember those poems and little plays you wrote and performed at Christmas and Epiphany?"

A ray of pleasure warmed Mariah's heart. "Yes, but I am surprised you do."

"You always were a creative girl. Writing. Playacting." Another shadow of a smile crossed her face. "I like a bit of drama myself, you know."

She crooked a finger, and Mariah obediently drew near the bed. "Closer."

She leaned over her aunt, nearly close enough to whisper in her ear. Then her aunt snaked up a trembling hand and dragged the key from her bodice. Miss Jones leaned over the other side of the bed and helped draw it over her head. Raising both hands slowly as though made of granite, Fran Prin-Hallsey reached the old chain up and over Mariah's bent head. Her arms shook from the effort.

Under her aunt's watchful eye, Mariah tucked the key into her own bodice, glad she had not worn a high-necked frock that day.

A sudden scratching sound from the door pulled Mariah's head around. Hugh Prin-Hallsey stood in the threshold, chin high, eyes alert.

"What has she given you? Nothing of my mother's, I trust?"

Mariah swallowed. "No, sir."

"Do not fret, Hugh," Francesca said languidly. "It is only a chain given me by my first husband. Its value is purely sentimental. Mariah admired it as a girl, and I thought she might like to have it."

It was lies. The lot of it. But Mariah did not refute a word.

Hugh held her gaze, then turned on his heel and disappeared from view.

Her aunt whispered, "He thinks I have a treasure hidden away somewhere."

Mariah chuckled. "Why would he think that?"

"I hinted at that very thing." Francesca's eyes glinted. "Did it to torment him."

"Have you a treasure?" Mariah asked.

Her aunt Fran lifted a faint shrug. "Haven't we all?"

Two days later, Jack Strong brought the news that Mrs. Prin-Hallsey had died in the night. Mariah was surprised at the cloud of loss and grief that hovered over her. She was further surprised when Hugh Prin-Hallsey appeared at the gatehouse a few days after the funeral, a black band on his sleeve.

"I know. Hypocritical, no doubt. But society expects it." He shrugged. "She was not a bad old girl, just had no place marrying my father. Can't say I am sorry she is gone, but I did not wish her dead. Well, I may have wished it, but rest assured I did nothing to hasten it."

"How . . . kind," Mariah said, making little effort to conceal her sarcasm.

"And here you are in black, Miss Aubrey. A horrid old gown, I must say. It doesn't suit you."

"I quite agree. But it is all I have for mourning."

"Well, do stay far from the great house in those weeds. I will be showing it to potential tenants and I don't want them seeing you and believing the place haunted."

His words held no rancor, and she found the man oddly amusing in spite of herself.

His face creased into a smile. "Unless you think that would give the place a certain gothic appeal?"

She was about to return the smile when his words registered. "Tenants? You are not selling Windrush Court?"

"Selling, no. At least not yet. But with the London townhouse, I have little use for this big place. And a great need for income."

"I see."

"Speaking of which. My steward tells me you pay not a farthing for the gatehouse. A situation I mean to redress. Nothing personal, my dear Miss Aubrey, you understand. I would say you are an ornament about the place and allow you to stay as you are, but not with black upon your person." He gave a theatrical shiver.

"I could change," she offered meekly.

One dark brow rose. "Could you, Miss Aubrey? Miss Mariah Aubrey of Milton? For I was speaking of more than the gown."

And then it was Mariah's turn to shiver.

Captain Matthew Bryant followed a man in livery across the entry hall of Windrush Court, his boot steps sending echoing reports through the high-ceilinged space. Might it all really be his one day?

He had first gone to Wesley Park, beyond Bourton, the day after he was thrown from his horse. But the elder Wesley had refused to sell or even to let his empty house to a naval captain, muttering complaints about how the navy "allowed men of low birth unnatural distinction." Matthew still bristled at the thought.

But from what he had heard, Hugh Prin-Hallsey held no such

compunction. He had let it be known he was looking to let his ancestral home. Rumor was he needed the money. And money was one thing Matthew had—naval captain or not. Matthew had already met with Prin-Hallsey's steward. He hoped today's meeting would finalize the bargain.

Ahead of him, the footman opened the door, and Matthew stepped into an impressive paneled library.

"Captain Bryant," the footman announced and withdrew.

Behind the ornate desk sat a gentleman perhaps six or seven years older than himself, with hair nearly black and features showing the first signs of dissipation.

The gentleman rose. "Hugh Prin-Hallsey. Welcome, Captain." The two shook hands, and Prin-Hallsey swept his gaze over Matthew's new civilian clothes, a Carrick coat with several shoulder capes and a simply tied cravat. "Out of uniform already?"

"Yes. Regulations—I am no longer on official duty nor on my way home. In fact, I have been on shore more than a fortnight."

Prin-Hallsey gestured toward a chair and reclaimed his own seat. "Discharged?"

"Paid off and without a ship at present. So, until another commission is offered me, it is time I find my land legs again."

"Have you no family?"

"I do. My mother and father live in Swindon." Matthew anticipated seeing his parents with a mixture of fondness and dread. He would wait until he had found a house before he visited again.

"But you are a bachelor, I take it?"

Matthew nodded. *But hopefully not for long.*

"What use has one man for such a large place?" Prin-Hallsey asked, steepling his fingers.

Matthew frowned. "What need have you in knowing my motivations, sir?"

The man spread his hands. "Motivations, none. Intentions, plenty.

Cannot have strangers dancing upon the pianoforte or using the family china for target practice, can we?"

Irritation surged. He was a captain in the Royal Navy. Not some pillaging pirate. Biting back a sarcastic retort, Matthew said evenly, "My intentions are this. I hope my parents may join me for a time—my mother is not in good health. Eventually, I also hope to host a house party with friends from London. Perfectly respectable."

"I will hold you responsible for any damage to the property."

"Understood. I also plan to invite a fellow officer to lodge here for the summer. He is scraping by on half pay and is injured as well."

Prin-Hallsey leaned back in his chair. "Charitable fellow, ey?"

"Not especially. He is no stranger, after all. And, now I think on it, my former lieutenant might feel more comfortable under his own roof. Are any estate cottages available?"

"No. But there is an old gatehouse we no longer use as an entrance. It is occupied at present, but I have reason to believe it will soon be vacant."

"How soon?"

"Very."

Matthew thought of the girl who had helped him recapture his horse. "Well, no hurry. I shall invite him to join me in the house for now. Certainly large enough for the two of us. It is a bit farther from the coast than I would like, but I negotiated a satisfactory sum with your steward. The terms are agreeable?"

"You are a man who likes a bargain, I see. And I will agree to the lesser amount on one condition."

"Yes?"

"That I am allowed to return, allowed access to the place even while you are in residence."

Matthew felt his brows rise.

"I will let it furnished and staffed as you requested," Prin-Hallsey explained. "But since the death of my father's second wife, I have had insufficient time to sort through many old family papers and ledgers and the like."

Matthew frowned. "You might box them up and take them with you. I shall have no need of such. You are leaving your steward to oversee the accounts."

"Yes, but . . . well, it is more than papers. There are several family heirlooms and things of that nature that have become, well, misplaced. The woman had a different idea of organization than did I, or my mother before her. I need to find . . . several items. I am not sure how long it will require, nor how exactly I will split my time between the task and my . . . responsibilities . . . in town."

Matthew studied the man. He knew there was more going on than he said, but had no interest in prying. He did not like the idea of paying rent to the owner and then having the man come and go as he pleased as if he still owned the place. But the truth was he did.

"I cannot stop you from coming," Matthew allowed. "It is your house, after all."

Prin-Hallsey casually crossed his legs. "True. But if you are agreeable to the terms, the place is yours for six months beginning April first."

Matthew said, "I don't suppose you would consider selling outright?"

Prin-Hallsey hesitated, twisting his lips to one side. "Afraid I can't, old boy. Not yet. Perhaps in future, if you are still interested, I might be able to part with her."

"Is the estate entailed?"

Hugh stroked his chin. "No. But it has been in the family for years."

"I see."

"I doubt it." Hugh rose, signaling the end of the meeting. "At all events, the steward, Hammersmith, will manage things for you and see to troublesome tenants, useless servants, and the like. He is a man who gets things done."

"Here he comes," Mariah whispered to herself, standing at the kitchen window with mounting dread. She realized she had unconsciously been awaiting the steward's call ever since Hugh Prin-Hallsey mentioned his intention to "redress" her situation.

She watched Mr. Hammersmith as he tottered up the drive, dressed in black, his round upper body and thin stockinged legs giving him the look of a stuffed goose on peg legs. One of his arms was crooked behind his back, the other bore a green ledger. Mariah's heartbeat began to quicken in time with the man's choppy, brisk steps.

When she opened the door to him, he lifted his black hat in the faintest of acknowledgements before replacing it on thin fawn-colored hair.

"Miss Aubrey. How do you do. I am Hammersmith, steward to—"

"Yes, I know who you are. Won't you come in, Mr. Hammersmith?"

"Thank you, no. This won't take a minute." He adjusted his spectacles but did not open the thick ledger. Mariah wondered if he carried it merely as a sort of shield. "I am here to inform you of an increase in your rent to twenty pounds per quarter, effective immediately. You have until the thirtieth of April to pay or vacate the premises."

Twenty by the thirtieth? Impossible. That was only six weeks away. It had been nearly a month since Henry took the manuscript, and she had yet to hear one word from him. Had the publisher even looked at the book yet? What else could she sell? She thought of her aunt's chest. But surely if Aunt Fran had possessed anything of value, she would not have left it in the gatehouse attic.

How could she raise the funds?

Mariah was on her feet, pacing. So when a knock sounded on the kitchen door, she answered it herself.

Her aunt's man, Jeremiah Martin, stood there, letter in hand, looking decidedly uncomfortable. There would be no further summons to Francesca's bedside. What could he want?

"Hello, Martin. May I help you?"

He breathed in slowly. "Unlikely, I fear."

There was a quiet dignity about him, Mariah noticed, though he could not be an educated man.

"Did you need something?"

"I don't need much, Miss Aubrey, you will find. And I am useful in my way."

"I am sorry. I don't—"

"Your aunt has left me to you."

Confusion buzzed in Mariah's brain. "Excuse me?"

The man sighed and handed her the folded paper in his hand. "I trust this will explain her wishes."

Frowning, Mariah unfolded the sheet and saw that it was a brief letter signed by her aunt. The words seemed out of focus, so little sense did they make.

Mariah,

I leave you my manservant, Jeremiah Martin. He has been with me for more than a decade, the only servant I brought with me when I remarried, for reasons which would take longer to write down than I have left.

Hugh has never liked him and will no doubt sack him before the last shovel of dirt fills my grave. So, I give him to you. I have left him a bit of money, and he shall work for you in return, for as long as he is able, or until Hugh runs you off the place. Insufferable boy. Never liked me, of course. And never approved of my letting you have the gatehouse. Did it to irk him, you know.

Well, until we meet again on the other side of that river.

Francesca Prin-Hallsey

"I don't know what to say."

"That's all right, miss. Never cared for chatty girls. Look, I know it's irregular. So either tell me where to sleep or send me on my way. Makes no nevermind to me."

Dixon appeared at Mariah's elbow and asked in a terse whisper, "What does *he* want?"

Wordlessly, she handed the letter to her. While Dixon read it, Mariah's eyes were drawn to the man's hunched shoulder and hook. It was difficult to look, but almost impossible to look away.

"Saints preserve us," Dixon muttered. "We don't want him here."

Mariah forced a smile. "Would you excuse us one moment, Martin?"

"Aye."

Mariah closed the door gently and turned to Dixon, a finger to her lips.

Dixon whispered, "The old lady must have lost her mind when she lost her health. Him, here, with the two of us? In this little place?"

"You read the letter; he'll have no place to go."

"I could tell him where to—"

"Dixon, that is not very kind in you."

"Have you smelt the man, Mariah?"

"Perhaps we can devise a way to . . . tactfully mention it. Consider all the work he could do around the place."

"With that hook? I don't see how. He didn't even help us move in here."

"It will be different now, if he lives with us. I am certain there must be some tasks he can do to ease your heavy load. You do too much."

"You're the one who does more than you should. Fine young lady like you . . ."

Mariah huffed a laugh. "Hardly." She said more soberly, "Remember that stormy night you were out and a strange man came to the door? I was frightened to be home alone. Having a man about the place might be wise in many respects."

"But this man is far stranger than the last."

Mariah held her gaze. "Looks can be deceiving, Dixon, as we both know."

Dixon hesitated, then threw up her hands. "Where would he sleep?"

"The pantry?"

"The smell of him, the stable would better suit."

In the end, they laid the options before Martin. He decided that as long as the weather was fine, he would make his bed in the stable loft, which was dry and private and where he might come and go as he pleased without disturbing the ladies. When the weather turned cold in the late autumn, he would resign himself to a cot in the narrow pantry, but he obviously did not look upon the prospect with relish.

"I suppose I have been spoilt all these years with your aunt. Become accustomed to having a room of my own. With not only a bed, but a desk and chair besides."

Mariah bit her lip. "I don't think any of us should become accustomed to our quarters here. Martin, I think it only fair to tell you, before you throw in your lot with us, that there is every likelihood we shall not be here much longer. Mr. Hammersmith has stipulated a rent beyond my ability to pay. Dixon and I are contemplating options, but I don't know how likely we are to succeed."

"Do you really think Mr. Prin-Hallsey would put us out?" Dixon asked.

Martin nodded. "I would not put it past him."

"I imagine he would have done so before now had my aunt not been here to sway him."

Dixon grimaced. "What can we do?"

Mariah straightened her shoulders. "I shall have to think of some way to endear myself to Hugh. Charm him into allowing a *dear cousin* to stay."

Dixon gave her a sidelong glance. "Careful, Miss Mariah."

"Don't worry, Dixon. I am not about to attempt anything foolish."

Martin cleared his throat. "I would not mention *my* being here, miss," he said. "It will not aid your cause."

❧

The footman led Mariah into the Windrush Court library, announced her, and took his leave.

Hugh Prin-Hallsey, seated behind a large carved desk, rose. "Ah. Miss Aubrey. What a surprise."

"Is it? I thought you might expect me."

"Not at all. Why, I barely see you, so rarely do you venture from your seclusion *en pénitence*." He gestured toward one of the chairs before the desk.

She sat and adjusted the skirt of her favorite gown of rose-pink, a color she had been told flattered her complexion. She had made a point not to wear the black. Her straw bonnet with a matching ribbon was tied beneath her chin.

She clasped damp hands in her lap. "I hoped to ask you for a bit of grace in the new rent your steward proposed. It is all such a surprise, when my aunt had so generously allowed me to live in the gatehouse *gratis*."

"Your aunt is dead, Miss Aubrey. And this is not a charitable institution."

She stared, stunned at his coldness.

He pinned her with a steely gaze. "Can you think of one reason I should forgo a reasonable income on my own property?"

She swallowed.

"You are no relation of mine," he continued. "I obeyed my father's wishes in providing for your aunt after his death, though it galled me to do so. Why do you think I stayed away in London so much of the time? I did not like the woman in my house. In my mother's rooms. But now she is gone and I am rid of any obligation to her. Extending charity to her wayward niece was never part of the bargain."

Mariah was horrified to find her eyes filling. "I see." She bit the inside of her lip to keep the tears in check.

He glanced at her, hesitated, then stared off in thought, his dark eyes speculative, and perhaps, softening. He spread his hands expansively. "If it were only up to me, Miss Aubrey, I might lower your rent, or at least allow an extension. But you see, the new tenant is a hard, unbending man. He shall be in charge for the next six months, though Hammersmith will no doubt administrate the new master's wishes. You understand, I trust? It is quite out of my hands."

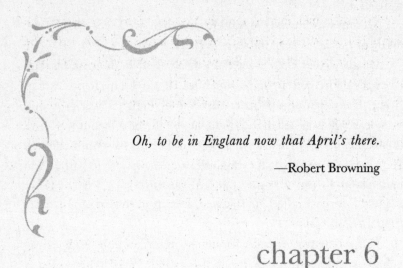

Oh, to be in England now that April's there.

—Robert Browning

chapter 6

s the April sun dispersed the morning mist, Captain Matthew Bryant strode across the grounds of Windrush Court, feeling like a man surveying his own land. He wore a new olive frock coat, striped waistcoat, cravat, and beaver top hat. And if the looking glass he'd consulted that morning could be trusted, he appeared every inch the gentleman.

A budding tremble of hope, of eagerness and pride, was growing within him. He could see himself here. Could imagine himself master of a grand estate like this. He wondered what his parents would say to find him living in such a place. What *she* would say. Would her certain surprise be coupled with admiration, with the acknowledgement that she had known he would succeed all along? Would she join him in exalting over the naysayers of his worth and suitability, her own father chief among them?

Ahead of him, Matthew saw a field of bluebells like a purple-blue sea. How lovely. He had spent so much of his life aboard ships that such sights still awed him.

A woman knelt there among the flowers. With her blue dress, he had almost missed her. Her dark hair was pinned in a thick coil at the back of her head. Her long fair neck curved gracefully as she bent over . . . what? . . . a letter? A book?

So still was she that she looked like a figure in a painting, a landscape of vivid green stems reaching up, her blue frock surrounded by bright bluebells nearly to her waist, her head bowed like the head of a lovely flower.

He stared, moved by the scene. Was she praying? Weeping? He stepped forward and a twig snapped. Her head turned at the interruption, mouth ajar.

Her profile was delicate, feminine—upturned nose, high cheekbones—and somehow familiar. Who was she? Prin-Hallsey had not mentioned a wife or sister.

"I beg your pardon," he said, feeling sheepish to be caught spying. "I did not intend to trespass on your solitude." He walked closer with hand extended to help her up, but she ignored it and rose to her feet unaided.

She gave her dress an ineffectual swipe with one hand. In her other, she held a folded letter. Her bearing, her gown, bespoke the lady, though her hands, he noticed, were less than pristine. Her complexion was fair. Her features finely formed. When she looked up at him, her eyes were large, amber brown, and fringed with dark lashes. He had spent so many years on ships filled with men that the sight of a beautiful woman still awed him as well.

Then he recognized her with a start. The girl from the gatehouse, who had assisted him in recapturing his horse. He was embarrassed to recall his ineffectual behavior that night, his display of timidity. But he was also grateful for her help all over again.

"It is you," he began foolishly. "I almost did not recognize you. Without the cap, I mean, and . . . well, you were dressed so . . . That is, I thought you were . . ."

"A maidservant?" she said easily.

He winced. "Forgive me."

"There is nothing to forgive. You came upon me in my jam-making attire." She smiled. "Yet I recognize you out of uniform, Captain Bryant."

What a charming smile she had. Such perfect teeth. He smiled in return, gratified she had remembered his name.

"And how is your horse?" she asked. "No worse for the experience, I hope?"

"No, he seems fine. Thanks to you."

"I am glad to hear it."

"And I am glad to happen upon you, so I might thank you again." He gave her a deep bow, and she curtsied in return.

"I was happy to help," she said, all warmth and friendliness. "I have always had a tender spot in my heart for horses."

"Have you? I own I am still growing accustomed to the creatures."

Her head tilted to one side. "You did not ride a great deal in your youth?"

"Not at all. I was sent to naval academy as a boy and have spent the greatest portion of my life aboard ships since."

"Ah." She nodded her understanding. "May I ask what brings you to Windrush Court? I had not expected to see you again."

"Then you don't know. I am letting the place for six months with an eye toward owning it one day."

Her smile fell. "You, sir? *You* are the new master?"

Her tone rankled. Did she, like so many others, believe navy men had no right to an estate like this? "I suppose I am. What about that, madam, strikes you as so farfetched?"

An angry flush marred her fair cheeks. "I would not have thought it of you."

"Why not?"

She stammered. "Because I thought you . . . I thought you a . . ."

His anger kindled. "Unworthy? Poor? A nobody?"

"No. I thought you a *gentleman*." Her dark eyes flashed. "I see I was wrong."

She turned and ran headlong across the field, unconcerned for the flowers she was crushing beneath her slippers. Yet, why did he feel as though he were the one who had just crushed *her*? Had she some designs on Windrush Court herself? Why was she so angry?

Matthew sought out Hugh Prin-Hallsey inside the house and found him shooting a solitary game of billiards.

"The girl in the gatehouse," Matthew began, still irritated. "Who is she?" He realized he had once again failed to ask her name. What an idiot he was. Especially where women were concerned.

Prin-Hallsey took his shot, then straightened to his full height, cue stick cradled in both hands.

"The lovely Miss Mariah Aubrey. The soon-to-depart tenant of the gatehouse, as I believe I mentioned. Some niece of my late father's wife, by her first marriage. The woman let Miss Aubrey have the old place for nothing, though she had no business doing so."

"Had she not some right, as your stepmother?"

Hugh grimaced. "You risk my sword, Captain, saying that. She was no mother to me. She managed to bewitch my father and seduce him into matrimony late in his life. Baleful woman. Never understood what the old man saw to admire in her."

Matthew was surprised Hugh did not plan to honor the woman's wishes in regard to her niece. "But she was his wife."

"Yes, and had her widow's jointure to prove it."

Matthew pondered this. "Is there some reason Miss Aubrey would not want me here? We crossed paths a short while ago, and she seemed quite vexed with me for no reason I could fathom."

Hugh gave him a wry glance. "Told her you were the new master, did you?"

"I may have done. She asked what brought me here, after all."

Hugh nodded. "I recently gave her notice of increased rent."

"What has that to do with me?"

"I may have let on it was your doing. Sorry to relegate blame, old boy, but you did say you wanted the gatehouse for a friend, if it could be had. And I didn't think you would mind the misapprehension. You two are strangers, after all, whereas I cannot abide having a beautiful girl cross with me."

"But . . . " Matthew began. "We have met twice now. She did me a good turn at our first meting, and I should like to return the favor. What would it hurt to allow Miss Aubrey to stay as she is? At least until another tenant might be found to pay the higher rent."

"It might hurt more than you think. Your reputation, for example."

"How so?"

Hugh eyed him curiously. "What do you know of Mariah Aubrey?"

Matthew shrugged. "Nothing. Only that she has a way with horses and is a well-spoken young woman."

"Then you are correct; you know nothing." Hugh drew himself up officiously. "But the letting of the gatehouse is not your concern. I need all the funds I can raise at present. She can pay up, or she can go."

Worried as she was about the future, Mariah warmly welcomed Jeremiah Martin as he entered the kitchen, still dressed in black. Without a word, he stepped to the kettle on the sideboard and spooned modest portions of mutton and potatoes onto his plate. He tucked fork, knife, and table napkin into his pocket, and then picked up his plate and carried it outside with him. She noticed he had left the door slightly ajar so that he could open it with his hook on the way out, as his lone hand was full.

When the door closed behind him, Mariah whispered to Dixon, "Did you tell him he could not take his meals with us?"

"Didn't have to. He certainly never ate his meals with Mrs. Prin-Hallsey—that I can tell you."

"But I don't mind. I am no fine lady that—"

"Of course you are, Miss Mariah. It is bad enough that you eat here in the kitchen with me."

It was an argument they'd often had last autumn, until Dixon finally conceded to Mariah's wishes. How ridiculous Mariah would feel eating alone in the drawing room.

Mariah stood at the window, watching as Martin placed his plate and himself on the garden bench, spread his napkin on his lap, and set his plate atop it. She wondered how he would manage to cut Dixon's tough mutton chop. She observed with admiration as he lanced the meat with his fork, propped up the utensil with the inner forearm of his hook hand, and then commenced to take up his knife with his good hand and saw at the mutton with vigor. She wondered why he did not simply impale the meat with his hook, undignified as that might appear. Did he realize she was watching?

Suddenly self-conscious, she turned her attention to her own bland meal and left him to his.

A few minutes later, Martin stepped inside once more and glanced about. "Might I trouble you for the salt cellar? I don't see it."

"And why should you need salt, Mr. Martin?" challenged Dixon.

"Ahh. You see, I am accustomed to food having, mmm, *flavor*, Miss Dixon. A weakness in my character, no doubt."

Dixon frowned darkly.

Oh dear. Mariah rose swiftly and retrieved the salt cellar from the cupboard. "Here you are, Martin."

While her back was to Dixon, Mariah spooned salt into her own palm before handing it to him.

He gave her a conspiratorial wink. "I shall do the washing up after, all right?"

"Thank you, Martin."

Though Dixon would have scolded had she known, Mariah stayed behind to dry while Martin managed the dishes. His hook seemed to hinder him only when it came to the silverware. These he swished about the dishwater with one hand. Mariah checked each piece carefully before drying it.

"Did you know our neighbor enjoys a bit of fame?" Martin asked.

She glanced at him. "Hugh Prin-Hallsey?"

"I said fame, not infamy," he huffed. "I meant Captain Bryant."

She was instantly alert, though she tried not to show it. "How so?"

Martin braced a carving knife against the basin with his hook arm and scrubbed at it with the cloth in his hand.

"Mrs. Prin-Hallsey let me have the newspapers after she was finished with them. I've saved all the interesting articles about the navy and the war in general. There were several about Captain Bryant."

"Really?" she murmured, hoping to sound nonchalant.

Apparently she failed, because Martin wiped his hands on the apron and pulled a piece of newsprint from his pocket. "Here's one that might interest you." Unfolding it, he read, " 'Captain Matthew Bryant, recently of the frigate *Sparta*, has lately returned to England after an absence of four years. Not only has Bryant achieved the rank of captain at a relatively young age, but he has also made a tidy fortune by the war. The reckoning of his prize money is said to surpass twenty thousand pounds. . . .' "

He read several more lines, but Mariah barely heard them, the staggering figure still echoing in her mind.

Martin set aside the clipping and picked up his dishcloth once more. "He's no Admiral Nelson, mind. Nelson made captain by age twenty. Did you know he had his right arm amputated and was back on duty thirty minutes later?"

Mariah shook her head.

"Still, Captain Bryant has quite a reputation for determination in battle. He captured several ships, both enemy and merchant, which outmanned and outgunned his smaller frigate. Impressive indeed."

Mariah had difficulty imaging such fierceness in the man, when he had seemed timid with a mere horse. But then again, was he not insisting on "prize money" of a sort from her?

"Sounds merciless, this Captain Bryant," she murmured.

Martin lifted the carving knife high to inspect it. In the sunlight streaming through the window, the blade glinted. "I don't know," he said. "But I for one would not want to be his enemy."

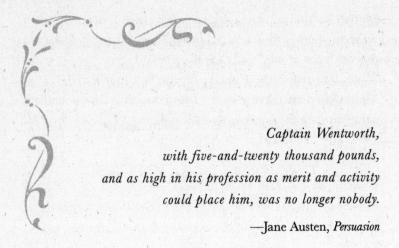

Captain Wentworth,
with five-and-twenty thousand pounds,
and as high in his profession as merit and activity
could place him, was no longer nobody.

—Jane Austen, *Persuasion*

chapter 7

The navy had been good to him. Not only had Matthew achieved the rank of captain before the age of thirty, but he had also made his fortune by the war. Now, having claimed his prize money of more than five-and-twenty thousand pounds, he was no longer nobody.

It was time he made this fact known.

His plan was a simple one: set himself up in a fine estate and enlist the help of his highborn friend, Captain Ned Parker, in reintroducing him to society. After all, it was through Parker that Matthew had first met *her* some four and a half years before.

In letting Windrush Court, he had accomplished the first item on his agenda. He had also ordered a gentleman's wardrobe and had resigned himself to submitting to the ministrations of Prin-Hallsey's valet, one of the many servants that came part and parcel with the estate.

Once he grew accustomed to his new environs and mastered the gentleman's life, he would invite that certain lady and several others of her set to a house party—two or three weeks of shooting, riding, balls, and fine dinners. She would see his success, his transformation, and realize that she had been wrong to reject him, to concur with her father's assessment that he was beneath her. And Matthew would win her at last.

Isabella.

She had been only eighteen when she'd rejected him, and was still young. He had been surprised and relieved to learn that she had not yet married. How he had worried she would. Yes, Parker confided, an engagement had recently been announced. But as long as she was not married, there was still hope—slim though it might be.

Matthew acknowledged he was likely deceiving himself. That in reality he had no chance. But he could not accept defeat. It was not in his nature. He was determined to wage one final campaign to secure her affections.

Matthew told himself his plan was not purely selfish. After all, he had written to invite Lieutenant William Hart, who had once served as his first officer, to reside with him. Hart had been injured in the line of duty, and Matthew felt responsible for the man. Besides, he truly liked Hart and looked forward to furthering his acquaintance with his brother officer.

But first, Matthew hoped to persuade his parents to leave their small, damp cottage and live with him—to allow his mother the comfort and care she so richly deserved after a lifetime of scraping by. That was a selfless wish, was it not?

Then why did his palms sweat at the thought of presenting the offer to his father?

❧

Matthew surveyed the small study of his modest childhood home, situated on an unfashionable side street in Swindon. He looked at his retired-clerk father, sitting in his favorite chair, one leg crossed over the other, a book in one hand, pipe in the other, a curl of aromatic smoke rising. In fact, whenever Matthew smelled that sharp sweet smell of tobacco he was instantly transported back to this humble room in which he had spent so many boyhood evenings before leaving for naval academy.

But instead of being struck with how familiar the scene was, his father in his favorite room, his favorite chair, engaged in his favorite pastime, Matthew was instead struck by how different his father looked. How aged.

His shoulders were stooped, and the hand holding the heavy volume trembled under its weight. His once thinning grey hair was now a snowy fringe around the back of his head. He still wore long side-whiskers, but these were now white as well. Age spots and wrinkles competed for preeminence over the top of his head, reminding Matthew of the naval chart of a busy trading route. A thick pouch of webbed wrinkles framed each eye, though his eyes at least were as clear and blue as Matthew remembered.

His mother, it seemed, had fared worse. Her appearance was much the same as ever—cheerful brown eyes, light brown curls threaded with silver, her frame slight but for the rounded middle that evidenced her fondness for sweets. But Matthew had not been home a quarter hour before he realized his mother was not well. Her breathing was audibly labored, as if she had just run in from the rain. There was also a wheezing sound in her chest that alarmed him.

"It is just the damp, my dear. No need to worry," she'd replied when he asked. "I shall be perfectly well, now you're home safe and sound."

He took her hand. "I have let a fine house, Mamma. Large enough for all of us and not as damp as this one. I would like you both to come and live with me. It will make a nice change for you, and a change might do you good."

"Your mother is fine here, as am I," his father said. "We are not about to be uprooted at our age. This is our home, Matthew. Not good enough for you now—is that it?"

Matthew felt deflated and defensive at once. "I did not say that, sir."

"You were born and raised here, don't forget. Our friends are here, our church is here, your brother's grave is here. We'll not leave so easily."

His mother bit her lip and squeezed Matthew's hand. "Thank you, my dear. You are very kind to think of us. But you need the society of other young people. People as successful and clever as you are. Not a couple of old fools like us."

"Mother, you are not—"

"We're fine, Matthew," his father interrupted. "We've not got one foot in the grave yet." He rose. "If your mother needs something, I shall be the one to provide it. We don't need your blood money buying us fancies and dainties." He strode through the door.

Matthew's objection followed him from the room. "Blood money? It is hard-earned prize money from His Britannic Majesty's Navy."

"Don't mind your father, Matthew," his mother soothed, patting his arm. "It's his pride talking—that's all. Hates the thought of not being able to give me the kind of life he thinks I want." Tears brightened her eyes. "Without Peter, I can never be truly happy, but I am content, Matthew. Especially now you're home. And I want you to be content as well."

His father reentered the room, teacup in hand. "Setting yourself up in a manor house like some lord, buying dandy clothes, and puttin' on airs to woo some fickle female? I'll have no part in that."

"John, please," Helen Bryant said, then turned plaintive eyes toward Matthew. "My dear, if a fine house is what you want, then I am happy for you. But if you feel you *need* to do all this to earn the affection of a certain lady, as your father says, then I must question whether this young woman is truly right for you. Truly loves you for who you are."

JULIE KLASSEN

Matthew sighed. "In the real world, Mamma, blood and money are all that matter. And if you are nobody by birth, then wealth and connection are all one has."

"Nobody?" his father echoed. "You dare sit in my house and call us nobodies?"

"That is not what I meant, Father. But in society—"

"I don't care a fig about *society*, nor did I raise you and your brother and sister to do so. Poor Peter would never have chased after temporal success the way you are."

A moment of pained and hallowed silence followed, as it always did whenever John Bryant mentioned the name of his deceased son.

"You'll be visiting your brother's grave before you leave, I trust?" he said hoarsely.

Matthew winced. Had he overstayed his welcome already?

His mother's big eyes beseeched his once more. "Do you really love her, Matthew? Or are you out to prove that she was wrong to refuse you before?"

Matthew rubbed a hand over his face. "Yes. On both counts."

A few hours later, Matthew rode to the market town of Highworth, some six miles northeast of Swindon. Once there, he dismounted before a small, tidy cottage near the church. As he tied his horse to the rail, the door burst open

"Matthew!" A dainty young woman ran to him and threw her arms around his neck.

"Lucy." He embraced her, then held her at arm's length to soak in the look of her. The caramel hair, several shades lighter than his own, the snapping brown eyes so like his, the deep dimples on either side of her grinning mouth. So much the same as ever, but different too. The years they had been apart had been very kind to his sister, and her face radiated joy and confidence.

He had been away at sea when Lucy was wed, but she had written to tell him of the happy event. He had been glad and relieved to hear of it for more than one reason.

"How wonderful you look," he said. "Marriage must suit you."

"Indeed it does. You, on the other hand, look awful." Her eyes sparkled. "I suppose you have been to see Mamma and Papa?"

"I have."

"Then it is good you have come to see me. I shall cheer you!" She took his arm and led him inside. "I suppose Papa was . . . distant, as usual?"

"Yes. One would think I was just home from prison instead of the war."

"He does love you, Matthew. Never doubt it."

But Matthew did doubt it.

While Lucy had not entirely escaped their mother's endless grief and their father's detachment, she had borne it better. Her constant cheerfulness and ready smile had garnered their unconscious affection, rather like a charming, obedient pug one mindlessly stroked for comfort. He supposed that was not fair—Lucy indeed brought warmth and consolation to John and Helen Bryant, while his own attempts to offer the same had been soundly rejected.

"And where is Charles?" he asked, seating himself on the worn but comfortable settee.

"Away on parish business—visiting the workhouse. I should have gone with him, but I was indisposed earlier."

"Indisposed?" He grinned. "You look in perfect health to me. Do not tell me you feigned some passing malady to avoid paying calls."

She settled herself in the armchair closest to him. "It is not some passing malady, Matthew. It is a baby."

His breath left him. "A baby?"

"Yes, or it will be, in seven months or so."

Matthew felt a strange combination of surprise, pleasure, and unexpected envy. He pushed the latter aside and smiled. "Lucy, what happy news! Still, I must say I am rather put out. It was one thing to marry before your older brother managed the feat. But to have a child before me as well? Unpardonable." He reached over and playfully tweaked her nose.

"It is not my fault, Matthew. If you were not so bent on winning the hand of a certain unworthy female . . ."

"It was I who was unworthy, do not forget."

"I do *not* forget. And what I remember is that she used you cruelly."

"Cruel? It was her father who refused my suit."

"Which she knew all along he would do. Far better never to offer you hope, to lead you to think she would wed you *if only* she were allowed. Had she never encouraged you and resigned herself to marrying at her level, you would have given up and fallen for some other girl long ago."

Matthew found himself frowning. "Lucy, I prefer you not speak ill of her. She may be your sister yet."

Lucy shook her head, a sad look on her pretty face. "The right woman for you is out there, Matthew. And she will not care if you are a baker, a cobbler, or a captain. I would not. Look at Charles and me. Talk about unworthy."

"Hush. Do not say that. You, who are suddenly so grown up, and so wise."

She smiled, even as tears brightened her dark eyes. "If I am wise now, I came to it late—as well you know."

He squeezed her hand. "Let us not speak of it. It is in the past."

"Yes." Lucy exhaled, pressing her eyes closed. "And thankfully so."

A few days after Easter, Mariah stood at the window in her bedchamber, staring out at nothing. Seeing nothing . . . except for her mounting problems.

Still no word from Henry.

She and Dixon had spent a quiet Easter together. It was the first year in memory Mariah had not traveled to visit family over the Easter holidays. Together the two of them had boiled eggs, saved from Lent, with red onion skins to dye them red. "To remember," Dixon said in reverent tones, "the blood Christ shed to cover our sins." Although her stalwart friend had not directed the words at her, still Mariah felt their pinch.

On Good Friday, they baked hot cross buns, and on Sunday, at Dixon's insistence, they attended church together in the village. It wasn't that Mariah disdained or blamed God for what had happened. She simply no longer felt worthy of Him. After the service, they had shared a modest dinner of mutton, turnips, boiled eggs, and left over buns with marmalade. As usual, Martin took his meal outside. No one mentioned the dry mutton. They all knew there was no money for ham.

Vaguely now, Mariah heard voices from below. Dixon and Mr. Phelps, discussing where the lilies he had divided and culled from his own plot should be planted in front of the gatehouse. Mariah felt like those lilies, a perennial cut from its roots, displaced. Transplanted in slipshod fashion. She wondered if she would have time to recover from the first upheaval before being yanked out again.

Mr. Hammersmith was not a man to be put off for long. Nor, did it seem, was Captain Bryant. And the thirtieth of April was looming ever closer on her calendar. Why did Henry not write? She supposed he had gone home to Attwood Park for the Easter holidays. That might have delayed him. Or perhaps the publisher had rejected her novel outright.

Mariah heard a distant door close and knew Dixon had come back inside. The two of them had begun reading aloud and editing her second manuscript in the evenings, in no doubt naïve anticipation of the publisher wanting it as well. If he did not, how else could she raise the money? And if she could not, where would they go?

As if the place called her name, she lifted her eyes, up past the trees greening with spring leaves, to that dreaded place of grey stone, with its flat roof guarded by an iron railing and spiked with chimneys. The poorhouse. Would she and Dixon end up there yet?

Suddenly, atop the poorhouse roof, motion caught her eye. Mariah leaned forward until her nose touched the cool, wavy glass. *What in the world?* A man was walking on the roof. His motions were not the regular, focused actions of a workman, but rather erratic and fast-paced as he . . . marched? . . . from one side of the roof to the other.

"What is he doing?" she breathed.

"If you mean Martin." Dixon strode in with laundered bedclothes. "Nothing useful. The man had the nerve to complain about my fish stew."

"Come here, Dixon," Mariah urged. "Do you see that man?"

"Where?"

She pointed. "There on the poorhouse roof."

"Good heavens! There is a man up there." Dixon squinted. "I can't make him out very well. . . ."

"What is he doing, do you think? Taking exercise?"

"Exercise?" Dixon snorted. "On the roof? More likely he's off in his attic. Men!" she grumbled.

Something in Dixon's tone snagged Mariah's attention. She studied her friend's agitated face and asked, "And how is Mr. Phelps today?"

"A bit too friendly, if you take my meaning."

But Mariah did not miss the blush in her thin cheeks. They both stared out at the distant man once more.

Dixon sighed. "What is it about springtime that makes men crazy?"

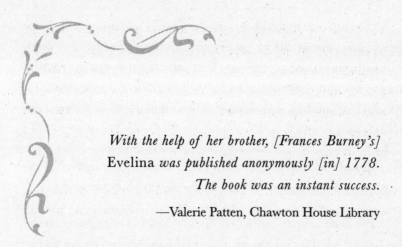

With the help of her brother, [Frances Burney's]
Evelina *was published anonymously [in] 1778.*
The book was an instant success.

—Valerie Patten, Chawton House Library

chapter 8

atthew spent Easter with his sister and her husband. While there, he was aware of how near he was to a certain family's estate on the outskirts of Highworth but did not pay a call. He was not yet in position to launch his campaign. Instead, he returned and settled in for his first full week as master of Windrush Court.

He was surprised to find the girl in the gatehouse often on his mind. Understanding now why she had been cross, he wished to apologize to her, hoped he might clear up the misunderstanding that had caused her to direct her ire at him.

That evening, as Matthew walked toward the gatehouse to call on Miss Aubrey, he heard voices coming from inside. Voices in earnest conversation. And there—a sharp exclamation. An argument? He did not alter his course but kept to the path. He had every right to be there, he told himself. In fact, he was paying handsomely for the privilege.

"You are very much like your aunt, child," said the gravelly voice of an older woman. "If you wore a wig, and had a fine tapered waist, I should almost conceit that I saw her again. Is it true that the ranting, raving captain is here again, and some other young scapegrace?"

A clear, youthful voice replied, "The captain is here, ma'am, with a Mr. Montgomery."

Matthew recoiled. *The captain?* The *"ranting, raving captain"*? Certainly they did not speak of him. And who was Montgomery?

The older woman continued, "In my days, if a young woman was seen to be speaking to a man, unless he happened to be her father, her brother, or at least her cousin, he was set down as her betrothed admirer, and it generally turned out that he became her husband. But now 'tis higgledy-piggledy, fiddling, acting, a parcel of fellows kept in the house of a young woman, for no earthly purpose that I see, but to make her the talk and the scandal of the whole neighborhood."

Matthew listened, increasingly disconcerted. A *"parcel of fellows kept in the house"*? Had Miss Aubrey so many male callers? What sort of a woman was she? Matthew had thought Miss Aubrey admirable, if not traditionally ladylike. He hoped his earlier assessment had been correct.

He had overheard one or two disgruntled comments from the steward, Hammersmith, and a few suggestive hints from Prin-Hallsey. But he had chalked them up to vicious gossip. He knew too well how cruel people could be, how quick to swallow any tale that hinted at a woman's loss of virtue. His own dear sister's misfortunes had taught him that.

The women in the gatehouse were speaking of someone else, he decided, and resolutely walked away.

Matthew determined to try again the next day. The rain, which had started as a gentle drizzle and no deterrent to a man used to standing on deck in all sorts of weather, was now pelting down with soaking regularity. Matthew was tempted to turn around, but since he had spent the better part of an hour working up his courage and allowing the fastidious valet to fuss with his cravat, he thought it best to make his apologies and have done.

As he walked down the ever-narrowing lane through the wood, he heard the reverberating *clunk* of wood upon wood and wondered who would be out working in this weather. He had yet to master the names and faces of all the staff, but he believed a carpenter lived in one of the cottages not far from the gatehouse. It was likely him.

But when he approached the back garden of the gatehouse, he was stunned to see none other than Miss Aubrey, bent at the waist, gripping an axe that was wedged into a chunk of wood, refusing to either cut through or come loose. *What on earth?* If there was a "parcel of fellows" in the house, why were none of them assisting her?

Her head was bare, and she wore the oilcloth coat he remembered from the night of their first meeting. Beneath it, her blue frock hem was quickly becoming a muddy mess.

"Miss Aubrey!"

She glanced up, and he saw tears on her cheeks before she could avert her face or wipe them away. Or was it only the rain?

She stiffened. Then, with a fierce expression, she turned back to her task. She lifted the impaled chunk of wood high over her head and brought it down on the chopping block with a solid *thunk*. Still the wood did not yield.

"Fiddle!" she half yelled, half sobbed.

Clearly more was wrong than one stubborn piece of wood. She made to toss the axe down, but he rushed forward and grasped it, fearing it might strike her foot. He tried to take it from her, but she held fast.

"Allow me," he said.

"No, thank you," she clipped between clenched teeth.

"Then at least wait and have your man do it."

"There is only Martin. He can't chop wood with one hand. Besides, he has gone to market. We are out of coal and I haven't money for more. I can't ask Mr. Strong to come out in this, when he has done so much for us already. The fires are nearly out and Dixon was chilled, so I've sent her to bed. I don't want her to catch cold or suffer another bout of the ague. . . ."

While her words accelerated and her voice rose, he gently pried the axe from her fingers and set it down. He firmly gripped both of her shoulders and spoke earnestly to her. He wondered at his boldness in touching her, and knew he would not have done so were she not so distressed. He felt the urge to comfort her, and hoped she would take no offense.

"Miss Aubrey, first allow me to say, I am not responsible for raising your rent. I believe Mr. Prin-Hallsey wished to transfer blame, not realizing I would care, or that we had even met. But I do care. And I regret you should think ill of me after your kindness with my horse. Do you believe me?"

She nodded, blinked rain and tears from her eyes. "I would believe that of Hugh, yes."

"I hope we shall be friends, Miss Aubrey. And as a token of my apology and friendship, I ask you to please go inside and allow me to chop this wood."

"But, I could not. It would not be—"

"Yes it would," he insisted. "I am not used to idleness and need the exercise. Please."

A rivulet of rain coursed down her forehead, crossed the bridge between her eyebrows, and ran onto her upturned nose.

She blinked again. "Very well, Captain. But just this once. Thank you."

He picked up the axe, but she turned back.

"And thank you for explaining. I should have known."

Inside the kitchen, Mariah hung up the coat and found a towel for her hair. She told herself she should have realized that Hugh, as owner, remained in charge of tenants. But she had no personal experience with such arrangements. And Hugh had been so convincing. Now she saw why Fran had called him a wicked boy.

From the window, Mariah watched Captain Bryant. He laid his coat over a barrel just inside the stable door. In waistcoat and shirtsleeves he lifted the axe and brought it down on the block, chopping the dense piece with ease. Again and again he set up a log, split it, and then tossed the pieces onto the pile at the back door. The rain had lessened now, but still the drizzle curled his brown wavy hair and dampened his shirt sleeves until they clung to his shoulders and biceps and forearms. She glimpsed fair skin and the swell of muscle beneath his increasingly translucent shirt.

Very masculine, this Captain Bryant, she thought. She admired his profile, the aquiline nose, strong cheekbones and chin. And she admitted to herself that she found him attractive, especially now that he was not the villain of this chapter in her life.

Mariah, she silently warned. Had she not promised herself she was finished with men and their untrustworthy ways? Even as she thought this, she knew the promise was a poor shield against the truth. For she felt certain no honorable man would ever love her now. She would be wise to steel her heart.

And avert her eyes.

❧

At the sight of Henry walking up the path to the gatehouse the following Saturday, Mariah's palms began to perspire. Why had he not written? Were the tidings so bad he wished to break the news in person, and be there to comfort her in its wake?

She forced herself to wait until he knocked, then took a deep breath and opened the door. "Henry, hello. Do come in."

He smiled but looked tired. She took his hat and indicated the best chair.

He sat down and she positioned herself on the settee near him, clasping her hands nervously in her lap.

"I shall not keep you in suspense," he began. "Mr. Crosby wishes to publish your novel."

She was afraid to believe it. "Really?"

"Yes, really. He will agree to either a flat payment for the copyright, or a commission at author's risk. As neither of us has the money to cover the printing upfront, I chose the former terms. I hope I did right."

Relief washed over her. "You did." She could hardly take it in. Her book would be in print for all of England to see—or at least a few hundred souls willing to take a chance on some unknown author. Joy surged within Mariah, but it was dampened by the reserve on Henry's face.

"What is it?"

He leaned forward, elbows on knees, fingers interlaced. "Mr. Crosby wants to meet you in person."

"What?"

"I am afraid so, Rye."

Her mind whirled. "But why? Why should he care? I am not the first authoress, nor author for that matter, to write anonymously or under a *nom de plume*."

"True. Though he says he would prefer to know all of his writers' identities even if readers do not. Apparently there has been public outcry against a particular male author, who has taken to writing under pseudonyms to pass off inferior work. And, as so many female authors seem to write moralizing, didactic tales these days, he feels an obligation to confirm their identities. He wants no surprises. Doesn't want to discover his latest bestseller was penned within the walls of Newgate, or the Magdalene."

"But this is terrible!" Mariah groaned. "I don't want anyone poking about my affairs. That is the very reason I wished to keep my identity secret."

"Just come down to Oxford and meet him. He will see you are a lady of education and refinement and all will be well. It is a formality only."

"I have no wish to go to Oxford."

"Have you no wish to be published either?"

Mariah stared at him. "He will insist upon it?"

"Yes, he was quite adamant. Though, perhaps . . ."

"What?"

"Mr. Crosby offered to call on you if that would be more convenient. Perhaps you would prefer that?"

Mariah hesitated. Did she? On one hand, she would much rather meet him within the security of her private retreat, away from prying eyes. How she dreaded the thought of traveling by coach, or even post, when who knew whom one's fellow passengers might be. But to bring Mr. Crosby here, to her place of exile? Would it not in its very unusualness—a young unmarried woman living separately from her family—raise questions Mariah longed to avoid? And, worse yet, once the man had visited the gatehouse, what was to keep him from letting it slip where Lady A lived and in what humble circumstances? What if word were to reach her parents of not only Henry's hand in her fledgling writing career, but of the endeavor itself, of which her father would disapprove nearly as heartily as her initial disgrace?

Considering her finances, she could honestly say it would be a hardship for her to make the trip. But if meeting him here in the gatehouse would open the door to publication and payment? She would have to do it. She would meet Mr. Crosby here, try her best to assure him she was a woman of quality, though she could hardly pretend to perfection, and hope he would be satisfied without requiring a detailed telling of her past. Perhaps she would even have the nerve to show him her second manuscript. She and Dixon were still reading aloud the most recent draft and polishing it as they went.

"Very well. If he is willing to come here."

"He has said as much. He is eager to meet you."

"When would he call?" she asked.

Henry squeezed her hand. "Saturday week."

Might the man bring payment then? Or send it later, assuming she passed muster? She had only a fortnight to pay the twenty pounds for rent. She dearly hoped the payment would be enough, and that it would arrive in time.

Before he took his leave, Henry handed her a letter. "From Julia. I confided that I would be seeing you."

"Oh . . . !" Mariah breathed. "She should not have risked doing so."

Unfolding the single page, Mariah's eyes skittered to the signature at the bottom, and there her attention was snagged by a postscript added in her mother's hand.

> *How relieved I was to hear you are well. My prayers are with you.*

Mariah's heart lifted to see it. Then she read her sister's enthusiastic note.

> *Dear Mariah,*
>
> *How cruel this separation is! I cannot tell you how I miss you and our bedtime talks. I know Papa will be cross with me if he learns I wrote to you, but I could not rest until I shared my fondest secret with my dearest sister.*
>
> *I am in love! Yes! I have met the most handsome, kind, and attentive young man. It is my hope that he shall very soon ask Papa for my hand. That is, once he rouses his courage—you know how hard it is to ask our father for anything! I suppose I should not say it, but I am still vexed. They will not tell me exactly what it is you have supposedly done, but knowing you as I do, I cannot imagine it is anything so bad. Not bad enough to justify sending you away. . . .*

Oh, but it is, Mariah thought sadly, feeling the pain and mortification of her wrongdoing anew. How sorry she was that her sister had to suffer for it too.

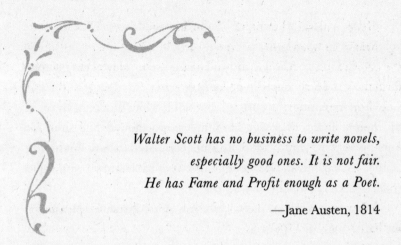

Walter Scott has no business to write novels,
especially good ones. It is not fair.
He has Fame and Profit enough as a Poet.

—Jane Austen, 1814

chapter 9

*T*he next Saturday, Mariah slipped into a long-sleeved day dress of ivory lawn with a high belt of lavender ribbon. She pinned her hair simply and neatly, hoping to appear ladylike. As the time of the meeting approached, she descended to the drawing room and sat down, trying not to fidget.

Dixon stood watching at the window. When the clock struck the hour, she whispered, "He's here!"

Mariah rose from her chair on rubbery legs and smoothed her skirt as Dixon opened the front door.

Mr. Crosby was a gentleman of middling height, but his thin frame made him appear taller. He wore his mink brown hair combed fashionably forward, silky fringes blending with dark brows. His light brown eyes were the largest she had ever seen on a fully grown man. His nose was thin and prominent and his cheekbones sharply evident beneath his pale skin. Still, the overall effect was pleasing. Mariah decided he had the appearance of a well-dressed ascetic. She felt quite voluptuous by contrast.

"A. K. Crosby, ma'am," he said and bowed. "Have I the pleasure of making the acquaintance of Lady A?"

"You have, sir." She curtsied, but not too low, suddenly aware of the modest display of *décolleté* her simple gown allowed. She surely did not appear a starving artist, at least not compared to him. But his fine clothes—crisp cravat, waistcoat, and coat of sable brown with velvet collar—were not a poor man's garb.

"An honor, madam," he said warmly, and Mariah felt pleasure at the earnestness of his words.

"Please, let us sit and be comfortable," she said.

"Thank you."

She made a mental note to offer him seconds of everything when refreshments were served. *Tea, Mr. Crosby? Muffins? Biscuits, butter?*

Dixon, she saw, had failed to take his hat. Smiling apologetically, she gestured toward the end table. He laid his hat there and sat down, pulling his coattails around himself as he did so. She sat as well, smoothing down the skirt of her gown. She hoped it was not conspicuously out of fashion.

She glanced up and found him watching her, eyes alight and a smile playing about his lips. Self-conscious, she glanced down at her bodice to assure herself all was as it should be. Why had she not worn a fichu?

He began, "I hope you do not mind my saying that you are younger and . . . um, more . . . graceful than I expected."

Graceful? Was that what he meant to say? His eyes said *pretty*, but she supposed it would be unprofessional to say something so personal and pedestrian.

"Are most of your authors older?" she asked, hoping to appear composed.

"Yes. I would say most are in their middling years, though some are quite old indeed."

"And how do they respond to having such a young publisher?"

She had not meant to ask that, but if the man was even thirty, she would have been very much surprised.

He looked down modestly and chuckled. "Touché, Miss . . . Do you mind if I call you by your real name?"

"No, I suppose not."

He tucked his chin apologetically. "Then . . . you shall have to tell me what it is."

Mariah felt her cheeks grow warm. "Oh, forgive me. I thought my . . . Henry might have told you."

"He is very protective of you, your Mr. Aubrey." He crossed one leg over the other and picked a piece of lint from his trousers. "He will be taking his fee from your earnings, I suppose?"

She shook her head. "He refuses to take any."

One dark brow rose. "No agent fee nor even allowance for expenses? A most generous man, your Mr. Aubrey."

Mr. Crosby is fishing, she realized. What was worse, having the man think Henry her lover, or admitting he was her brother and risk their father finding out Henry was helping her?

Tentatively, she asked, "Henry did not explain the nature of our relationship?"

The man looked taken aback, and if she was not mistaken, the hint of a blush tainted his pale cheeks.

This will never do. She made her decision. How likely was her father to meet this young Oxford publisher in any case? She said, "Henry is my brother, Mr. Crosby. He acts as my man of business out of the goodness of his heart."

His expression was, she thought, incredulous and perhaps relieved. "If he is your brother, then why not tell me? Why all the secrecy?"

She bit her lip. "It is our father, you see. He would not approve of Henry having any part in my new life."

Fortunately, he misunderstood. "Your father does not approve of novel writing?"

That is an understatement, Mariah thought. Her father had lamented ever allowing the volumes into his house, blaming them in part for the "romantic fancies" that had led to her fall. She said only, "He does not. And so, Mr. Crosby, if I could ask you to refrain from mentioning Henry Aubrey's connection to Lady A, or mentioning him at all for that matter, we would both be very grateful. And of course I wish to remain anonymous as well."

His brown eyes sparkled. "And as I have yet to learn your name, your anonymity is assured."

"I am Miss Aubrey."

"Miss?"

She nodded.

"And might I learn your Christian name, though, of course, I would not presume to use it?"

"I don't know, A.K." She grinned. "Might I learn yours?"

He smiled appreciatively. "Anthony King. But as it was my father's name as well, I prefer to go by A.K."

"I see. My given name is Mariah."

"Miss Mariah Aubrey. A lovely name."

She felt her cheeks warm once more. "Thank you."

He leaned back. "I appreciate your willingness to meet with me, Miss Aubrey. I believe I understand, at least in part, your reluctance—"

A single knock sounded, and Mr. Crosby glanced toward the kitchen door. Martin opened it for Dixon, who came in bearing a tray of tea things. Martin followed a few moments later with the teapot itself.

"Will you take some refreshment, Mr. Crosby?" Mariah asked. "I am sure you must be hungry after your journey."

"Tea would be lovely. Thank you."

With pleasingly steady hands, she poured a cup, which he accepted with a distracted smile. But when she offered him sugar, milk, or lemon, he declined them all. Likewise, he declined her offer of muffins or cheese biscuits. Inwardly, Mariah sighed. Abstemious people were such a trial. She could not eat if he did not. It would be quite unladylike—an impression she wished to avoid this of all days.

She sipped her tea, missing the sugar immediately.

When Dixon and Martin closed the door behind them, Mr. Crosby continued. "I hope Henry told you how much I admire your novel."

"It pleases me to hear it. Though I suppose I assumed some level of approbation, considering your interest in publishing it."

He nodded. "And allow me to say that you are not the first lady to shy away from the public eye, for fear of exposing herself to scrutiny and perhaps censure."

Mariah felt her smile tremble. She had already exposed herself to both. Need she tell him?

Instead she asked, "Are you meeting with all of the authors you publish?"

He sipped politely before setting his cup in the saucer. "The new ones, yes. Many have been with Crosby and Company for years—long before I took over the firm in my father's stead."

"And what is it you hope to ascertain in meeting new authors?"

"Primarily, that they are who they say they are."

Mariah took a sip to wet suddenly dry lips. "But clearly, many women and even some men publish under pseudonyms. Few of us are who we say we are. Even Walter Scott fools almost no one with his books by Captain Clutterbuck or Crystal Croftangry."

He nodded. "Though I am not speaking of appellation alone, Miss Aubrey, but rather of a genuineness of character. There was quite a furor when Miss Pinkley, author of *Advice to Rosina and All English Ladies* fame, turned out to be none other than Mr. Eugene Fowler, lately of debtor's prison."

"I am not a man, Mr. Crosby, I assure you."

His expression did not change as he regarded her. He blinked, then blinked once more. "Of that I have no doubt, Miss Aubrey." Leaning forward, he said, "In fact, now that I have met you and spoken with you, my mind is relieved on that score. You are clearly an educated woman of quality."

"Thank you," she murmured, feeling like a fraud.

He set down his teacup. "I confess I would prefer to use your real name instead of Lady A, which is so impersonal, so similar to the standard *by a lady*. It is one thing for authors with several books to their credit. Then we simply print *by the author of such and such* on the title page of the latest novel. But as this is your first book . . ."

She felt her jaw tighten. "I publish anonymously or not at all."

He studied her for a moment, as if gauging her resolve. "Very well." He reached into his pocket and extracted several bank notes, which he set upon the table without comment. Then he took a deep breath and rubbed his hands together. "Now, tell me about this second novel your brother mentioned."

Half an hour later, Mariah saw Mr. Crosby out and paused on the front doorstep to bid him farewell. She was startled to see Captain Bryant tethering his horse to the gate.

"Captain Bryant," she acknowledged dully, chagrined to be seen during her "secret" meeting.

"Miss Aubrey." Captain Bryant glanced quickly at her but then trained his gaze on the slight, well-dressed man beside her.

Mariah looked from Mr. Crosby to Captain Bryant, trying to decide what best to say. "Mr. Crosby, may I present Captain Bryant, my neighbor and landlord of sorts. And this is Mr. Crosby, my . . ." She faltered as she took in the captain's expectant, searching look. "A family friend."

Captain Bryant's eyes narrowed, clearly unsatisfied with her answer. "How do you do, Mr. Crosby?"

"Well, I thank you. But I had better take my leave." Mr. Crosby consulted his pocket watch. "The Oxford coach departs from the Mill Inn at four, I understand."

"Are you walking, sir?" Captain Bryant asked.

"I am."

"Then allow me to offer my horse. Leave it with the hostler at the inn and tell him I shall call round for him in an hour or so."

"That is very generous of you, Captain. But I shall have no trouble arriving on schedule. I timed myself on the walk here, you see. I shall have four minutes to spare if I leave now."

"As you wish."

Mr. Crosby bowed, smiled at Mariah, and then turned smartly on his heel.

Mariah and the captain watched him depart in silence, the tension of unasked and unanswered questions pulsing between them.

Suddenly a ball bounced across the lawn and rolled up Captain Bryant's boot. He bent to retrieve it just as George Barnes ran into view from the poorhouse lane.

Eyeing the strange man, George stopped where he was.

Captain Bryant raised the ball and, seeing the lad ready, threw it true. George caught it easily.

Mariah waved the boy over, glad for the distraction. "Come and meet our new neighbor." When George stood before them, Mariah turned to the captain. "Captain Bryant, may I present George Barnes. He and his sister live in Honora House, there across the road."

"Hello, George."

"Hello, sir. What sort of captain are you?"

"Royal Navy."

George scratched his ear. "You are a long way from the sea, sir."

The captain grinned. "As I am daily aware."

Once George had run off again, Captain Bryant asked, "What is Honora House?"

"The parish poorhouse."

Relieved he had not persisted in asking about Mr. Crosby, Mariah explained the little she had learned from Jack Strong and Mr. Phelps.

Honora House was not a workhouse, where able-bodied persons

were required to labor strenuously to earn their keep—breaking stones or picking oakum—or carted off for factory work. This poorhouse took in only the elderly, the lame, the simple, and children. They were not forced into hard labor, but all who were able were required to complete chores to keep the place running and as self-sustaining as possible. One might be assigned duties in the gardens, the kitchen, the laundry, or the knitting room, where hands young and old, male and female, were kept busy knitting socks, stockings, and mufflers to sell in the village. The institution also received funding from the church and wealthy benefactors—the Prin-Hallsey family primary among them.

Mariah wondered if Hugh Prin-Hallsey still managed to contribute.

"An odd location for a poorhouse," the captain said. "So close to the estate, I mean."

"Yes," Mariah agreed. "I thought so too."

And now that she had received payment for her first novel, she would not have to go there. At least, not yet.

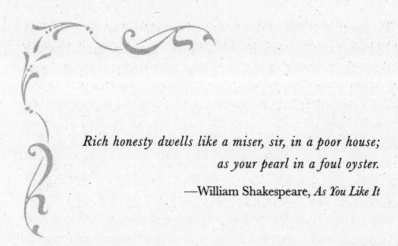

Rich honesty dwells like a miser, sir, in a poor house;
as your pearl in a foul oyster.

—William Shakespeare, *As You Like It*

chapter 10

rom her bedchamber and sitting room windows, Mariah glimpsed the man on the poorhouse roof several times over the next two weeks. She wondered if he was employed by the institution, or was one of its residents. If the former, the roof must be in poor condition indeed to require such regular attention.

After one of these sightings, Mariah saw George and Lizzy Barnes walking along the road, coming from the direction of the village. Their father, George had told her, had once owned one of the mills in Whitmore. But three mills in one village had proved one too many, and the mill had gone under. Mariah could imagine George grown, a spotless apron over his ample belly, fine white powder in his hair and in the creases of his hands, cheerfully serving customers at the mill that would have been his one day, had his father not lost it.

Their mother now lived as companion to an elderly woman in Bourton. Mariah had asked George once why their mother did not come to live with them at Honora House. George shook his head. "Says it would kill 'er to enter a poorhouse. Her a gentleman's daughter and all. Nearly killed her to send me and Lizzy. But after Papa died, she couldn't afford to feed us, could she? And the ol' tabby she works for hasn't room for us and can't abide children either."

George's sister, Lizzy, was a girl of seventeen with golden-brown hair a shade lighter than her brother's and blue eyes a shade darker. She was a slender girl, not much taller than her brother, though six years his senior. George would no doubt soon surpass her in height, as he had already done in girth. As the daughter of a miller and a gentle-woman, Lizzy would likely have married well, thanks to a generous dowry or at least an endless supply of bread and other good things to eat. Instead, she whiled away her youth in the poorhouse, her bloom radiant, though few had opportunity to see it.

Mariah wondered at the liberty George Barnes seemed to enjoy. She had heard that poorhouse children were required to attend three hours of school each weekday, when the old village schoolmaster came out to teach basic reading, writing, and arithmetic. And each child had chores to attend to, depending on age and ability. But George seemed to roam about the countryside at will.

Mariah saw Lizzy less often. By rights, Lizzy should no longer have been in the poorhouse. When boys turned thirteen, and girls sixteen, they were considered able-bodied adults and were sent off to the workhouses in Cirencester or Stroud, or the "house of industry" in Oxford. Grim fates indeed compared to the life of relative ease afforded by Honora House.

But Lizzy had been kept on, employed by the poorhouse matron, and so was allowed to remain with her brother.

Mariah unlatched her window and pushed it open. "George?" she called down.

He smiled, altering his course toward the gatehouse. "Yes, miss?"

"May I ask you a question?"

"Of course, miss. You know I'll do anything for a biscuit."

"Greedy boy," she teased. "I haven't any biscuits today. But come back tomorrow."

His small eyes lit in anticipation.

She asked, "Who is the man who walks about the poorhouse roof?"

George's smile instantly faded. "Couldn't say, miss."

"You don't know his name?"

He ducked his head in uncharacteristic unease. "No, miss."

Lizzy walked over and put her arm around George. "Please don't ask him. We are not meant to know about any man on the roof, and definitely *not* to speak about him."

"But why?"

Lizzy's brow furrowed, her normally sweet expression sparking with irritation.

Mariah winced. "Sorry. But I cannot help wondering. I cannot abide a mystery." *Unless I am the one writing it,* she added to herself.

Mariah bid farewell to the Barneses and closed the window. She heard Dixon's half boots in the passage and called out to her. "That man is up on the roof again."

Dixon stepped into the room and joined her at the window. Watching the distant man, she shook her head and clucked her tongue. "If he isn't careful, he'll fall to his death. Crazy fool."

Mariah grew alarmed. "Do you really think he is in danger? Perhaps I should walk over and make sure the matron knows he's up there."

Mariah knew the poorhouse was overseen by a board of guardians, but left the day-to-day running of things to its matron, a Mrs. Pitt.

She added, "I'd hate for him to be hurt when we might have prevented it."

Dixon turned on her heel. "Take Martin with you. Perhaps he'll oblige me and fall off instead."

A few minutes later, Mariah walked up the path to the poorhouse.

The building rose three stories high, topped by the flat roof and myriad chimneys she could see from the gatehouse. But this was the first time she had viewed the poorhouse at close range. While Windrush Court and most of the buildings in the village were constructed of the honey-colored limestone typical of the Cotswolds, Honora House was built of stark grey stone. Tall rectangular windows lined all levels on each side. A pair of spindly yew trees flanked its otherwise unadorned entrance.

Several yards to the left of this entrance sat two women on a bench. How small they appeared against the backdrop of the tall box of a building. As Mariah drew closer, she saw the ladies were older, perhaps about sixty years of age. The dark-haired one was knitting, while the white-haired woman simply sat with her face raised to the spring sunshine.

"Good day, ladies," Mariah greeted them. "A lovely day to be out of doors."

"Indeed it is," the white-haired woman replied.

"Clouds rolling in," her dark-haired companion amended.

Mariah looked from one woman to the other. And even as she formed her next sentence, she knew it to be only partly true. Feature to feature the resemblance between them was remarkable, yet beyond the hair color, there were striking differences. "You two are so alike," she said. "You must be sisters."

"And you must be a genius." This from the woman with dark hair mixed with strands of steel grey, whose mouth and eyes were framed by the deep grooves carved by hard times and bitterness.

The white-haired woman smiled. "We are indeed. Twins. I am the younger, but my hair is white while Sister's is still dark. Where is the justice in that, I ask you?" Her eyes twinkled.

Mariah smiled in return. "I am Miss Mariah Aubrey. I live in the gatehouse across the way."

"Ah, yes." The cheerful woman nodded. "The children have mentioned you. You are as lovely as they said you were."

Her sister frowned. "They never said that."

"Well, not in words. They are boys after all. But they said as much with elbows to each other's ribs and blushing faces."

Mariah grinned. "I know only a few of the children by name. George and Sam and George's sister, Lizzy."

"George is such a dear. He brought back that pot of jam you gave him and shared it all round the table of a Sunday morning."

"Did he? I am glad to hear it."

"My portion would barely cover a crumb," the dour sister said. "Though it was tasty."

"When Dixon and I make more, I shall bring you your own pot," Mariah offered.

"That is very kind, my dear. Is Dixon your maid?"

Mariah shrugged. "I prefer *companion*. Miss Dixon was our former nursery-governess but stayed on with the family after my sister and I were grown." She hurried to change the subject before they might ask about her family. "And might I know your names?"

The cheerful white-haired woman smiled and gestured toward her sister. "This is Miss Agnes Merryweather and I am Miss Amy."

"How do you do?" Mariah curtsied to each sister in turn. Amy smiled beatifically while Agnes studied her with narrowed eyes.

"I was hoping to speak to the matron here. Do you know if—"

"Out," Agnes said, her mouth pressed in a thin line until her lips had nearly disappeared.

"Mrs. Pitt has gone into the village," Amy said. "Invited to dine with the vicar's family and the undersheriff. Isn't that nice?"

Agnes snorted softly.

"Perhaps I might wait inside?" Mariah suggested.

"No visitors are allowed inside when Mrs. Pitt isn't here," Agnes said. "Afraid someone will see what it is really like."

Mariah felt her brows rise.

Amy Merryweather said carefully, "The matron is naturally . . ."

"Suspicious," Agnes supplied.

Her sister amended, "Cautious."

"Miserly."

"Officious."

Mariah felt like a spectator at a battledore and shuttlecock match, looking from sister to sister as each returned the other's volley.

Agnes scowled. "Miserly I said, and miserly I meant. You can't tell me some of the parish funds didn't end up in that ridiculous feather-stuck hat Mrs. Pitt wears, or on the private table of her overstuffed husband—God rest his soul. Why, I smelt roast goose on Christmas, when all we had—"

"You cannot know that, Agnes," Miss Amy said patiently. "I saw no goose."

"I know roast goose when I smell it, Amy. Never say I don't. I may not have tasted it in many years, but well do I remember that golden smell!"

Miss Amy turned to Mariah. "Her nose has always been her best feature—it is true, Miss Aubrey."

"And what did we feast upon that holy of days? Boiled chicken. From an old cock what had been strutting the earth longer than the man on the roof."

Flashing her eyes at Mariah, Amy Merryweather laid a warning hand on her sister's arm. Agnes darted a glance first at her sister, then Mariah, before looking away.

"Man on the roof?" Mariah echoed.

Amy swallowed, the bony ball moving up and down her withered neck. Agnes sullenly refused to meet her gaze.

"That is actually why I've come." Mariah pointed to the roof. "About the man up there."

Agnes Merryweather clasped slender, veined hands in her lap and pinned Mariah with a meaningful gaze. "None of us knows about any man on the roof, Miss Aubrey. There *is* no man on the roof."

Mariah protested, "But—"

"Did one of the children say something?" Miss Amy whispered, face tense with worry. "You must tell me if they did, so I might warn them. The Pitts have been very pointed in their instructions."

Mariah shook her head. "They haven't said a word, I assure you. But I have seen him myself from the gatehouse."

"Who else knows?" Agnes asked. "Has anybody else seen him?"

"Only Dixon. I don't know if she told anybody."

"The less said the better, my dear," cautioned Miss Amy. "If the Pitts hear talk, they are sure to suspect one of us."

"And they will line us up and not feed us until one of us confesses."

Mariah felt her mouth slacken. "But that is preposterous. You may tell her *I* saw him. Or send her to me and I shall tell her myself."

"Us, send Mrs. Pitt somewhere?" Agnes nearly grinned. "That I should love to see."

Miss Amy chewed her lip in thought. "Does it not wonder you, Sister? For years, nothing. The gate locked, the house abandoned. But now that the gatehouse is inhabited . . . ?"

Agnes nodded. "It does wonder me."

"Why did they lock the gate? Do you know?" Mariah asked.

Agnes Merryweather's lip curled. "We know the reason given. They said some of us were stealing. Which was not true."

"You mustn't forget, Agnes," Amy said gently, "there was Harry Cooper and those strawberries."

"Three strawberries! Poor lad had never seen strawberries before. Had one in his mouth and two in his hand for his sisters before I could say a word. If they locked the gate for that, well, I don't know what that says about Christian charity."

Miss Amy looked at Mariah. "You see, my dear, at first they left the gate open and we could stroll about the grounds. Not near the house, mind. Such lovely gardens. That young Mr. Phelps took such pleasure in showing us his prized specimens. Even gave Sister a posy on more than one occasion."

Even now Agnes's wrinkled cheek pinkened.

"The family hosted a harvest festival our first year here and invited us all to join in. What dainties! What music. They brought in fiddlers from the village. We danced right there on the lawns. Such a happy time."

"But then they said we were stealing from the kitchen garden and the henhouse."

Timidly, Mariah added, "I heard poaching mentioned as well."

"Poaching! Never say so. I think we would know if anything of that sort was going on, sitting here all day as we do."

"But, Sister, we only sit out when the weather is fine."

"Do you think the old men here have fowling pieces? Or are spry enough to go traipsing about the wood setting traps? We would know. I'd not miss that biting gamey smell."

Amy shook her head. "She would not. It is true."

"It seems a pity the gate remains locked," Mariah mused.

Both sisters nodded.

"Well." Amy sighed. "I am relieved it was not one of the children. If word gets round, there isn't much they can do to two old crones like us."

"Except forget to purchase coal for the fires," Agnes said. "Take our shawls to launder and never return them. Like last time."

"Hush, Sister. Miss Aubrey has not come to hear our troubles—the worst of which are long past in any case."

Mariah was indignant at the thought of these two old women facing deprivation. Punishment. "But that is not fair."

Amy Merryweather eyed her knowingly. "Life is not fair, Miss Aubrey. Who ever said it was?"

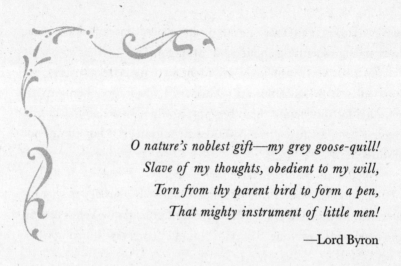

O nature's noblest gift—my grey goose-quill!
Slave of my thoughts, obedient to my will,
Torn from thy parent bird to form a pen,
That mighty instrument of little men!

—Lord Byron

chapter 11

ords seemed to flow more slowly now that the rent was paid. Feeling stymied about the last scene in her second novel, Mariah set down her quill, wiped ineffectually at the ink stains on her fingers, and slipped her arms into a long-sleeved pelisse. She decided an evening stroll around the grounds was in order. Motion always seemed to spur creativity, and she was in definite need of that ability at present.

She was halfway around the rose garden when Captain Bryant's voice startled her. "Miss Aubrey. Was that you I heard talking to yourself?"

"Oh. Was I?" She felt her face flush and was grateful for the veil of dusky twilight. "Dreadful habit."

Captain Bryant was dressed casually in trousers and coat over an unadorned shirt. No waistcoat, no cravat. No doubt he had not expected to encounter anyone out-of-doors after sunset. He said, "You were saying something about a Mr. Montgomery."

Oh dear. "You mustn't pay any attention to me, Captain," she said hurriedly. "At Miss Littlewart's seminary I was forever being repri- manded for distracting the other pupils, when I had no idea I had made a sound. I fear it is a habit deeply ingrained. I hope I did not disturb you."

"Not at all. Shall we take a turn together?"

She nodded and fell into step beside him as they strolled the perim- eter of the reflecting pond. Mariah looked up and saw Venus among the first stars of evening. She said, "I find I do my best thinking while I walk."

"And what do you think of?"

"Oh . . ." She hesitated, realizing she had asked for that. "Whatever my mind is working on at the time, I suppose. A solution to a problem, new ideas . . ."

Gravel crunched beneath his boots. "You are not afraid to walk in the dark?"

Relieved for the change of topic, Mariah shook her head. "One of the advantages of living within a walled estate. One feels unreason- ably safe."

"My being here does not hinder you?"

"Not at all."

"I am glad to hear it."

They walked for several more minutes in easy silence. He bent and picked up a stone and skipped it across the surface of the pond, disrupting the reflection of the moon on the silver plane of water. One bounce, two, three. He started to walk on but turned back when she sank to her haunches on the bank, sorting through the rocks until she found two smooth, flat stones. She stood and gave the first a side- armed toss. *Plunk.* It sank directly. She bent her knees and tried again. One bounce, two, three.

"Bravo," he said. "I never knew a girl who could skip rocks."

She smiled and moved on, deciding not to mention that her brothers had taught her.

"May I ask about your family?" he said, as though reading her thoughts. "Are your parents not living?"

It was a natural question. Why else would a single woman be living out from under her father's roof?

"On the contrary, they are both alive and well," she answered brightly, hoping to avoid more questions. "Mother is no doubt enjoying spring. It is her favorite season. And yours?"

"My parents, or my favorite season?"

She chuckled. "Both, if you like."

"I suppose I prefer summer. And my parents are both living. In Swindon."

He paused before a bench and gestured toward it. She sat down while he remained standing, arms crossed.

"Have you no brothers or sisters, Miss Aubrey?"

"I do. Two brothers and one sister." To steer the conversation to less painful ground, she added, "My elder brother is stationed in India."

"That must be quite an adventure."

"For him, yes. I don't think his wife quite agrees. And have you brothers and sisters?"

He grimaced. "My mother had six children who did not survive infancy and one who lived to see the ripe old age of seventeen. All I have living is one younger sister. Recently married and quite happy in her choice."

"I am glad for her."

"Is your sister married?" he asked.

How polite he is, Mariah thought. To dance around her family situation carefully, to avoid stepping on her toes.

"No. She is only nineteen. But my father hopes for news of an advantageous match by the hour. And she is a sweet-natured girl who will no doubt oblige him."

He stiffened and looked away. What had she said to offend him? Surveying his profile by moonlight, Mariah saw him nod.

"Yes, fathers can be quite persuasive when it comes to daughters. They wield great influence, and overpower her true feelings with arguments of 'not rich enough, not well-connected enough, no decent prospects.' "

He sat down heavily on the other end of the bench.

"You know this from experience?" she asked gently.

He nodded, resting his elbows on his knees. "Painful experience."

For a moment, they sat without speaking. An unseen insect landed on her arm and she swatted it away. A turtle dove cooed a gentle *turr, turr*, while a wood pigeon warbled mournfully.

She said quietly, "It is not only young men who are scrutinized by fathers and found lacking. Young women are also rejected for not being rich enough nor well connected enough. And no matter how fervently the young man professes his love, in the end, he obeys his parent."

He looked over at her, likely hearing the wistful catch in her voice and having no need to ask if she spoke from painful experience of her own. "I am very sorry to hear it, Miss Aubrey."

Disconcerted to realize what she had revealed, she looked away, staring out at the pond once more.

As if trying to cheer her, he said, "We have that in common, at least." He paused. "Is there no hope your young man might change his father's mind?"

She uttered a bleak laugh. "None. He is married."

He winced. "Ah."

"And you, Captain. Is there any hope your ladylove will change her mind, or her father's?"

He nodded. "I have great hope. In fact, Miss Aubrey, that is precisely why I am here."

Before she could ask him to elucidate, he rose, offering his arm. "It grows late. May I walk you back to the gatehouse?"

She hesitated. Now that he had declared his intentions toward another woman, she felt there was nothing improper in his gesture, nor in her accepting it. She did not fear he would misunderstand or take advantage. Rising, she tentatively placed her hand on his. "Thank you."

He tucked her hand beneath his arm, and the two walked companionably along the curved drive. She relished the warmth and friendly affection the connection delivered. It had been too long since someone had touched her, except for Henry's brotherly embrace, or the practical touch Dixon might bestow while dressing her hair or fastening her frocks.

Dixon was not the demonstrative person Mariah's sister was. Julia was forever throwing her arms around Mariah in some triumph or dramatic woe. How she missed her. Their mother was mildly affectionate as well. Enjoyed brushing her daughters' hair and having her own brushed in turn. And the kiss on the brow before bedtime. Her father, however, had never been openly affectionate. Like many men, he was reserved and conscious of decorum. Mariah had not once seen him kiss his wife or any of his four children.

The gatehouse came into view, a candle left glowing in the kitchen window. How thoughtful Dixon was.

She pressed Captain Bryant's arm. "I wish you every success in your endeavors here, Captain."

For a moment, he kept hold of her hand, squeezing it gently. "And I wish your heart might one day heal."

She quirked a brow. "Would yours?"

"Ah. I have yet to acknowledge defeat, so I cannot allow myself even to contemplate the need to heal. For now, it is one step, one day at a time. Ever keeping my eye on the prize."

She gave him a lopsided grin. "Then I bid you good-night, Captain. And sweet dreams of her."

As soon as she stepped inside, Dixon lurched from the kitchen table and released an airy whoosh of relief.

"Miss Mariah, are you all right? I have been fretting and praying for the better part of an hour. What can you be thinking, out all hours with him?"

"There is no need to fear, Dixon. He has made it perfectly plain he has his heart set on another woman." Mariah slipped off her pelisse. "In fact, that is why he is here. To prove to the world that he has come up in its ranks. And to convince the girl's father he is now good enough for her."

"Is that what he's about? I wondered."

"Well, we need wonder no more."

"Just be careful," Dixon warned. "I would hate to see you break your heart all over again."

Mariah blinked back sudden, unexpected tears. "I know, Dixon. I know."

On a Sunday in mid-May, Mariah wrote a letter to Henry, thanking him again for his help with Mr. Crosby, and inviting him to visit at his next opportunity. Noticing the nib of her quill was fraying, she paused and laid it aside. She would need to cut a new one.

While the goose feather soaked in hot water, she sharpened her penknife. Dixon had offered to mend pens for her, but it was a task Mariah liked to do herself. She was admittedly picky about her writing implements.

First she stripped away the barb where the quill would rest against her forefinger. Then she cut away the tip at a steep angle and removed the membrane from inside. She made a slit in the center of the barrel, sliced a U from its underside, and angled off the nib on each side of the slit. Her last step was to "nib" the pen, thinning the tip by scraping it with her penknife.

After the tedious operation, Mariah rose and stretched her stiff neck muscles. The house was quiet with Dixon gone to church. Too quiet.

Church . . . Why did Mariah suddenly feel as though she were in the hallowed place herself? She had gone only once since her arrival—last month on Easter.

Mariah cocked her head to one side, listening. What had she heard?

She stepped to the partially opened window and pushed it wide. There it was, more clearly now. A distant melody, sung by a voice so sweet, so pure, it stilled Mariah's soul. For a moment, she simply closed her eyes and savored.

Curiosity rising, Mariah skipped downstairs and stepped outside. She followed the sound of the voice across the road, toward the poorhouse.

The crunch of her feet on the gravel path disrupted the sound, and she was torn between wanting to stop and listen, and wanting to discover its source. She stepped from the gravel to the spongy moss verge and, in the resulting quiet, could make out a few words.

> "Time, like an ever rolling stream,
> bears all who breathe away. . . ."

Mariah emerged from the tree-lined path, and there sat the two old sisters in their customary places before the poorhouse. And standing before them was a small girl with long, reddish-gold curls. In one hand she held a long twig with a gossamer ribbon tied to its tip, swirling it about, forming loops in the air as she sang. She focused on the whirling ribbon and not the sisters, as if she had no conscious awareness of an audience. But perhaps this was illusion, for her voice was pitch-perfect. Hauntingly beautiful.

> "They fly forgotten, as a dream
> dies at the opening day. . . ."

Mariah's slipper skimmed a rock and sent it skiffing across the path. At its small sound, the girl looked over her shoulder, then darted around the side of the poorhouse and out of view as quickly as a startled hare.

"Oh! Forgive me," Mariah said to the Miss Merryweathers as she approached. "I did not mean to interrupt. In fact I hoped to listen. I heard her singing from the gatehouse. What a voice she has!"

"Sings like an angel but flighty as a bird," Agnes said.

Amy added, "Terribly shy, poor girl."

"I am sorry. I shall go, and perhaps she will return."

"Never mind, my dear," Miss Amy said. "Now that you are here, do stay and chat. It is such a treat to have a caller."

"Very well." Mariah sat on a wooden slat chair angled toward the bench. "Who is that girl, if I may ask?"

Amy answered, "Her name is Maggie, but most of the children call her Magpie."

"Magpie?" Mariah chuckled. "How unjust. She sings like a nightingale."

Amy nodded. "She is an orphan, poor dear."

"I am sorry to hear it. I suppose there are no orphanages in the parish?"

Agnes shook her head. "None that I know of. Not for girls her age, at any rate."

"Does she often sing for you?"

"Most every Sunday. Have you never heard her before?"

"No."

Amy eyed her speculatively. "Then perhaps you were not ready to listen before now."

Mariah felt her brow wrinkle at that odd statement. More likely she had simply not had her windows open before the weather turned warm.

"Do you not attend church, Miss Mariah?" Amy asked.

"I . . . used to. Do you?"

"Not anymore. Some folks here walk to the village church, but my days of country walks are over, I'm afraid. Now and again, the vicar or an itinerant revivalist comes by, but otherwise, we are content to commune with our Maker here, and listen to sweet Maggie sing."

Miss Amy closed her eyes and continued the hymn in a high, reedy warble.

> "O God, our help in ages past,
> our hope for years to come . . ."

Her voice was a stark contrast to the girl's but still oddly beautiful. From somewhere out of sight, the girl joined in, her rich voice complementing and completing the old woman's.

> "be thou our guide while life shall last,
> and our eternal home."

The final note held, shimmered on the air, and burned Mariah's eyes. *Home.*

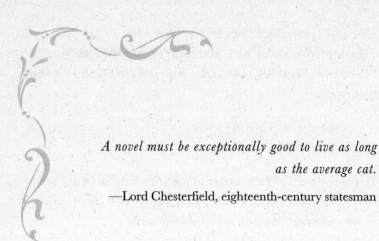

A novel must be exceptionally good to live as long
as the average cat.

—Lord Chesterfield, eighteenth-century statesman

chapter 12

At dinnertime the following week, Mariah paused at the rain-streaked kitchen window. She saw Martin dash across the yard from the stable, hat pulled low against the spring shower. She had almost expected him not to bother, considering the weather and his obvious dislike of Dixon's cooking.

A whiff of rain and Martin's odd herbal scent followed him inside.

"Hello, Martin."

"Miss."

He wiped his boots, hung his hat on a peg, then eyed the sideboard with suspicion. There, a pork pie belched steam as well as a slightly off odor.

"The day is wet, Martin," Mariah began. "Will you not take your meal with us? We need not stand on formalities here."

Martin looked at Dixon, her back stiff as she attempted to pry an overcooked pudding from its mold.

He glanced back outside at the rain.

"We do not mind," Mariah assured him. "Do we, Dixon?"

Dixon turned and set the lopsided, scorched pudding on the table. "You are the mistress."

Sigh.

Mariah set an extra place while Martin prodded a sleepy Chaucer off the usually unoccupied third chair.

The meal passed in awkward silence, Mariah now and again attempting conversation.

"Do you find it difficult to climb into the loft?"

Martin took a sip of water. "I manage."

"And have you everything you need?"

Martin nodded, eyes on his plate. "Jack Strong helped move my things up there. Even offered to build a few bookcases and the like."

"How kind."

Mariah paused to take a bite and conversation lagged. Martin seemed to be concentrating on arduously chewing and swallowing each mouthful. Finally, he set his fork down, his plate still half full.

"Miss Mariah," he began. "I wonder if I might make myself useful in the kitchen. I served the Royal Navy as seaman, cook, and steward in their turn."

Dixon's mouth became a prim line. "Do you think we want your ship's biscuit and salt beef here?"

Mariah privately thought it might make for a nice change.

"Spoken by the chef who produced this pottage?" Martin lifted a gelatinous piece of . . . something . . . from his plate.

Mariah winced, realizing the situation could quickly become hostile.

"There is nothing wrong with my cooking." Dixon bristled. "It is basic, I admit, but perfectly nourishing. Is it not, Miss Mariah?"

She forced a smile. "Of course, Dixon. But you do not enjoy the task. How often I have heard you lament it. And if Martin wishes to try his hand—er, sorry—then I don't see the harm. Perhaps just for a week to start?"

Dixon sat back, lips puckering.

Martin dipped his head. "I am much obliged to you, miss." Seeing Dixon's sour expression, he placated, "Now, Miss Dixon. I have a hankering to be back among the pans and kettles, I do. Perhaps I might prepare dinner, and you might continue with breakfast?"

"An excellent suggestion, Martin." Mariah glanced hopefully at Dixon.

But she refused to look at either of them. "Very well."

Martin tried again. "And you are right, Miss Dixon. Shipboard fare was monotonous indeed: boiled beef or pork, dried peas, cheese, duff, lemon juice, and weevil-infested ship's biscuit. But now and again, the captain would allow us to fish from the deck. Then what delights we would have—shark, swordfish, even turtles. How the captain enjoyed my turtle soup. But what he liked most of all was my figgy dowdy, which I made on Sundays when we had the stores for it: biscuit, pork fat, plums, figs, rum, and currants all baked together."

"Sounds delicious," Mariah said.

"It was indeed. Shall I prepare one tomorrow?"

"That would be excellent," Mariah enthused. "My brother Henry is due to call again tomorrow."

He was coming to finish the read-through of *Daughters of Brighton* with her and Dixon before delivering it to Mr. Crosby. In fact, Mariah added to herself, perhaps Henry would visit more often if someone else were doing the cooking.

The next morning after Martin had done the washing up of the breakfast things, he began pottering about the kitchen, apron folded over and tied around his thick waist. At first Dixon fastidiously stayed away, as if allowing him to sink on his own. She settled herself before the drawing-room fire with mending basket and spectacles, wincing every time pots clanged or a cupboard door slammed.

Martin emerged once or twice to ask where some utensil or staple might be found, and eventually she got up with a long-suffering sigh and followed him into the kitchen, muttering about how his cooking was supposed to *save* her time.

Mariah followed as far as the door and pressed her ear to it, her anxiety increasing as she listened.

"You will have lumps, adding flour like that!" Then, "Is something burning? Oh, it's you. What is that pungent odor of yours, by the way?"

"An ointment for my arm," Martin replied. "And thank you for noticing."

"Ah . . . Well," she faltered. "Better use a larger pot or that will boil over."

A lid clanged, followed by a rapid chopping sound.

"Miss Mariah does not like leeks."

Finally, Martin's voice rose. "Hush, woman, and taste this."

Mariah peeked through the crack in the door in time to see Martin all but shove a spoon past Dixon's lips.

Waiting for her reaction, he tasted the sauce himself. "Hmm?" he asked, brows tented high.

Dixon hesitated, and then defeat crossed her features. "I own it is very good." She dipped the spoon into the pot and sampled it once more. "What did you say you called it?"

He was drawn, he supposed, like a hound to the scent of fox, or a cat to cream. Once more, Matthew's evening stroll took him to the gatehouse, with its padlocked gate and candlelight glowing from the windows. Not to mention its attractive occupant.

As he approached, he again heard voices—Miss Aubrey's, as well as the low, deep-pitched tones of a man.

A man . . . in the gatehouse at night? It must be their manservant. The odd man with the stooped shoulder and hook hand.

But the deep voice he heard did not agree with his supposition. It seemed younger than that man would possess, and more cultured.

"Can you be so barbarous to dismiss the man who lives but in your smiles? Oh, my dear! Do not break my heart. If I must leave you, let me bear with me your forgiveness. Let me hear you say you do not hate me."

"Hate you!" repeated Miss Aubrey. "Hate you! Oh no! I never hated anyone; but you know too well that I—"

"Proceed," said the man. "Proceed, dear one. What is it I know? That you love me?"

Who *was* this man? Matthew wondered, alarmed. Was it that Mr. Crosby he had met by chance? Was he forcing his attentions on Miss Aubrey?

After a pause, the man added, "That look speaks yes; then why refuse to make me happy?"

Should he intervene? It was none of his business, of course. Except . . . he *was* master of the estate, at least temporarily. And as such, was not Miss Aubrey entitled to his protection? His sister's face flashed in his mind. If only he might have protected *her*. He doubted Miss Aubrey would welcome his interference. And yet, in good conscience he could not walk away until he was certain.

He knocked sharply on the door.

The raised voices within fell instantly silent.

He knocked again, less sharply this time. He was tempted to peer in through the windows, but the knell of approaching footsteps kept him where he was. The door creaked open a few inches, and the servant woman's face appeared, wearing a jaundiced cast in the golden light of a candle. Her eyes were wary but softened fractionally upon seeing him.

"Captain Bryant. We did not expect you."

"I was just walking by and heard a man raising his voice. Is everything all right?"

"A man? No, sir, you are mistaken."

Matthew hesitated. "I distinctly heard voices. Miss Aubrey's and a man's."

"There is no man here, unless you count Martin. And I don't."

"If Miss Aubrey wishes to entertain male callers in her home, at night, well, that is her prerogative, but—"

"Male callers? Good heavens. What an imagination you have! She hasn't any male callers, Captain. If you heard a man, then it must have been Martin. Old fool is always fussing and complaining about something. It was him, no doubt, giving us all a bellyful of woe."

"But Miss Aubrey sounded upset. If the man frightens her, she ought—"

"She wasn't frightened. Not really. Mostly bluster, Martin is." She began to edge the door closed. "You are very kind to worry, Captain, but there is no need."

Miss Aubrey appeared at her maid's side. "What is it, Dixon?"

"It's Captain Bryant. He thought he heard voices—you arguing with a male caller of all things. I told him it was only Martin."

"Oh . . . Martin. Yes."

Matthew felt his ire rising. Why the subterfuge? "But the man spoke of love."

"Oh!" Miss Aubrey sputtered. "That was not . . . We were not speaking, we were reciting."

"Reciting?"

"Lines from a . . . play. A theatrical. Our family has always enjoyed performing theatricals, especially at Christmas and Epiphany."

"It is May."

"I know, I know. You must think us very foolish."

He studied her face. "Are you well, Miss Aubrey? You look pale."

"Do I?" She brushed a tendril of dark hair from her face. "I assure you I am perfectly well, Captain."

He hesitated. "Well, if you are certain you are all right."

"I am. But thank you for your concern." She formed an unconvincing smile.

He bowed and turned to go, disheartened to conclude that Miss Aubrey had not been honest with him.

Matthew did not intend to spy. Not really. Yet he returned to the gatehouse the next morning before heading to church, compelled to test his suspicions and make certain the occupants of the gatehouse were all right after last night's odd encounter. After he had left them, he had imagined some masked bandit within, threatening violence should they reveal his presence. *A bandit speaking of love?* Foolish notion, he knew, yet he could not rest easy until he assured himself Miss Aubrey was well.

As he neared the back garden, he once again heard voices and, through the bars of the gate, saw two figures on its other side—Miss Mariah and a well-dressed man a few years younger than himself. This was no disembodied voice. No ghostly man. Not that Mr. Crosby he had met and certainly not old Martin. She could not make this man disappear with explanations and excuses. *A man who stayed the whole night in the gatehouse?*

As Matthew stood there, unnoticed, the man enfolded Miss Aubrey in a quick embrace. An unexpected, nauseous dread filled Matthew's gut at the sight. Illogical jealousy? Distaste at having the rumors he'd dismissed confirmed?

Miss Aubrey handed the man a parcel wrapped in brown paper, which he tucked under his arm. He smiled at her and gave the parcel a reassuring pat. A gift perhaps, or something to sell. He knew Miss Aubrey struggled to pay her rent. He had even talked with Hammersmith, trying to persuade the steward to extend a bit of grace. But the man had only grumbled that he need not concern himself. She must have managed this quarter's rent, at least, to still be living in the place.

Miss Aubrey stood where she was, watching the man as he walked to the road, turned toward the village, and disappeared from view. Whatever Matthew's initial feelings, anger now filtered in to replace them. She had lied to him. She and her servant both. No doubt they thought they had fooled him with their little performance last night.

Before he had consciously chosen to do so, Matthew stepped close to the gate and said archly, "Hello, Miss Aubrey."

Mariah whirled, eyes wide. "Oh! Captain Bryant. You startled me."

He leaned his shoulder against the gate. "And why is that?"

"I . . . was not expecting to see you."

"I imagine not. Not when your gentleman caller had his arms about you in broad daylight."

She frowned. "Would you prefer a nighttime tryst?"

"What? No. I was not suggesting . . ." Why did the woman always put him off balance? He was a wobbly-legged midshipman all over again in her presence.

She lifted her chin. "And he was not a gentleman caller, per se."

"No? Then who was he?"

She hesitated. "My . . . friend, who . . . assists me in matters of business."

"What sort of business?"

"That is none of your concern."

"Is it not? If it takes place on this estate?"

"Nothing *took place* anywhere. He spent the night at the inn and only called this morning to bid us farewell. I assure you I have been the picture of propriety since I came to Windrush Court."

"Have you? And before?"

She stared at him, apparently taken aback. Her discomfort,

her evident grief and embarrassment, smote his conscience. "Please forgive me, Miss Aubrey. I ought not have implied anything untoward."

She swallowed, but the tart reply he expected did not come.

chapter 13

On his way inside to shoot billiards—to shoot something—a frustrated Matthew spied Hugh Prin-Hallsey in the dim gunroom. The man was on his knees, digging through the contents of a dusty old cabinet. Behind him was a stack of antique guns, some in and some out of a large packing crate. Hugh, leaning halfway into the cabinet, peeled down the cloth covering from an ornately framed oil painting. Matthew caught only the quickest glimpse of the portrait—a man's face—before Hugh rewrapped the frame. Had Hugh now stooped to selling his family history as well as heirlooms?

It unnerved Matthew to have the man underfoot. How could he make Windrush Court his home if the owner was forever loitering about? He hoped the man would return to London before Lieutenant Hart arrived. And stay there.

Matthew leaned against the doorjamb. "Hello, Prin-Hallsey. Lose something?"

Hugh's reply was an artificial grin bordering on a grimace. As he rose to his feet, one of his knees cracked.

"You know anything about Miss Aubrey having a man of business?" Matthew asked, and quickly wished he had not.

"Man of business?" Hugh's brows formed a dark V. "What sort of business would she have to conduct?"

"I don't know. I saw her speak with a man as he was leaving the gatehouse, and hand him a parcel. She mentioned he was her friend who assists her in matters of business."

Hugh's voice rose. "You saw her give the man a parcel?"

Matthew nodded.

"A large parcel?" he asked eagerly.

Matthew marked off a rectangle with his hands. "Fairly large. About the size of a book, I would say."

"A book?" He frowned. "Did you get the man's name?"

"No. She did not say. I asked her maid when I passed her, but she either could not or would not tell me. Seemed to make her nervous when I asked."

"I wonder why." Hugh's eyes were far away in thought. "What is Miss Aubrey up to?"

When Dixon showed Hugh Prin-Hallsey into the drawing room, Mariah quickly tucked her page of new story ideas inside a volume of Johnson's dictionary. "Hugh! I mean, Mr. Prin-Hallsey. This is a surprise." She rose and curtsied. "How do you do?"

He swept off his hat, giving her a stiff, perfunctory bow. "I could be better, Miss Aubrey."

"Oh? Might I help you with something?"

"Indeed I hope you can." He turned his hat around in his manicured hands. Hands that did not match his lank, unwashed hair and unshaven face. "I am looking for something, you see. Something that belongs to me."

"And what is that?"

"Something your aunt had in her possession before she died. I wonder if, perhaps, she gave it to you? Not realizing she had no right to do so."

She stared at him, thinking back to the things her aunt had brought over, and to her warnings about Hugh.

"She did give you something?" he asked eagerly. "Never fear, I will not blame you. You may not have realized your aunt's error. How could you?"

Mariah slowly shook her head. "My aunt gave me nothing of value, if that is what you mean. She only came to call on me once, soon after I moved in here. To see me settled."

"And she made you a gift?"

"Only a few small things for the house."

"What? What?" His eyes were feverish. Nearly manic, she thought.

Mariah shrugged uneasily. "Only a basket of kitchen things. A tin of tea, another of coffee. A few candles, and a packet of biscuits."

"A tin? Have you it still?"

She hesitated. "I think so."

"Then let me see it." He turned to the kitchen door through which he had so recently stepped, and held it open for her. She had little choice but to precede him into the kitchen.

Dixon spun around from her place at the worktable as they entered, her softly lined face grimacing. "Bless me, but you startled me."

"I am sorry, Dixon. Might you put the kettle on? It seems Mr. Prin-Hallsey has a sudden longing for tea." She turned to the man. "Or would you prefer coffee?"

"I don't— Whichever you prefer is fine. The tin, Miss Aubrey?"

Mariah led the way to the larder, feeling Dixon's concerned gaze on her back. She quickly located the ornamental tea tin—they had reused it over and over again, as the original few ounces of Ceylon had long since been used up.

He grabbed the tin from her, pried open the lid, and began shifting the loose tea this way and that as though to see to the bottom.

"Here." She took it from him, dumped the tea leaves into a bowl, and then handed it back. He looked inside the now-empty tin.

"Nothing," he murmured.

What had he expected to find?

She had more difficulty finding the old coffee tin.

"Dixon? Do you remember what we did with that blue enamel coffee tin my aunt gave us when first we came?"

"Oh." Dixon wiped her hands on her apron. "Just a moment and I'll fetch it."

She returned from her own room a few moments later and offered the blue tin as though one of the magi presenting a gift.

Hugh pulled it from her and carelessly ripped off the lid, sending a clattering shower of buttons and pins scuttling across the kitchen floor. Dixon's face crumpled as though her last few shillings had been cast upon the sea, irretrievable.

"There is nothing here," Hugh announced. "What else did you say she gave you?"

"Just some biscuits, wrapped in paper, which are long gone I am afraid."

Dixon added, "And your aunt gave us a candle—"

"Several candles," Mariah interrupted quickly, with a warning look at Dixon. "But those are long gone as well."

"Dash it." Hugh dropped his head, rubbed his long-fingered hand over his unkempt hair, and fought for control. "Well." He straightened abruptly. "Pardon the intrusion. I trust, *cousin* Mariah, that should you remember anything else your aunt gave you, you will not hesitate to let me know?"

Mariah nodded, but the promise would not come.

Once Hugh had gone, Mariah helped Dixon gather up the spilled buttons. Then she lit a candle and walked slowly upstairs to the attic. There, she pulled the old key from around her neck and knelt before her aunt's chest. She had resisted opening it to this point. But now . . . What in the world did he think was inside? Surely there was nothing to her aunt's jest about "treasure." Was it possible Hugh had believed it?

She slid the key into the lock and tried to turn it. It would not give. She jiggled it in the slot and tried again. *Click.* She raised the lid and lifted her candle high to see inside. On top was a lace shawl, curiously like the one she kept in her own trunk. She set it aside. Under it, she found two pairs of gloves, a stack of old ledgers, two novels, and two miniature portraits—one of Aunt Fran's son and one of Mariah's uncle Norris, both long dead. She peered more closely at the one of her mother's brother. How bittersweet to see his face again after so many years. What a funny, lovable man he had been.

Setting these aside, she picked up the first of what appeared to be several large, heavy ledgers. Household accounts? Journals? She had no interest in the former and wondered if it would be proper to read the latter. But had Francesca Prin-Hallsey not left them in her care? What had she said . . . ? *"Wait until after I am dead and buried, and then you may sift through my things."* Something like it, at any rate.

She lifted the cover of the first volume and began to read.

> *The Prin-Hallseys wish everyone to think they are from an old, good family with close connections to the nobility. But the truth of the matter is that old Horace Hallsey made his living as a tailor. But after listening to his patrons—many of them personages of quality—he acquired several useful investment strategies, the ability to mimic an upper-crust accent, and a style of conversation pleasing to the ton. He added the Prin to his surname, taken from his mother's maiden name, because he thought it made him sound aristocratic, and to distance himself from the name of his family's well-known London business, Hallsey and Sons. He met his first wife at Covent Garden. An actress . . .*

Mariah shook her head. No wonder Aunt Fran didn't want these journals to become public until after her death. Did it also explain why she had given them to Mariah—did she fear Hugh would destroy them, should they fall into his hands?

The candle guttered, and Mariah's knees began to ache. She decided she would take the journals down to her room to read them in greater comfort at her leisure.

When a hired post-chaise stopped before the gatehouse three days later, Mariah hurried to the window, fearing who it might be this time.

It was Henry. What was he doing back so soon? She was not expecting him, especially midweek. And why the carriage to her door instead of taking the coach from Oxford to Whitmore and then walking the rest of the way as usual? Why the hurry, the added expense?

She could tell nothing from his expression, hat pulled low against the drizzle, frock coattails whipping in the wind. He carried a parcel under one arm and held a valise in the other. Had Mr. Crosby rejected her second manuscript already?

She hurried to the door and flung it wide. "Henry, what is it? Is everything all right?"

A slow smile lifted one side of his mouth. "You tell me." He handed her the brown-paper-wrapped parcel, and she took it in her arms like a mother takes a child. It was solid, rectangular. Her heart began pounding. Could it be? So soon?

Henry said, "Am I to come in or stand in the wet?"

"Oh. Do come in," she murmured as she stepped back, her eyes and thoughts on the parcel. She set it on the table and carefully began to pull away the paper.

Henry wiped his feet and removed his hat. "Come on, Rye, for once in your life, just tear in."

She felt slightly offended at his remark but was too distracted to do more than shoot him a look. She ripped the paper and let it fall to the floor. She stared, eyes wide, nerves jangling.

There it was. In her hands.

A Winter in Bath
by Lady A

"Is it real?" Mariah breathed.

"No, my dear, it is fiction." Henry grinned. "At least, I hope it is."

"Goose." She glanced at him, but her eyes were quickly drawn back to the book. "I did not expect it so soon."

"And that is not all. Crosby says he is interested in *Daughters* as well, though he wants to read more before he commits. Is that not good news?"

"Yes."

Henry smiled and tapped the book cover. "Then I say this calls for a celebration."

Happiness bubbled inside her. "And I say you are perfectly right."

They were sitting around the kitchen table—Mariah, Henry, Dixon, and even Martin—when Captain Bryant appeared at the back door, propped open to allow the rain-washed air to cool the kitchen, still overly warm from the cooking fire.

"Captain Bryant!" Dixon, cheeks flushed from the champagne Henry had brought, rose quickly to open wide the door.

There was nothing else to do. He wasn't at the front door, where one might send him away with a manufactured excuse. He was right there at the kitchen door and had already seen them sitting together, talking and laughing.

While Captain Bryant exchanged greetings with Dixon, Mariah slid the book from the table onto her lap.

"Excuse me, I did not mean to intrude," he said, shifting the basket he held to his other arm.

"Never mind," Dixon said. "We are only doing a bit of celebrating."

"Oh? Celebrating what?"

They all looked at Mariah.

She faltered, "I . . . that is . . . does one need an excuse to celebrate?"

"Normally, yes."

Mariah noticed the speculative challenge in his eyes. What could she say without giving away her secret?

Martin leaned back in his chair and casually crossed his arms. "It is my birthday, Captain. I don't like a fuss, but there's no reasoning with women. Not when they've got their minds set on something."

Mariah was surprised and relieved at Martin's quick thinking. Or was it true?

"Well. Happy birthday, Mr. Martin." The captain directed his disconcerted and disconcerting gaze on Mariah. "I shan't keep you. I have caught several trout and a few grayling as well. More than Cook can use at present. I thought you might like them."

"That was very kind of you, Captain Bryant. Was that not kind, Dixon?"

Dixon nodded vigorously. "Very."

Captain Bryant eyed Henry, who nodded a greeting, but no one offered an introduction.

"Martin has made a cake," Mariah said brightly instead. "Will you not join us, Captain?"

"I thank you, no. I had no intention of intruding on your . . . celebration." He set the fish basket on the sideboard, gave a curt bow, and let himself out.

An awkward silence followed his departure. Henry and Mariah regarded one another somberly as Dixon busied herself with the fish and Martin rose to help her.

"Tell him what you must, Rye," Henry said. "I had rather risk my small inheritance than your reputation."

Mariah shook her head. "No, Henry."

"It's all right."

Mariah blew out a puff of air. Excusing herself, she threw on a shawl and ran sprightly outside and toward the great house, careful to avoid the worst of the puddles.

She saw him ahead on the curved drive.

"Captain Bryant, wait!"

He turned and stood where he was as she approached. She noticed with chagrin that he did not meet her partway, nor with a welcoming smile.

"May I ask, Captain," she began, pausing to catch her breath, "if you have any acquaintance in Cambridgeshire?"

He frowned. "Not that I recall. Why?"

"Then I will tell you. That man is my brother. I am sorry I did not introduce you. That was rude of me."

His frown remained. "If he is your brother, why did you not tell me before, when I all but accused you of entertaining a lover?"

She hesitated. Chewed her lower lip. "My brother is not supposed to be visiting me. Our father has forbidden it."

"Why?"

"He has his reasons; that is all I wish to say. But I do not want word getting back to him that Henry has been to see me."

The captain shook his head. "I shall not breathe a word, but I think it devilish unfair of your father."

"Do not judge him harshly. It is not his fault. It is mine. Only mine."

Captain Bryant opened his mouth as if to ask her to elaborate but apparently thought the better of it. Instead he simply thanked her for telling him, and bid her good-night. Mariah watched him walk away with the dismal realization that he was also saying good-bye.

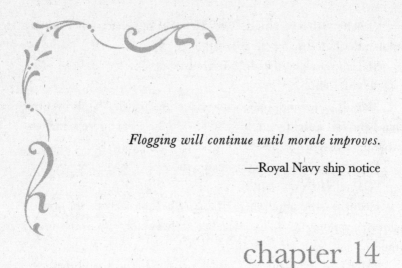

Flogging will continue until morale improves.

—Royal Navy ship notice

chapter 14

Matthew helped himself to a solitary breakfast from a sideboard that could easily have satisfied a dozen hungry midshipmen. As he selected sausages, eggs, and muffins, he thought about last night's encounter with Miss Aubrey. The inhabitant of the gatehouse was certainly intriguing, but something was not right there. He wondered why he thought of her so often. Was he so bored? In truth, he had found his life as a gentleman to be exceedingly tedious so far. And, he admitted to himself, lonely. While not fully staffed, Windrush Court teemed with any number of servants and estate workers. But no friends. At least aboard ship he had enjoyed the companionship of commissioned officers at meals. Here, he dined alone.

On his way to the stables later that morning, Matthew heard a horse trot up the drive. Through the arched portico, he saw the rider was a fair-haired man in dark blue coat and cocked hat. His heart buoyed.

William Hart had arrived.

The young groom hurried out to greet the visitor and take his horse. Matthew winced as his friend gingerly dismounted, his foot catching at the stirrup in an ungainly fashion. The waiting groom took the horse's reins and offered a steadying hand.

Matthew hurried down the front stairs and across the drive. "Hart!"

The fair-haired man limped forward to meet him. "Hello, Bryant."

The two men shook hands, then slapped shoulders in a half hug. Apparently self-conscious, Hart pulled away first. He looked up, surveyed the house, and whistled. "Nice quarters, Captain."

"Temporary quarters. At least for now. Do come in and I'll show you around. I am so glad you've come, old friend."

Matthew gave Hart a tour of the house, careful to moderate his pace, and was relieved not to see Prin-Hallsey about. He offered his guest his choice of several bedchambers, suggesting one at the top of the stairs to limit how far Hart would need to walk several times each day, and then sent a footman to bring up Hart's kit. After William was settled, they shared a meal together, exchanging news of men they had served with and each other's families—Hart had only an invalid mother living, and Matthew knew the two were quite close.

But what began as a pleasant afternoon seemed to change at some point. Matthew became aware of a mounting tension between himself and his former first lieutenant. The reunion was certainly not proving to be the amiable one he had anticipated.

"Shall we ride?" Hart offered. "You can show me your vast domain and exercise your new horse in the bargain."

"You must be tired from your journey," Matthew said. "How about a game of chess instead?"

Hart grimaced. "You despise chess."

"I don't mind. Whatever you want to do."

"I want you to stop treating me like an aged invalid."

Longing to escape the confines of the house and the clock-ticking tension, Matthew suggested a walk through the grounds and gardens. He added, "If you think you can manage it."

"Of course. I have a stout stick and the surgeon's assurance that exercise will benefit the leg."

As they walked, Matthew pointed out the ivy-covered stable block with its unusual central clock tower, the rose garden sporting early yellow roses, the shaped hedges, and reflecting pond. As they circled its placid shore, Matthew bent and selected a flat stone and skipped it across the silvery surface, thinking back fondly to his nighttime stroll there with Miss Aubrey.

"I want you to stay here with me, William," he said. "For as long as I have the place."

William frowned. "Why?"

Matthew was taken aback. "Well, there is certainly more room here than one bachelor like me needs. And—"

Hart cut him off. "And I am on half pay and crippled in the bargain."

"Well . . . yes."

"And you feel sorry for me."

"Of course I am sorry, man. If I could have taken that bullet for you, I would have."

Hart's usually smiling mouth twisted. "Ever the heroic Captain Bryant. Do you really think yourself so much stronger? That you would have overcome such a *minor* flesh wound and been up dancing the mazurka by nightfall?"

"I never said—"

"Said what? That I am the weaker man? You thought it. Why else have you invited me here but to offer charity. Pity."

"Hart, how defensive you are. What has come over you?"

"Months of stares and condescension—that's what. But I can still best you, old man."

"Hart, I hardly think—"

"Don't think I can? You think a bad leg will hinder me sufficiently? I bested you at academy, and I'll best you now."

"We were boys then, William. And that was before—"

William Hart shoved him hard, nearly toppling him into the water.

"Hart!"

"Will I be hung for striking a superior officer?"

"We are not commissioned at present."

"Good. Just checking." He shoved Bryant once more.

Matthew felt his balance slip and managed to grab Hart by his lapels and pull the man down with him. Both hit the water with a splash.

Matthew sat up in the shallow pond, sputtering and muttering. "Thunder and turf, man, what has got into you?"

Hart sat up as well, panting and out of breath. "I don't need your pity, Bryant. Never have. Never will."

Matthew peeled off his sopping coat and tossed it on shore. "Was it so wrong of me to offer you a home here?"

Hart wiped the water from his eyes. "Offer me friendship, Matthew. Nothing more. Nothing less."

At that moment, Miss Aubrey strolled into view and was no doubt startled to see two men in the pond—one fully dressed, the other in soaking wet shirtsleeves.

"Oh! Forgive me," she murmured, quickly averting her gaze.

"Miss Aubrey," Matthew said. "There is nothing to forgive. We were, um, simply . . . bathing."

"Then, pardon me. I will leave you to it." She walked quickly away, clearly stricken.

Dash it, Matthew scolded himself and stood, sloshing out of the pond and jogging after her.

"Miss Aubrey, please wait," he called. When she did, he paused beside her, trying to catch his breath. "It is I who should apologize. It was thoughtless of us."

She kept her face averted. "You have nothing to apologize for. It is your home, is it not?"

"We are *both* tenants here," he said gently. "I ought to have shown more consideration."

"Think nothing of it." She looked at him, then her gaze skittered away. "I grew up with two brothers, after all. I have seen nothing so very shocking, I assure you."

He glanced down at his clinging white shirt. *No wonder . . .* "But we have embarrassed you. And for that, I apologize on behalf of both Mr. Hart and myself. I would introduce the two of you, but considering . . . uh . . ."

"I understand. Apology accepted." Still, she looked uncomfortable and would not meet his gaze as she turned and walked away.

Idiot, he chastised himself yet again.

When Dixon showed Captain Bryant into the drawing room the next morning, hat in hand, Mariah felt her cheeks warm instantly. For though he was fully dressed in golden-brown riding coat and buff trousers, she recalled how she had seen him last, in clinging, translucent shirtsleeves.

"Ah, I see you have not forgotten yesterday's embarrassment. I have come to apologize more formally, and to assure you that my friend and I shall refrain from . . . bathing . . . in future."

"Not on my account, I beg you. I shall simply avoid trespassing so close to the house."

"Now, that I should not like, Miss Aubrey," he said earnestly. "I wish you to be free to roam the estate at will." He took a step nearer. "In fact, why do you not come and join Mr. Hart and me for dinner tomorrow? We are at each other's throats already, and he has only just arrived." His brown eyes glinted. "A lovely female companion might be just the civilizing influence we need."

The thought of having dinner in Windrush Court with two men

caused Mariah to feel ill at ease. He seemed to notice this as well, for he amended his invitation.

"Your Miss Dixon might accompany you, if you like."

Mariah doubted Dixon would be comfortable with that arrangement either.

"You are very kind, Captain. But instead, why do you and Mr. Hart not join us for dinner here in the gatehouse? We can use the larger table in this room and fit quite comfortably. Martin is an excellent cook."

"Miss Aubrey, I had no intention of coming here to beg an invitation nor to inconvenience you in any way."

"No inconvenience, Captain. It would be a pleasure. If you and your friend will not mind our more humble surroundings?"

"Not at all. If anything we shall be more comfortable here than in that echoing space."

Once they had settled on a time, he thanked her again and took his leave with "until tomorrow, then."

Dixon overheard his parting words. "Tomorrow? What is happening tomorrow?"

Mariah said wanly, "You and I are hosting our first dinner party."

"What?" Shock lengthened Dixon's already long, angular face.

Mariah sighed. "Let us hope Martin is up to the task."

Mariah found Martin and presented the plan. To her relief, he accepted the challenge eagerly.

"Thank you, miss. You have no idea what a pleasure it will be to cook for a captain again."

While Martin planned the menu, Mariah and Dixon began a flurry of cleaning and straightening, enlisting George Barnes's help with some of the heavier tasks. They sought out Jack Strong to repair the leg of a wobbly chair and Mr. Phelps for flowers for the table. A list for market was prepared, Dixon dispatched to fulfill it, and Mariah's purse lightened to pay for the required foodstuffs.

Early the next morning, Martin donned an apron and began humming about the kitchen. He requested Dixon's help in peeling, cutting, and chopping. Mariah feared her old friend would take offense, but was relieved to see Dixon put aside whatever resentments she felt and work beside Martin without grumbling.

Pausing to wipe her hands between tasks, Dixon handed him a small jar she had purchased the day before.

"What's this?" he asked.

"Ointment for your arm with a pleasanter smell, if you please."

Mariah cringed, but was doubly relieved when Martin took no offense either.

"Thank you." He lifted the lid and took a trial whiff. "Why, Miss Dixon, I shall smell like a lady."

"An improvement, sir, I promise you. Now, let's get busy. These ducks will not pluck themselves."

Captain Bryant and his friend appeared at the designated hour in half dress, and both looked so elegant, Mariah was relieved she had worn her best rose gown and allowed Dixon to curl and pin her hair. Captain Bryant had brought claret, and for the cook, a pouch of pipe tobacco.

"Miss Aubrey, may I present Mr. William Hart. Hart, this is my kind neighbor, Miss Mariah Aubrey."

Hart bowed, an appreciative gleam in his pale blue eyes. He appeared a few years younger than Captain Bryant, but that might have been due to his fair hair and boyish, innocent features, which made his limp seem all the more regrettable.

She curtsied and welcomed both men to the gatehouse. She introduced Miss Dixon as her companion, as well as Martin, though she stumbled over what title to bestow upon the man.

All were seated in the drawing room, Mariah and even Martin insisting that Dixon sit down with them and leave the serving to him.

Expressions of delight followed a first course of spring soup and crimped salmon, then crescendoed to groans after courses of ragout of duck and green peas, garnished tongue, beetroot and cucumber salad, and gooseberry tartlets. The wine and conversation flowed comfortably for more than an hour. Finally, Dixon rose to help Martin clear away the main meal and carry in the coffee and desserts.

"Miss Aubrey tells us you served as captain's steward, Mr. Martin. A Royal Navy man, like Hart and myself."

"That I did, sir—though it was a long time ago." Martin began pouring coffee as Dixon reclaimed her seat.

"I never ate half this well on any commission, I assure you. Well done, man." The captain raised his coffee cup in salute, then insisted Martin sit down and join them.

"Thank you, sir."

"Whom did you serve under?" Hart asked.

"Oh, I doubt you've heard of them. I became a steward when I was quite young. Not long after I lost the hand. I first served a year under a Captain Stone. Man as hard as his name. Big man. Cared more about the quantity than quality of his meals. Hard to take pride in your work under a master like that.

"The second captain was far different. He appreciated the finer things, and counted my cooking among them. I served under him for only one journey more than thirty years ago now. But what a journey it was! Six months at sea without landfall. And then, only some wild coast to take on fresh water. What adventure. What danger. But you young men know all about that. Don't want to bore you."

"Not at all." Hart poured Martin a glass of claret and gestured for him to continue.

Nodding his thanks, Martin said, "I shall never forget the last night I served under Captain Prince."

Mariah noticed Captain Bryant and Mr. Hart exchange knowing glances and wondered why. Did they know the man?

"The captain was fearless and kindhearted both. The night it happened, he was visiting a young midshipman who'd taken ill. That's why he was belowdecks when the Frenchies boarded our ship. They must have used some spell or poison darts on the watch, for none of us heard a single shot. They cut down the first men who rushed on deck, then closed and barred the hold, trapping us like smelt in a barrel. But that didn't stop Captain Prince. In no time we had a plan and were battering the hatches from below. But them Frenchies, they pointed our own cannons at us and fired down the hold. Many men were killed on the spot, but Captain Prince, he charged up the stairs, cutlass blazing, and killed the French captain and two other officers before they knew what hit them."

Martin sipped his wine while the others drank coffee. "But you see, we were so caught up in the fight that we failed to notice two things." Martin held up his good hand and raised his index finger. "First—the captain had been hit on the side of his head. The man was so wild with bloodlust that he didn't know it, and we followed blindly after him."

Martin raised another finger. "And second—while we were trapped in the hold, a fierce gale had blown up. And by the time we realized it, it was too late. The boarding party had damaged our masts and cut the sails, and even though we fought off the Frenchies, there was little we could do to fight off that storm. After all that brave fighting, we lost the ship. We went down, every last one of us. I managed to sink my hook into a floating mizzenmast and hold on for dear life. A few others grabbed on to some wreckage, and we managed to stay afloat until a passing ship picked us up. The coxswain, the carpenter, and a few midshipmen—that ailing lad among them."

Mariah watched the story unfold in her mind in vivid, awful detail. "And the captain?"

Martin shook his head. "With that massive head wound? No. I did once hear a rumor that he'd been found, but I cannot credit it. I never saw him again. Nor saw any mention of him in the newspapers as having received either court-martial or another commission."

Again Mariah saw Captain Bryant and Hart exchange amused looks.

"Well, sir," Captain Bryant said, "I give you credit as a skilled storyteller, though of course we all know that such tales of a 'Captain Prince' are mythical."

"Mythical?" Martin frowned. "Are you telling me I dreamt going down with the *Largos?*"

"The *Largos* was real and lost, that much is true. But a Captain Prince . . . ?" Bryant ended his thought with a shrug.

Martin bristled. "And I am telling you, I served under the man myself. And I still have his glass to show for it." Ignoring their protests, Martin rose and hurried from the room.

A few minutes later he returned, breathing hard. He shoved the glass toward Bryant, who reluctantly accepted it.

"Gave it to me just as the first alarm was raised. Thrust it into my hands and asked me to watch over that poor young midshipman with my life. I don't know how I managed to keep hold of it in the waves, but I did."

"A fine piece," Bryant allowed.

Hart added, "Forgive us, Mr. Martin. We certainly do not mean to repay your excellent meal by casting doubts on your story."

"Perhaps they blotted out his record for some reason," Martin defended. "For all his bravery, he was not a conventional officer. Perhaps he crossed the wrong admiral."

"Did you ever sail again?" Captain Bryant asked, clearly attempting to move the conversation away from controversy.

"Indeed I did. I was not yet five and twenty when it happened. After we were rescued, I went on to serve another twenty years. But never did I meet the equal of Captain Prince, God rest his soul."

With another glance at Captain Bryant, Hart asked, "And after the navy . . . ?"

Martin shrugged. "I drifted about for a time, sorry to say. But then I met up with Miss Aubrey's aunt, and chose a different course for my life." He straightened. "But that is another long story, and I've already bent your ears long enough. Now, who wants more coffee?"

It is this delightful habit of journaling
which largely contributes to form the easy style of writing
for which ladies are so generally celebrated.

—Jane Austen, *Northanger Abbey*

chapter 15

*T*hough the evening had been a success, and Mariah was exhausted, she slept fitfully. In the morning, she felt too tired to rise immediately. Instead, she pulled out one of her aunt's journals from her bedside table and began to read.

> *I first became acquainted with the Prin-Hallsey family when I was a girl of seventeen. My father had already passed on by this point, and my mother was also suffering with the lung fever. Friends counseled her to seek the care of physicians in Oxford. They feared she would succumb to the disease otherwise. I urged her to follow their advice, not only for her sake, but for my own. How bored I was of life in our small, sleepy village. Mother of course was loath to leave our snug cottage, even for the summer, but being exceptionally persuasive, I managed to convince her.*
>
> *We traveled post to Bourton and from there managed to hire a boy and cart to take us the rest of the way. The road from Bourton was very rough, and I feared we should lose all our belongings. But at last*

we turned and passed through an old castle of a gatehouse and into Windrush Court, the home of one of Mamma's friends.

This friend was rather a fine lady and, in comparison, my mother rather shabby. We were definitely the poor charity cousins to the grand lady. I wondered how my mother was acquainted with such a personage, and I came to understand that they had been at school together.

Mrs. Prin-Hallsey was not in the best of health either and so felt compassion on my poor mamma. She arranged for her to be cared for by her own Oxford physician, a Dr. Dartmore.

Mrs. Prin-Hallsey had a grown son, Frederick. But he barely took notice of me. His mother confided that he had set his sights on some fine lady of quality and she expected news of an engagement any day.

I remember thinking, she is welcome to him!

He was attractive, it was true. Tall with dark hair and admirable address. But he clearly thought a great deal of himself and his own prospects, and I decided to have as little to do with him as possible, even though we resided under the same roof. It was easy enough to achieve, for I was busy as my mother's companion and nurse. When I did have time to myself, I befriended the daughter of the porter, who lived in the gatehouse. She was a quiet, malleable girl a year my junior, and she was quite willing to accompany me for walks, or play at draughts, or read gothic novels together. . . .

Mariah never knew Francesca had met Frederick Prin-Hallsey when she was young, even before she had married Uncle Norris. And how interesting to have this glimpse of the girl who had once lived in the gatehouse. Was it her swing Mariah still enjoyed, now that Mr. Strong had repaired it? She wondered what had happened to the girl. Had she lived there with her parents until the Prin-Hallseys decided the north gate was no longer needed and her father lost his post? Or had she already married and moved elsewhere by then?

Laying aside the journal, Mariah rose, dressed, and went into the sitting room adjoining her bedchamber. She should have been writing. Instead, she stared out the window, squinting at the crazy old man on the poorhouse roof as he came in and out of view between the trees.

It had been easier to see him before the trees were in full leaf. What was he waving? Was he trying to communicate with her?

Suddenly a footstep scraped the floor nearby. She jumped.

"Oh, Martin! You startled me."

Without missing a beat, and with no change in expression, he handed her his old ship's glass.

"Don't care for spying myself. But if you're going to keep a lookout, might as well do it proper." He turned without another word.

She sputtered, "I wasn't—"

But he was already gone.

She looked at the glass in her hand. No, she was not spying. She set it down on the small table only to pick it up again. It was no use. She could not resist. She stood once more at the window and raised the long glass to her eye, fiddling with it to find the poorhouse roof once more. Trees, chimneys, there! She sucked in a sharp breath and lowered the glass as if her eyes had been burned by the sun. For she had seen an old man holding his own glass, looking back at her.

Late that afternoon, George and Lizzy Barnes passed by, likely on their way back from visiting their mother in Bourton. Seeing them, Mariah invited them in for tea and biscuits. George accepted readily, while Lizzy hesitated, then said, "Only for a few minutes."

As they sat at the little kitchen table together, Mariah could not resist mentioning that she had again seen the man on the roof. Remembering the warnings of the Miss Merryweathers, she did not press them. But while George studied the plate of biscuits and carefully selected the largest, he offered, "I hear him sometimes but never see him. He is kept apart from the rest of us."

"Is he a criminal or something?" Mariah asked before she could stop herself.

Brother and sister exchanged harassed looks.

Lizzy said, "No, miss. I am certain he's not. All we have been given to believe is that if he were to be found out, it would not go well for him. That we are protecting him to keep him secret-like."

"But why?"

"Don't know, miss," George said as he wiped his sleeve across his mouth.

Lizzy pulled his arm down with a frowning shake of her head. "Could be just a rumor. Lots of tales are whispered when Mrs. Pitt isn't around."

Mariah slid the plate of biscuits closer to George. "You said you sometimes hear him, George. Hear what?"

Again George stole a look at his sister. He shrugged. "Shouts a lot of nonsense, he does. Can't make out most of it."

"Shouts?" Mariah echoed. "Is he hurt, in pain?"

"No. Not that sort of shouting." George leaned forward. "His favorite is, 'Hands to the braces!' or something like it. Old loon."

"That's enough, George," Lizzy gently reprimanded. "Now, head on back. See if Cook needs help peeling potatoes or some such. Be useful."

He groaned under his breath but rose, thanked Mariah, and trudged across the room.

When he had gone, Mariah smiled apologetically at Lizzy. "I am sorry if I pry too much."

Lizzy's smile was tight. "It's all right. We just need to be careful about the Pitts."

"Mrs. Pitt?"

Lizzy nodded, her focus distant, distracted. "And her son, John."

Something about the look discomfited Mariah. She asked, "How old is John Pitt?"

"Nineteen."

Mariah bit her lip, treading cautiously. "And what manner of man is he?"

The girl shrugged. "Not a bad sort, exactly."

"What does that mean?"

Lizzy frowned. "It just means that the Pitts are people to be kept on the good side of. To please or pay the consequence."

Mariah's stomach knotted. "Lizzy, have either of them threatened you?"

The girl's expression buckled with incredulity. "No, miss! Nothing like that."

Still, there was something in the girl's guarded expression that made Mariah ill at ease.

In the poorhouse office the next day, Mariah sat in the begrudgingly offered chair. She reached into her basket and handed Mrs. Pitt a jar of jam. The woman was in her late forties or perhaps fifty, with a bony chest, sharp clavicle bones, prim lips, and stiffly curled dark hair.

Mrs. Pitt eyed the jar skeptically with muddy brown eyes. "Rhubarb? How . . . healthful. That was very good of you, Miss Aubrey. Not that I am in need, but—"

"No, of course not. A small gift, that is all."

"Then, I thank you."

"I wanted to ask you, Mrs. Pitt . . . You see, from the gatehouse, we have seen a man on your roof. Which is no problem to us, I only wanted to make sure you knew he was there and that he is safe."

The woman's smile was wooden. "All our inmates are quite safe, Miss Aubrey, I assure you. Most are in their right minds too—though not quite all of them, I'm afraid. If there is any risk, we do what we can to keep the potential miscreant apart from those he might harm, even unintentionally. We are a small parish after all, and there is no asylum for such poor souls elsewhere."

"You are very good, Mrs. Pitt, to shelter him here."

She dipped her head in acknowledgement. "It was my late husband's goodness, God rest his soul. I was not privy to the details of the arrangement, but—"

A knock sounded on the threshold, and Mrs. Pitt's face instantly brightened into a genuine smile, which shed ten years from her visage. "Mr. Lumley!" She glanced back at Mariah. "Miss Aubrey, are you acquainted with our vicar?"

Mariah turned to look up at the man in black suit and tabbed white collar. "I have seen him in church, but we have not been formally introduced."

The man gave a perfunctory dip of his head. "Miss Aubrey."

If he had heard of her, or remembered her from Easter Sunday, he gave no indication.

He looked back at Mrs. Pitt. "Forgive me—I have only come to discuss accounts. But if you are busy . . ."

Mariah rose. "I was just leaving, Mr. Lumley." She conjured a smile. "Good day to you, Mrs. Pitt." The woman began to rise, but Mariah gestured her to stay. "No, no. You go on and have your meeting. I shall see myself out."

But outside the office door, Mariah hesitated. Instead of turning toward the front door, she turned farther into the main entry hall. From her brief visit and conversations with George and Lizzy, she knew that the kitchen, larders, and laundry rooms were in the basement below and that a schoolroom, sickrooms, offices, and the entry hall comprised the main level. At the end of the hall was a large stairway which led up to two floors of bedchambers. Mariah walked quietly over to it. At the base of the stairway, she paused. Hearing no objection from the office, and believing herself unnoticed, she gingerly mounted the stairs, reached the first landing four or five stairs up, and then turned sharply to climb the longer staircase to the first floor above. She stepped lightly, and her slippers made barely a sound.

Suddenly a stair creaked a protest and she froze. But as she listened in silence she heard only the faintest sound of Mrs. Pitt's obliging laughter at something the vicar had said.

She rounded the stair rail of the first floor, glancing through doors left standing ajar into small tidy bedchambers. Empty. She guessed the majority of residents were busy at their chores in the laundry, kitchens, or gardens outside. She continued on.

Seeing a narrower set of stairs to the next floor, she climbed these as well. Here, more doors stood open. From one of these, she heard muffled voices. One male and one female, but so low she could barely make out the words. She tiptoed closer and heard the man's voice rise. "Lizzy . . ."

Mariah slipped though one of the open thresholds and peered around the door, just as Lizzy Barnes strode into the corridor from a few doors down. In her arms, she carried a basket of linens. "Let me go about my work, John," she hissed.

"But, Lizzy . . ." A barrel-chested young man appeared in the threshold, paused long enough to shut the door behind him, then followed Lizzy down the stairs.

Mariah looked at the closed door. Could that be *his* room?

Tiptoeing forward, Mariah tried the knob, fearing it would be locked. It turned easily, and she peered inside. Seeing no one, she stepped in, closing the door behind her. She found herself inside a small antechamber, like a dressing room separate from a larger bedchamber. But instead of clothing, there was only a small table and chair on one side and an old stuffed chair with several books and magazines piled beside it on the other. A candle lamp glowed weakly from the table.

She crossed the narrow antechamber and pressed her ear to the inner door. At first she heard nothing, but then she made out a few words of an old ditty she'd heard somewhere before, sung in a low masculine voice:

> "My father's got an acre of land,
> Blow, blow, blow, ye winds, blow,
> You must dig it with a goose quill,
> Blow, ye winds that arise. . . ."

Mariah knocked very softly. Inside the singing stopped. She knocked again.

"Hello?" she whispered. "Are you all right in there?"

A shuffling sound. Then a melodic baritone replied, "I am as I am. But who do you be, madam? I recognize not your fair voice."

"I am your neighbor. I have seen you on the roof. That was you, was it not?"

His voice lilted in discovery. "Ah . . . the girl in the gatehouse. A pleasure. How kind of you to call." The door rattled but did not open. "I am afraid I am not to have the pleasure of inviting you in, nor of meeting you in person. That is to be regretted."

Mariah hesitated, not sure how to address a potentially feeble-minded or even dangerous man. "Are you . . . in distress?"

"Distress? Corporeally, no." His tone grew philosophical. "When you have lived the life I have, such circumstances are the most minor of inconveniences. All I lack is . . ."

"Yes?" Mariah wished she might somehow give him the bread in her basket.

"There is a certain lady here, you see. If I could but speak with her, my island of solitude would be paradise."

"Who is the lady, if I may ask?"

"Miss Amy Merryweather. A dear friend. How I miss her."

Miss Amy! How had he met her? "Shall I pass on a greeting to her? I shall likely be seeing her soon."

"Then how fortunate you are! Yes, please give her my fond felicitations and best regards."

"And . . . whom shall I tell her the greeting is from?"

"Why, Captain Prince, of course."

Mariah was taken aback. The mythical, or at best dead, captain? "Captain Prince . . ." she repeated dubiously.

"Yes. Is it not an apt name for a man who roams the ramparts of his castle, looking down with benevolence upon his domain below?"

Mrs. Pitt was right. The old man was not in his right mind. Poor soul.

"I shall tell her," Mariah whispered.

She stepped back into the corridor and closed the door behind her. Suddenly John Pitt loomed above her. "Oh! Mr. Pitt."

"What are you doing up here?" he asked, expression thunderous.

"I . . . I was looking for you, of course."

His eyes narrowed. "Me. Why?"

"I have a small gift for you—that is all." She reached into her basket with trembling fingers and drew out the wrapped loaf of cardamom bread she had hoped to give to the man on the roof.

"I have given your mother jam and thought you might like the bread. I made it myself."

He made no move to accept it. "You are not to be up here, miss."

"Am I not? I wonder why?"

His eyes were mere slits now. "How did you know to look for me here?" His gaze flicked to the closed door before returning to search her face.

His superior glare put starch in her backbone. She was not the only person doing what he ought not. "Why, I followed your voice, Mr. Pitt. Yours and Lizzy Barnes's. You two were conversing. Dare I say, disagreeing. I shouldn't wonder if the whole house heard."

His brows rose, and for a moment he looked ill at ease. Caught.

Good, she thought. Perhaps he'll leave Lizzy alone in future, though she doubted it. More likely, he would just be more careful. At least he might think twice before telling his mother he had discovered Miss Aubrey abovestairs. And how his voice had led her to that particular room.

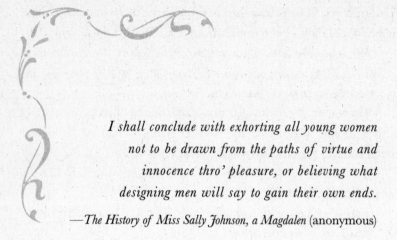

*I shall conclude with exhorting all young women
not to be drawn from the paths of virtue and
innocence thro' pleasure, or believing what
designing men will say to gain their own ends.*

—*The History of Miss Sally Johnson, a Magdalen* (anonymous)

chapter 16

he Frenchmen kept coming. One after another, like stinging ants from their hill. One after another he cut them down, his cutlass swinging red, his arm so tired, so heavy, so numb with death. And still they came. Some barely more than boys.

"S'il vous plaît, non!"

"Please, sir. Let me go home."

Frenchman, Spanish, Dutch. Appendages piled up on the deck, blood flowed over the tops of his boots, and still they came. *Lord almighty, will it never end?* And there, another young man fell to his knees before him, begging for mercy. He raised his cutlass once more. At the last second, Matthew recoiled, shocked to recognize the young man's face. It was his own brother. Peter. But the cutlass was in the air, the blade flying in its silver and red arc, ready to deliver the deathblow.

"Noooooo!" Horrified, Matthew shot up in bed, hearing the echo of his own cry. He was drenched in sweat, bedclothes tangled around his limbs, his right arm in numb needle pricks from lying on it. His chest heaved, his heart raced.

Footsteps drummed down the corridor and, after a quiet knock, his bedchamber door creaked open. "Matthew? Are you all right?"

He inhaled and exhaled deeply, trying to regain his breath. "Sorry to wake you, William."

Hart stepped tentatively inside, candle lamp high. "Another nightmare?"

"Yes."

"Want to tell me?"

Matthew shuddered. "Not really. Same old thing. Killing, bodies, regret." He rubbed a hand over his eyes as though to erase the lingering images.

"It was war, Matthew. You are not a killer—you are a decorated captain in His Majesty's Royal Navy."

"Then why do I feel guilty?"

"You have done nothing wrong."

"Tell my conscience that." Matthew expelled a harsh breath. "Look, Hart. Go back to bed. We'll talk more in the morning. I am sorry to have disturbed you."

Hart chuckled, trying to lighten the moment. "The nightmares don't bother me, Matthew. It is the snoring I can't abide. I should have chosen a room farther down the passage."

In the morning the two men went riding together, Matthew handling Storm with relative ease now. They rode across the estate, and then through the front gate and out onto the open road, startling birds into flight and dogs to barking as they went.

Matthew gave his friend a sidelong glance. "You really don't regret any of it?"

Hart shrugged. "I regret getting in the way of that French bullet, and squandering my prize money, but otherwise, no."

As captain, Matthew received the greatest share of each prize. The scheme of percentages had grown increasingly complex, but on average, Matthew knew he received eight or nine times what Hart had for the same captures. And then of course Hart had been injured and sent to the naval hospital, while Matthew had gone on to capture several more ships, including a Spanish frigate loaded with gold specie.

"Can you really say it was all for the sake of winning the war, for king and country?" Matthew asked. "I cannot. Warships are one thing. But what about those merchantmen?"

"It was all for the good of our cause."

"No, it was unmitagated greed. I killed for prize money. What does that make me?"

Hart pursed his lips. "Rich? In line for promotion?"

Matthew argued, "Our prime directive was to destroy enemy warships, not to capture rich merchantmen, no matter how profitable."

Hart shook his head. "I disagree. The Admiralty knows the lure of prize money is its best recruiting tactic. Heaven knows it is not the regular wages."

Matthew knew this. Knew that most captains, at least of fast frigates like his, keenly sought such prizes, for the value of a captured ship was often more than a year's pay for the crew, and earned by only a few hours of fighting. The capture and eventual sale of a seaworthy or at least repairable ship increased the size of the prize. It was the reason boarding and hand-to-hand combat remained the attack of choice, even though cannons could be used to sink the enemy from afar.

"I do not lose sleep over the warships, their officers and crew. What wakes me at night are the thoughts of all those young men pressed or in trade, whose mothers, whose wives and children, still cry because they are not coming home."

"Even that shortened the war, Matthew," Hart insisted. "Anything that hindered France's ability to trade served to weaken the country and Napoleon's supply routes. You must believe that."

"I do. Usually." Matthew grinned weakly. "At least, by the light of day."

But inwardly, he wondered for the hundredth time if it had all really been worth it. *It might be*, he told himself, if it allowed him to finally win Miss Forsythe.

Mariah did not see the Miss Merryweathers after her encounter with the man from the roof, so she returned to Honora House the next day hoping to deliver his message.

She walked up the lane in time to see Agnes and Amy stepping gingerly from the house toward their customary place outside. As Mariah approached, Amy's legs seemed to give way and she crumpled into her sister, who grabbed hold of her arm and tried to keep her upright. Mariah ran forward and took Miss Amy's other arm, and together she and Agnes helped her onto the bench.

"Are you all right?" Mariah asked in concern. "Shall I fetch Mrs. Pitt, or run into the village for the apothecary?"

Miss Amy put a hand to her chest to catch her breath and still managed a smile. "Thank you, my dear, but there is nothing either of them can do. My old body is just giving out—that is all."

Mariah did not think the woman past sixty. Had she always been sickly?

"She will be right as a trivet in no time, out here in the sunshine," Agnes said, the hollow look in her eyes belying her bravado.

"Nonsense, Sister. It is only a matter of time. After all, we have already outlived most of our friends and relatives." She looked at Mariah. "How do you think we ended here?"

Agnes explained, "We managed on our own for many years after Father died. Sold our house and moved into a small pair of rooms together. Our few friends did what they could, but Amy's health began to fail and eventually . . ." She shrugged to punctuate the inevitable.

"That is what happens to women who don't marry," Miss Amy added. "Unless you have family to provide for you, of course." Her concerned blue eyes fastened on Mariah's. "You do have family, I trust, my dear?"

Mariah hesitated, not wishing to add to Miss Amy's worries. "I have family," she said, sounding unconvinced in her own ears. Well, she did have Henry.

Miss Amy asked abruptly, "You haven't need of any help around the gatehouse, have you?"

Mariah hoped Miss Merryweather wasn't looking for a post in her present state of health. "I . . . What did you have in mind?"

"You are acquainted with Lizzy Barnes?"

"Yes, I have met her several times. I understand she has worked for Mrs. Pitt since her sixteenth birthday."

Miss Amy nodded. "She has, yes. But, well, you see . . . that is . . ."

"The Pitt boy has his eyes all over her." Agnes showed none of her sister's delicacy. "And where eyes go, hands are sure to follow. And you know what follows after that."

Mariah's cheeks burned.

Amy whispered, "Perhaps she doesn't, Aggie."

Agnes frowned. "Oh, she knows, and so do you. Just look at her."

Mariah shifted, uncomfortable. "And has Lizzy told this young man to leave her alone?"

"Of course she has," Agnes said. "Or tried to. But she's afraid to lose the position, so she's had to be nice about it. And you know how convincing 'nice' refusals are with a young buck like John Pitt. Not at all. But if she had another place, then she could be out from under his eye and his power, see?"

"I do see," Mariah said. She considered the situation. If only Mrs. Barnes were on hand to advise her daughter. But Mariah knew Lizzy and George were only able to see their mother every few months or so. "I haven't much extra money for wages at present, but I shall see what I can do."

"You would have to call on Mrs. Pitt first," Amy apologized. "All employers must gain her approval before engaging one of the residents."

"But whatever you do, say nothing against John," Agnes warned. "He is her angel, and woe to anyone who forgets it."

A few moments later, Mariah took her leave. She walked away, her mind filled with images of Lizzy Barnes, barely able to keep John Pitt at bay. And of Miss Amy, barely able to walk and with no family except her sister. So deep in thought was she that Mariah was back in the gatehouse before she realized she had forgotten to deliver the message from "Captain Prince."

She went to find Dixon, but the kitchen was empty. Through the window, she saw her in the garden shelling peas, and went outside to help. She sat on the bench and scooped a handful of peapods from the basket. Dixon sent her a grateful smile before returning to her work.

Mariah split several pods with her thumbnails, releasing the peas with a soft *pling, pling* into the bowl between them. Suddenly she stilled. Here she and Dixon sat, very much like Amy and Agnes Merryweather. Too much alike. Miss Amy's words echoed in her mind, *"That is what happens to women who don't marry."* She and Dixon were unmarried. Two peas in a pod. Dixon had no family that Mariah knew of, and she was connected to her own family by only a spindly thread. Would they end as two old women living alone, or worse—if her books did not sell—side by side in the poorhouse?

"Dixon," Mariah said abruptly. "If you have opportunity to marry one day, or to take a better post, promise me you won't forgo that chance on my account."

Her friend turned and studied her face. "What is it? Has something happened?"

"No. It is only that I worry about the future. What might become of us."

Unperturbed, Dixon continued to shell peas, long fingers steady, as confident about the future as if each green orb were a priceless pearl.

"I don't worry," she said. "All our days are in God's hands."

Mariah wondered if that were true. Or had she fallen from His hand, and taken Dixon down with her?

The gardener ambled up the lane as they finished the last of the peas. He carried his latest offering—a basket of scarlet berries.

Mariah sent Dixon a knowing smile. "What have we here, Mr. Phelps?"

"Only the best fruit in England, miss." He lifted his chin with pride. "*Fragaria elation.* I have kept aside the choicest berries for you ladies."

"How kind, Mr. Phelps. Was that not kind, Dixon?"

Dixon halfheartedly agreed.

"Miss Dixon adores strawberries," Mariah said. "Did you know it?"

Albert Phelps ducked his head, his ruddy cheeks darkening further. "She may have mentioned it."

Dixon rose and tossed the spent husks on the compost heap. "We are much obliged to you, Mr. Phelps."

He beamed. "They are rinsed and ready. A pleasure not to be missed."

As she and Dixon stepped to the door, Mariah noticed the gardener made no move to hand over the basket. The wily man was waiting to be invited inside.

She obliged him. "Please join us, Mr. Phelps."

Sitting at the kitchen table together, the three of them selected and nibbled one berry, then another, Mariah enthusing over the flavor and even Dixon allowing they were sweet indeed.

The berries reminded Mariah of what the Miss Merryweathers

had said, about the boy who had stolen three strawberries. She asked, "Mr. Phelps, how long have you been at Windrush Court?"

"Oh, more than twenty years now."

"So you were here when the gate was locked?"

He nodded. "And sad I was to see it happen too."

"Do you recall the Miss Merryweathers?" Mariah asked. "Two sisters you once showed about your gardens?"

He screwed up his face in recollection. "Twins, were they?"

"Exactly so. They remember you as well, and fondly. But they also recall a small boy helping himself to a few strawberries and wonder if that was the reason the gate was locked all those years ago."

Mr. Phelps grimaced. "I hope not, miss. I never said a word about it. The master himself complained, said the folks over there had a mind to steal the place blind. Never saw evidence of that myself." He popped another berry into his mouth. "The old porter who lived in the gatehouse before you, he said he had other ideas about why they locked the gate."

"What ideas?" Mariah asked.

He shrugged. "Lost his post before I could ask him. He and his family were living here one day and gone the next."

"How strange," Mariah murmured.

Suddenly the strawberries did not taste as sweet.

A few days later, Mariah sat under a tree with drawing pencil and notebook, trying to outline a story idea while enjoying the fine early June weather. She was soon distracted from her purpose. The tree peonies were in flower, and their fragrance hung sweetly on the air. A titmouse, with blue head and wings, olive-green back, and yellow breast, perched on a flimsy branch, and Mariah began sketching the nimble bird when she should have been writing. Not far away, George Barnes sat leaning against the gate, dangling a string before a pouncing Chaucer, as if he had nothing more important to do either.

Lizzy strode over from the poorhouse, scowling and shaking a finger at her brother. "George! The schoolmaster is threatening to report you to Mrs. Pitt if you are not in your seat in five minutes."

"Dash it," George muttered, lumbering to his feet and sprinting across the lawn.

It was the word *threatening* that reminded her.

"Lizzy, do you have a minute?"

The pretty girl looked at her and shrugged, wary. Even so, when Mariah beckoned her over, she came.

"Is John Pitt pressuring you or threatening you in any way?" she asked, laying aside her pencil and notebook.

Lizzy's mouth twisted. "Hardly that. Unless you call courting a threat."

Mariah felt her brows rise. "John Pitt means to marry you?"

The girl looked flustered. "I did not say that, miss. He has made it clear he . . . likes me, is all."

"And do you like him?"

Lizzy met Mariah's gaze, but hesitated. "No. But please don't tell anyone I said so."

Mariah frowned. "I don't understand."

"You would, if you lived in the poorhouse. Mrs. Pitt is the queen and John the prince. They make the rules and hand out the rewards and punishments. There have been extra helpings for George and extra blankets for us both since John took an interest. I won't take food from my brother's mouth by outright refusing him. Besides, Mrs. Pitt pays me now, so I've a few shillings to put by in hopes of getting out of there someday."

Mariah rose and gently but firmly took Lizzy by the shoulders. "Lizzy, look at me. You are worth far more than food and blankets or a few shillings. Don't value yourself so cheaply."

Lizzy said archly, "You think I should ask for more?"

"That is not what I meant, and you know it. Lizzy, you do realize men will profess love and hint at marriage only to gain their own ends, don't you? Not all men. But many."

Lizzy looked down. "I know. John says he loves me, but I don't think Mrs. Pitt would ever allow him to marry the likes of me."

Mariah hesitated, wanting to tread carefully. "And does Mr. Pitt . . . demonstrate . . . his feelings?"

Lizzy again ducked her head, but Mariah saw the telltale blush.

"He tries to kiss me," Lizzy allowed. "But only when we are alone. In the pantry or storeroom."

"Then stay out of the pantry and storeroom."

"It isn't that easy, miss. Like I said—I can't turn him against me."

"But neither need you accept his advances. Lizzy, your virtue, your character, are so valuable. So important. Without her character, a girl has nothing and will never secure marriage with an honorable man." This Mariah knew all too well. "If word gets around of the two of you alone together behind closed doors the worst will be believed, and what decent man will have you for his wife then?"

"What decent man will have me *now*?" Lizzy asked tartly. "Carrying the shame of the poorhouse upon me, not to mention my father's ruin. I've no dowry, no money of my own, and no prospects. Why should I not take the only man I am ever likely to have?"

Mariah lowered her voice, though no one was near. "And if he uses you and does not marry you? What then?"

Lizzy's face clouded. "You don't understand! It is easy for you to speak of honor and character when you need not wonder where you'll sleep or where your next meal will come from if the poorhouse turns you out."

Mariah slowly shook her head. "I do understand. More than you know. Believe me when I tell you the loss of your character is a terrible price to pay." She bit her lip to keep from saying too much. Too many people knew already.

Mariah took a deep breath and continued. "Now. You have admitted you don't like John Pitt, let alone love him. What happens if you give yourself to him and the next day a man you *could* love appears at your door?"

Since meeting Captain Bryant, Mariah could well imagine that particular torment.

Lizzy laughed dryly, and Mariah cringed to hear the cynical, desolate sound from one so young. "At the poorhouse door? That will be the day. The only men who come there are the ancient apothecary and schoolmaster, the married vicar, and the oily undersheriff. John Pitt looks a prince indeed compared to any of them."

Mariah grasped the girl's hand. "Lizzy, you are only seventeen. Be careful. Wait and choose wisely. For once your choice is made it cannot be made again."

Disheartened, Mariah watched Lizzy trudge back toward the poorhouse. She wished she could offer Lizzy a post to get her out from under the Pitts' influence. But she could not. Not yet. Most of the money she'd received for her first book had gone to Mr. Hammersmith, as well as the greengrocer and the butcher. And she'd yet to receive a farthing for her second.

Was there nothing she could do? So many girls were in danger of falling victim to manipulative men or their own naïve vanity. Just as Mariah had been. It was too late for her, but there was *something* she could do. She could warn them. Mariah decided then and there that her next book would be a cautionary tale based on her own experiences. She would change the names and some circumstances. This, coupled with the fact that she was not publishing under her own name, would serve to protect her identity. She did not want readers to reckon her as the injured character, or guess the identity of her heartless betrayer. Or did she? Might he then share in her shame, if only in part? Not likely. She was grateful anew that Mr. Crosby had agreed to publish her as Lady A, even though he would have preferred to use her real name.

Going inside, she pulled out a fresh sheet of writing paper, opened her inkpot, dipped her quill, and began her third novel.

The Tale of Lydia Sorrow
by Lady A

Lydia was wearing a nightdress of lawn and lace, the one her mother had purchased for the occasion. Her first house party. What high hopes her mother cherished for the event. Several eligible gentlemen from good families would be on hand, and she felt certain Lydia would capture the brightest and best among them. Or at least the wealthiest and best connected.

But Lydia cherished her own secret hope. She had come to Somerton not with a desire to form some new acquaintance, but with a desire to see the man who had already won her heart. To spend time with him—far more time than she had been allowed before, out from under the watchful eyes of her parents and with only a permissive chaperone between them.

Lydia had listened politely to her mother's many entreaties— reminders of decorum and proper behavior—with outward acquies- cence. All the while thinking only of him.

But the man Lydia longed to see was tardy in arriving at Somerton. Just when she began to fear he would not attend the house party at all, she spied him entering the hall after dinner, as the ladies were shepherded into the withdrawing room. Her pulse quickened. She would see him, speak to him, the very next day. She was sure of it. . . .

Mariah paused and took a deep, shuddering breath. If only she had taken her mother's entreaties to heart.

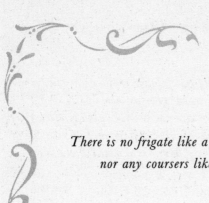

There is no frigate like a book to take us lands away
nor any coursers like a page of prancing poetry.

—Emily Dickinson

chapter 17

atthew rose from behind the desk as Miss Aubrey entered the Windrush Court library and stood stiffly before him.

"You sent for me, Captain?"

Matthew winced. "How officious that sounds." When would he learn he no longer commanded a large crew—that he need not delegate such tasks?

He stepped around the desk. "Miss Aubrey, I beg your pardon. Hammersmith mentioned he was bound for the gatehouse. I only asked him to inquire if you might call here sometime at your convenience." He pulled a grimace. "Though I suppose on Hammersmith's tongue it came out rather like a command?"

She nodded with a telling lift of her brows.

Matthew noticed a small beauty mark above her left eyebrow, near her temple. He found his gaze lingering on her brow, her cheeks, her lips, before he abruptly shifted his focus. He must stop staring before he gave the wrong impression.

"I am sorry. If this is not a convenient time, you must feel free to say so."

"I am here now."

"Very well. I . . . I have a favor to ask of you."

"Yes?"

How direct, how steady, were her golden-brown eyes. Disconcertingly so.

He swallowed. "I have been away at sea the better part of four years. And even before that, I was not very good."

She was staring at him, clearly confused. A wariness tightened her jaw and stiffened her feminine mouth.

Matthew sighed. "Never mind. It was likely too presumptuous."

"What, Captain?"

He licked his dry lips. She already knew he was a novice horseman. Would her opinion be so much lowered by a confession of another wanting skill?

She must have sensed his self-consciousness, for a mischievous glint lit her brown eyes to amber. "Do you wish me to teach you to ride?"

He grinned. "No. Not to ride, Miss Aubrey." He inhaled deeply. "To dance."

She tilted her head to one side. "You do not know how?"

"Oh, I had lessons in my academy days and spent a night or two dancing very ill in London. But that is years ago now. I am hosting a house party later this summer and fear I may be called upon to dance. I was hoping you might help Hart and me polish our poor, half-forgotten skills?"

She smiled. "I shall help you with pleasure, Captain." Her eagerness dimmed as she glanced from him to the empty room. "But I shall need some assistance."

᚛

It was arranged for Saturday. Lizzy agreed to come over on her half day as a second woman, though she did not know many dances either. Dixon would accompany them on the pianoforte.

Captain Bryant and Mr. Hart rose as they entered the salon, each man appearing as nervous as a schoolboy at his first ball.

"Shall we begin with a country dance?" Mariah suggested. "Perhaps, Pleasures of the Town?"

"To what tune, Miss Mariah?" Dixon asked, settling herself at the pianoforte.

Mariah paused. She was an accomplished dancer, but her sister, Julia, was the family's musician. "I have no idea."

Martin walked in behind them and sat in one of the chairs near the pianoforte. Without looking at anyone, he announced, 'The Fair Maid of the Inn.' "

Mariah glanced at Dixon. Her friend's stunned expression no doubt mirrored her own.

Ignoring them, Martin opened a small case and from it extracted and fitted together the pieces of a simple three-holed pipe. With it, he played the opening notes of the jaunty tune with his one hand. Dixon raised her brows high.

"Mr. Martin," Mariah said for them both. "We had no idea you were a musician."

He shrugged. "A bit. Now, are you going to dance or not?"

She and Dixon exchanged a look. What other surprises had the odd man in store?

"Very well. Let's begin," Mariah said. "Gentlemen there. Ladies facing them."

Hart pushed himself off the wall and limped forward. Captain Bryant stood beside him.

Mariah painted a circle in the air with her hand. "First, gentlemen ring around the ladies."

Captain Bryant gave his friend a sidelong glance, saying dryly, "I am not holding your hand, Hart."

Mariah bit back a smile. "Step lively. And one, and two, and one and two. Very nice, gentlemen."

Surprisingly, Hart's limp did not seem to much hinder him. When they returned to their places, Mariah continued. "Now we ladies join hands and circle the other way around the men."

"While we look admiringly on," Hart quipped, eyes on Lizzy.

Lizzy grinned and blushed prettily.

"Take your partners in the promenade hold," Mariah instructed as she and Lizzy returned to their places.

When the captain hesitated, she stepped to his side. "The lady's right hand in your right, her left hand in your left."

"Ah."

Captain Bryant's hands enveloped hers, and Mariah endeavored to appear unaffected.

She glanced instead at Hart and Lizzy. "She should stand at your right side, Mr. Hart. Your right hand *above* your left. That's it. Now allemande in a circle around the room. Though this is a bit tricky with only two couples."

"Then let us have three."

Mariah looked across the salon, surprised to see Hugh Prin-Hallsey lounging against the doorjamb.

The music and dancing stopped as Hugh straightened and walked over to the pianoforte. There he bowed to Dixon. "May I have this dance?"

"Oh my. I don't . . . That is . . . I shouldn't . . ." Dixon blustered and blushed and tried not to look as pleased as she clearly felt.

"Go on, Miss Dixon," Martin said. "Enjoy yourself. I shall provide what music I can single-handedly." He waggled his brows and grinned at his own joke.

Miss Dixon smiled in return. "Oh, why not. Very well, Mr. Prin-Hallsey."

If Captain Bryant was displeased with the intrusion, Mariah noticed that he was too polite to show it.

"Now, where were we," Mariah resumed. "Right. Face your partner. Gentlemen, keeping hold of the lady's right hand, switch places with her. Ladies step forward and form a circle, left hands high. And finally, gentlemen, turn your partner once more. Good. Again."

Hugh danced with effortless skill, grinning at Mariah whenever she caught his eye. Dixon moved gracefully, and it was easy to imagine her the lithe young woman she had once been.

Mr. Hart hobbled through his steps but managed to keep up better than Mariah would have expected. She wondered, however, how Captain Bryant's London guests might react to such an imperfect performance. She dearly hoped they would not laugh at him. Surely, no friends of Captain Bryant's could be so cruel.

As for Captain Bryant, he seemed to dance quite competently beside her, step for step, sides occasionally brushing, hand in hand. But he was too close, and she too aware, to risk looking at him often.

As Matthew held Mariah's hands in his as she'd directed, he admitted to himself he liked the feel of her smaller hands in his and the warmth of her shoulder tucked close to his side as they danced in the promenade position. He regarded her lovely profile and upturned nose several inches below his. She darted a glance up at him and blinked, as if surprised to see him so near. He smiled down into her brown eyes. Even at this close range, her complexion was pure cream. The skin of her brow and cheeks smooth, but for that small beauty mark. That point of punctuation on her delicately arched brow.

Matthew found himself thinking, *She looks good. She smells good. She sounds good* . . . and fought the irrational desire to lean down and kiss her brow, or at least her pert nose.

Steady, Bryant, he warned himself. *Keep your eye on the prize.*

On Monday, Mariah realized her inkpot was running low and set about making another batch of purple-blue iron gall ink. She ground oak apples, iron sulfate, and gum arabic, purchased from the village apothecary, and added these to stale beer and a little refined sugar. She corked the bottle of this preparation and carried it into the drawing room. She would leave it standing in the chimney corner for a fortnight, shaking it a few times a day until it was ready to use.

From the drawing room window, Mariah glimpsed coppery curls. The young singer from the poorhouse lingered across the road, watching George and Sam as they erected a makeshift wicket and cricket pitch. The girl—what was her name? Magpie? No, Maggie—looked very much as if she would like to join them but was afraid to. Mariah remembered Miss Amy saying how shy the girl was, and that she was an orphan.

Wiping her hands on her apron, Mariah walked back into the kitchen. There, she wrapped several biscuits in paper and then let herself out the front door.

George and Sam rushed over at the sight of her, the brown paper as a red cape before bulls. Once the boys had shoved biscuits into their mouths and returned to their play, Mariah cautiously approached little Maggie.

"Hello there," she began, walking slowly across the lawn. "Would you like a biscuit?" The girl stayed where she was, alert eyes reminding Mariah of a frightened doe—or storm-frightened horse—about to take flight. "Well. I shall just leave it here on this paper. If you don't want it, the birds will."

Mariah turned, the faint music not registering at first, as she listened for any indication that the girl had accepted her offering. She glanced over her shoulder. Saw the girl pick up the biscuit but not stop to eat it. Instead she carried it with her, walking forward, following the music. Reaching the gate, Maggie put her free hand on one of the iron bars while the biscuit dangled in the other. She swayed gently to and fro to the tune from Martin's flute as he sat on the garden bench on the other side, playing an old sailing song.

Mariah stood several feet from the girl, careful not to get too close. "That is Mr. Martin. You like his music, do you?"

If Martin saw the girl there, watching him, he chose to ignore her, assuming no doubt that she would run away, shrieking in silly tones about the hook-handed pirate, as other children had done. Or that she would simply grow bored and move on.

When she still stood there several minutes later, he paused in his playing and looked at her through the bars.

She looked placidly back.

"Do you like the way the flute sounds?" he asked.

The girl nodded, her curls bouncing.

"You can come closer if you like," he said. "In fact, you can go right through the house and join me in no time. You shall be perfectly safe. Miss Dixon and Miss Mariah are here. And there are George and Sam just there. All right?"

Warily, Maggie looked from person to person, then nodded once more and bolted through the house, doors open on the fine summer day, and emerged on the other side in seconds. Mariah followed her but stopped in the kitchen to watch from the window.

Once outside again, Maggie slowed and approached Martin cautiously. He had gone back to his playing, as if sensing this would be the best way to put the girl at her ease. He scooted over on the bench without looking her way as he played another ditty.

Silently, Maggie sat down at the far edge of the bench.

Dixon, on her knees working in the garden, called over, "Don't be teaching her any of your bawdy songs, now."

Martin ignored her but paused in his playing to say to the girl, "I shan't sing you one of those songs. All about Davy Jones's locker, rum, and the pox."

"Mr. Martin!" Dixon reprimanded. "A girl her age does not need to hear words like *the pox*."

"She's heard it twice now, madam, thank you."

Martin coaxed a sweet, reedy melody from his wooden flute. Then he paused again. "When I was a young man, I played a transverse flute—like this." He lifted the flute from a vertical to horizontal position, balancing it in his hook, while miming the fingering of many holes with his good hand. "Now, that was a beautiful sound." He played a bit more, then turned to her. "Would you like to try?"

Her eyes grew large. She nodded.

He pulled a handkerchief and a small vial of oil from his pocket. "We shall have to clean it good and proper first, or Miss Dixon there will accuse me of fouling your wee self with scurvy, the typhus, and I know not what."

He handed her the vial. "Uncork that for me, will you? Devilish difficult with one hand." She did so with her small, nimble fingers. "A few drops here, if you please." He held forth his handkerchief. "On my perfectly clean handkerchief," he said loudly in Dixon's direction. "Which I know for a fact Miss Dixon boiled in lye."

Dixon looked up, rolled her eyes, and scowled before returning to her work.

He cleaned the mouthpiece thoroughly, inside and out, with the oiled cloth. Then he repositioned it and handed the girl the slim instrument. "That's right. Your fingers there, and there, and there. And your thumb at the back for support. Good, now blow long and slow, like a whistle."

An airy note shrieked from the flute.

"Excellent. Now close your fingers over each hole one by one and see how the sound changes."

She did this, and if possible, her blue eyes grew larger yet.

When she handed the flute back to him, he asked, "Do you know what this is called?"

She shook her head.

"Some call it a one-handed or three-holed flute. The French call it a *galoubet*, but I haven't cared for the French since the war. It was not invented for one-handed gents like me. It was made to be played with one hand so that the other hand would be free to play a small drum.

That way, some enterprising musician could make a tidy living playing for country dances and the like. Of course, not being an ambidextrous fellow myself, I play it alone."

The girl was no longer looking at the flute. She was studying his hook. She asked softly, "Does it hurt?"

So, Mariah thought, *Maggie can talk as well as sing.*

"What, this?" He raised the hook. "Not anymore. Though now and again I awake with my fingers aching, only to remember those fingers are long gone. Isn't that strange?"

She nodded solemnly. "Where are they?"

"Ah." He nodded as if it were the most natural question in the world. "At the bottom of the sea, I suppose."

"Why?"

He regarded her. "Are you sure you want to know?"

Again, the solemn little nod.

Mariah listened as attentively as the girl. Even Dixon, she noticed, had paused in her work.

"You see, I was not always a steward, brushing the captain's uniform and preparing his meals. Before that, I was a proper seaman, battling with the best of them. Now, the yarn I tell the other jack-tars is longwinded indeed. But suffice it to say, cutlasses were crossed. A Frenchman lost his head and I lost my hand, so I got the better end of the bargain."

"Mr. Martin!" Dixon complained.

Martin leaned closer to the girl. "But I shall tell you the real version. The Frenchies were firing on us, see. And the nine-pounders were coming in like hailstones. I turned and saw a young midshipman standing there just a'staring up as a ball was about to strike. So I stuck out my hand and shoved him out of the way." Martin shrugged. "There went the hand, but at least I lived to tell the tale, and so did he."

He glanced at her, found her staring at his arm in fascination. "Sometimes itches, where the hook facing laces to my arm. Otherwise, it's naught. An apothecary gave me some foul-smelling ointment, but it was useless. Miss Dixon there gave me a new pot. Now I smell like a flower shop."

Martin looked from his arm to the girl. "Would you like to see it? It isn't too gruesome, at least I don't think so. But then, I'm used to it." He rolled up his loose sleeve and showed her how the leather bindings wrapped around his forearm, just below the elbow. "A nice smooth stump. Ship's surgeon did a good job. I've seen far worse anyway."

Maggie swallowed, and he quickly rolled his sleeve back down.

"Sorry, lass," Martin apologized. "Ought not to have shown you. That's more than enough for one day, ey?"

He rose from the bench and Maggie hurried back through the gatehouse. Her "thank-you" followed her out, so that Mariah was not sure if it was meant for her or Martin.

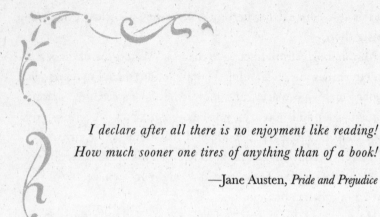

I declare after all there is no enjoyment like reading!
How much sooner one tires of anything than of a book!

—Jane Austen, *Pride and Prejudice*

chapter 18

Hart was holed up in the library, reading one of two new books he had brought with him from London. Matthew had begun to read the other volume offered but could not sit for hours on end as Hart seemed capable of doing. He rose and paced about the room. When Hart cleared his throat, Matthew took the hint and let himself out into the hall.

From the windows at the front of the house, Matthew watched as Hugh Prin-Hallsey directed the loading of a cart of belongings, which the man was selling to raise funds. Matthew still didn't like Prin-Hallsey rummaging about the place, clanging and carting furnishings, paintings, and the like while he was paying good rent to live there. Especially now that he had a guest. But he kept his objections to himself, still hoping to curry the man's favor until he agreed to sell Windrush Court to him outright.

The portly agent from some auction house marked each item in a ledger as the servants carried out piece after piece. Matthew hoped he and Hart would still have beds to sleep in when the man was through.

Mariah Aubrey hurried up the drive, hand atop her bonnet to keep it in place. Thinking something might be amiss, Matthew quickly let himself out the front door and onto the covered portico.

"Mr. Prin-Hallsey." She paused to catch her breath, cheeks flushed. "Mrs. Strong mentioned you were . . . parting . . . with a few things. I should like to purchase something I saw when last I visited my aunt."

She turned her head, looking among the heap of articles waiting to be catalogued and loaded, and pointed to a wheeled invalid chair. "There it is!"

"What, that?" Hugh frowned. "I do hope you are in good health, Miss Aubrey."

"Oh, yes. It is not for me. It is for the dearest old lady in the poorhouse. She is weak as a foal but always so cheerful."

Hugh inhaled thoughtfully. "Your aunt's nurse had it taken up to her room, but the old girl was too proud to use it. It was built for my father near the end of his life."

Miss Aubrey bit her lip, likely fearing this meant Prin-Hallsey would not be willing to part with it cheaply. Perhaps Matthew would buy it for her.

"So . . . how much, do you think?" she asked.

Hugh looked down at her, his expression inscrutable. Suddenly he reached out and tweaked her chin. "Oh, take it for nothing for your dear old lady."

"Really?" she asked.

Watching the exchange, Matthew was as surprised as Miss Aubrey clearly was.

Hugh shrugged. "My mother, Honora, would have approved. Besides, it wouldn't fetch much, and I plan never to need it."

A look of wonderment crossed her face. "How good of you, Hugh.

Thank you." In a flash, she reached up and kissed his cheek and hurried past before Hugh could react. In fact, the man looked mildly dazed.

Miss Aubrey grasped the chair by its handles, then pushed it down the drive before anyone might offer to help. Or change his mind.

Matthew observed Miss Aubrey's gratitude and hurried departure with an odd sense of envy and bemusement.

Prin-Hallsey shook his head as though to clear it, climbed the front stairs, and stood beside Matthew. Together, the two of them watched Mariah push the chair across the lawn, evidently finding the graveled drive too jarring.

"Singular creature, our girl in the gatehouse," Hugh mused. "You would think with all her troubles, it would not be the best time to concern herself with the problems of others."

"Perhaps that is the best time of all."

Hugh's lower lip protruded. "You may be right, Bryant. I own a strange lightness in my own crusty heart at having given her the old thing."

"Any particular reason for the sudden largesse?"

Hugh inhaled deeply. "You might say I have experienced a recent windfall."

"At cards?"

"No, not cards. Not this time."

"I have never cared for games of chance myself."

The man looked at him wryly. "Oh, come, Captain. Do not deceive yourself. You are in the midst of a very risky game of chance as we speak, are you not? For what else has brought you to Windrush Court? Risking all that hard-earned prize money, and for what? The smallest chance a certain lady will jilt her well-connected suitor to marry you, when she rejected you once before. What are the odds?" Hugh smirked and shook his head. "I would not bet on you, old boy. No, I would not."

❧

Mariah delivered the invalid chair to a grateful Miss Amy. Even Agnes seemed pleased. Mariah also delivered the belated greeting from Captain Prince, which made Miss Amy beam and her sister look nervously over her shoulder.

While she was there, Mariah looked about for little Maggie but did not see her. On the way home she wondered if Martin had succeeded in frightening the girl away, but was pleasantly surprised when she appeared at the gatehouse door a few days later. Without a word, she looked up at Mariah with clear appeal in her eyes.

Mariah opened the door to her. "Well, go on." She smiled and followed behind as the girl ran through the gatehouse.

Dixon was already standing at the kitchen window, and Mariah joined her there. Outside Martin sat on the garden bench, again playing his flute. Maggie sat down to watch and listen.

After a few minutes, Martin lowered his instrument. "I hear you are a singer," he began. "I'd play something you could sing to, but I understand you like hymns and I don't know many of those."

Maggie shrugged and asked, "Will you get your hand back in heaven?"

He considered her, head cocked to one side. "I don't know. Do you think I shall?"

She nodded, reddish-gold hair bobbing up and down.

"Well, then I shall look forward to going there. I sure miss that hand and wouldn't mind seeing it again." He grinned. "How I would shake my hand should we meet once more."

Maggie giggled. "You can't shake your own hand."

"Could happen." He regarded her a moment. "How old are you?"

She shrugged again. "Seven or eight. I don't know my birthday."

Martin lifted his chin, appraising her. "I think eight. Do you know why?"

She shook her head.

"I had a sister once, and you remind me of her. The last time I saw her, she was eight years old. I was older and already gone to sea when the letter came, saying she had died. My mother was laid very low over it. But when I got shore leave two years later, there was already another babe to take her place. But I never forgot my sister. In my mind, she is ever eight years old."

"What was your sister's name?" Maggie asked in her quiet voice.

Martin smiled wistfully, eyes distant. "Mary. But our mother was Mary as well, so we called her Mary Jane."

"Mary Jane," she repeated.

"And may I have the honor of knowing your name?" Martin asked, though Mariah had already mentioned her name, she was sure.

The girl bit her lip in a bashful smile. "Maggie."

He offered her his good hand and she shook it.

"I don't know my mother's name," she added.

"That's too bad. And your father's?"

Maggie shook her head. "I lived with my grandmamma, and that's all I called her."

"As well you should." Martin looked into Maggie's sweet, accepting face and seemed to hesitate. "You know, I still have my old flute. Should have sold it years ago, but couldn't bring myself to part with it. Perhaps I could teach you to play it. At least, I think I could. Would you like that?"

Maggie smiled and nodded.

"Well, give me a few days to find it. I believe it's buried in my seaman's chest. But I shall unearth it, shall I?"

"Yes, please."

Martin rose from the bench with a groan and a stretch. "Well, I had better get back to work, before Miss Dixon calls me a sluggard and worse. A good day to you, Miss Maggie."

She bounced a small curtsy. "And to you, Mr. Martin."

At the kitchen window, Dixon breathed, "Oh dear . . ."

Alarmed, Mariah asked, "What? What has he done now?" She

looked into the stricken face of her old friend and what she saw written there surprised her. "Don't tell me he's gone and made you like him."

Dixon pulled a grimace. "Foolish girl. Not 'like him.' Not in that way, of course. But . . . he does surprise one, doesn't he? Maggie speaks more to him than to the two of us put together."

Mariah nodded. "Children who are not frightened by him seem drawn to him like bees to honey."

"Or manure," Dixon murmured, as though that were the next line in the script, but she no longer possessed the asperity to do the part justice.

The next day, a pony cart came rumbling up the gatehouse lane, driven by Jack Strong. Martin sat beside him and was the first to climb down when the cart came to a halt. Mariah stepped outside to see what the men were about, and Martin gestured her over. He reached into the cart and hauled out a large canvas bag and tossed it to her. She caught it gingerly, but the bag was far lighter than it looked. Then Martin and Mr. Strong began hefting an old trunk off the back of the cart. Maggie, George, and Lizzy appeared at the other side of the gate, grasping the iron bars and watching the bustle with interest. Mariah waved George over, and the boy came running through the gatehouse, hurrying forward just in time to help with Martin's end of the trunk.

"Couldn't stand to see your aunt's things burned in the rubbish pile, or pilfered by the maids," Martin explained, puffing and straining. "Thought you might like to have them—what Hugh didn't manage to sell, that is. I suppose what's left is not very fashionable."

"Thank you, Martin. That was very thoughtful."

Mariah carried the canvas bag toward the house just as Dixon opened the door for them. Martin, George, and Jack Strong bore the trunk inside, then went out for a load of bandboxes, another bag, and an old mahogany cosmetics case. The men left everything in the drawing room for the ladies to peruse at their leisure, but Mr. Strong offered to return the following day to haul the trunk upstairs if they wished. George lingered behind after the men departed.

Maggie and Lizzy appeared at the drawing-room window, Maggie's nose pressed against the wavy glass. Dixon gestured them inside. As the girls entered, Mariah smiled her welcome and unlatched the trunk. "Come and see. What is your guess? Pirate treasure? Mr. Martin did deliver it, after all."

Maggie giggled. George rubbed his hands together.

Mariah pushed back the lid and looked inside. "No treasure, I am afraid."

George peered over her shoulder. "Clo-o-othes," he muttered in disgust. He tipped his hat and was out the door in two seconds.

His sister rolled her eyes, and the women shared a smile.

Mariah pulled out a feathered mask from some long-ago masquerade ball, followed by a pleated betsie. "Martin was right, these do look a bit dated."

"Oh, I don't know." Dixon tied the betsie around her neck. The ruff was so stiff she could barely turn her head.

Mariah laughed. "You look like Queen Elizabeth in her lace collars."

Mariah wrapped a mantle of moth-eaten mink around her own shoulders and set a tall chimney-pipe hat upon her head. "What do you think?"

Dixon regarded the ensemble. "It is not quite the thing." She replaced the hat with a gauze turban sporting a jaunty egret plume. "Oh yes, infinitely better."

They put a faded, tunnel-like poke bonnet on Maggie, who disappeared within it, laughing all the while.

Eyes wide, Lizzy lifted out a silvery wig from one of the bags, a high Cadogan hairdo with roll curls.

"Well, go on," Dixon urged.

Lizzy giggled and settled the confection upon her head, and was utterly transformed into an imperial lady.

Soon, an all-out game of dress-up and charades ensued as four females indulged their playful feminine natures.

Dixon pulled on a pale satin tunic over her day dress. She fitted her head with a Grecian style coronet complete with attached snood to cover her pinned hair.

Mariah helped Lizzy into a velvet spencer jacket with fur-trimmed collar and flared cuffs. Then she handed her a soft muff of matching fur.

She extracted a gold-braided Hussar jacket for herself and pulled it on. Near the bottom of the trunk she spied a riding habit—long skirt and short jacket. There was nothing extravagant or amusing about those pieces. In fact they brought a stab of regret, reminding her of her fine riding habit, and fine horse, at faraway Attwood Park.

She left those garments where they were and instead pulled out a wide mushroom-shaped muslin hat with eyelet trim and bow, a fashion from at least twenty years ago, though it seemed familiar. Why had Aunt Fran kept it? And then she remembered her aunt showing her this very hat when she was a girl, and telling her it had been what she was wearing when Uncle Norris proposed. How sweet that she kept it after so many years, even after another husband.

With a grin, Mariah removed the bonnet from Maggie's head and replaced it with the ballooning hat. "Adorable. The hat and the girl wearing it."

Maggie ducked her head but could not conceal her delight.

Martin walked in, eyes focused on the bottle of oil in his hands—on his way to refill the lamps, no doubt. His eyes lifted, then widened, as he looked from the mound of clothes, to bandboxes spewing tissue paper and ribbons, to Lizzy, Mariah, Maggie, and Dixon dressed in musty finery. "I feel as though I have walked into the pages of *La Belle Assemblée*," he said. "You all look like fashion plates."

Maggie and Lizzy giggled.

Martin's eyes lingered on Dixon. "May I say, Miss Dixon, the coronet suits you. You look like a goddess."

Dixon bit back a smile, clearly pleased yet self-conscious. "Oh, go on with you."

But Martin was right. She did look like a goddess. And it was at that moment that the idea struck Mariah. They should put on a theatrical for the children of Honora House. She remembered her aunt saying she recalled the "little plays" Mariah wrote and performed as a girl. She would no doubt approve of them putting her old things to such good use.

ᔑ

Mariah walked across the grounds and spotted Captain Bryant and Mr. Hart reclining on a picnic cloth spread beneath a leafy oak. Remnants of a repast were tossed haphazardly in a basket on one corner. Both men were reading in casual, relaxed poses, but Captain Bryant straightened when he saw her approach.

Mr. Hart remained propped on one elbow. "Miss Aubrey, come and have pity on us. We are reading novels and feel our manliness diminishing by the moment. Come restore our vanity, do, and tell us we look the dashing officers we once were."

What cheek, Mariah thought, amused. But as Mr. Hart reminded her of an overgrown little boy, she smiled at him. "Hello, Mr. Hart. Captain Bryant. What are you reading?"

Hart cocked his head in Captain Bryant's direction. "Bryant here is reading a new novel, reported to be all the crack in London."

Mariah felt her brows rise. "Captain Bryant reads novels? I am surprised."

"Yes." Hart sat up and crossed his legs. "You see, I happened to meet a certain young woman he admires, and she told me she *adored* it and thought it 'everything romantic and thrilling.' "

Captain Bryant rolled his eyes and looked very much as though he wanted to kick Mr. Hart's foot. His bad foot.

"And so you purchased him a copy," Mariah said. "How kind."

William Hart's eyes shone with mischief, and he leaned forward conspiratorially. "I don't believe *he* sees it as a kindness. For if Bryant here has ever read more than his ship's log and the newspaper accounts of his own exploits, I should be very much surprised."

"Thank you, Hart," Captain Bryant said dryly. "I am afraid it is not to my usual taste, but I am endeavoring to enjoy it." He lifted the book in his hand. "Have you read it, Miss Aubrey? Perhaps you could give us a summary and pithy commentary, so we can have done. I have not shot nor ridden in two days, and I feel my legs turning to pudding."

"I may have read it. What is the title?"

"*A Winter in Bath*, by Lady A. Do you know it?"

Mariah started, her stomach knotting. "Well . . . yes. I suppose I am familiar with it." She suddenly felt dizzy. "You say you don't find it to your liking?"

"How can I? Listen to this." Captain Bryant began to read.

And Mariah began to squirm.

"The wind whipped his raven hair and black cloak about him. He stared at her with smoky grey eyes, fiery with intensity. She could not look away. She was ensnared all over again, caught in the brambles and powerless to escape.

"She thought of what her aunt had said, about the blackberry being a symbol of lowliness and remorse. She felt both of these emotions now, trapped as she was in a bramble of her own making. The thorns had caught her, tripped her, held her. She had fallen among them. Or had she been pushed?"

He snapped the book shut. "It is all so much gentlewoman gibberish to me."

Hart lifted one shoulder as he idly picked and twirled a blade of grass. "I like that bit about the thorns."

Captain Bryant regarded Mariah frankly. "You are a woman, Miss Aubrey. Tell me. What did that certain lady mean when she said she found this 'everything romantic'? Must I have raven hair and grey eyes to win her heart?"

"*Smoky* grey eyes," Hart amended.

He grimaced impatiently. "Who has grey eyes, anyway? Light blue or brown or green, or any combination thereof, but grey?"

"I have seen grey eyes," Mariah defended.

"On an *Englishman*? In any case, I am afraid I find the book frightfully dull."

"Let me guess," Hart said. "No swordplay, no gunfire, and no horse races."

"Exactly. Lots of long looks and deep discussions."

Hart raised one finger high. "And therein lies the void between the sexes. Women want long looks and deep discussions, and men want to ride and shoot."

Captain Bryant nodded. "I know I do. Can we lay aside novels for a few hours and go shoot something?"

"Oh, very well."

Captain Bryant got to his feet and gave Hart up a hand up. "But you are my witness, William. I did try to read *A Winter in Bath*."

Mariah felt her throat tighten. "And you, Mr. Hart. Is your novel frightfully dull as well?"

"Actually, mine is excellent. Most diverting. *Euphemia's Return* by a Mrs. Wimble. I shall be finished soon, Matthew, and we might switch if you like."

Captain Bryant groaned. "No. If this is her favorite novel, I shall read it. Or die trying."

"Well." Mariah formed a brittle smile. "I was going to ask you and Mr. Hart to take part in a theatrical we are putting on for the poorhouse children, but no doubt you would find that frightfully dull too."

Captain Bryant looked wary. "What sort of theatrical?"

"Is there to be swordplay?" Hart asked eagerly.

Mariah looked from one man to the other, and then answered carefully, "There . . . can be."

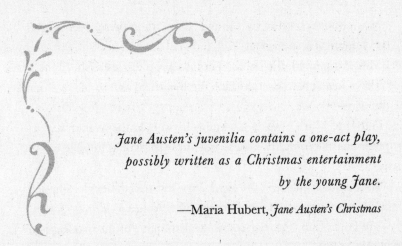

Jane Austen's juvenilia contains a one-act play,
possibly written as a Christmas entertainment
by the young Jane.

—Maria Hubert, *Jane Austen's Christmas*

chapter 19

nowing she would need permission to hold the theatrical, Mariah
spent the morning working up her courage to go and see Mrs.
Pitt. On her way to the poorhouse, she stopped to speak with the Miss
Merryweathers. The sisters advised her to involve the matron in the
production somehow, saying she was more likely to grant her approval
if given a role. Mariah thanked them but was secretly reluctant to ask
Mrs. Pitt to take any part.

In the poorhouse office, Mariah stated her case. As she spoke,
the matron's mouth tightened, her eyes narrowed in obvious dis-
approbation.

Desperately, Mariah added, "And you might even take part in the
theatrical, if you like."

The woman hesitated. Mariah was sure she was about to refuse
outright, when a voice from the door startled them both.

"A theatrical! Excellent notion."

Mariah looked up to find the vicar standing there, eyes bright. "The children will so enjoy it."

Mrs. Pitt paused, then said, "I am glad you think so, Mr. Lumley. For I have just agreed to introduce the theatrical and to narrate one of the plays."

Had she? Mariah was not certain she wanted the woman to participate. She faltered, "I . . . was not sure you would be able to get away."

With a quick glance at the vicar, Mrs. Pitt smiled her close-lipped smile. "The poorhouse is not a prison, Miss Aubrey."

"Of course not," Mariah murmured, thinking of the man kept on its top floor. But she thought it best not to mention him.

Mrs. Pitt intertwined her bony fingers atop the desk. "Yes, I think I must take part, to assure the performance is suitable for the children and all the inmates."

"Wonderful," the vicar said. "I shall look forward to it."

Mariah smiled weakly, wondering if Mrs. Pitt would have agreed to the production at all had the vicar not arrived when he had.

"And in my brief absence," Mrs. Pitt added, "my son, John, is more than capable of overseeing the institution. Now, when is the first rehearsal to be?"

Mariah glanced across the drawing room yet again. How strange it seemed that Mrs. Pitt should be there in the gatehouse, seated in the best chair. The mantel clock struck the hour and Mariah jumped. The woman made her nervous. She glanced instead at the others in the room, Dixon and four young people from the poorhouse— Lizzy, George, Sam, and Maggie. The children were clearly nervous as well.

Mariah stood as Captain Bryant and Mr. Hart entered.

"Bryant and Hart reporting for duty," the captain said.

Hart added a cheeky salute.

"Hello, gentlemen," Mariah said, hands primly clasped. "Thank you for coming."

At that moment, Chaucer loped down the stairs and across the floor, leaving a trail of inky paw prints. Had she forgotten to close her inkpot again?

"Chaucer, no!" Mariah lunged to pick up the cat, all poise forgotten, but he quickly skulked through the kitchen door and out of sight.

Dixon rose. "Never mind, Miss Mariah, I shall attend to it. You go on."

"Thank you." Mariah pushed a stray hair from her face and attempted to recover her dignity. "You gentlemen know Miss Dixon and Miss Barnes, I believe."

The officers bowed and Lizzie curtsied, a becoming pink rising to her cheeks. Dixon was too busy wiping up the ink to acknowledge the men's gesture.

Mariah continued. "And this is Mrs. Pitt, matron of Honora House, who has kindly graced us with her presence."

Mrs. Pitt dipped her head in condescension.

"And our other players here are George, Sam, and Maggie. Everyone, please take a seat and be comfortable. George, do you mind sitting on the floor? Thank you."

Hart sat in George's place, but Captain Bryant remained standing. The crowded drawing room had never felt so small.

Mariah took a deep breath and addressed the group. "Miss Dixon and I have decided upon a selection of *Aesop's Fables* for our performance. 'The Peacock's Complaint,' 'The Lion, the Bear, and the Fox,' and 'The Fox and the Crow.' "

Mr. Hart raised his hand. "I shall take whichever part has the fewest lines."

Lizzy giggled.

Mariah said, "Actually, I had two parts in mind for you, Mr. Hart."

"And what role shall you play, Miss Aubrey?" Captain Bryant asked. "The peacock? You certainly have the feathers for it."

Mariah hesitated, for a brief second thinking the captain had complimented her, but then he gestured toward a pile of feathers on the table. She had neglected to gather them up before the children arrived and then had forgotten all about them. "Oh! Yes, a lot of feathers. I fear I am very particular about my quills."

"You must write a great deal of letters."

"Yes. A great deal." She looked away from his speculative gaze. "Now, where were we? Mr. Hart, I would like you to play the lead role in 'The Peacock's Complaint.' "

Hart grinned. "You think me a preening peacock, Miss Aubrey?"

"Not at all. I think you a good sport."

"I must be, to have put up with Bryant here all these years."

Mariah smiled. "And as reward, you shall also play the bear and fight the lion over the fawn."

"And Captain Bryant is the lion, I suppose?" Hart asked wistfully. "Yes."

"Why, I wonder, do all ladies see *him* as the valiant lion and me as the grouchy bear? I promise you that in reality, our roles are quite the opposite."

Captain Bryant crossed his arms.

"There, there, Mr. Hart," Mariah soothed. "You may fight him and show us all how valiant you are. You may even use swords, though I shall ask the carpenter to fashion wooden swords for the spectacle, what with so many children about. But you may practice with steel all you like beforehand."

George and Sam whooped while Hart nodded. "That is something at least."

"If you are not to play the peacock, Miss Aubrey, what role will you play?" Captain Bryant asked. "The goddess Juno?"

"No. Dixon shall do the part more justice than I. I shall be busy reminding people of their cues, helping on with costumes, et cetera."

In fact, Mariah had already begun fashioning costumes from odds and ends in her aunt's trunk. She added, "By the way, Captain, I would also like you to play the fox in 'The Fox and the Crow.' "

He tilted his head and looked at her, eyes alight with challenge. "If you will play the crow."

"Why?" Mariah asked, surprised.

He gave her a lazy grin. "I want to hear you sing."

"You shall hear me *caw*, a slight improvement on my singing voice, but at least I should have an excuse."

"All the better." His grin widened.

"Maggie is the true singer here." Mariah placed a hand on the girl's shoulder, and Maggie bit back a smile.

"Besides," Mariah added. "I already asked Lizzy to play the crow."

"Go on, miss, you play the crow," Lizzy urged. "I am frightened to death at the thought of playing the dove as it is."

"Very well, if you are certain. And Mrs. Pitt has kindly offered to narrate the piece."

Again that lady dipped her head, and Mariah wondered once more why the woman had agreed to participate.

Mariah bent and pulled her creation from a basket on the floor—a headdress she had crafted from one of her aunt's hats. "I made this for the crow to wear. The beak can hold a wooden block of cheese."

"Ingenious, Miss Aubrey," Hart said, all admiration.

Bryant studied her all too closely. "What other talents have you hidden away, I wonder?"

In the actual performance, the poorhouse stairway would serve as the "tree" in the entry hall, which Mrs. Pitt thought best suited for staging a theatrical. But for the rehearsal, Mariah stood on a kitchen chair to play the crow.

Mrs. Pitt held the script near the candle lamp. She cleared her throat and began, " 'A crow, having stolen a bit of cheese from a cottage window, perched herself high in a tree and held the choice morsel in her beak.' "

Mariah had to admit the woman had a good, if affected, speaking voice.

Wearing the crow headdress and her aunt's fur mantle, Mariah stood gingerly on the chair, swiveling her head from side to side so that everyone might see the beak and "cheese" from the best angle. George guffawed. Even quiet Maggie giggled. Hart, she noticed, was too busy staring at Lizzy, and Lizzy too busy *not* looking at him to react at all.

Mrs. Pitt waited for silence, then continued, " 'A fox, seeing this, longed to possess the tasty morsel himself, and so devised a wily plan to acquire it. He would compliment the crow on her beauty.' "

Captain Bryant, wearing the velvet ears Mariah had sewn from one of her aunt's old collars, and an authentic fox tail tucked into the waist of his pantaloons, walked casually over and stood beneath the "tree."

He glanced up from an idle inspection of his "paw," and reacted as if he had just noticed her there. He exaggerated his look of surprise with wide open mouth, bugged eyes, and sputtering. The children laughed again.

" 'How handsome is the crow,' " he exclaimed. " 'I protest, I never observed it before, but your feathers are a more delicate white than ever I saw in my life.' "

"White!" George objected. For Mariah's headdress and mantle were black.

" 'And what a fine shape and graceful turn of the body is there!' " Captain Bryant continued.

Mariah smiled and turned from side to side in mock modesty. She noted that, although she had given Captain Bryant his lines only five minutes before, he seemed to barely need to look at the page in his hand.

Mrs. Pitt took up her cue. " 'The crow, tickled by his very civil language, nestled and preened, and hardly knew where she was.' "

Captain Bryant sighed dramatically. " 'If *only* you had a tolerable voice. If only *it* were as fair as your complexion.' "

Mariah frowned in faux disapproval, planting her hands on her hips.

" 'Oh, if her voice were only equal to her beauty, she would deservedly be considered the queen of birds!' "

Mrs. Pitt said, " 'Realizing the fox was dubious as to the particular of her voice, and having in mind to set him right on the matter, the crow opened her beak and began to sing.' "

Mariah let out a loud "Caw!" and dipped her head to dislodge the cheese.

" 'And in that instant the cheese dropped from her mouth,' " Mrs. Pitt said. She looked up at Mariah, squinted her eyes, and then repeated, " 'The cheese dropped from her mouth!' "

Beside Mariah's chair, Matthew beamed up at her with a lopsided grin. She shook her head again and finally felt the lightening of her headdress as the yellow-painted wood fell.

Captain Bryant caught the wedge neatly and pretended to take a lusty bite from it.

" 'This was exactly what the fox had planned and hoped for,' " Mrs. Pitt read. " 'And he laughed to himself at the credulity of the crow.' "

Matthew laughed and slapped his thigh in exaggerated hilarity. He called up to a pouting Mariah, " 'My good Crow, your voice is fair enough. It is your wit that is wanting!' "

With this, Captain Bryant jogged off with his prize. The small audience began to clap. Before Mariah could step down from the chair, the captain circled back and offered her his hand. Self-consciously, she placed her hand in his. He helped her down but did not release her. Instead he held her hand high and led her to "center stage," where they both took their bows. The children, Lizzy, Mr. Hart, and even Mrs. Pitt applauded good-naturedly for the simple performance.

Mariah was buoyed by the promising beginning and hoped the rest of the rehearsals and the performance itself would go as smoothly. She looked forward to bringing cheer into the lives of the poorhouse residents. And into her own life as well. Perhaps it would help her forget, at least for a little while, her remorse over the past. . . .

Lydia was surprised late that first night when she heard a scratch at the door of her bedchamber. She knew instantly it was him. She paused in the brushing of her long dark hair. For just one moment, she sat as a statue, meeting her amber eyes in the looking glass. She saw the light, the hope there.

Her chaperone was asleep in the adjoining room. At least Lydia hoped she was.

She rose and padded in bare feet to the door. Pressed her hand, then her ear and cheek against its cool, smooth grain.

"Yes?" she whispered, never imagining what she was agreeing to.

"It is me," his muffled whisper replied. "I must see you. Talk to you."

Lydia thought quickly. "Meet me in the arbor before breakfast."

"No. Now. I must speak with you now."

"We cannot."

"We can!"

"Shhh . . ." Lydia urged, fearing he would awaken the whole house.

"You don't understand, Lydia. I am afraid. My heart aches to see you. One more time. One more time before I must . . . depart."

Stricken, she opened the door. "Depart?" she echoed. "But you have just returned."

"I know. But . . ." His words faded away. His eyes widened, darkened, as he looked from her face, to the hair tumbling loose around her shoulders, to the lace bodice of the nightdress.

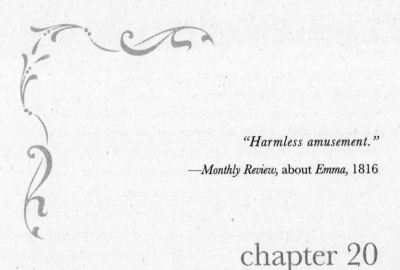

"Harmless amusement."

—*Monthly Review,* about *Emma,* 1816

chapter 20

The following week passed quickly with another dance lesson at Windrush Court, a second theatrical rehearsal in the gatehouse, and a third in the poorhouse itself. On the evening of July first, Mariah went over to Honora House early to make certain everything was in order for the performance.

Mrs. Pitt, well dressed in a jaunty feather cap and a green gown that complemented her thin frame, met Mariah at the door.

"Good news, Miss Aubrey. The undersheriff is here visiting. He is an old friend of the late Mr. Pitt, and he has promised to stay for the theatrical. He does us a great honor, does he not?"

"Indeed," Mariah said, feeling sheepish. "I only hope you mentioned our humble entertainment is meant primarily for the children. Though, of course, all are welcome."

A stout bearded man appeared in the office doorway. "Never fear, miss. I haven't fancy tastes. I'm sure your spectacle shall prove amusing."

"I hope you find it so, sir."

Captain Bryant and Mr. Hart arrived even earlier than she had requested.

"We walked through the gatehouse instead of riding around," the captain said. "I hope you don't mind."

"No, of course not," Mariah said. But inwardly she felt ill at ease. Why hadn't she anticipated that? She certainly hoped she had covered up the pages of the new book she was writing. In any case, there was nothing she could do about it now, and much to do to get ready.

Together they hung blankets from the storeroom all the way to a structural post near the "stage," creating a narrow passage that would allow the actors to don costumes in the storeroom and enter the stage without being seen by the audience. Around the stage, they placed gas lamps to illume the scene. The candle chandelier, rarely used, was lit for the occasion.

At the appointed hour, the eager audience came in, some from out-of-doors, some from abovestairs. Children sat on the floor in front, older folks in chairs behind them, and able-bodied guests—the vicar, Martin, Mr. Phelps, and the Strongs—stood at the back. The under-sheriff and John Pitt stood at the side of the stage, arms crossed as if the king's bodyguards.

When all was ready, Mrs. Pitt positioned herself at the podium. She introduced the undersheriff with great fanfare, warmly thanked the vicar for attending, and warned the children to behave. Then, clearly enjoying the attention, she arranged her note cards and announced, " 'The Peacock's Complaint.' "

Miss Dixon entered, swathed in Aunt Fran's pale tunic, the Grecian coronet atop her head, and carrying a branch as scepter. She sat regally upon the worn chair at stage left, instantly transforming it into a throne.

From her place near the stage but behind the curtain, Mariah noticed Mr. Phelps grin and elbow Jack Strong.

Mariah felt someone near and glanced up to find Captain Bryant standing beside her in the narrow, shadowy corridor. Captain Hart and

Lizzy stood a few feet away, exchanging low whispers. Seeing them, Mariah felt a pang of unexpected jealousy. Where had that come from? She reminded herself that she was resigned to life without romantic love. She had already had her chance and squandered it.

Captain Bryant leaned across to sneak a look at the assembled crowd, brushing Mariah's arm as he did so. When he settled back against the wall, she noticed he stood nearer yet, his shoulder touching hers. She found she did not mind. In fact, it sparked in her a secret thrill, being in such close proximity to a tall handsome officer, people all around them yet out of view, only Hart and Lizzy as chaperones— too preoccupied with each other to notice.

It was a silly, romantic notion, and Mariah enjoyed it even as she upbraided herself for it. His heart belonged to another. And even if it did not, he would never court her—and nor could she blame him. At least she had her own secret outlet for romance. Her novels. And that was enough, she told herself. It was. It would be.

Little Maggie climbed the stairs and stood at the rail. She swallowed and glanced down white-faced at Mariah. Mariah nodded and smiled reassurance. Jeremiah Martin stepped forward and played the opening measures on his flute. Taking a deep breath, Maggie stared straight ahead and began to sing. The audience hushed instantly.

> "Alas, my love you do me wrong
> To cast me off discourteously. . . ."

Mariah did not expect the tears, but there they were, wetting her cheeks. The beautiful voice, the lyrics of love and loss, struck her more painfully than she could have anticipated.

> "And I have loved you so long
> Delighting in your company. . . ."

Mariah did not wipe at her tears, did not want to bring them to Captain Bryant's notice. But then she felt it. Her hand, by her side, taken in his warm fingers. Gently pressed and held. And with that simple act of empathy, her heart squeezed and her whole body longed to be held.

When the song ended, the hushed crowd drew a collective breath, and a smattering of applause grew as the dumbfounded spectators returned to themselves. Mariah extracted her hand from Captain Bryant's to join in the applause, and the moment between them passed.

"Mr. Hart!" Mariah whispered.

Mr. Hart looked up, startled, and quickly donned his mask as little Maggie grinned and darted down the stairs.

Then, as the peacock, with the masquerade mask of jewel-blue feathers and a feather fan besides, Mr. Hart swaggered onto the stage and addressed the crowd. "Sure, sure, you all love the voice of the nightingale, do you not? I cannot compete. Oh, Juno, goddess Juno, listen to how they adore the voice of the nightingale. While they laugh at my ugly screeching voice."

He screeched for effect. The children laughed. The ladies winced or covered their ears.

Hart pouted. "I thought *I* was your favorite bird."

"Of course you are, Peacock," Dixon, as Juno, said patiently.

"Then I beseech you. Give me a voice as beautiful as the nightingale's."

Juno shook her crowned head. "Tsk, tsk, Peacock. Are your beautiful feathers not enough for you?"

"No." He crossed his arms and pouted once more. Again the children laughed.

"If the nightingale is blessed with a fine voice, you have the advantage of beauty and largeness of person."

Watching her former nanny, Mariah was reminded of all those days in the nursery, when she would scold Mariah for pining for Julia's musical ability, or some other girl's superior beauty. How wise Dixon had been.

"Ah," Peacock said, "but what avails my silent, unmeaning beauty when I am so far excelled in voice?"

"Selfish bird. The properties of every creature are appointed by the decree of fate." Juno turned her head and lifted her branch-scepter. "Behold the mighty eagle."

George, as the eagle, with shirt stuffed with stocking "muscles," swooped by, flexing. His comrades guffawed.

"Would you also have his strength?" Dixon asked.

"If I could."

Martin stepped forward again, this time wearing a colorful shawl about his shoulders and flapping his arms with a stoic lack of enthusiasm.

He groused under his breath to Dixon, though Mariah and likely the entire front row heard. "Oh sure, make the ol' tar play the parrot. That'll serve 'im right." Then more loudly, he squawked, "Brack! Polly want a biscuit. Brack!"

Juno rolled her elegant eyes and once again addressed Mr. Hart. "Behold the parrot. Would you also have his power of speech?"

"If I could."

Martin returned to his place with apparent relief. Behind the curtain, Lizzy stepped near Mariah. Mariah took her hand and found it trembling.

"And lastly, behold the gentle dove with her sweet innocence of character."

Lizzy, wearing Fran's translucent, silvery shawl over a gown of white muslin, took small dainty steps across the stage, eyelashes fanning her pale cheeks and golden hair ringing her face. Mariah conceded the casting perfect. Lizzy glowed in innocence and loveliness both.

Juno raised an arm toward the dove. "Would you take this from her as well?"

Mr. Hart seemed particularly struck by Lizzy's loveliness, for in fact he merely stared, forgetting or neglecting his line.

Juno cleared her stately voice.

"No," Mr. Hart breathed. Then ad-libbed, "She is perfect as she is."

Mariah saw John Pitt frown.

Juno rose and stretched out her arms. "Each of these is contented with his own particular quality, and unless you have a mind to be miserable, you must learn to be content too."

But Mr. Hart was still staring at Lizzy.

Juno poked him with her scepter.

"Ah . . . yes. Yes, I shall."

The players bowed, Hart taking Lizzy's hand and raising it high, then bowing with great flourish. Again John Pitt frowned. But Hart did not release Lizzy's hand even as the two exited the stage. His limp, Mariah decided, had never been less noticeable.

Mariah took her place at the podium. She would narrate the second play and Mrs. Pitt the last. "Next we shall have 'The Lion, the Bear, and the Fox.'"

She waited until Mr. Hart removed his mask and both he and Captain Bryant picked up their wooden swords. They each stood in frozen pose of menace while she read.

"There once was a mighty, fearless lion and a strong, brave bear. One day, as they roamed the forest, they each spied a fawn at the very same moment, and each wanted her for himself."

Young Sam pushed the wheeled invalid chair bearing Amy Merryweather to her place stage left, out of range of the swordplay. Atop her white hair, she wore a pair of brown velvet ears. She looked charming as she waved to the audience. Hands and smiles rose in return from around the room.

Mariah continued. "What followed was an epic duel of claws . . . um, cutlasses, as the lion and bear each fought to prove his supremacy."

Captain Bryant and Lieutenant Hart lifted and clashed their wooden swords in an echoing crack. One parried while the other struck. One struck while the other ducked. They moved through the steps of an intricately choreographed fight, and Mariah noticed that they had arranged it so that Hart stood primarily in one place and pivoted around on his good foot, while Captain Bryant made larger dives, turns, and spins. The two must have spent hours rehearsing. It touched Mariah that they would do so. Or had they really been so bored?

She watched for several moments, then read, "The battle was severe on both sides. They worried and tore at each other for so long that both grew too weary to strike another blow."

Both men fell slowly, theatrically to the ground, groaning as they descended.

Mariah continued, "Thus, while they lie on the ground unable to move, panting . . ."

She waited for them to pant. "And with tongues lolling." Barely covering a smirk, she waited until each man obliged her.

Then, glancing up to see that Martin was at the ready, she went on, "At that moment a fox, who had been watching the battle from a safe distance, came and stood very impudently between the bear and the lion."

Martin, now wearing ears and tail, walked forward and stood between the prostrate men. He gave each a little bow, and said in a courtly manner, "I thank you, gentlemen." He then took up the handles of Miss Merryweather's chair and wheeled her smartly down the aisle.

The lion and the bear looked on, sputtering protests, lifting their torsos from the floor and reaching out, but then falling back down in exhaustion.

Before Mariah could read the next line, a shout and cries of alarm shot up from the crowd. Mariah looked up in time to see a man throw back the draperies from the window at the first landing. He ran forward and, with one hand on the banister, leapt over the stair rail and onto the stage below as though he were an athlete of twenty instead of a man of seventy, which his face showed him to be. The gaslight illuminated droopy features, unkempt grey hair, and a weathered visage.

He appropriated one of the wooden swords from the still-prone Hart, leapt onto Juno's throne, and bellowed, "Unhand her, you cur, or I shall have your head."

Near the back of the room, Martin whirled to face this unexpected foe.

What a sight the man made in his blue coat faded nearly white with more golden buttons missing than present, wearing old-fashioned knee breeches and stockings, but no shoes. His stance atop the chair was impressive, menacing and elegant both, as he held his sword in the *en garde* position, the other arm aloft for balance. A fire lit his droopy eyes, and his soft jaw clenched in challenge.

Martin gaped. In surprise, yes, and in recognition. If there was a measure of fear there, it was not the primary emotion. "Captain Prince!" Martin exclaimed. He snapped his shoulders back and stood at attention, offering the man a salute on the invisible brim of his missing hat. One of the fox ears flopped forward at the gesture.

The man lowered his sword. "Great Poseidon! Can it be?"

The lowering of the sword seemed the signal for a melee. Mrs. Pitt screeched a command, and her son and the undersheriff lunged forward and took hold of the old man and began hauling him across the floor toward the stairs. His stocking feet sought footing in vain, slipping and dragging as the two larger men all but carried him up the first flight of stairs.

Amy Merryweather had gotten herself up out of the chair and, holding on to its arms for support, turned in time to glimpse her would-be rescuer as the men hauled him from view. She made a movement as though to follow, but Agnes put a staying hand on each of her slight shoulders. With a glance at Mrs. Pitt, Agnes leaned close and whispered to her sister. Though Mariah could not hear the words, she imagined them. "Remember. We don't know about the man on the roof."

For that's who the man was. The man kept locked on the top floor had somehow stolen downstairs to watch their "harmless" entertainment. And because of it, Mariah feared he had just tasted his last morsel of freedom.

In the mayhem that followed, the rest of the performance was forgotten.

Mrs. Pitt continued her terse orders and began shepherding the residents back to their quarters. Mariah was sorry they'd had to forgo "The Fox and the Crow," especially considering all the work she had put into that headpiece. But Mrs. Pitt made it perfectly clear she wanted all visitors out and order restored as quickly as possible.

Martin appeared shaken and was silent as they walked, dejected, back to the gatehouse. Had he really recognized the man? Or had he imagined the likeness, only to remember his former commander was long dead?

Even Captain Bryant and Mr. Hart walked in silence. At the gatehouse, Mariah thanked them for being willing to help and apologized for the way the evening had turned out.

"Are you joking, Miss Aubrey?" Hart said. "That is the most fun I've had since coming to Windrush Court."

"Thanks, Hart," Captain Bryant said dryly, then pressed Mariah's hand. "You did a good thing for those children, Miss Aubrey, and we were pleased to be a part of it. Don't let the ending spoil the whole."

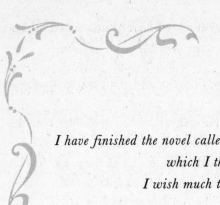

I have finished the novel called Pride and Prejudice,
which I think a very superior work.
I wish much to know who is the author,
or ess as I am told.

—Annabella Milbanke, 1813

chapter 21

*M*r. Crosby *wrote to ask if he might* call again the following
week, and Mariah felt she had little choice but to write
back and accept. She felt self-conscious about posting a letter to the
man, and refrained from inscribing the word *Publisher* in Mr. Crosby's
direction.

In his letter, Mr. Crosby had expressed interest in publishing her
second novel, as Henry had indicated he would. So what was the purpose of this call? She hoped it wasn't to continue his interrogation.

Mariah glanced out the window at the appointed hour. Nothing.
That was odd. The man had said he prided himself on his punctuality.
Mariah paced across the room, then paused before the small looking
glass, checking her appearance again. She had taken more time with
her hair than usual, brushing it until it shone, pinning it into a neat
coil high on her head, and then even using the hot iron to sear curls on

either side of her face, which she rarely bothered to do. The day was damp. She hoped the curls lasted through Mr. Crosby's visit.

Again crossing to the window, she saw a flicker of movement through the trees lining the road. She was surprised to see not one man but two standing there. The first wore the telltale brown coat of Mr. Crosby. The second, a taller man, held the reins of a black horse. This man threw his head back in laughter and Mariah recognized the profile of Hugh Prin-Hallsey. She found herself frowning. *That's odd.* Did the two men know one another? Or had they met by chance in the village and walked this way together?

She did not like the idea of Hugh discovering that a publisher was coming to call at the gatehouse. He would probably raise her rent again. What excuse would Mr. Crosby give? She hoped he would not confide in Hugh, foolishly choosing to trust the man due to his family's distinction. Mariah shivered at the thought.

As she watched, Hugh swung himself up into the saddle and rode away back toward the village and the turnpike which led to the estate's main entrance. Mr. Crosby lifted a hand in farewell and stepped from the road onto the gatehouse lawn, carrying a thin valise. Was that a small smile on his face, or a grimace? She wished she might decipher his expression.

At the door, he greeted her warmly. "Miss Aubrey, how good to see you again."

"Mr. Crosby, you are most welcome. Do come in." Dare she ask about Hugh? Admit she'd seen them talking and appear a nosy spy?

Instead, she said, "I was beginning to worry when you did not arrive at the time you mentioned in your letter."

His full eyebrows rose. "Am I tardy? I did pause to speak to a fellow traveler . . ." He checked his watch. "I *am* five minutes late. Imagine that." He looked back at her, eyes alight. "It was good of you to worry, Miss Aubrey. I hope that means you look forward to my visits."

Her cheeks heated. She had walked right into that. How forward he must think her. She attempted to cover her embarrassment with a carefree smile.

He smiled warmly in return, handed her his hat, and sat on the settee as he had during his first visit. Chaucer jumped up and tried to climb onto his lap, but Mr. Crosby gently but firmly pushed him down. "I am afraid cats make me sneeze."

Once again Dixon and Martin brought tea, and again Mr. Crosby declined all but a solitary, unadulterated cup. Mariah did not mind. She had eaten ahead of his call this time.

"I have good news and bad news," he said, pulling out a pile of clippings and a few periodicals from his valise. A corner of his mouth quirked. "Or should I say good reviews and bad reviews. Which should you like first?"

Mariah pulled a face. "Horrors. I am not certain I wish to hear the bad reviews at all. Scathing, are they?"

"Decide for yourself." He picked up a clipping and began to read. " '*A Winter in Bath* I do not very much like. Want of interest is the fault I can least excuse in works of mere amusement.' "

"Want of interest?" Mariah sputtered. "Work of mere amusement?"

He selected another. "This one is not so bad. 'A clever novel. And though it ends stupidly, I was much amused by it.' "

Mariah regarded him suspiciously. "You are enjoying this, Mr. Crosby, are you not?"

"Very well, I shall leave off tormenting you. But one good review first." He lifted *The Critical Review* high. " 'Well written. The incidents are probable, highly pleasing, and interesting.' "

"That one is more palatable, thank you." Feeling self-conscious, Mariah changed the subject. "I was very pleased to hear you will publish *Daughters of Brighton* as well."

He nodded. "Yes. And since we've found a few errors in the printing of *A Winter in Bath*, I will want you to correct proofs for the next book. But we shall cross that bridge later. I am here today because I have another proposal for you."

"Oh?"

"I have come to understand, from your brother's unspoken more than spoken hints, that additional income would not be unwelcome."

Her cheeks heated anew.

"Now, now, no need to be embarrassed before the likes of me. Am I not in business for profit?"

She braved a smile.

"That is better. Now. I represent a playwright who is stymied to devise his next script and who would pay handsomely for another writer to create a first draft in his stead. Your name would appear nowhere on the work, and you would receive no credit should it succeed, and only his censure should it fail. But either way you would earn a substantial sum for your efforts."

Mariah's head spun. "Is it not unethical? I mean, to pass off one person's work as another's?"

"Only if plagiarism is involved—if one steals the work of another without his or her consent. I would need you to sign a contract agreeing to the terms."

"It still seems deceptive."

"Happens all the time, Miss Aubrey, with novels, plays, operas. One of our authors supported herself by writing poems and love letters for gentlemen before she was published. Whether ethical or not I cannot judge, but it is certainly legal and smart business to marry a well-known author's name with a skilled author's work."

She was too stunned to be flattered. "I have never written a real play before."

"Your brother mentioned you are quite adept at theatricals."

"Well, yes, but those were only for our family, or for the local children."

"Very much the same. Here. I have brought the playwright's outline and the few pages he was able to produce 'before the muse deserted him,' as he says. Read them over and see if you think you might be game for the challenge."

She glanced at the scrawled words. "I don't know. . . ."

"I realize you are likely writing a third novel, and there will be proofs to correct for the second, but I am hoping you can fit this in." He withdrew a calling card and handed it to her. A figure was penned on the back. "This is what he is prepared to pay you."

It was more than she would have expected. Not quite the amount her novel had brought her but nothing to dismiss lightly either. Her rent would be paid for the next quarter. She and Dixon would have enough fuel and food for the winter. Better yet, she could hire Lizzy.

Mariah smiled at Mr. Crosby. "I find I am 'game' after all."

She went to see Mrs. Pitt that very afternoon, for the first time since the ill-fated theatrical. The woman greeted Mariah with her prim, close-lipped smile and a vague wave toward the guest chair before returning her attention to a ledger on the desk, her bony forefinger resuming its glide down a neat column of figures.

Sitting across from her, Mariah licked her lips and announced, "I should like to employ Miss Lizzy Barnes."

Mrs. Pitt stilled, her hand midair above the ledger. "Lizzy? But she already has a position here, working for me. Surely one of the other girls would suit just as well."

"Perhaps. But I specifically wish to engage Miss Barnes."

The woman's eyes narrowed. "Why? What has she told you? Has she said she doesn't like working for me?"

"No, Mrs. Pitt. Nothing like that, I assure you." Mariah hesitated. "I . . . I think she would like a change of, um, scenery and . . . society. After all, she has lived and worked within these walls for some time."

"And what is wrong with these walls?" Mrs. Pitt challenged.

"Nothing."

Fire lit the matron's muddy eyes. "Has she said something about my son? Has she accused him of anything? Ungrateful chit!"

"Accused him, no. She has not said a word against him. I did hear from . . . someone. . . . that he pays her unwanted attention, but—"

"Those Merryweathers told you. Is that it? Told you my John is sniffing after the likes of Lizzy Barnes. Vile imaginations! Well, let me tell you something, Miss Aubrey. You cannot trust everything the Miss Merryweathers tell you." The woman leaned forward across her desk. "Don't let them fool you. Proper matrons, ha. One of them was sold into prostitution by her own father as a young woman—and that's a fact. It's no wonder they imagine lust in the eye of every male they see."

Stunned, Mariah felt bile rise in her throat. "Which one?" she asked weakly, guessing she already knew the answer.

"I'll say no more. I only confide it to prove that you cannot credit everything that pair tells you. You've heard how the pox affects the mind, I trust?"

Mariah stared at the woman, shocked speechless that she would say such a thing about anyone.

Mrs. Pitt leaned back and pursed her lips. "I will speak to Lizzy and leave the decision to her."

Mariah was taken aback by the matron's glower and what could only be described as hatred glittering in the woman's eyes. Hatred aimed at Lizzy and the Miss Merryweathers . . . or her?

She left Honora House feeling unsettled and concerned. She wondered what sort of manipulation Mrs. Pitt would use to keep the girl from accepting.

Crossing the road to the gatehouse, Mariah paused, marveling at the exuberant scene before her. Children from the poorhouse were spread across the lawn—George, Sam, and even Maggie, along with several other children whose names Mariah could not recall. And there was Lieutenant Hart, standing with bat ready, while Captain Bryant bowled the ball at him.

Thwack. Hart hit the ball and the children scrambled after it. Hart converted the bat to a makeshift walking stick and ran-hopped toward the opposite wicket, while George, the other batsman, ran to swap places with him, becoming the next to bat.

"Join us, Miss Aubrey?" Captain Bryant said. "We could use a wicket keeper."

"Very well."

His dark eyebrows rose. He had clearly expected her to demur.

She walked across the lawn and stood not far behind the striker's wicket, awaiting his next delivery. George gave it a whack, but Captain Bryant caught it after a single bounce. He threw it hard and hit the makeshift wicket before George and Hart could again swap places, and Hart was declared out.

They had insufficient players for a proper game, but the children enjoyed running about on the fine July day. They eventually switched sides, even though not everyone had been called out on the first.

Mr. Hart took over as wicket keeper as Mariah stepped up to bat. George and Sam both begged for turns as bowler, but after several consecutive wild deliveries, Captain Bryant again took to the pitch.

He rubbed the ball on his trouser leg, gave her an impish grin, and spit on the ball.

She wrinkled her face at him.

Holding the bat low, she tapped the ground in preparation. Only belatedly did she realize she was unconsciously swaying her hips as she did so. From his appreciative glance, Mariah knew Captain Bryant had not failed to notice.

He took his running start and bowled the ball. It bounced once in line with the stumps. Perfect.

Thwack! She hit it dead on.

Captain Bryant's mouth dropped open. "I can't believe it. My best delivery."

The ball flew past Sam, past George, and past Maggie—who

was picking dandelions, in any case—all the way to the road, their boundary "fence."

An instant four runs. She didn't even have to move.

Mariah raised her bat high in triumph, then smiled at Captain Bryant. "Did I not tell you I grew up with two brothers?"

The joy and sun-filled afternoon faded and with it Mariah's mood, which darkened as each hour passed with no sign of Lizzy Barnes. Mariah's insistence on hiring Lizzy had obviously irked the matron, and the thought of an angry Mrs. Pitt discomfited Mariah. Ensconced in her sitting room, she read the outline and sample pages from playwright Simon Wells, then pulled out several sheets of fresh paper to begin drafting the script. But she soon found she could not concentrate. Worries about Lizzy kept distracting her. Exasperated, she pulled out one of her aunt's journals instead.

My days at Windrush Court are more peaceful, though certainly more boring now that Frederick Prin-Hallsey has gone to London for the season. This is a quiet place for a girl, with no men to flirt with, save the dashing but cheeky footmen. I did see a man in his late twenties about the place a few times visiting Mrs. Prin-Hallsey, but we were not introduced. There was also an artist, at least I guessed he was, evidenced by the easel and canvas he brought with him, but again Mrs. Prin-Hallsey did not consider a bored young houseguest worthy of introduction.

My mother's health is improving and I believe she is beginning to chafe under the kind, though stifling attentions of "dear Jane," as she calls Mrs. Prin-Hallsey, always ending her friend's name on a sigh. For, while kindly meant, the lady does overbear one with itineraries of exercise and endless lists of herbals and medicinals one ought to take. I think, increasingly, Mother misses her own home and longs to be mistress of it, and of herself, once more.

I cannot say I blame her.

Mariah flipped ahead several pages.

Mother continues in health now that we are home, though I do not think she will ever be her old robust self again. I rarely think of Windrush Court and Frederick Prin-Hallsey now. I have met another man. A man who considers me worthy of his attention. A kind, warmhearted man who makes me laugh. And even though he is several years older than I am, I believe I shall marry him.

Mariah realized she was probably reading about her uncle Norris, her mother's brother.

Perusing her aunt's journal reminded Mariah of the new novel she had begun. Eager to return to it, she went into her room and retrieved the few scribbled pages. She reread what she had written so far and then sat back down to continue *The Tale of Lydia Sorrow.*

Lydia grasped the door between them like a shield, both thankful for it and wishing it away in the same thought.

"Lydia . . . You are beautiful," he breathed.

Her lips parted to say . . . something. But the words were forgotten before they could fully form, so struck was she by the revelation in his eyes. The deep awe and unexpected . . . Was it loss? Longing?

"Thunder and turf, Lydia, you will kill me yet."

"Shh. If Miss Duckworth should hear or anyone see you . . ."

"Then let me in. For I am not going away. Not yet. Not until I can speak my heart. I must, Lydia. I must."

She hesitated. "Very well. But only for a moment. And keep your voice down, I beg of you."

The sweet, heady delight Lydia had felt upon seeing him earlier in the hall, and at the anticipation of being alone with him in the garden, perchance, or dim library, now lurched into something else.

Fear.

Mariah laid down her quill. Even reliving that much of the experience was enough to make her worry for Lizzy all over again.

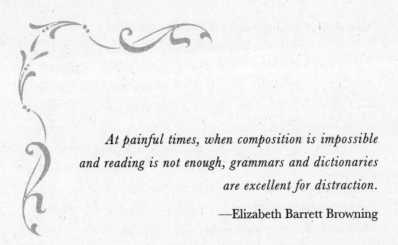

At painful times, when composition is impossible
and reading is not enough, grammars and dictionaries
are excellent for distraction.

—Elizabeth Barrett Browning

chapter 22

*H*oping a change of scenery might help, Mariah took her blotter, pages, ink, and quill down to the drawing room the next day. There she worked on the play for several hours, following the prescribed outline of love and deception between a man who must marry for money, and a poor, widowed countess feigning wealth. For some reason the drama left her unmoved. Perhaps it was because, as much as she might empathize with a woman hiding the reality of her situation, Mariah struggled to admire her. The climactic love scene, one of the few the playwright had scratched out, seemed overwrought and disingenuous to her. She had tried several drafts to improve upon it, but still felt it was not right.

She was standing at the front window, murmuring possible lines of dialogue aloud, when a rap startled her. She turned to find Captain Bryant grinning in the kitchen doorway.

"Caught you talking to yourself again, Miss Aubrey. I hope you don't mind; Miss Dixon invited me in."

"Of course not."

He glanced down, his gaze snagged by something on the floor. Before she could prevent him, he stepped forward and picked up one of the playwright's pages that had fallen from the table. Glancing at it, his brows rose. "Writing another theatrical, Miss Aubrey?"

Oh dear. What to say? She decided to be as truthful as possible. "Ah. This time the playwright Simon Wells receives the credit."

"And why, may I ask, have you Simon Wells's script?"

Mariah swallowed. "Mr. Crosby, whom you met, is a friend of his. I gather he wants a woman's . . . reaction." Hoping to divert him, she picked up another page and went on hastily, "His love scene doesn't strike me as quite right."

He nodded, apparently accepting this explanation. "Shall we read it aloud?" he suggested. "See where the false note lies?"

"Um . . . that is very kind of you. But not necessary."

He shrugged. "Might be amusing. I admit I was disappointed not to perform our little drama together at the poorhouse."

Nerves fluttering, she admitted, "It would be helpful. If you are certain you do not mind?"

"Not at all."

Palms damp, she handed him the marked-up original in Simon Wells's hand and kept the version in her own hand for herself.

Again using the quick memory he had demonstrated during the rehearsal of "The Fox and the Crow," Captain Bryant spent a few minutes reading the lines, then began abruptly, " 'Look at me. Why will you not look at me?' "

Mariah started in surprise. Pulling her eyes from his, she belatedly found her line and cleared her suddenly clogged throat. " 'I cannot. Not now. When you know I am not the woman you thought me.' "

" 'Not a widowed countess?' "

" 'A countess, yes, but a poor one.' " Mariah swallowed again, her throat desperately dry. " 'And you must marry a rich woman. An heiress to save your family's estate. Go. She is better suited to you.' "

" 'You are correct. She is.' " Script between thumb and forefinger, Captain Bryant grasped Mariah's shoulders with both hands.

She gasped, stunned by his intensity, never expecting him to so fully act out the script's stage directions.

" 'Why can I not leave?' " he said. " 'Why am I drawn back to your door? Your arms?' "

Wistfully, Mariah thought, *Would that you were.*

" 'I came here to win one woman,' " he continued, " 'and instead am lost to another.' "

" 'Go,' " Mariah croaked out. " 'Go while you can.' "

" 'It is already too late. Only promise me you will never again deceive me.' "

He traced a finger along her cheek and Mariah felt a thrill of pleasure. *He is only acting, foolish girl!*

" 'I promise,' " she murmured, feeling like a hypocrite even as she delivered the line.

His voice dropped to an intimate whisper, " 'Well then, my winsome, ethereal girl, you have but one promise left to make.' "

His straight nose neared her short, upturned one. His sweet breath tickled her cheek, and the scent of shaving soap warmed her senses. *He is acting*, she reminded herself again.

The tip of his nose touched hers. He angled his head, lowering yet closer. His mouth dipped nearer, ever nearer to hers. She could not breathe. Could not move. His lips touched hers, and a flood of warmth filled her chest and made pudding of her knees. He pulled back only slightly and looked into her face. His brown eyes were warm, his pupils large black orbs.

"There is no kiss," she said breathlessly, "in the script."

One side of his mouth lifted. "There should be."

Remembering his intentions toward another, the momentary thrill dissolved. What had he heard? Was he trifling with her because of her reputation?

His smile faded. He winced and pulled back. "This was a bad idea. I knew it even as I suggested it. Please forgive me, Miss Aubrey."

"Of course." She swallowed, struggling to regain her composure. "So, what do you think of the scene?" Her voice wavered. "Awful, is it not? Melodramatic? Overwrought?"

"I don't know. I found it quite . . . effective." He cleared his throat. "A word of advice? Tell Simon Wells that a real man would not describe a woman as 'winsome and ethereal.' Not if he truly admired her, at any rate."

Defensiveness flared at this criticism of her work. But she was too shaken to reply.

Matthew left the gatehouse directly after that, knowing he had better retreat quickly before he lost his head. What had he been thinking? Why had he toyed with her like that? He had already told her of his intentions toward another woman. How little Miss Aubrey must regard him now, for thoughtlessly flirting with her, all the while hoping to marry another. How inconstant he must appear. Was he? All he knew with certainty was that he did not like himself very much at the moment. It was time, past time, to get back on course and begin planning his campaign in earnest.

His first step would be to contact fellow officer Captain Ned Parker and his highborn and fashionable mother. Mrs. Parker had been the one to suggest a house party in the first place. *"Why do you not let me plan the party?"* she had said. *"Nothing like it to launch you into society—at least into the specific circle you have in mind."*

It was time to take her up on her offer.

He wrote to her the very next day, inviting her and her son to visit Windrush Court, or if they preferred, he would travel to London and call upon them there.

Mrs. Parker accepted his invitation by return post and informed him that she and Ned would arrive the following week.

In the meantime, Matthew gave the gatehouse a wide berth.

When the Parkers' coach-and-four rumbled up the drive, Matthew walked out to meet it. Captain Parker, he saw, rode his own Arabian beside the carriage.

The groom handed down the elegant middle-aged woman, and Matthew bowed low. "Mrs. Parker, how good of you to come." He looked up at her dashing, fair-haired son. "Ned old man, enjoying your leave as much as I?"

"No doubt more." Parker dismounted with athletic grace.

Matthew led the way inside to the drawing room, where refreshments awaited. William Hart waited as well.

Matthew began the introductions. "Mrs. Parker, may I present William Hart, my good friend and former first officer."

Hart bowed over her hand. "Mrs. Parker. A pleasure."

Matthew turned to Ned. "You remember Lieutenant Hart?"

Parker nodded and Hart saluted. "How do you do, sir."

Matthew smiled once more at Mrs. Parker and gestured her into an armchair upholstered in apple green velvet. "Thank you again for coming."

"I am happy to be here," she said. "Life in town had grown tiresome. I embrace the challenge of hosting a man's first house party. It will be a resounding success or my name is not Catherine Steadman Parker."

"And we gents shall leave you to it, Mamma," her son said, pouring himself a tall drink. "Give us leave to visit the cellars, and we shall give you leave to arrange the rest."

"Naughty boy. You might at least help with the guest list."

Keenly interested, Matthew sat in a matching armchair opposite

Mrs. Parker. With a dramatic sigh, her son slumped onto the crimson silk settee. Hart joined him.

"I have a few ideas and have begun a tentative list, of course," Mrs. Parker said, producing a small pocketbook.

"Of course," Ned Parker echoed with an indulgent smirk.

Mrs. Parker opened the book. "You three, of course. And we must have James Crawford."

Matthew frowned, but Mrs. Parker said gently, "I am afraid we simply must, Captain." Then she went on more brightly, "And perhaps Bartholomew Browne for interest."

"The widower poet? What rapture." Sarcasm curled Ned Parker's words, and Matthew bit back a smile.

His mother lifted her chin. "It will not hurt you to keep company with a little culture and accomplishment, Ned."

Privately, Matthew was surprised Mrs. Parker wished to invite a fairly recent widower and doubted the man would come.

Mrs. Parker returned to her notes. "For the ladies, we shall have Isabella Forsythe and Miss Ann Hutchins, a friend of hers. Most eligible."

"You can keep throwing her in my path, Mamma," Ned drawled. "But I shan't change my mind."

Mrs. Parker ignored him. "I still need a few more ladies. There are any number of young debutantes we might consider, Helen and Millicent Mabry, for example. And the ladies must have chaperones."

Mrs. Parker regarded Matthew. "Are you acquainted with any other accomplished young ladies we ought to consider?"

The truth was Matthew was not. Whom else could he invite to make up the party? And what would his guests do at Windrush Court? There would be shooting, which the men would enjoy, and billiards and cards. But how would the women occupy themselves? There would be dinners, of course, and he could ask Hammersmith to arrange for local musicians to play for a ball. But would Isabella and her friend be content with only the society of the Mabry sisters, agreeable girls though they might be? He thought suddenly of Miss Aubrey. She was clearly educated and accomplished. He wondered if she might be persuaded to come over in the evenings. . . .

In the end, Matthew told Mrs. Parker to invite whomever she thought best, as long as Isabella Forsythe was among the party. Anyone else, he knew, was only there to disguise his real purposes.

After a visit of a few days to tour the estate, make plans, and take stock of what needed to be done before the house party, the Parkers returned to London. They left Matthew with lists of tasks to be done and supplies to be purchased before their return in August. He grew weary simply reading all that must be accomplished in the next few weeks. But it would be worth it, he assured himself. As long as she was there.

He saw Miss Aubrey taking a turn around the gardens and went to join her.

"Captain Bryant." She hesitated as he approached, her gaze meeting his, then awkwardly flitting away. She faltered, "I have not . . . seen you . . . in some time."

Dash it. Was she still feeling embarrassed about that kiss?

It was on the tip of his tongue to say he had missed her, or to apologize again, but he refrained. "I have been occupied with guests," he said instead. "A friend from town and his mother."

She nodded her understanding, visibly relieved, and they walked on.

He said, "I believe I mentioned that I am hosting a small house party in August. You would be most welcome to join us for . . . well, whatever you like. Dinner, riding, dancing."

"I love to ride, but a house party?" Miss Aubrey shuddered. "No thank you."

He was taken aback. "You don't approve of house parties?"

"No. I don't."

"The young ladies will be chaperoned," he defended. "And my friend's mother—a very respectable lady—will act as hostess. It will all be above reproach, Miss Aubrey. Quite innocent."

"In my experience, house parties are never completely innocent."

He paused to look at her. "Oh?"

"I do appreciate the invitation, Captain. But parties and large gatherings are not for me. I prize my privacy and prefer to live quietly."

Matthew was surprised by her vehement objection. He had not taken her for shy and retiring. "Well then, you must pardon me, Miss Aubrey. My calls to your door must have been repugnant to you."

"Not at all, sir! I was happy to make your acquaintance, and you and Mr. Hart are welcome at any time. But I have no wish to meet with strangers." A shadow of concern crossed her lovely face. "At least," she murmured, "I assume they are strangers."

They walked on. "As you wish, Miss Aubrey. We shall not burst in upon you. But if you change your mind at any point, you are most welcome."

"Thank you, Captain. But I will not change my mind."

The next morning, Captain Bryant came trotting up the gatehouse lane on Storm, leading a second horse of dapple grey.

Mariah met him in the back garden. "Good morning, Captain."

He lifted his hat. "Miss Aubrey, I wonder if you might like to go riding with me? You mentioned you enjoyed it."

A surge of excitement was followed by myriad reasons why she should or could not. She had not brought her riding habit, had no proper hat, a script she ought to be writing, not to mention questions of propriety.

But before she could demur, Dixon stepped out of the house and answered for her. "She would be most delighted to accompany you, Captain. Just give us a few minutes, please."

Dixon pulled her inside, but Mariah objected *sotto voce*, "But, Dixon, I can't. I don't—"

"Of course you do."

A "few minutes" became half an hour, after which Mariah descended in her aunt's old riding habit of voluminous skirt, trim-fitting jacket with velvet collar, plumed hat, and short leather gloves. She felt self-conscious as she stepped outside, but Captain Bryant's eyes lit appreciatively, putting her at ease.

The dapple-grey mare was saddled with a quilted black sidesaddle with single pommel. In the absence of a mounting block, Mariah would need the assistance of a groom to mount. In the absence of a groom . . .

"May I?" Captain Bryant asked as she approached. He bent and cupped his hands, offering her a leg up. She hesitated, eyeing his pristine gloves.

"Go on, I don't mind. My valet needs *something* to keep him occupied. Meticulous fool spent twenty minutes tying this dandified cravat."

"It looks well on you. You . . . look well," she faltered. He did indeed. In fact, he looked quite handsome in his cutaway riding coat and black boots with contrasting tan cuffs.

Placing her foot into his interlaced hands, she allowed him to assist her up onto the horse. Settling onto the sidesaddle, she hooked her right knee over the pommel and rested her calf behind the horse's shoulders. She felt Captain Bryant's gloved hands gently guide her slippered left foot into the single stirrup. Warm pleasure threaded up her leg at his touch, innocent and pragmatic though it was. She smoothed her long skirt down the left side of the horse, making sure her legs were fully covered. Then she took up the reins.

Captain Bryant remounted Storm, who shied and danced but submitted to his firm, gentle commands. He had come a long way as a horseman since the night they first met.

Mariah could not wait. Eager as she was to ride again after so long, she clicked the horse forward into a walk. She wondered if anyone rode her horse, Lady, at Attwood Park. Did they leave it to the groom to exercise Mariah's bay mare? Or had they sold her, that reminder of their daughter gone astray? Tears pricked her eyes at the thought, but she blinked them away, determined to enjoy this ride, this day, and this companion.

Captain Bryant was beside her in a moment. Together they rode through the grounds at a stately walk, then at a modest trot out the main gate and along the turnpike as Mariah found her seat and rhythm. Taking the lead, Captain Bryant turned his horse down a rural lane. Here they urged the horses into a smooth canter. Mariah's mood soared. Ah, the freedom of the rolling gait, the wind teasing the hair at her temples, strands coming free and dancing in the air and catching at the corners of her mouth. . . .

Her grinning mouth.

Captain Bryant's eyes gleamed. "Are you enjoying yourself, Miss Aubrey?"

She smiled. "You know I am."

Mariah knew it was foolish to feel this little flutter about Captain Bryant. How futile to open her heart to a man bent on pursuing another. And if he showed romantic interest in her, would she not then be obligated to reveal her past? How she hated the thought of watching the admiration fade from his shining brown eyes. It was better this way, she told herself. Since he had made his intentions toward another woman so clear, she needed not say a word.

They rode through a gently rolling meadow, and then along a narrow stream, whirring and whispering over rocks and around bends, sparkling in the sunlight and leading them farther and farther from Windrush Court. Mariah had not ventured this far from the gatehouse since arriving last autumn. It felt good to lengthen her tether. To fill her lungs and savor new sights and sounds.

At a spot where the embankment flattened, they allowed the horses to pause and drink. Mariah held Captain Bryant's gaze, hoping her eyes expressed the depth of gratitude and warmth she felt, feelings she thought wiser not to put into words. She said only, "Thank you so much for today, Captain. I cannot remember when I have enjoyed myself more."

"Then we shall have to ride again."

But with the house party looming near, Mariah had the foreboding sense that this ride might very well be their first and last.

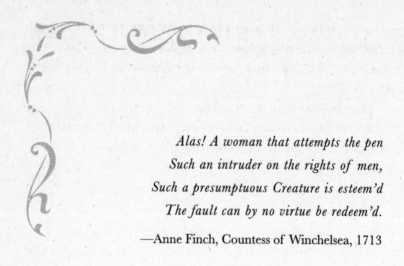

Alas! A woman that attempts the pen
Such an intruder on the rights of men,
Such a presumptuous Creature is esteem'd
The fault can by no virtue be redeem'd.

—Anne Finch, Countess of Winchelsea, 1713

chapter 23

Mariah was sitting on the garden bench a few days later when Hugh Prin-Hallsey sauntered up the lane. She had not laid eyes on him since she had seen him talking to Mr. Crosby on the road a fortnight before and had assumed he had gone back to London. What had he returned for this time?

She rose. "Mr. Prin-Hallsey, hello."

"Please. Call me Hugh. Are we not practically cousins?" He smiled expectantly, but she only stared at him, wary.

"Will you not invite me in?"

"Oh. Of course." She stepped to the back door, opened it, and gestured him inside. "Please."

Feeling the kitchen too humble for such an august guest, she led Hugh into the drawing room. Chagrined to find a copy of her novel on the table, she quickly stacked other books atop it, preparing to stash it from view. But he moved more quickly than she.

"Ah . . . Lady A's novel. Did you enjoy it?"

"I . . . did, yes."

"They were full of it at the Whites. But between you and me, I shouldn't be surprised to learn that Lady A is really no lady at all."

Had he somehow guessed? Pinpricks of shame and dread riddled her body. "What makes you say that?"

He shrugged. "I imagine Lady A is really a Mister A in disguise. All the best writers are men."

Relieved to have misunderstood, she said faintly, "Are they?"

"I think so." He glanced around the room. "But I have not come to talk about books, Mariah. May I call you Mariah?"

"I . . . suppose so."

"You see, I have exhausted my search of the house, and Bryant is quite vexed with all my comings and goings. So, I think, I believe, I *hope*, that what I am seeking is here in the gatehouse. Has been here all along."

"But . . . ?"

"I know I called once before and you did not recall any particular item your aunt might have left here. But you haven't the devious mind of your aunt. Nor of Hugh Prin-Hallsey. I think if I might look about myself I am more likely to find what I am searching for."

He regarded her, eyebrows high, smile nearly convincing. Still she hesitated.

He leaned toward her. "You haven't anything to hide, I trust."

She clenched one hand in a tight fist, fingernails biting into her flesh. "Not specifically, but as a gentlewoman, I have natural reservations about a man pawing through my private things."

His dark eyes glittered. "That's right. You are a woman with a secretive and colorful past."

She felt her cheeks burn. "Perhaps you had better leave, Mr. Prin-Hallsey."

He studied her flushing countenance with apparent pleasure. "In good time, Mariah. After all, this gatehouse is my property. Is it not?"

He was watching her carefully, and Mariah wondered if he expected an answer to his rhetorical question.

He surveyed the room, then said, "I believe a top-to-bottom search is in order—starting with the attic in the turret."

Mariah guessed that the young footman had finally confessed to carrying a chest up to the gatehouse attic last fall. She wondered if he had been forced or bribed to divulge Mrs. Prin-Hallsey's secret mission.

Hugh strode toward the stairs, not awaiting her reply.

Mariah swung around with a pleading look to Dixon. A look that said, *What do we do now? How can we stop him?*

They heard his Hessians echoing across the floor above them and then creaking up the attic stairs.

Her love letters! Early drafts of her novels. The promise she made to her aunt . . . These thoughts stirred a surge of panic in her bosom. Her bosom . . . where the key still lay secure. Would he smash open the chest?

A few minutes later, she had her answer. Hugh clomped back down the stairs, looking piqued. With apparent effort, he restrained his frustration and demanded calmly, "I require two things from you, madam. A candle. And a key."

Glancing through the gatehouse windows to discover if Miss Aubrey was within, Matthew was astounded to see Hugh Prin-Hallsey looming ominously over her. He hurriedly let himself inside in time to hear the man say, "Shall you give me the key, or shall I wrench it from your neck?"

"What is going on here?" Matthew demanded.

Both heads snapped his way.

"Are you all right, Miss Aubrey?"

"I . . ."

"Miss Aubrey is perfectly well," Prin-Hallsey said. "Merely confused. She has something of mine and refuses to relinquish it."

Miss Aubrey lifted her chin. "I have nothing of yours, sir."

"How do you know? Have you looked inside the chest?"

"Have you?"

"An omission I am seeking to correct this very moment."

Miss Aubrey addressed her next words to Matthew. "Captain, my aunt, Mrs. Prin-Hallsey"—Hugh flinched and his jaw tightened, but Miss Aubrey continued undeterred—"gave me only a few personal mementos. Nothing of value and nothing that belongs to Mr. Prin-Hallsey."

"Then why not show me and prove it?" Hugh said.

"I do not like the thought of you going through Mrs. . . . . my aunt's private things, nor my own."

"What exactly are you looking for?" Matthew asked.

"I don't *exactly* know. But I shall know it when I see it."

"Oh, very well!" Miss Aubrey suddenly relented, her face a grimace of frustration and something else Matthew could not identify. She handed Prin-Hallsey a stout old candle lamp. Then she grasped the chain around her neck and fished the key from the hollow between her breasts. Watching the key slide across her skin, Matthew forced himself to avert his gaze. She did not hand over the key, but gestured for Hugh to lead the way upstairs.

Holding the lamp, Hugh Prin-Hallsey preceded them up to the first floor and then up the narrow stairway to the turret attic.

Once at its door, Hugh gestured Mariah in before him and followed her inside. Matthew stayed in the doorway, the small space already crowded with the two of them and an assortment of trunks. Mariah quickly bent before an ornate chest, unlocked it, and stepped back.

Hugh handed her the candle lamp. Then he fell upon the chest like a starving man at a banquet, digging in with both hands. His frantic motions soon slowed, and he turned an angry profile toward Mariah.

"There is almost nothing here." He lifted a fine old shawl with careless disdain. "You cannot expect me to believe she delivered this chest to your care with only this piece of nothing, two miniature portraits, and a few Edgeworth novels."

Mariah said, "There were a few other articles of clothing—gloves, for example. But I have since incorporated them into my own wardrobe. You may see them if you like."

"No letters? No . . . journals?"

Mariah stared at him. Allowed the question to resonate through the stifling silence. "And if there were, how should that concern you? What right have you to them?"

With a quick glance at Matthew, Hugh hedged, "Well, if there were papers dealing with the estate, or with family . . . concerns."

"I promise you there were no legal documents. No deeds, no bank notes or stocks, no gems, or gold or silver either."

Matthew wondered if Mariah had already removed whatever it was Hugh was looking for. Was that why she had initially resisted, guessing Hugh would suspect that very thing had she given in too easily?

Hugh studied her, as if testing her sincerity, or as if the words were slow to penetrate. He inhaled through his nose and exhaled heavily. Then, with another glance at Matthew, he rose and gestured for Mariah to lead the way back down.

But on the next floor, Miss Dixon called to them from the sitting room, where she stood at the window. "That crazy old captain is up on the roof again."

Miss Aubrey hurried over and, curious, the two men glanced at each other then crossed to the window as well. Mariah picked up Martin's glass and took a look, shaking her head. Then she handed the glass to Hugh, beside her.

"Spying on our neighbors? How diverting." Hugh peered through the glass, but his amused smirk instantly fell away. "Thunder and turf . . ."

"What is it?" she asked, alarmed. "Do you know him?"

Hugh hesitated, then handed the glass back. "No. How should I know him?"

"But . . . from your reaction, I thought—"

"No. I was merely shocked. Anyone would be, seeing that lunatic waving his arms from the ramparts."

Matthew took his turn with the glass and saw the old man who had disrupted their theatrical. "He appears to be waving a white flag." He lowered the glass and looked at her. "He is surrendering to you, Miss Aubrey. Any idea why?"

Mariah sat at the writing table and tried in vain to put the events of the day from her mind. How relieved she had been when Captain Bryant intervened during Hugh's manic visit. Considering she had already removed her aunt's journals, she had thought it wise to put up a show of resistance before unlocking the chest. She must have put her childhood playacting experience to good use, for it seemed to have some effect. Though Mariah was convinced that had Captain Bryant not been on hand, even her theatrics would not have kept Hugh from tearing through the entire gatehouse in his search. Was he so afraid of what Francesca's journals might reveal about the family? Or did he truly believe her aunt had hidden some valuable treasure here in the gatehouse?

At all events, she was happy Hugh was gone, and the gatehouse was peaceful once more.

Taking advantage of the quiet, she dipped her quill and continued *The Tale of Lydia Sorrow.*

Was he about to ask for her hand, Lydia wondered, as he had all but done several times before? Would he speak those longed-for words in that melodic, mesmerizing voice of his? Was he then going to kiss her with all the banked passion she saw in his eyes?

But with the excitement came an icy terror of being found out. Of being caught with him in her bedchamber. How quickly they would be forced to marry if they were! But surely even that would not be the end of the world, would it? Yes, it would be devastating for her parents to learn of it. And her character would be tainted, but only until he redeemed it by marrying her. Which he meant to do. Of that she had no doubt. But what was this talk of departing? He had just returned from several months on the continent.

He took her hands in his. "My dear, how I have longed to see you again. How I missed you, ached for you while I was away."

"And I you." By the candlelight which danced with the flickering firelight, she eagerly surveyed his countenance, noticing he was already in need of a shave.

He squeezed her hands almost painfully tight. "I thought I could take my time. Court you. But my father insists. He wants to see me married. Settled."

She was ready to marry him at a moment's notice, or at least as soon as the banns might be read. "I don't mind," Lydia said.

He looked up at her, apparently taken aback.

His father was unwell, she knew. He would not defy him at such a time.

Emboldened by the look of timidity, of near-defeat in his big, expressive eyes, she whispered, "I am ready."

She leaned forward, intending to place a comforting kiss upon his cheek, but he mistook her intention. Pulling her into his arms, he met her lips with his own and kissed her deeply.

Abruptly, he drew away. "Forgive me. I am the vilest creature I know, but I could not help myself."

She was surprised by the ferocity of his self-rebuke. While a gentleman, he was not often severe with himself. She longed to kiss the bleak expression from his face. Instead, she asked, "What is it? What is the matter?"

He shook his head, lips pressed in a grim line.

"It is all right," she murmured. "You know I would marry you tomorrow."

"I know," he whispered. Taking her hand, he turned and led her to the bed.

Mariah set down her quill and sighed. How wearying, how painful it was to remember that night.

She set aside the novel and instead brought out the script for Simon Wells, which she should have been working on in any case. But for a moment she just sat there, thinking of Captain Bryant. She could not work on the play without recalling the day he had read from the script . . . and kissed her.

Mariah sighed. Forcing her mind back to her task, she dipped her quill once more. She needed to finish the play, and she needed to finish it soon, for Mr. Crosby was calling in three days' time to pick up the script. He had written to let her know when to expect him. He had also written to say that he wished to address a few other matters of business with her—though he did not specify what these were. She hoped it wasn't more bad news . . . or reviews.

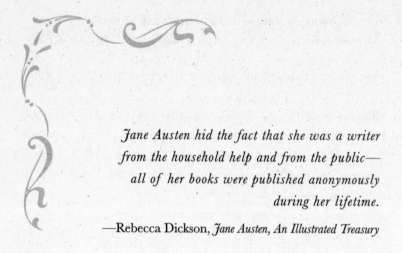

*Jane Austen hid the fact that she was a writer
from the household help and from the public—
all of her books were published anonymously
during her lifetime.*

—Rebecca Dickson, *Jane Austen, An Illustrated Treasury*

chapter 24

Three days later, at precisely the appointed hour, A. K. Crosby walked across the gatehouse lawn, tucking his pocket watch away with one hand, while carrying a parcel under his other arm.

Mariah met him at the door. "More frightful reviews?"

He shook his head. "Not this time."

Once they were seated, teacups in hand, Mariah asked, "How is the first book selling?"

"Fair, I would say." He took a sip of tea. "Not as well as I should like."

To change the uncomfortable topic, Mariah handed him the script. He briefly perused it, then pulled a bank note from his pocket. "Excellent. Here is half. I shall send the rest once Mr. Wells approves the script."

Setting down his teacup, he lifted the parcel and handed it to her.

"I am making you a small gift. Now, you need not hesitate to accept. It is only two other books I have had the privilege of publishing. One is a book of travel writing—quite popular these days."

Mariah opened the parcel and read the inscribed title. "*Enchanting Views of Italy* by Mrs. Elizabeth Rushford. Is that *her* real name?"

"It is. I have met both Mrs. and Mr. Rushford. She travels with him and writes while he conducts his merchant business. But the second one, a novel, I am especially keen for you to read. It is *Euphemia's Return*, by our rising new star, Mrs. Wimble."

Mariah frowned. Was that not the name of the book Mr. Hart had been reading? "I have heard of it."

"You are not alone in that, for I have sold out my first printing and have ordered a second."

"How nice for you and Mrs. Wimble," Mariah said dryly. Inwardly she chastised herself for not wishing another female writer every success—even if more success than she herself enjoyed.

He cocked his head to one side. "Have you given any more thought to using your real name on your second book?"

"I have not changed my mind, A.K."

"Is there some reason for your secrecy—beyond ladylike modesty— that you are not telling me?"

She stiffened. "I am telling you I wish to remain anonymous."

He held her gaze a moment, then looked away. "Well. Only one more piece of business, then." He looked at his pocket watch and, satisfied, snapped it closed once more. "I have been contacted by another of our authors, a man who sold a good deal of books in his day, and he wishes to meet Lady A. He is involved with a respected periodical and wishes to offer you advice, to publish reviews, perhaps even serialized excerpts of your work. It would be a boon to sales, Miss Aubrey. A veritable boon."

Nerves and delight wrestled within her. "Who is it? Would I have heard of him?"

"That is the rub, Miss Aubrey. This author also published under a pseudonym, a name I think you would recognize. In fact, I have reason to believe you may already know the man."

"Know his work, you mean," Mariah clarified.

He shook his head. "The man himself."

But Mariah was not acquainted with any authors. Unless . . . might Bartholomew Browne write novels as well as poetry? But why would he use his real name for poetry and a pseudonym for novels? *Foolish girl*, she thought. Did not Walter Scott do that very thing? Mr. Browne did not contribute to any periodical, as far as she knew, but he could easily have begun doing so without her hearing of it. She heard so little of society news these days. Besides, who else could it be? She ticked off the men she knew. Surely not her brother, or Captain Bryant, or Hugh Prin-Hallsey, or Mr. Crosby himself. Might it be the man who broke her heart?

She asked, "Why would you think I know him?"

Mr. Crosby shrugged. "Just something he mentioned in his letter. I could be wrong. Does the name Thomas Piper mean anything to you?"

Mariah vaguely recognized the name. "Did he not write *The Golden Prince Adventures*?"

"Exactly so."

"My brother read those several years ago." Mariah paused, frowning. "Thomas Piper wants to meet me?"

"Yes."

"But that is not his real name?"

He shook his head. "I suppose he thinks that if the two of you meet and learn each other's identities, that will ensure you keep the other's secret."

"I see. . . ." But Mariah was torn. As much as she wanted her books to succeed, she was nervous about opening her sanctuary to this unknown author, having no idea what manner of a man she was inviting into her life.

"May I think about it?"

Mr. Crosby rose. "Yes, but do not tarry too long. I shall soon have to decide whether or not I can afford to continue to publish your work. I would hate for you . . . for either of us . . . to miss this opportunity."

After Mr. Crosby had taken his leave, Mariah flipped idly through *Enchanting Views of Italy*. She thought it most unlikely she would ever have the opportunity to travel to Italy or anywhere. She decided she would save this book for a day she felt like traveling to foreign shores in her mind, if not in body. She placed the volume on the sparse bookshelf, then sat down with Mrs. Wimble's *Euphemia's Return*.

> *For one strange and sunlit summer, Euphemia Dellwood resided at Primrose Park, a friend's London estate, with her mother, to be nearer medical care in that prosperous city than she was likely to receive in their small village. Mrs. Dellwood had been offered the use of the estate gatehouse by the dowager Lady Dartmore, whom she had known when both women were young and boarded at Mrs. Rathbone's Seminary for Girls. The dowager was not in the best of health herself and so felt compassion on Mrs. Dellwood when she learned of her ongoing ailment and the inability of the local apothecary to bring about noticeable improvement. It was at Primrose Park, as her mother's companion, nurse, and housekeeper, that Euphemia first met the dashing and socially superior Lord Dartmore, the dowager's son.*
>
> *Tall, black-haired, and brooding, Lord Dartmore was a widower with a sickly child. He regarded Euphemia with all the interest a stallion might appropriate a common dewberry blossom. Until the day he was shot through the heart by one of her fatal thorns. . . .*

How strange that the book should be set in a gatehouse. She would never choose a setting so indicative of her own situation for fear someone would find her out.

Mariah read for some minutes longer, and what began as a mild awareness—as of a gnat buzzing about a lamp, or a distant drumming of rain—grew less amorphous. The vague sense of familiarity, of comfort with the words, became something more specific, and

Mariah realized she felt as though she were hearing a tale recounted by a friend. But why should that be? She looked at the copyright date, checking to be sure this was not some new edition of an older book she had read in the past. No, it had been published this very year—new, as Mr. Crosby had said. Why had he given her this particular book? Perhaps because the heroine resided in a gatehouse as Mariah did? Or had he some other reason to believe she would enjoy it? Mariah shook her head. Why did it seem so familiar?

Matthew wrote to his father, reiterating his invitation to visit Windrush Court. Unless Prin-Hallsey changed his mind about selling the place to him, Matthew had only two months left on his lease, and he truly wished to share this beautiful place with his parents.

As he wrote, he was reminded of his younger days, when he would write and ask his father to come to some academy event or commissioning. Most often John Bryant sent a terse reply in his stead.

Matthew posted *this* letter with all the anticipation of an opening salvo, already dreading return fire.

He was surprised when Hugh Prin-Hallsey sought him out a few days later. He joined Matthew in the library as Matthew drank his coffee and perused the London papers.

"I have been giving it a great deal of thought, old boy," Hugh began. "And I have decided I am willing to part with Windrush Court after all. Assuming you still have a mind to buy the dear place?"

Matthew felt a rush of satisfaction at his words. When Isabella arrived next week, he could tell her he was the owner of Windrush Court, her future home, if only she would consent to be his wife. But this happy thought was followed immediately by a thread of suspicion.

"Why the sudden change of heart?" he asked. He considered the notion that he had proved himself worthy of the grand estate in Hugh Prin-Hallsey's eyes, but somehow he doubted it.

When Hugh hesitated, Matthew added, "Has it something to do with whatever you failed to discover in the gatehouse?"

"Failed to discover . . . ?" Hugh screwed up his face in thought. "No, not in the least."

Matthew regarded the man, trying to gauge his sincerity. If he could buy Windrush Court, did the man's reasons for selling matter? Unless . . . had the man recently discovered some structural defect Matthew was unaware of? He would consult Hammersmith and Jack Strong before he decided.

"Name your terms," Matthew said. "And I shall consider it."

Matthew and William Hart were paying a call on Miss Aubrey later that afternoon when Mr. Martin thundered down the stairs into the drawing room. Miss Aubrey looked up in some surprise, clearly taken aback to see Martin coming down from abovestairs. As far as Matthew knew, the odd man rarely ventured beyond the gatehouse kitchen.

"Captain Bryant. Mr. Hart. Glad you are here. Are you on board?"

"On board?" Matthew asked.

"The plan. The mission. I mean to rescue Captain Prince tonight. Are you in?"

"Rescue?" Matthew felt his brow furrow. "Is he in peril?"

Incredulous, Martin sputtered, "Is he in—?" He ran a hand over his balding head. "How would you like to be locked up way up there in that poorhouse, all alone?"

"I shouldn't."

"Well then?"

Matthew asked, "How do I know he isn't just some crazy old man who has been locked up for his own good?"

"Come with me." Martin hurried back up the stairs.

Matthew glanced at Miss Aubrey for approval, saw her nod, and then followed reluctantly behind, Hart at his heels.

At the window in the small sitting room, Martin nodded toward the poorhouse roof. "That's how."

When he squinted to see clearly, Martin handed him his glass.

Matthew focused the instrument and saw the perfectly executed signal flags hoisted on a line strung from a chimney. These were no layman's signals, as that white surrender flag might have been. First came a blue-white-blue striped flag over a solid red flag—*I've run aground*.

The distant man followed this with a numerical signal from the closely guarded Admiralty Book. Yellow over red over yellow. *One.* Diagonal from lower hoist to upper fly, white over blue. *Six.* Sixteen— *Engage the enemy more closely*.

"Well?" Martin asked.

Matthew lowered the glass and handed it to Hart. "I'm in."

When they described their plan to Miss Aubrey, her charming mouth opened in stunned alarm. "We are not at war with the poorhouse."

"Miss Aubrey, you know that I am a peace-loving man," Martin said. "But I cannot sit by while the captain is locked away against his will. I owe him too much."

"Could we not civilly go to Mrs. Pitt and demand, *civilly*, to see him? To ascertain his true situation and wishes? For all we know he likes haunting the rooftop."

Matthew crossed his arms. "Then why all the signaling?"

"Attention? Look, he managed to come down for the theatrical, so could he not manage to escape if he really wanted to?"

Martin shook his head. "I don't know. All I know is I shall not rest until I speak to him myself and do whatever I can to help him."

In her distress, Miss Aubrey put her hands on her hips, causing her billowy dress to cling to her curves. "Captain Bryant, may I remind you that the undersheriff and his bailiff have jurisdiction in this matter? I would hate to see you locked away in the Stow jail."

"I gave my word to Mr. Martin that I would help him. Hart has also agreed."

William Hart nodded eagerly. "Truth is, Miss Aubrey, we are bored to tears. If we don't see some action soon, there is no accounting for our behavior."

She turned those liquid amber eyes on first Hart, then him. "Promise me you won't shoot anybody. Or run anybody through, or whatever it is you do with those swords."

"Oh, very well," Hart said with shuddering sarcasm.

But Matthew found no humor in the comment. He did not wish to think of all the bloodshed he had been responsible for in the commission of his duty.

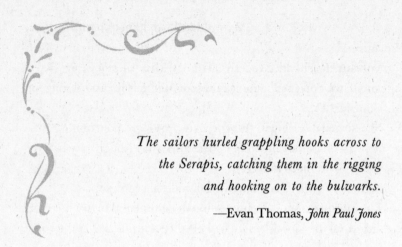

*The sailors hurled grappling hooks across to
the Serapis, catching them in the rigging
and hooking on to the bulwarks.*

—Evan Thomas, *John Paul Jones*

chapter 25

When night fell, the men reconvened at the gatehouse, where young George Barnes joined them. There, they took turns blackening their faces with a burnt cork. Watching him, Miss Aubrey shook her head. "You are enjoying this, aren't you?"

"Yes, actually." Matthew grinned and tapped the tip of her nose with the blackened cork. "I didn't realize the life of a gentleman would be so mind-numbingly boring."

She looked adorable with a spotted nose. "Has it all been boring?" she asked.

He tucked his chin in mock disapproval. Knew she was fishing for a compliment. "Not all, minx, as well you know."

The three of them, Martin, Hart, and Matthew, followed George, their self-appointed guide, into the darkness toward the poorhouse. Hart stayed near George, and Matthew overheard him whispering to the boy, asking after his sister. Martin carried a long coil of rope and something under his arm. But they carried no lamp, or fatal weapon either. Matthew hoped and prayed Mrs. Pitt and her son did not sleep with guns at the ready.

When they reached the side of the poorhouse, George pointed up to the top floor. "See that open window? That's his room there."

From under his arm, Martin drew forth an iron treble hook.

Matthew felt his brows rise. "A grappling hook, Mr. Martin?"

"Oh, I have quite a collection of weapons and navy paraphernalia. Never imagined this old thing would be put back into service."

Matthew was relieved that they would not have to break in to see the man. Hart, always better with knots than Matthew, secured the rope to the grappling hook.

Martin handed him the heavy coil of rope. "Captain Bryant, might you do the honors?"

Matthew supposed he was the most able-bodied among them, and hoped he had the strength for the task. He laid the coil on the ground beside him and lifted a loop of slack in his left hand, while in his right he began swinging the heavy hook like a pendulum, gaining momentum. He and his crew had done the like innumerable times in preparation for boarding enemy ships, but that distance had been horizontal versus the more difficult vertical throw required now. He took one last swing, and released the hook with a heave and a grunt. It flew true and landed on the roof with a *clank*. Matthew winced, waiting for lights to be lit or dogs to bark, or a head to appear in the open window. But after the echo died away, all was silent.

"Well done," Hart breathed.

Matthew tested the hold of the hook. Finding it anchored, he took a deep breath and lifted his foot against the rough stone. Using the rope, he climbed laboriously up the side of the building.

A few months of easy living had already softened him. Matthew was sweating profusely, and his arms and legs shook by the time he reached the third row of windows. He gained footing on the ledge and paused at the open window, trying to catch his breath. He could see almost nothing inside the room, save for the glow of embers in a hearth. He was surprised the old man had slept through the clang of the hook landing on the roof above his room. Was he ill? Or not in the room at all? Perhaps he had escaped on his own without their help.

The window casement was thrust straight out, and he was relieved that, although he was clearly no longer in peak condition, at least he was still trim enough to slide through the opening.

He landed in the room with a thud, but before he could gain his bearings, he was knocked off his feet in a forceful whoosh and crashed to the floor. For a dazed moment, he thought he had been felled by "wind of ball," the passing air from cannon shot that could knock a man senseless. But this was no mere wind that pinned him to the ground. This wind had flesh and sinew and a fierce grip around his throat.

"Thought I wouldn't hear your grappling hook catching on the rigging and hooking on the bulwarks, but I did," came a gruff whisper from above him. "Try to board my ship, will you? Who are you? A Frenchman, I suppose?"

Matthew fought to breathe, pushing at the hands that held him. His attacker loosened his grip enough for Matthew to say, "No, sir. Captain Bryant of the Royal Navy, lately of the Frigate *Sparta*."

"What's this?" His captor released his hold, stood, and moved to the fire. A moment later a stick of tinder had been kindled in the embers and a candle lamp sparked to life.

"You saw my signal?" the man asked.

"We did, sir." Matthew rubbed his smarting throat. "We are not a boarding party, sir. Rather, an escape party, come to free you, if you wish it."

The man lifted the candle lamp higher and peered into Matthew's face. "Do I not look free? When was a captain's cabin ever so fine?" He swung his lamp in an arc around the room—and indeed the upholstered settee and chair, table, and floor-to-ceiling bookshelves were as fine as any gentleman's library.

"And how do you attain the roof from here, sir?" Matthew asked.

"The name is Captain Prince," the old man said sternly. "And I would appreciate if you would remember that."

"Yes, sir—that is, Captain."

The man's expression softened and he lifted the candle lamp toward one corner of the ceiling, where a rickety ladder led to a trapdoor. "There's the hatchway there. I come and go as I please. Though John locked it for a time after my, em, guest appearance downstairs. Only recently managed to persuade him to unlock it again. He reinforced the door lock as well."

So much for walking out of here, Matthew thought on a sigh. "Would you like to climb down with me, Captain? That is, if you are able?"

"Of course I am able. I am not an invalid."

Perhaps not, but the man was surely nearly seventy. "Mr. Martin awaits below, Captain."

"My former steward? I thought it was him that night. I am sorry I confused him with a kidnapper."

Matthew hesitated. "An . . . honest mistake."

The man shrugged on his coat and stepped toward the window.

"Um . . ." Matthew wondered if he should mention it. "Shoes, Captain?"

The man frowned. "Can't abide the things. Now, let us be off."

Recalling how the man had leapt over the stair railing the night of the theatrical, Matthew should not have been surprised at the ease and agility with which he descended the side of the poorhouse, but he was. Matthew followed after, less gracefully. But he told himself that he'd already had to scale the wall, which was the more difficult feat.

The man leapt to the ground and landed before Martin. Martin knuckled his hat brim. "Captain Prince."

"It is you, Mr. Martin. How good to see you again after so long." The two men shook hands.

Hart saluted as well. "Lieutenant Hart."

The older man nodded his acknowledgement.

Hart clapped the shoulder of the boy in front of him. "And this is George Barnes, who served as our guide tonight."

"George, is it?" The man shook the lad's hand.

Martin said eagerly, "With your permission, Captain Prince, I have prepared your favorite treat—figgy dowdy."

"Figgy dowdy! How that takes me back!"

Martin gestured with his good hand. "If you would like to follow us across the road to the gatehouse . . . ?"

"Lead on, Mr. Martin."

George decided he'd better turn in for the night, but the others walked away, leaving the rope where it was, with the old man's promise to toss down the grappling hook upon his return. *So he already plans to return*, Matthew thought. *So much for our "rescue."*

"Are you really Captain Prince?" Hart asked as they walked, but Bryant elbowed his side. He had no wish to offend the man. Mad though he might be, he had clearly served the British Navy in some capacity to have gained such skill in signal flags, not to mention ship vernacular.

But the man answered Hart's question without asperity. "That is a long story, Mr. Hart. Ply me with figgy dowdy and port and I shall happily oblige you."

Mariah was relieved to see the would-be rescuers return unscathed, and with their object among them. She was somewhat nervous about having the strange man in her home. Was he insane, as Mrs. Pitt suggested? He had certainly seemed coherent and well-spoken when she had talked briefly with him through the door, but she could not forget the way he had charged from behind the curtains and onto the stage, wooden sword blazing.

"Miss Aubrey," Martin began. "May I present Captain Prince?"

"How do you do?" She curtsied and he bowed gallantly before her.

"Ah, the kind young lady who came to visit me. What a pleasure to meet you face-to-face."

Mariah opened the door wider and stepped back. "Welcome. Come in."

Captain Bryant ran back to the great house for the requested port, which Mariah did not possess, while Martin set about brewing coffee and whisking up a sauce for the figgy dowdy.

While Mariah set the larger table in the drawing room, Captain Prince surveyed her movements, hands behind his back.

"Were you able to deliver my message to Miss Amy?"

"I did, sir."

"I have not seen her since the night of the . . . uh . . . drama. How does she fare, do you know?"

"Last I saw her she was a bit frail. But her spirits seemed as cheerful as ever."

"Yes. They always were."

She wanted to ask how long he had known Miss Amy but did not press him with Mr. Hart and Dixon in the room.

Soon Captain Bryant returned with the promised port and Martin set his masterpiece on the table before them along with a sauceboat.

"What a sight for these poor eyes," Captain Prince said.

Martin beamed.

The figgy dowdy was just as delicious the second time, Mariah thought. Even Dixon admitted it. Captain Prince was excessive in his praise, which clearly delighted Martin. The older man raised his glass of port in salute, while the others sipped coffee. And when Captain Bryant refilled his glass, Captain Prince neatly wiped his mouth and began his tale.

"The *Largos* was my first command. I shall never forget her. We undertook a long voyage to the Horn, amassing several victories with which I shall not bruise your ears. Mr. Martin, I would guess, has told you of our final battle and the storm that was our ruin?"

Heads nodded around the table.

"Then you know the mighty *Largos* was lost. It still pains me to think of her, there at the bottom of the sea, rotting away. Not unlike me, in my chamber. My useful days, my glory days, gone. But, I digress." He sipped his port.

"I was determined to go down with my ship to her watery grave. I don't know exactly how it happened, but one minute I was standing on deck and the next the ship had rolled and I was tossed into the sea. I seem to remember a mermaid slipping her arm around my neck and telling me to float on my back while she pulled me to that beautiful shore. I suppose I assumed she meant heaven. Then my vision began to darken like a shrinking tunnel, like a ship's glass fouled or broken, and I could see nothing but blackness. How long I inhabited that blackness I cannot say."

His faded green eyes grew misty. "My earliest memories of that time are of voices. Unfamiliar, birdlike voices, speaking in a tongue I did not recognize or comprehend. Soft hands, tending me, interspersed with searing pain in my head and eyes. I would guess now that I was in and out of consciousness for quite some time, months even. I do not know. When I finally awoke, I felt a long beard on my formerly clean-shaven face. I opened my eyes to see two beautiful brown women. It seemed as if I should know them. And in a strange way, I did. I had come to know their voices, their touch, even their aromas over the months I had drifted on the waves of unconsciousness. It was a pleasure to put faces to people I already knew. Much as I felt upon seeing you, Miss Aubrey."

He smiled, and Mariah returned the gesture.

"Were these women my family? My friends?" Captain Prince continued. "I did not know. I was not bewildered initially. That came later when shards of memory from my former life began to return. But at first, when these women smiled down at me as if they knew me, and talked excitedly to each other in their language saying, or so I imagined, "Here he is! At last he has returned to us!" I felt only relief and contentment. A newborn child in his mother's arms. And, in many ways, Fara, the older of the two women, was very like a mother to me. Her daughter, Noro, the sister I never had.

"Slowly I regained strength and began to take in my surroundings. Fara and Noro lived in a small village on a large island they called Madagasikara, but I later realized it must be the place we sailors called the Island of the Moon."

"Is that where you washed ashore, Captain?" Martin asked. "The rest of us survivors were picked up by a passing ship and taken to Mauritius."

"Well, Martin, you did not have a mermaid to guide you, then, did you?" He smiled, and it was difficult to tell if he was joking or not.

Then Captain Prince clasped his hands and asked tentatively, "Did many survive?"

Martin shook his head. "Only a few. But that young midshipman you bid me watch over was counted among us. Mind, I take no credit. Why God spared some while so many others were lost, I cannot know."

Captain Prince nodded, then lowered his head. A moment of respectful silence followed before Captain Prince once more looked up and continued.

"I do not wish to wear out my welcome with longwinded tales, so suffice it to say, I began a new life there. Learned the language, worked alongside the Malagasy people—fishing, hunting, building. Men were scarce after years of skirmishes with *kindoc*, the pirates who made the island their port. So I was begrudgingly accepted by the surviving men and eagerly accepted by the women."

He paused to scrape the last bite of figgy dowdy into his mouth. "Since I had no idea who I was or what my name might be, they called me *lahy lava*, which I later learned meant tall man. Though the less kind among them called me *vazaha ratsy*—ugly white man." He chuckled. "I could not blame them. My head wound healed very poorly, and even now I keep my hair long on the sides so others might not be burdened to see it." He patted his hair. "What a row Mr. Pitt and I had when he tried to cut it short!"

His smile soon faded, and he said, almost reverently, "I am glad Miss Amy is not with us to hear the next part. For Noro eventually became my *vady*. My wife. We spent many happy years together and even had a child." Here he paused, his voice thickening. "A little girl. Jane."

"Jane?" Dixon asked. "Was that a name in their language as well?"

He shook his head, as if not trusting his voice. Then he cleared his throat. "That was the first faint thread of memory: I wished to name my daughter Jane, though I was not certain why. That was how it started. Like raindrops—or bird droppings—falling from the sky. How many falling memories had I missed? Or failed to attend to? Perhaps my memory would have returned more quickly, more completely, had I tried. But the truth was I . . . I didn't really care. I was happy where I was. In fact, I began to dread what I might remember, fearing it might rip me away from my peaceful new life."

He grimly shook his head. "Something did rip me away, but it was not a threat from the past. Rather one from the present. Other *vazaha* began coming to the island. Traders primarily. Most of them honest and well-meaning, but not all. They gave me strange looks, I can tell you, but none seemed to recognize me. But in the end they brought strife, infighting, and foreign disease to our small world. I might be there yet had God not seen fit to . . ." His voice broke and tears ran unabashedly down his cheeks. "To allow Noro and Jane to perish."

Mariah's heart plummeted.

Captain Prince stared down at his clasped hands once more. The room was silent as his hearers exchanged pained looks.

Eventually he whispered, "If I do hide from reality, let the fog and mist settle in my mind from time to time, do you blame me?"

Mariah, tears running down her own face, put her hand on his arm. "No, Captain. We do not."

He wiped a table napkin across his face, sniffed, and went on briskly. "Injury and pain wrought the loss of memory, and injury and pain began its restoration. Suddenly, I remembered Amy Merryweather. The sweet angel awaiting me in England. Hope flamed in my near-dead heart. At the very least I had promised to return to visit her, and I would keep my promise, though I knew it would be many years tardy. But even once I had pieced together enough of my past to know I needed to return to a place called Bristol, it was several months more before I was able to get passage on one of the traders' ships. He in turn decided to press me into service to compensate for my passage. And so began another long series of misadventures. I finally managed to return to Bristol, if one can trust calculations done in this head, some fourteen or fifteen years after I set sail from its port."

As if reminded by the word, he finished the remaining ruby liquid in his glass.

"I found my way to the boardinghouse where I had last seen Miss Merryweather. Surprisingly, I remembered the location quite plainly. But, alas, Amy was no longer there. I should have known she would not be. And yet . . ."

Captain Prince rose abruptly, his chair teetering behind him before settling back on all four legs with a clatter. "I need to find her. Miss Amy used to come to speak with me once or twice a week. Yet she has not come in quite some time and that troubles me. Very unlike her. I pray nothing is amiss." He turned toward the door.

Mr. Hart asked, "Shall you be able to scale that wall? To regain your room?"

At the door, Captain Prince turned and boldly declared, "I shall go in through the front door, as God intended."

"But . . . you have not told us how you came to be in Honora House," Martin protested.

Captain Bryant added, "Or why, when 'Captain Prince' was lost at sea, and the authorities tried to locate his next of kin, they could find no trace of anyone named Prince to notify."

"Ah!" Captain Prince said, eyes alight. "Another story for another day. And another figgy dowdy!"

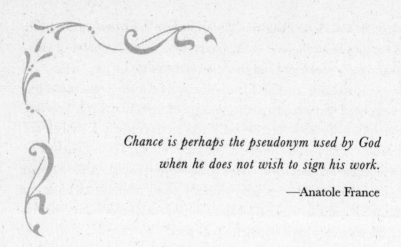

Chance is perhaps the pseudonym used by God
when he does not wish to sign his work.

—Anatole France

chapter 26

or several minutes after the old captain left them, the rest of the party stayed at the table, finishing dregs of cold coffee and rehashing the man's wild tale. Matthew had his doubts about it, as did Hart and Miss Dixon, but Martin and Miss Aubrey clearly believed every word. If Matthew remembered his academy lessons correctly, the *Largos* sank more than thirty years ago. If he were nearer to town, he would have searched the naval records to see what he might discover about the ship's crew. But in all truth, he had other more pressing matters to occupy his mind. For the days were passing all too quickly and there remained much to do in preparation for the house party.

Eventually Martin eased himself up and said he would just stroll over and make certain Captain Prince had managed to get himself back inside the poorhouse.

"I shall go along if you don't mind," Miss Dixon said, laying aside her table napkin. "A walk is just what I need after that rich food."

When they left, Miss Aubrey rose to begin clearing the table.

Matthew and Hart offered to help, but she waved them away. In truth, Matthew was glad to take his leave, for Mrs. Parker's long list of tasks had begun to enumerate themselves in his mind.

The household staff of Windrush Court moved like a set of rusty cogs in need of a great deal of greasing. It was clear they had not been obliged to undergo the arduous work of preparing for a party in many years, so they grumbled and slowly creaked into the higher speed needed to complete all the cleaning, cooking, and polishing required.

While Hammersmith stoically planned the replenishment of the cellars and negotiated with the local musicians, the housekeeper, Mrs. Strong, proved to be Matthew's greatest ally. She took on Mrs. Parker's list of tasks, ordered additional ice, commissioned footmen on shopping excursions, negotiated with local musicians, and tallied the incremental household expenses—for which Matthew would be responsible. She cheerfully bustled about, working hard herself, but also delegating endless duties to the maids, laundresses, and cook. She apparently relished the thought of airing the entire house, preparing bedchambers not used in several years, consulting Mr. Phelps about flowers, et cetera, et cetera.

Mrs. Strong's cheerful labors went a long way toward motivating the sluggish staff, but Matthew himself provided extra greasing with the promise of bonuses for a job well done. After all, this was not a frigate awaiting his Sabbath inspection, where the bosun would strike any slackers and a flogging would await any man who shirked his duty. No, other means must be employed, and if Matthew had learned anything about this new world of gentlemen, it was that money spoke.

Beyond preparing the house itself and planning lavish menus, entertainment needed to be considered. There were insufficient horses for the entire party, even though ten guests was a modest number, according to Mrs. Parker. The hostess would not ride, and he, Hart, Parker, and likely Crawford and Browne would have their own mounts. The stable also housed Prin-Hallsey's black, when he was in residence, the dapple-grey mare Miss Aubrey had ridden, and a pair of matched bays for the carriage. But he doubted the suitability of team horses for saddle riding. He would have to ask Parker. He also made a note to check how many sidesaddles were in the tack room.

With the help of Mr. Phelps and Jack Strong, they groomed the back lawn for ninepins and set up an archery range. Hart himself offered to devise a treasure hunt about the estate grounds. Matthew thought of Miss Aubrey's theatrical and guessed the party would greatly enjoy putting on their own production. He would have to ask her if she would be willing to loan them the scripts and costumes. Or perhaps even participate herself, though he doubted he could convince her to join them.

Four days before the other guests were due to arrive, Mrs. Parker and Ned returned to Windrush Court to oversee the final preparations. While her son lounged about, Mrs. Parker bustled about, inspecting the house, assigning bedchambers to each guest, and planning the dining room seating assignments. Now and again Hart would disappear for an hour or so, and Matthew wondered what he was up to—until he spied him out walking with Lizzy Barnes. He had hoped his friend might find some kind young lady among the guests who would overlook his lame leg. But perhaps Hart had already met such a girl.

Two days before the party, Matthew received a reply from his father.

> *Thank you for reiterating your invitation. Please allow me to reiterate my reasons for refusing. . . .*

Refusing. People seemed to make a habit of it in Matthew's case. He crumpled the brief letter in his hands, telling himself it didn't matter. That the emotion he felt was mere irritation and not the pain of rejection.

৶

Hugh Prin-Hallsey returned to the gatehouse, all smiles and politeness—as though his forceful search of the attic had never occurred.

Mariah begrudgingly opened the door to him. "Hello, Hugh."

"Mariah. What a pleasure to see you again. Thought I would see how you were getting on. Also, Captain Bryant asked me to absent myself from dinner." He smirked. "Curmudgeon. I see now why we won the war."

She did not ask Hugh to leave, but nor did she intend to invite him to join her for a meal.

Still, he made himself at home, sitting on the settee and crossing his long legs—legs that bounced with excess energy. Or nerves.

His gaze alighted on a book lying on the end table. "I see you are reading *Euphemia's Return*. What do you think of it?" One brow rose high as he studied her face. He clearly did not ask idly but was eager for her opinion.

"I find much to admire in it," she allowed. "Though I am only about halfway through. I understand reviews have been very good."

He smiled, eyes glinting. "Did you see the review in *Gentleman's Magazine*? No, I don't suppose you would subscribe to that. They described it as a 'work so skilled as to be suspect.' "

"Suspect?"

He chuckled. "They believe it beyond the grasp of a writer of the female sex. That the author must be a man."

"And that, I suppose, is the highest praise," she said dryly.

"Of course. Isn't it delicious?"

"Why should it be?"

He looked about the room as though an editor from the *Quarterly Review* might jump from the cupboard at any moment. "Can you keep a secret, Mariah? Why am I asking? Of course you can." He winked and announced, "They are right. The author is a man."

She stared at him, dreadful realization pricking through her. "How do you know?"

He leaned near, face bright with youthful pleasure. "Because I am that man."

Awash with incredulity, Mariah felt her mouth fall ajar. "*You* are Mrs. Wimble? I don't believe it."

His pleasure dimmed. "And why not?"

She shook her head, her mind refusing to accept that what she had read—the feminine thoughts and feelings—had been conjured by this man.

But had they not seemed familiar? And now that she thought about it, had she not seen Hugh talking to Mr. Crosby that day?

Fellow traveler indeed!

After a quarter of an hour of gloating, Hugh apparently realized Mariah was not going to offer him anything to eat and finally took his leave.

When he had, Mariah went upstairs to her bedchamber and pulled her aunt's journals from her dressing chest. She felt compelled to peruse the volumes in which Hugh was often mentioned, to see if there was any hint about his writing stories as a younger man.

> *I learned that Frederick Prin-Hallsey married the wealthy, well-connected girl as his family had hoped. Her name was Honora Whitmore, a descendant of the local gentry from whom the village long ago took its name. I also learned that the couple had one son, which is all I managed to bear for Mr. Norris. In a day where families of eight, ten, or twelve children are common, Providence had given us each only one. Alas, Providence also saw fit to take mine from me, while their son still lives.*
>
> *I never met Honora Prin-Hallsey. I heard a great deal about her from Frederick, and attempted to piece together an accurate description of her character from the varying accounts of husband, son, neighbor, and servant. Whatever Honora had been, Frederick apparently thought me an improvement as a wife, which may not speak very highly for her demeanor or warmth. Of course, in Hugh's eyes, I was nothing to her and never would be. Nothing I did or didn't do found favor in his eyes.*

I was surprised when I learned Honora had been responsible for the donation of funds and lands for the poorhouse adjacent to the estate. Nothing in her son's behavior nor her husband's devotion led me to credit her with Christian charity. And this knowledge of her good deed caused me to regret my uncharitable thoughts.

How sad, Mariah thought, that such a generous and charitable woman had ended up with a son like Hugh.

Reading about the poorhouse brought Lizzy Barnes to mind, and Mariah wondered yet again if Mrs. Pitt had even told the girl about Mariah's offer of a post. How she wished she could pluck Lizzy from the institution—and from John Pitt's reach.

Coming to the end of that journal, Mariah reached down and extracted a second volume from nearer the bottom of the stack, to see if it was more of the same. She opened it and began reading.

Lord Masterly's eyes bore into Jemima's limpid green gaze. His hand reached across the gravestone to grasp hers.

"I knew you would return to me. I have cast a spell upon you. One you could no more resist than the tide can resist licking the waiting shore."

"No, my lord, you are wrong. I am only here to find my grand-father's map, and with it your ruin."

What in the world? Mariah flipped a few more pages, surprised and somehow amused to see pages and pages of some gothic novel written in her aunt's loopy hand.

She smiled.

What had Aunt Fran said? *"You and I have more in common than you might guess."*

✥

Mariah received another letter from Mr. Crosby—this one reiterating author Thomas Piper's wish to meet her and to publish reviews or excerpts of her next novel in a leading periodical.

Why did the man wish to help her? Or did he? What if he had some other motive, one he conveniently neglected to mention to a young and perhaps gullible A. K. Crosby Junior? Her encounters with the man who betrayed her, and even with devious Hugh Prin-Hallsey, had left her skittish and unable to trust her instincts—or the assurances of others.

Mr. Crosby had intimated that her first book was not selling as well as he wished, and that he planned a smaller printing on the second. He said reviews by Thomas Piper might help her career, might help him justify publishing a third Lady A novel. But was success worth the risk of giving up her anonymity, of her family discovering her work, and the public discovering Lady A was no lady at all?

Mr. Crosby said she might know the man. If so, could the secret author be Hugh Prin-Hallsey himself? He had admitted to one pseudonym already. But could—would—Hugh help her? She doubted it was worth the risk of finding out.

Mr. Crosby ended his letter by saying he would write again in a week's time with specifics of when and where the proposed meeting would take place. She would need to decide by then.

Knowing she thought more clearly while she walked, Mariah left the gatehouse, intending to take a brisk stroll around the grounds.

Martin, sitting on the garden bench with pipe and newspaper, lifted a hook in casual greeting.

"Hello, Martin."

"Miss." He turned a page of his newspaper. "Napoleon has finally sailed for his long-anticipated exile on the island of Elba."

"That is good news. Why don't you seem happy about it?"

"Elba is not far enough away, to my way of thinking."

She stepped nearer, glancing idly at a second periodical on the bench beside him. "What is this?"

He lifted his odd half-shrug. "*Gentleman's Magazine*. Mrs. Strong is good enough to save Master Hugh's copies for me once he is through with them."

Surprised, Mariah shook her head. "First the newspapers and now magazines as well. If you tell me you read novels, I shall faint dead away."

He turned another page. "Well, you won't find me reading epic poems. Cannot abide the longwinded things."

"I shall tell Mr. Scott you said so."

He looked up quickly.

"I am only teasing, Martin. How should I know the man?"

"I don't either. Still wouldn't want to offend him." He picked up the *Gentleman's Magazine* and opened it to an earmarked page. "There is something in here that might interest you. A review on that novel you've been reading. *Euphemia's Return?*"

"More glowing praise, I suppose?"

"Rather, yes. It has less glowing things to say about *A Winter in Bath*, but I don't suppose you would care to hear it?"

"No, Martin. I would not."

He nodded. "If you are headed up to the great house, take heed. Last I heard, Captain Bryant and some other fellow were shooting archery blindfolded."

Oh dear.

Mariah walked gingerly down the gatehouse lane, careful to look in all directions as she neared the new archery range. She saw no one about.

Continuing on, she spied Mr. Hart sitting alone under a tree, portable writing desk on his lap and quill in hand. "Mr. Hart."

Startled, he looked up, then quickly slid the paper beneath a blank sheet, his eyes flitting, his expression awkward. It was something she might have done. Could it be . . . ? Sweet Mr. Hart, the secret novelist?

"May I ask what you are doing, Mr. Hart?"

"Oh, uh . . . nothing really."

Why did he appear so sheepish? So guilty? She raised her brows in expectation.

He said, "I was only writing a letter."

"It must be quite a letter to cause you to blush so."

He ducked his head. "I am afraid you have caught me out, Miss Aubrey." He attempted a chuckle, but it came out as a pitiful *huh*.

She waited.

"You will think me very foolish. As I no doubt am."

"Perhaps not."

"It is all a lot of nonsense. A man like me, trying to be . . . eloquent. Captain Bryant is so much better with words than I am."

"Is he?" *Surely not Captain Bryant,* she thought. He would have told her. But then again, she had not told him.

Hart confessed, "I was trying to write a love letter, you see, with a bit of verse. But I have not a poetical turn of mind. I don't suppose you would take pity on a poor besotted creature?"

Not a novel. A letter. She thought of what Mr. Crosby had said, about female authors earning extra money by writing love letters and poems for gentlemen. Still the notion struck her as wrong.

"May I ask whom the letter is for?"

He met her eyes. "Miss Barnes. I thought you would have guessed."

"I did. But I am glad to hear I was right."

"Are you?"

She nodded. "But a girl like Lizzy does not need fancy words or poetry written by another. Write what is in your heart." She reached over and briefly touched his shoulder. "She will like that, I think."

Mr. Hart squinted off into the distance. "What is in my heart is neither poetic nor, I daresay, likely to sweep a girl off her feet. I . . . I want her to meet my mother."

Mariah knew Mr. Hart's invalid mother lived with her sister in a small pair of rooms on the coast. And that mother and son were close.

"Tell me, Miss Aubrey. Do you judge such a suggestion foolish or premature? Will Miss Barnes think I presume too much?"

"No," Mariah assured him. "She will think you a man with honorable intentions."

Did Thomas Piper, whoever he was, have honorable intentions toward her?

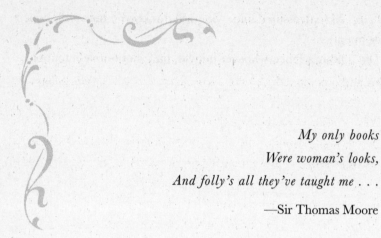

*My only books
Were woman's looks,
And folly's all they've taught me . . .*

—Sir Thomas Moore

chapter 27

*M*ariah sat at the kitchen table, lingering over coffee and her manuscript. Just outside, Albert Phelps was chatting, advising,
and lending a hand as Dixon worked in the garden. His voice carried
clearly on the still day, and Mariah overheard much of the one-sided
conversation.

"Know why I like plants?" Mr. Phelps asked.

Dixon made no reply, but clearly none was needed.

"Because I like being surrounded by living things. Makes a man . . .
a widower . . . a bit less lonesome, you see." He cleared his throat.
"Do . . . you ever get lonesome, Miss Dixon?"

My goodness, Mariah thought. The man was smitten indeed.

Mariah rose to refill her cup. Through the window, she watched as
a lad from the great house jogged up the lane, calling for Mr. Phelps.
Apparently the housekeeper, Mrs. Strong, wanted yet more flowers

for the house party. The gardener dutifully hurried away, waving his hat in farewell.

Martin ambled out from the stable and picked up the hoe Mr. Phelps had abandoned. "Hello, Miss Dixon. Have you seen Maggie today?"

"No. Wonder what is keeping her."

For several moments, the two worked companionably together, Martin managing the tool somewhat awkwardly with his hook. Then he hesitated. "Miss Dixon, I have been wondering. . . . Do you mind when people address you as Dixon?"

Mariah stiffened. He meant when *she* addressed Dixon by her surname.

Dixon said easily, "I am used to it. The girls' father started it, when I elected to stay on as general companion and dogsbody after Miss Julia went away to school. Before that, it was Nanny Dixon."

"May I ask your Christian name?"

She tilted her head to look at him. "Susan."

"A lovely name."

"Is it?" She resumed hoeing. "I admit I like hearing it—it's been so long. It is, of course, what my parents called me, and sometimes I miss it."

"I should be honored to call you Susan," Martin said. "If you give me leave to do so."

Susan Dixon smiled. "Yes, I should like that very much."

Feeling sheepish and chagrined, Mariah returned to her chair.

Several minutes later, Dixon came into the kitchen, removing her gardening gloves as she did so.

"Hello, Dix—Miss Dixon."

Dixon looked from the kitchen window to Mariah's no-doubt-guilty expression. She slanted her a knowing look. "I don't mind when *you* call me Dixon, Mariah. But Martin asked, and from a man, I would prefer Miss or my given name."

"I understand." Mariah winked. *"Susan."*

But Susan Dixon did not smile. Instead she sighed, not looking at all happy.

"I have never had one suitor, Mariah, and now, it seems, I have two. I thought it would be pleasant. But it is not. I do not wish to hurt either of them."

"Of course you don't," Mariah soothed. "But neither can you make them both happy."

Dixon stared off at nothing. "I know. But I don't like it. Perhaps I had better stay clear of them both."

Mariah shook her head. "You needn't sacrifice your own happiness, Dixon. I must admit it warmed my heart to see you and Martin working together in the garden, discussing Maggie. Like a little family you were, and I the interloper."

"You? Never say so. It is your house, after all."

"It is *our* house, Dixon, and shall be for as long as I can keep you." She added thoughtfully, "Though I fear that shall not be for long."

Finally, the much-anticipated day arrived. Matthew awoke in a sweat of nerves and ordered a bath for himself, though he'd had one the night before. He spent extra time on his ablutions and patiently endured the fussy valet's interminable shaving, combing, and cravat-tying without complaint. He walked through the house, his polished top boots echoing through the grand entry hall, and noted with approval how bright and tidy all appeared. Yes, he could get used to being the master of such a place.

The thought gave him pause. Could he really? A man like him, who'd spent his life in a humble cottage and cramped ship's quarters?

Horse hooves clattered up the drive, and Matthew stepped out onto the portico. *Yes,* he decided. *With the right woman at my side.*

And there she was—her fair face, wide at the brow and pointy at the chin, framed in the traveling coach window. Her hair still was as golden as he remembered, curled at her temples beneath a high-perched hat.

Matthew's heart began to drum in hard, slow thuds as regular as a death knell. *What have I done?*

What had he been thinking to bring her here, to invite her to reject him all over again? To reopen the deep and still-painful wound?

He recalled the last time he had seen her, her wide eyes gleaming with unshed tears. How his chest had ached to see it. . . .

Isabella had smiled bravely up at him, the expression pushing a tear from each blue eye. The tears trailed down her fair cheeks; and his heart, his hopes, plummeted with them. "I know you will be a great success, *Captain* Bryant," she said, emphasizing the new title to which he was still growing accustomed. He had achieved the rank, but not the wealth required by a man like Stanley Forsythe.

He took her hand. "I will talk to your father. Make him see reason."

"No, please don't." She shook her head, blond ringlets bouncing. "It will only anger him. And I know him too well to hope he will ever change his mind."

His whole body ached to hold her, to make her his. "I will not insult you by suggesting we elope. . . ." He let the notion hang in the air between them, praying she would insist but knowing how desperate and foolish and scandalous the idea was.

She shivered and pulled her hand from his.

He knew then. It wasn't merely her father rejecting him. She was rejecting him as well.

"Is there someone else?" he asked, hating the edge in his voice.

"No!" she cried, adamant, nearly offended.

Relieved, he grasped her shoulders. "Isabella, listen to me—"

"I am sorry, Captain." She stepped back, shaking her head once more. "We have always known Father opposed the match, and I . . . I am at last persuaded he is right. I am not fit to be a naval officer's wife. I would detest living alone in some port town far from London while you were gone to sea. I would die of boredom."

She gave a lame little laugh, and he was reminded of how young she was. Why did he have to fall for a girl barely eighteen? He was nearly eight years her senior. But age was the least of what divided them.

Realizing he had lost her, anger and grief battled within him.

And battled still.

Matthew stood there on the portico, dumb, frozen, as the groom opened the coach door and let down the step. Matthew should be there. It should be his hand reaching up to her, offering to help her down. *Idiot!*

From behind, he felt a push. Hart, no doubt. He could always be counted upon to deliver a well-timed shove. Matthew's legs came to life beneath him, catching up quickly with the rest of his body.

What would he see in her expression? Revulsion? Forced politeness? Admiration? Regret?

He would not act the fool. He would not. He would remain cool. Friendly, but detached. Past it. Over her. Had not four years passed, after all?

She looked up as he approached. "Captain Bryant!" Her voice rang out, her blue eyes brightened, and her smile was instant and apparently sincere.

His every nerve tingled to attention. "Miss Forsythe." He bowed, then straightened, his gaze lingering over the planes of her face, as beautiful as he remembered.

"How good to see you again." She looked from him to the house behind. "My, my, this house suits you. I always knew you would be a great success one day."

He felt a surge of pleasure akin to the thrill of victory. "Thank you. You are very welcome. I am glad you could come."

"I was delighted to receive your invitation."

She was all warmth. All admiration and approval. If only she were not engaged, this might all be quite easy.

But little in life, Matthew knew, ever was.

Miss Forsythe turned to her companion, who was smoothing her skirts beside her. "Miss Ann Hutchins. You remember Captain Bryant, I trust?"

The rather officious-looking young woman had dark auburn hair and a polite smile. "I do. Though I believe it was Commander Bryant at the time."

He managed to breathe. "Miss Hutchins, you are most welcome. And may I present my friend, Lieutenant William Hart."

He turned. But when William stepped forward, though making every effort to minimize his limp, Ann Hutchins's smile dimmed. Pretending not to notice, William bowed and the ladies curtsied.

Miss Forsythe clucked sympathetically. "Such noble men we have, Ann, serving our country." She offered William her gloved hand. "Allow me to thank you, Mr. Hart, as one grateful subject of His Majesty."

William smiled and bent over her hand. What a pretty speech from a very pretty lady. It seemed even defensive William could not help but be charmed.

As much as it galled Matthew to mention Isabella's intended, he knew he ought to do so, to demonstrate that he held no jealousy, no ill will toward the man. Matthew had never met James Crawford, but Parker said he was rumored to be a rake. Matthew knew he should hope it wasn't true, but the flaw somehow fanned his hope. "I am afraid Mr. Crawford has yet to arrive, Miss Forsythe, but we expect him very soon."

She gave a dismissive wave. "Oh, I am not surprised. Mr. Crawford will make a late but fashionable entrance as usual, I don't doubt. Who else is to join us?"

"Captain Parker and his mother, who has kindly undertaken the role of hostess. We also have Bartholomew Browne with us."

"Bartholomew Browne!" she echoed. "Wonderful notion. He shall prove diverting, I don't doubt."

Matthew noticed she did not ask about the females, but said nonetheless, "I have left Mrs. Parker in charge of the guest list for the female ranks, as a naval man hasn't the privilege of making the acquaintance of a great number of ladies whilst at sea."

Miss Forsythe raised one fair brow. "Debutantes to make Ann and me feel ancient, I suppose?"

Since she was no more than two and twenty herself, he knew he ought to compliment her, to reassure her that she had nothing to fear from any debutante, but he bit his tongue. "She did invite the Mabry girls, now you mention it."

"Pleasant, accomplished girls," Miss Forsythe allowed.

Beside her, Ann Hutchins nodded her approval. Clearly the Mabry girls posed no threat to their superior feminine charms.

So far, so good.

Matthew directed a pair of footmen to unload the ladies' things and carry them to two of the best rooms in the house.

"Perhaps, ladies, after you are settled, we might go riding together? The grounds here are lovely."

Isabella smiled at him, and Matthew's chest expanded with pleasure. William Hart had apparently disappeared. Ann Hutchins was invisible. Matthew had eyes only for her.

"Ann doesn't care to ride, Captain," Isabella said. "But I do. I would be happy to join you. Assuming I might borrow a horse?"

"Of course." He would request the dapple-grey mare and quilted sidesaddle Miss Aubrey had used, since she had praised both. "Shall we say, in an hour's time?"

Perhaps it was selfish, reckless, to maneuver a private rendezvous even before Crawford arrived. But Matthew had not risen to his position in the Royal Navy by hanging back and being cautious.

After the ladies were led inside by the servants, Matthew took himself into the house to change into riding coat and breeches. Mounting the stairs, he glimpsed Mrs. Parker standing at a rear window.

Hearing his tread, she crooked a finger at him. "Captain Bryant. Who is that girl?"

Matthew strode to the window and peered down at the back lawn, groomed for ninepins and bordered by fruit trees. He glimpsed a woman disappearing around the corner of the house and into the wood.

He frowned. "I am not certain, but I think that was Miss Aubrey."

"Aubrey? I don't recall inviting any Aubreys here."

"This Miss Aubrey lives . . . nearby."

The woman's face creased in concentration. "I believe we had a Miss Aubrey to our own house party last year. Such a disappointment."

"Oh?"

"Of course, I had hoped Ned might form an attachment with Miss Hutchins, but he would pursue other girls to spite me. May you never so torment your own mamma, Captain."

"I shall endeavor not to."

"Aubrey," she repeated. "What was it about a Miss Aubrey? Something not quite right there, but I cannot recall what it was."

Mariah was falling. She was in one of those disturbing dreams when one is falling from a height, a tower, a turret, the weightless panic in her stomach, the bloodless limbs, the disorientation, thoughts spiraling as the ground rushed to meet her.

He is here.

How had he found her? It did not matter. He had come. Come for her at last. To right the wrong. To show the world he loved her. Her mind whirled again. Her stomach collapsed. *Foolish girl.* For a rash second she had forgotten. He was married. Gone forever.

He was standing with two other men beside the new archery range, talking and laughing. He turned as if hearing her approach, smiled, and lifted a hand. Her own hand tingled to attention and began to rise in response, but in slow motion, again like a dream. Then a cold bucket of reality splashed her face and iced her veins. The sound of trotting hooves broke through her fog. Captain Bryant had ridden into view astride Storm. A woman rode beside him on the dapple grey. But Mariah barely saw her as realization struck.

He was waving at *them*. Smiling at *them*. He had not even seen Mariah, or if he had, was ignoring her.

Mariah turned sharply, embarrassment creeping up her neck and heating her cheeks. *Dear God in heaven, let him not see me. Let him not witness my mortifying reaction, my foolish, foolish hope. Stupid presumption. Stupid, stupid girl!*

Mariah attempted to walk naturally, to not draw attention to herself, but her feet would not obey. They strode faster and faster with her heartbeat, farther and farther from the man who once had the power to save her. But had walked away instead.

Matthew watched Miss Aubrey hurry away, cheeks flaming. Had one of the men said something to her? Had they even seen her? Captain Parker, Mr. Browne, and a man he assumed was Mr. Crawford seemed to be conversing companionably enough. Why was she so embarrassed . . . unless . . . did she know one of them?

What was it Hugh had intimated—that Miss Aubrey had caused a scandal, or was, perhaps, not the picture of propriety she appeared? It would explain why she was not married, yet living out from under her father's roof. Mariah herself had admitted she did not like house parties, that they were not, in her experience, "innocent." But that didn't necessarily mean the rumors were true.

Matthew wondered if one of these men was involved in the supposed scandal, whatever it was. If so, how unthinkable that he had brought the scoundrel to her own backyard. A sudden irrational urge to trounce the man rose up in him. But was Miss Aubrey really as innocent as he wanted to believe? In war, rarely was one party completely innocent while the other bore total blame. And Matthew knew from long experience that after battle both vessels were likely to be damaged.

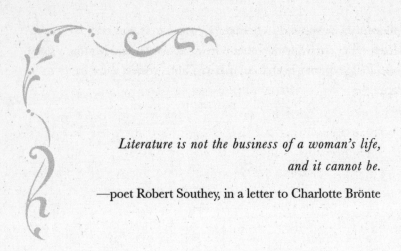

Literature is not the business of a woman's life,
and it cannot be.

—poet Robert Southey, in a letter to Charlotte Brönte

chapter 28

On the first Sunday in August, Mr. Phelps knocked on the kitchen door and asked if he might walk Miss Dixon to church. Dixon, in her Sunday dress and bonnet, prayer book in hand, nodded her assent.

Once they had gone, Mariah felt more isolated than ever, especially now that Captain Bryant and Mr. Hart were occupied with the house party. And worse, she guessed they would likely distance themselves from her permanently, once their mutual acquaintance made known every titillating detail of her fall.

Lonely, Mariah walked over to the poorhouse, seeking company. The Merryweather sisters were sitting out of doors as she'd hoped, Amy in her wheeled chair, and Agnes on the wooden bench beside her. Both women held long needles and balls of knitting wool in their laps.

"Hello, Miss Merryweather. Miss Amy."

"Miss Aubrey! Maggie was just here, singing that hymn you liked."

"Oh, I am sorry I missed it." As she drew near, Mariah saw how thin Amy's cheeks had become and how her fingers trembled as she stoically knitted on. While Agnes knitted what appeared to be a stocking of grey wool, Amy's yarn was a bright, orangy-red.

Mariah sat on the end of the bench nearest Amy and asked gently, "How are you, Miss Amy?"

"Failing, my dear," she said with a resigned little smile, her needles in constant motion.

Mariah's despondency must have shown on her face, for Amy unwound her fingers, reached over, and patted her hand. "Don't feel sorry for me, Miss Mariah. I don't."

At the woman's touch, tears burned Mariah's eyes.

Miss Amy squeezed Mariah's fingers, then lifted a second ball of cochineal-red knitting wool from her lap. She pinched a gnarled finger and thumb around a small knot at one end. "Do you see this tangle?"

Mariah nodded.

"This is my life on earth. And this—" with a stunning burst of strength, Amy tossed the ball in a long arc, still holding the knotted end. The ball flew, bounced, and then rolled, leaving a trail of colorful yarn behind. It topped a small rise before disappearing from view, no doubt rolling still—"is my life to come."

"Amy! What a waste!" Agnes clicked her tongue disapprovingly. "You and your metaphors. What nonsense."

"Perhaps," Amy allowed. "But I like to think of them. Keeps the mind occupied." Her eyes, focused on the red trail, grew distant. "The body might be engaged in the most base drudgery, but always the mind can be thinking on whatever is lovely, pure, noble. . . ."

Mariah wondered if that was the secret to Miss Amy's cheerfulness.

Agnes propped one hand on the arm of the bench and groaned to her feet.

"Sit, Miss Merryweather," Mariah urged. "I will be happy to retrieve the wool."

Mariah took the knotted end of yarn from Miss Amy and followed the trail, rewinding it as she went. When she returned, both sisters thanked her.

Miss Amy studied the red wool. "I was going to make a muffler for myself," she said. "I think everyone here has one of mine already. But I shall make one for you instead, Miss Mariah, if you like."

"Oh, no, Miss Amy, you must make one for yourself. This cheery red color will be so charming on you."

Amy smiled, running the vivid yarn through her bent fingers. "I do like it—though Agnes says it is a color for a Jezebel."

Mariah recalled the awful past Mrs. Pitt had mentioned. Yes, Mariah thought, Agnes Merryweather might very well link such a color to a colored past.

Mariah stayed and chatted with the Miss Merryweathers for several minutes more. She asked about Lizzy Barnes, but the sisters said seeing the girl was unlikely, as Mrs. Pitt kept her busy morning to night most days.

They also confided that a certain gentleman had come to visit them after his nighttime "rescue" the month before, and that the same gentleman had not been seen or heard from since. Mariah realized that she had not seen Captain Prince on the roof since then either. She hoped he was all right and wondered what had become of Martin's rope and grappling hook.

The next afternoon, while Martin cooked and Dixon cleaned up after him, Mariah energetically swept the drawing room. She wished she could sweep away the lingering mortification over her recent—and past—encounters with a certain man as easily.

Lizzy Barnes came to the door, little Maggie with her. Mariah had all but given up on Lizzy coming to work at the gatehouse.

She greeted them warmly. "Lizzy, how I hoped you would come!

And Maggie too. I know Dixon and Martin will be delighted to see you. Go on back to the kitchen and say hello."

Maggie grinned and dashed through the door.

Once they were alone, Mariah led Lizzy to the settee. "Did Mrs. Pitt mention that I asked to hire you?"

Lizzy nodded. "Last week."

Mariah wondered why Lizzy was just now coming to see her. She certainly did not seem as pleased as Mariah had anticipated.

"It's not that I'm not grateful, miss," Lizzy began. "I would be glad to say good riddance to John Pitt and his mother both. But . . ."

"But?"

"I fear what might become of George. I don't want to leave him alone. And then there's my mother."

"Your mother?"

Lizzy nodded. "It would break her heart if I entered service. She was a gentleman's daughter, see. Married beneath her when she married a miller, and never tires of reminding me."

"Yes, George mentioned it."

"She said her only options were becoming a companion or governess—the only proper occupations for ladies."

"But surely, compared to the poorhouse . . ."

Lizzy shook her head. "I know. But I tell her I am Mrs. Pitt's assistant, see? I'm not a *servant*, am I?"

But Mariah did not need another assistant—Dixon already assisted her admirably in her secret occupation. She thought a moment, then suggested, "Perhaps I might call Dixon my assistant and you my companion?"

"Perhaps," Lizzy said, but still did not appear convinced. Pressing her lips together, she looked down at her hands. Mariah noticed a small stain on her sleeve.

"Mrs. Pitt said it would be . . . bad for me to live here."

Mariah frowned. "Bad . . . how?"

"For my . . . reputation. She said unmarried women don't live alone unless their family put them out for good reason."

Mean-spirited woman! Mariah thought, yet guilt tugged at her. Mrs. Pitt might have a point, as much as Mariah hated to acknowledge it. Which was worse—working for a disreputable woman or living on parish charity? She said softly, "I did make a mistake in my past, Lizzy. A mistake with a man. It is why I wished to help you avoid my error. I do not think living here will bring you any harm, but you will have to decide that for yourself."

Lizzy nodded, thoughtful and quiet.

Mariah invited her to stay for dinner. The girl declined but did stay for half an hour longer, helping Martin and Dixon, who were scurrying about the kitchen trying to get several courses prepared at once. All the while, Maggie sat on a stool at the work counter, ostensibly helping, but mostly humming, swinging her legs, and snitching bites of whatever food passed within reach.

Lizzy proved a hard worker and a calming person to have on hand. Mariah wished again the girl might live and work in the gatehouse.

Before she took her leave, Lizzy whispered, "I am not saying no, miss. I am saying not yet."

That night at bedtime, Mariah found Dixon staring into her looking glass, running her hand over the fine creped skin of her neck.

"Maggie said I reminded her of her grandmother. A *grandmother.* When did I grow so old? I have never even been a mother. And, as much as I don't wish to look like one, I shall never have the privilege of being a grandmother either."

There were no words expected, and none to give. Mariah touched her friend's arm and left her.

Miss Aubrey, Matthew noticed, had been careful to keep her distance from the house and gardens since that first afternoon. This seemed to add credence to the rumors he'd heard, and as much as he'd enjoyed her company, he was relieved he had not gotten more involved with her.

But several days into the house party, Hart's treasure hunt brought his guests near her domain.

The group congregated around the gardener's cottage. Mr. Crawford and the Mabry girls undertook a search of the hothouse, while the rest of them—he, Parker, Browne, Miss Forsythe, and Miss Hutchins—lifted pots and looked under wheelbarrows in the yard, hoping to find the next clue.

Abruptly, Captain Parker straightened. "I say, who is that?"

Matthew turned and followed the man's gaze down the gatehouse lane in time to glimpse the retreating figure of Miss Aubrey.

Matthew waited to see if anyone else would acknowledge her, but no one responded.

"Do you know her, Bryant?" Parker persisted.

"Yes, I have made her acquaintance. Pleasant girl. Lives on the estate."

"But what is her name?" Ann Hutchins asked, staring down the wooded lane. "She looked familiar."

Matthew had hoped not to have to mention her name, but now could not avoid it. "A Miss Aubrey."

"Not Mariah Aubrey?" Isabella said, alarmed.

Matthew's stomach clenched. "Yes. Why?"

Isabella appeared stricken. "Mariah Aubrey is living *here*?"

"Nearby, yes."

Ann said archly, "I wondered what became of her."

Bartholomew Browne scratched his dark beard. "What do you mean?"

Ann scoffed. "Oh, come, Mr. Browne." She turned to Captain Parker. "You must remember, Captain, for it happened in your house."

"That was her just now?" Parker twisted his neck so far around, Matthew heard it pop. "How surprising she should be here."

Isabella murmured, "Surprising and upsetting."

"Why should it be?" Matthew asked.

Ann Hutchins looked at him as though he were a simpleton. "Why? Because she—"

Isabella shot Ann a warning look. An awkward silence fell over the group, and the conversation died. Perhaps they had just remembered the presence of the other person involved in the scandal, if scandal it was.

"We found it!" Helen Mabry ran out of the hothouse, waving a small square of paper. Her sister and Mr. Crawford followed behind.

"Come, Ann, let us go back," Isabella said. "I want to freshen up before dinner."

"Of course," Ann replied, eyes lowered in chastisement for her unnamed social gaffe.

"Captain Parker, you will escort us?" Isabella asked, her tone transforming the question into a command.

Parker dragged his gaze away from the lane. "Oh. Of course, if you like."

Matthew was both sorry and relieved to see him go. On one hand, he wanted to ask Parker what had happened at his house. But on the other hand, he was not really sure he wanted to know.

Parker and the two ladies retreated while the others hurried away in search of the next clue.

After the treasure hunt, the group dispersed, some to the house, some to the stable, some to the gardens. Matthew decided to call on Miss Aubrey and ask if any of his guests distressed her. To offer to keep them away from the gatehouse if she liked. But as he neared the wooded lane leading to the gatehouse, he heard voices and paused. Through the trees, Matthew was taken aback to see Miss Aubrey standing near Bartholomew Browne. The man's hair was too long, Matthew thought, especially as he did not tie it back. But he supposed poets need not concern themselves with fashion.

The two were speaking earnestly together, as though well acquainted. Miss Aubrey did not appear at ease, however. In fact she appeared agitated. And why would that be?

Bartholomew Browne was a married man, or had been, until his wife died some six months or so before. Matthew was still surprised the poet had accepted the invitation. Was six months long enough to grieve the loss of a spouse? Perhaps if one had married for reasons other than love. Or perhaps one grew lonely after a half year of mourning and longed for society. Matthew decided he should not judge the man too harshly.

"Mr. Browne, please," Miss Aubrey said. "Do not tell anyone. It was a long time ago."

"And you have put all that behind you, now you are older and wiser—is that it?" His tone was mildly teasing and lilted with a Highland brogue.

"I don't know about that."

"What does that say for me? For I have not given it up, irresponsible though it may be."

Matthew turned and walked out of hearing range, chagrined and in a state of denial. Surely it did not mean what it sounded like. Surely not. Not Miss Aubrey and Mr. Browne—whose wife had still been alive and well last summer.

Standing there in the gatehouse lane, Mariah felt her frustration rising. Would that she had never met this Scottish poet! Why had she ever confided in him? She had imagined some bond of empathetic trust between them as likeminded individuals. Clearly she had been mistaken.

"I wish you would not press me so," she said. "If I were the woman, would I want it known? Clearly whoever she is, she has gone to some effort to conceal her identity."

"I knew it." His dark eyes glinted. "It *is* you."

"Mr. Browne . . . !"

"Mum's the word, my dear. Mum's the word. But well I remember our first meeting. And your confession of your secret desires . . ." He waggled his brows suggestively. He certainly did not comport himself like a man in mourning.

"You make it sound so scandalous. I was still quite young and—"

"And the young must be forgiven their foolishness, I know."

Staring at facetious Mr. Browne, Mariah recalled the night she had been cursorily introduced to him, along with several other young ladies, at a ball a few years before. His wife, the ladies whispered, was home in her confinement. Mariah later saw him standing alone, looking bored. So she plucked up her courage to speak to him, expressing admiration for his new volume of poetry, and defending it against critical reviews. Flattered, he engaged her in a long conversation during which they discovered a shared love of several authors, poems, and novels. Her interest was so keen that he asked if she harbored her own secret desire to write. In confidence, she admitted that she had written a few plays and a story set in Bath—intended only for her brother and sister's amusement. How she wished now that she had kept her mouth shut.

"Mr. Browne," she tried again. "I beg you would not speak of this. Of me at all, with the other guests, or your host. I am acquainted with others in the party, and I should not like them knowing I am here."

"And why not?"

"I am not an invited guest, Mr. Browne. Do you wish to embarrass me, and your host?"

"I don't care if I do embarrass that lot. But no, I should not like to embarrass you."

"Thank you."

"You are more than welcome." He winked. *"Lady A."*

Matthew returned to the house, wanting to put the whole episode from his mind, but Parker met him on the portico, glass in hand. "I was astonished to learn Miss Aubrey is here."

"So I gathered," Matthew drawled.

"Remember when I said you might yet have a chance with Isabella, because her intended was rumored to be an immoral rake? *Miss Aubrey* is the woman he was supposedly involved with."

Matthew's stomach soured. His jumbled thoughts rattled into different slots in his mind. Not Browne. Crawford. "If that is true, why did you not tell me long before now?"

"Why should I, when I had no idea you had ever heard of Miss Aubrey, let alone shared an estate with her?"

Matthew huffed but did not protest further. He knew he had no reason to take the news personally. But that did not stop the bile of disappointment from rising up his throat.

"It happened at our house party last summer," Parker continued. "I flirted with Miss Aubrey myself when she first arrived, but unbelievable as it seems, she somehow resisted my many charms." He smirked. "I did not witness the events myself. I was in my cups that night and slept like the dead till noon. But from what I heard, she was found in bed with Crawford. And him an engaged man . . . or rather, nearly engaged at the time. In any case, not with me—and more's the pity. Found by Miss Forsythe herself. I gather Isabella raised quite a row that night, though since has tried to hush the thing up."

Matthew grew increasingly nauseated as the man prattled on.

"Spoilt the party, I am afraid." Parker crossed his arms over his chest and sighed. "These things go on, of course, but when the future wife walks in, well, that's sure to ruin the fun for everybody else. No wife for me, thank you. No matter what form of coercion *Mamma* tries next."

Parker slowly nodded his head. "Miss Aubrey, ey? Now the party is looking more interesting." He elbowed Matthew. "You old devil. Where do you keep her?"

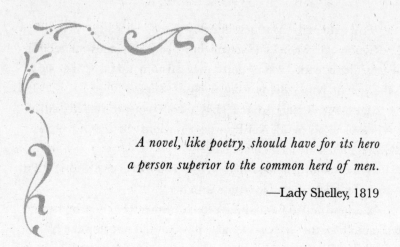

A novel, like poetry, should have for its hero
a person superior to the common herd of men.

—Lady Shelley, 1819

chapter 29

Instead of writing back in a week's time, as promised, Mr. Crosby appeared at the gatehouse in person, unannounced. Maggie and Dixon were off picking gooseberries together, so Mariah answered the door herself. Seeing him, Mariah conjured up a smile and invited him in.

"I thought this might be better," he said. "I did not wish you to waste several days in anxious worry that you could otherwise use in writing."

How thoughtful, Mariah thought sourly, dreading his next words.

"Here is what I have arranged. Thomas Piper will meet us in the Mill Inn at three o'clock today. I shall go along as chaperone, and for the sheer pleasure of seeing two authors I admire become acquainted."

Mariah's heart pounded erratically. *Today?* "Have *you* met Mr. Piper?"

Mr. Crosby screwed his lips to one side. "Not in person, no. My father met him, and I have exchanged several letters with him, but I look forward to making his acquaintance. My father thought him a colorful and interesting personage—that I do recall. There is nothing to fear, I assure you."

Mr. Crosby had not met him either? Having seen the two men on the road together, she had begun to feel quite certain the secret author must be Hugh Prin-Hallsey, who claimed to be the indomitable "Mrs. Wimble." After all, he was the only author she knew, save the poet Bartholomew Browne. Did Mr. Crosby not know the identity of the man behind Mrs. Wimble *or* Mr. Piper?

She asked, "You have met Mrs. Wimble, I trust? When you were making the rounds to meet all of your new authors this spring?"

He frowned. "Actually, I was unable to arrange to meet that author. It is still an outstanding item on my agenda."

"I see. . . ." Mariah murmured.

That meant Hugh *could* still be Thomas Piper as well as Mrs. Wimble. What would Hugh do if he learned she was Lady A? She did not think he would evict her, as he admitted to being a writer himself. Or, what if the author were someone else acquainted with her family? Mariah wondered which would be worse, her father finding out she was further damaging her reputation by scandalous novel writing, or Mr. Crosby learning the sordid reputation of the woman he was publishing under the guise of a lady.

Mariah rose, rubbing her fingers, and paced across the room. "I think I may know who Thomas Piper is. Is it Hugh Prin-Hallsey?"

"Prin-Hallsey?" Mr. Crosby frowned in concentration.

"I saw you speaking to him on the road when you called here last month. A man on horseback—tall, dark hair?"

"Yes, I remember him now. But I don't think he could be Thomas Piper. I am under the impression from what my father said, and from the fact that he did the majority of his writing more than a dozen years ago, that Thomas Piper is an older man."

"But you do not know that for certain?"

"I suppose it is possible that Mr. . . . "

"Prin-Hallsey."

"That he wrote *The Golden Prince Adventures* as a young man, but it would surprise me exceedingly to find them the work of an inexperienced youth. Has he ever been at sea?"

But Mariah did not answer immediately. His mention of the title had caught her attention and was busy echoing through her mind, bringing her up short. *The Golden Prince Adventures. The Golden Prince. Prince . . .*

Mr. Crosby asked, "Have you read his books, Miss Aubrey?"

She shook her head.

"They are tales of the sea," he explained. "Swashbucklers, pirates, castaways—you know."

"Oh . . ." she breathed. Could it be? Had Captain Prince written stories based on his own life upon returning to England?

Was that why Thomas Piper had not written anything in so long? Had he not the freedom to do so any longer? Mariah wondered if he would even be allowed to correspond with Mr. Crosby from Honora House or to contribute to periodicals. It seemed so unlikely. She doubted he even had the funds to post and receive letters. And if it was him, did he plan to escape his room this very day to meet Lady A in the village? He had certainly managed to free himself before. If so, she would not want to disappoint him.

But it seemed too fantastic. More likely it was Hugh, or even Bartholomew Browne, poet-turned-novelist. Both were at Windrush Court, after all, and could easily slip away for the meeting.

Finally, Mr. Crosby rose and said, "I don't think you have anything to be concerned about, Miss Aubrey, but I will not pressure you further. I will walk into the village now and leave you to think. I for one look forward to meeting the man. He hasn't written anything in far too long. Perhaps I can reinspire him." He grinned, then extracted and consulted his pocket watch. "If you are not at the inn by half past three, I will make your apologies to Mr. Piper and take the coach back to Oxford." He patted his pocket. "Oh, and before I forget, here is the remainder of your payment from Simon Wells. He is very pleased with your script and says rehearsals will soon begin."

Distracted, Mariah blindly accepted the money. "Thank you, Mr. Crosby."

Mariah went upstairs to stew in private but could not sit still. Instead she paced the sitting room, her soul not at peace. Was it worth the risk? Could revealing herself to someone like Hugh Prin-Hallsey or even Bartholomew Browne, who already believed she was Lady A, really help her? And what if it was Captain Prince? Kindhearted though he might be, would it be wise to trust her secret to such an unpredictable man?

Martin knocked on the sitting-room door, hat in hand. "I heard you pacing from belowstairs. Are you all right, miss?"

"I should be, but I am afraid." She told him of Mr. Crosby's request, the meeting she was already late for, the unknown man waiting to meet her right now in the Mill Inn.

Martin stepped in and stood before her. "Miss Mariah, you needn't go if it upsets you."

"But Mr. Crosby wishes it. If only I knew what manner of man this Thomas Piper is. That he intends no mischief." She thought once more of last summer's house party and winced. Was she opening herself to more humiliation?

"Of course he means you no harm," Martin said. "I assume Mr. Crosby assured you of that?"

She threw up her hands. "Then why am I so frightened?"

"The unknown needn't always be frightening, miss. But never you mind—you needn't wonder anymore."

"You are right. I should just meet him and have done." She paced across the room once more.

"Only if you want to. I shall walk with you, if you like."

"If only I knew I could trust him!"

"I think you can. He must have seen something in your writing he admired, and though he hasn't written much in years now, his name meant something once, and he thought he might help you. Advise you a bit."

"If his intentions are so honorable, why does he not reveal himself?"

Martin sat on the spare chair. "Perhaps he wanted to test the waters from the safety of shore. Perhaps he didn't want to inflict his presence on you. To invade your privacy, your life, more than he has. This way, going through Mr. Crosby, you have the right to refuse. And if you do, he will respect that and let it lie."

Mariah only half heard what Martin was saying; knew he was trying to calm her, to give her a way out. Only slowly did his words begin to print themselves sensibly on the pages of her mind.

Mariah whirled to look at him, to gape.

Unperturbed, Martin leaned back patiently, scratching his forearm with his hook. "And I can tell you what manner of man he is," he said easily, as if unaware of her stunned expression. "A washed-out old tar who never meant you any harm. Who's not worth two hairs on your head. Who can hardly believe anybody ever wanted to read the bawdy adventures he wrote, but they did. In great numbers, at one time."

Mariah sucked in her breath. "You . . . ? Are you saying that *you* are Mr. Piper?"

Suddenly the name resonated with meaning.

He smiled, his eyes crinkling at the corners. "Aye, miss. That I am. Based many of my yarns on the tales of Captain Prince, which is why I feel I owe him so much."

"I never guessed! Why did you not tell me?"

"As I said, miss. I didn't want to foist myself, my help, on you—if it was unwanted."

Mariah stared at him in wonderment. "Does Dixon know?"

He shook his head. "Nobody except you knows. Your aunt Fran knew. In fact, she was the one who suggested I write down the tales in the first place. But she took my secret to the grave with her. And I've kept hers as well."

Her secret . . . Mariah studied the face of this former seaman, steward, manservant, and . . . author . . . as though for the first time. How wise and knowing the weathered face, the steady blue eyes.

"Martin, may I show you something?"

She retrieved her copy of *Euphemia's Return*. "Remember this book, the one that received all those effusive reviews?"

Accepting the volume, he glanced at its spine. "Yes."

"I think Francesca wrote it."

His brow furrowed. "Did she? She never let on she had got one of her novels published."

"That is because she didn't. Hugh did. I believe he posed as its author and took the money for himself."

His eyes narrowed in thought. "She *was* vexed with Hugh, I recall. Accused him of taking some of her things. . . ."

"I think that is why she stowed her other manuscripts and journals here in the gatehouse. And may explain why Hugh has been poking about."

Martin nodded and drew himself up straight. "What time is it?"

She checked the mantel clock. "Half past three."

Martin rose. "Let's see if we can catch Mr. Crosby. Thomas Piper wants a word."

The next day, Miss Forsythe—wearing a wide-brimmed bonnet to shield her fair face from the sun—took Matthew's arm as they strolled through the rose garden. Miss Hutchins, perched on a garden bench, and the Mabry sisters, playing at shuttlecock nearby, provided chaperones aplenty. Enjoying the warmth of her gloved hand against him, Matthew walked blindly ahead and along the drive, until he realized they had unintentionally neared the gatehouse. At least, it had been unintentional on his part.

Isabella swept her gaze over the place. "So this is the mysterious gatehouse."

Matthew nodded. "Yes. My first introduction to Windrush Court. I stumbled upon it during a storm, before I had even let the place." He did not mention being thrown from his horse.

"Ah . . . that explains it."

"Explains what?"

"Well . . ." She darted him a cautious look. "You and Miss Aubrey seem quite close."

"Close? How do you mean?" Prickles of alarm began creeping through his body. True, he had mentioned the poorhouse theatrical, and Hart had amused the ladies with a story of their gatehouse dinner prepared by a one-armed cook. But surely that was not enough for Isabella to come to such a conclusion.

"A single man and a single woman living on the same estate, sharing meals and charitable causes, working side by side . . ." She let her words drift away, as though they spoke for themselves.

"You make more of it than it is," he insisted. "We are neighbors, yes, but we are not intimates. We are not, as you say, close."

She swiveled around to face him, turning her back on the gatehouse. "That is not the impression I have." She blinked her wide eyes. "I wonder, is it the impression Miss Aubrey has?"

"You are quite mistaken," he said. "Miss Aubrey and I are only acquaintances."

"Friends?"

"Well, perhaps, but I . . . I barely know the woman. Hart and I are friends, for example, but we have known one another for years."

She hesitated. "Do you . . . think it wise, considering her, well, reputation, to involve yourself so closely in her exile?"

No, it hadn't been wise. He saw that now. "She and I are not involved, as I said. We are not really even friends, in that sense—"

He broke off. For there she was. Over Isabella's shoulder, he glimpsed Miss Aubrey. Face stricken. Mouth slack. Eyes . . . betrayed. Instantly, his gut filled with bile. *Dash it.* He had not seen her behind the laundry line stretched from stable to woodshed, and now she had disappeared once more.

"We should return," he said abruptly. "The others will wonder what became of us. Crawford especially."

"Oh, let him wonder."

Had he not been wracked with guilt, he would have taken Isabella up on that enticing suggestion, would even have stopped to consider what she might be offering. But instead, he was consumed with regret and the need to take his leave from Isabella so he might return, explain, and apologize to Miss Aubrey.

Half an hour later, he found her on the old swing, as he had hoped he might. She swung idly, propelled by the toe of one slipper. She looked so young, so innocent. He could not really believe she had been involved with Crawford. In the twilight, he could see that she had been crying and felt like the cruelest stinging insect God ever created.

"Miss Aubrey, I am sorry you heard that."

"I am not. Now I know what you really think of me."

"No, you don't. I spoke rashly. You know how I feel about her. I did not want her to think that you and I . . . That any impediment stood between us. At least on my side."

She regarded him with those wounded amber eyes, and his heart constricted to see the pain he had caused.

"No, Captain. I heard what you said. The words you spoke. Though not so long ago you said to me, 'I hope we shall be friends.' Words are important to me. I listen to each one, weigh and measure it. If I cannot trust your words, how can I trust you?"

Right or wrong, Matthew realized he was fond of this woman and prized her friendship. "You *can* trust me, Mariah." He gave her a lopsided grin and attempted to tease her into a lighter mood. "Will you forgive me for sacrificing our friendship on the altar of love?"

She stared at him, face puckered, and shook her head. "That is the problem, exactly."

His grin faded. "I don't understand."

"I know." She sighed. "But thank you for coming to apologize anyway."

After Captain Bryant had bid her good-night, Mariah stayed on the swing, staring after him. She had been stilled by his odd words. He had said them lightly, jokingly, but they struck her as the crux of the problem between them. Matthew Bryant would sacrifice anything to win in love.

The word *altar* seemed chillingly apropos.

The voice of the woman with him had seemed familiar, but with her back turned and that deep coal-scuttle bonnet, Mariah had gotten only a glimpse of her profile. What was it about her that Captain Bryant found so irresistible?

Rising and threading her way through the shadowy garden, Mariah realized she needed to put thoughts of Captain Bryant from her mind. It would not be easy. But she believed a visit with Lydia Sorrow might help.

Lydia's heart pounded painfully as he sat on the edge of the bed and pulled her gently down beside him.

"You know I would marry you tomorrow, if I could," he said. "Tell me you know that."

Lydia nodded.

He leaned forward, kissing her temple, her cheek, her ear.

She shivered.

"How I have dreamed of this. You and I. Man and wife. Free to live and love."

His hand cupped her shoulder, then slowly slid down her arm, grazing the side of her body, the swell of her, as he did so.

Had she locked the door which separated her room from Miss Duckworth's? What if the woman entered at this moment? She would be shocked. Would sound the alarm and awaken the whole house. Or would she? No . . . to save her position, her reputation as trustworthy chaperone of young ladies, she would quietly propel the trespasser

*from the room, all the while extracting promises of utter secrecy, and
demanding immediate announcement of a betrothal.*

He kissed her neck and collarbone. Again, she shivered.

*"You are cold. Here." He straightened and pulled off his coat,
settling it around her shoulders. Then he proceeded to warm her
with kisses and caresses until her body felt molten and her brain
languorous. . . .*

༺~༻

In the morning, Dixon set a basket of produce on the worktable
and began untying her bonnet strings. "Mariah, if Mr. Phelps should
happen to call, please tell him I am otherwise occupied."

Mariah looked at her friend. "What don't you like about Mr.
Phelps?"

Arms crossed over her bosom, Dixon rubbed her hands up and down
her forearms. "He looks at me as though he'd like me for pudding."

Mariah grinned. "He likes you, Dixon. Nothing wrong with having
an admirer." She added to herself, *as long as he isn't bound to another.*

Dixon frowned and began unloading her basket. "He prattles on
endlessly about stamens and pollen, seeds and germination. And he
always has dirt beneath his fingernails."

"He is a gardener, Dixon."

"Mr. Montgomery hasn't such flaws."

"Mr. Montgomery is a fictional character."

"What about Captain Bryant? Surely he does not prattle on or
have unsightly appendages."

Appendages? Mariah thought. Were they speaking of Mr. Phelps
or Martin?

Dixon added, "And he is very handsome."

"True," Mariah acknowledged. "But there is something not quite
right there."

"What do you mean?"

"He is so . . . driven. To a fault."

Dixon inspected a cabbage from her basket. "It is good for men to have a sense of purpose. Better than some spineless male without a will."

"True. But it seems he would do anything to get what he wants, regardless of the cost to himself or others."

"To win a certain lady, you mean."

Mariah nodded.

Sighing, Dixon said, "I shouldn't mind being the object of such determined pursuit."

Mariah glanced out the window. "I think you may be, for here comes Mr. Phelps now."

In one hand the gardener carried a flowerpot; with the other he removed his hat as he neared. His bristly grey hair, Mariah noticed, was slicked down.

Dixon retreated to the larder, gesturing wildly to send the man away.

Mariah shook her head, whispering, "He's already seen you through the window."

Dixon groaned, narrowed her eyes at Mariah, and dragged herself to the door. When she opened it, Mariah saw that Mr. Phelps wore a tweed coat over a clean white shirt and dark trousers. Only his shoes were not as well polished as they might be. She could not see his fingernails.

Mr. Phelps handed Dixon a potted tea rose. "Miss Dixon. I wonder. Would you be so kind as to accompany me for a stroll about the gardens? The new dahlias are in bloom, as are my bachelor's buttons, and I should very much like to show you."

His *bachelor's buttons*? Mariah wondered at the significance of his mentioning that particular plant.

When Dixon hesitated, Mariah parroted the words Dixon had used to prod her into going riding with Captain Bryant. "She would be most delighted to accompany you, Mr. Phelps. Just let me fetch her shawl."

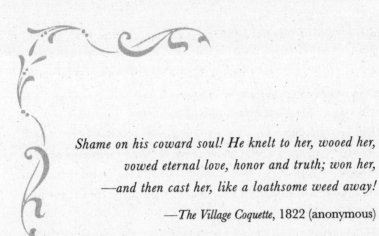

Shame on his coward soul! He knelt to her, wooed her,
vowed eternal love, honor and truth; won her,
—and then cast her, like a loathsome weed away!

—*The Village Coquette*, 1822 (anonymous)

chapter 30

ariah walked across the gatehouse lawn and bent to retrieve a crumple of biscuit-stained brown paper one of the children had discarded. She was wearing her ivory day dress again, this time with a modest lace fichu tucked into the neckline.

A man on horseback came trotting down the road. She ducked her head, but it was too late. He had seen her.

"Mariah? Excuse me—Miss Aubrey. I . . ."

That voice. His voice. She would know it anywhere. Instantly, her pulse quickened.

She looked up, but as soon as her eyes met his, she self-consciously ducked her head once more. Squeezing the wad of paper into a tiny ball, she forced her chin up and feigned nonchalance. "Hello, Mr. Crawford. What brings you here?" She wished the words back as soon as she uttered them.

"I am visiting Windrush Court. A Captain Bryant invited us."

Us. The word was an arrow.

He looked over his shoulder. "In fact, he and I were out riding together, but he stopped to greet a neighbor. He should be along directly." James Crawford looked around, and seeing no one, added, "I must say . . . I did not expect to find you here."

Did he think her a latecomer to the party? She had been certain Mr. Browne or someone else would have alerted him and his wife to her presence. Or had they not, wishing to shield the couple from that uncomfortable knowledge? "I am not one of the guests, Mr. Crawford. You need not fear."

He expelled a rush of breath. "Oh. Right. Of course not. That would be devilish awkward. Are you—"

She cut him off. "I fare well, Mr. Crawford. Thank you for asking." If he was about to ask a more personal question, she did not want to hear it. "And you? Are you well?"

"Um . . . yes. Quite well, thank you."

"Excellent. I hope you and your wife have a lovely time here." Mariah turned toward the gatehouse.

"Wife? Ah. Yes. We are engaged, but not yet married."

She spun back around, mouth ajar. "But . . . you said she was your betrothed. And that was . . . nearly a year ago now."

It was Crawford's turn to duck his head. "I know. We were about to be engaged at the time, but after the, uh, row, at the Parkers', she called things off. But she has forgiven me, I am happy to say, and we are officially engaged—announcement puffed off in the *Gazette*, banns read, all that."

Mariah stared at him. He had been free. He could have come to her. Married her. Rescued her. But he had not. Her father might have *worked* on him, had she not assured him the man involved was already attached. But it was all too late. Now that there had been a formal announcement, a gentleman had no honorable way to withdraw from an engagement.

"You lied to me."

He winced. "Not exactly. She is my betrothed and soon to be my wife. My father is most adamant."

Mariah's heart sank anew, but her ire rose. "Have you any idea what you have done to me? The price I have paid? I was stunned that I had not seen your supposed 'engagement' in the papers, but then, you had been out of the country for several months."

"It was my feeble plan. I thought if you believed me already engaged, I could remain resolved. You wouldn't be able to tempt me, to sway me from my course."

"I, tempt you?" She stepped nearer his horse. "You came to *my* room that night."

The words he had spoken—words she had committed to memory—replayed in her mind, mocking her. *"I thought we had time. That I could court you. But my father wants to see me married. Settled. . . . You know I would marry you tomorrow, if I could. . . ."*

He nodded, face grim. "I came to your room to tell you I could not marry you."

"Your chosen method was *most* ineffectual." Her words scorched with sarcasm.

He winced again. "I know. Once I was alone with you, I could not help myself."

Mariah slowly shook her head, over and over again. Why had she ever loved him? He was no gentleman, no man of honor. She had wasted herself. Her heart, her life, on a selfish, lying, manipulative man.

She took a deep breath and squared her shoulders. "Thank you, Mr. Crawford, for setting my mind at ease."

"Oh?" His eyes were wary, clearly anticipating another verbal blow.

"I feared you were about to renew your addresses to me. How relieved I am to find I was mistaken."

At that moment, Captain Bryant galloped up the road, and James Crawford, suddenly self-conscious, turned his horse's head. "I had better head back." He rode past Captain Bryant, a few words were exchanged which Mariah did not hear, and the captain looked inquiringly in her direction.

As Mr. Crawford rode away, Captain Bryant trotted Storm over to her. "Is everything all right?" he asked.

Did she look as shaken as she felt? She must, but she nodded affirmation anyway.

He glanced over his shoulder at the retreating horseman before returning his speculative gaze to her. "I take it you know Mr. Crawford."

Mariah shrank back as if pricked by a hidden needle. Had Captain Bryant learnt of the scandal? How exposed and sullied she felt at the thought.

"We are acquainted, yes." Then before he could inquire further, she asked, "And how are you acquainted with him?"

He dismounted. "I am not. Never met him before the party."

She frowned in surprise. "Then why invite him?"

He seemed to study his riding gloves. "It is always wise, Miss Aubrey, to get the opposing ship in one's sights, to size up the enemy, before determining the best battle plan."

She cocked her head to one side. "How came Mr. Crawford to be your enemy when you have never met him?"

"Quite easily."

She studied him through narrowed eyes. "Has this something to do with a certain lady?"

"It has everything to do with a certain lady—Miss Isabella Forsythe. I believe the two of you are acquainted?"

She stared at him. *Isabella Forsythe?* It couldn't be. *She* was the woman Captain Bryant longed to win? The woman she had believed married to her former love this twelvemonth gone? Isabella must have been the woman she had seen riding with Captain Bryant. Mariah had not recognized her from such a distance—would never have paired the two of them in her mind.

"We . . . have met," she murmured. "Briefly."

Captain Bryant patted the horse's damp withers. "If you wish to tell me your version of the tale, I promise to believe you."

She gave a dry laugh and looked away. "And why should you?"

He grimaced. "I am some acquainted with Mr. Crawford's reputation."

She turned. "Are you? Or are you merely willing to believe anything against the man engaged to the woman you want for yourself?" She was suddenly irritated with the captain. Must every man she admired fall for Miss Forsythe?

"Touché, Miss Aubrey. But there is another reason as well."

"Oh?" She waited, brows high.

"Will you keep what I tell you in confidence?"

She met his somber gaze and nodded.

"My own sister, who is, I am thankful to say, safely and happily married, had an unfortunate acquaintance with someone very like Mr. Crawford in her youth."

"Oh . . ." Mariah breathed.

"You see why I am keen on keeping it quiet."

She nodded.

The captain's confidence about his sister was kindly meant but did little to soothe Mariah's pain. Seeing James Crawford again had poured salt into a raw, freshly reopened wound. The salty tears burned her eyes, and she quickly excused herself to shed them in private.

When Miss Aubrey had retreated into the gatehouse, Matthew rode back around to the main entrance of Windrush Court. Trotting up the drive toward the stable, he saw Miss Forsythe wave to him from the portico and descend the stairs to meet him. His pleasure at seeing her was dimmed by his troubling encounter with Mariah. No wonder Isabella had warned him against associating with her.

Miss Forsythe smiled warmly up at him. "James returned ten

minutes ago and has already gone inside. What kept you? I was afraid you had met with some calamity."

"I stopped to speak with Miss Aubrey." He dismounted, realizing he probably should not have mentioned her.

Isabella winced. "Captain Bryant . . ." She hesitated. "I know it is not my place, but . . . must she be allowed to roam the estate?"

"Miss Aubrey is a tenant here." Keeping hold of Storm's reins, he looked about for the groom, then realized he must still be busy with Crawford's horse.

"I find the timing most . . . troubling," Isabella said. "That she should be here, at the very same time James is."

"Miss Aubrey has lived here for nearly a year."

She pondered his words. "So, she must have come here almost directly after . . ."

He decided to feign ignorance. "After what?"

"Surely you heard? The Parkers' house party last summer?" She shuddered, cheeks flushed. "I am mortified even to think of it."

Matthew faltered. "I . . . may have heard . . . something."

Miss Forsythe continued. "I suppose she told you she and James had an understanding? It is not true, no matter how much she wanted to believe it, or imagined it. James admits he may have allowed her to believe him fonder of her than he was, because he hated to injure her feelings."

Matthew considered this. "If he is not attached to her, why should you care if she is here? Are you not secure in his attachment to you now?"

"Of course I am. I do not doubt him, but nor do I trust her."

"You think she may try to ensnare him, and he shall be helpless to resist?"

She apparently missed his sarcasm. "It happened once before."

"Miss Forsythe. A gentleman would not—"

She huffed and wrinkled her elegant nose. "Oh, don't tell me what a gentleman would and would not do. I have eyes, haven't I? And a father and brother besides. I know James means to marry me. But that does not mean he shall be chaste in the meantime, nor faithful to me after the wedding. It is too much to expect of mortal men, or so Mamma has always said."

He shook his head. "You are wrong, Miss Forsythe. You have every right to expect fidelity from the man you marry. There are men who take their vows before God seriously. Who would love and cherish you and only you forever."

She glanced up at him from beneath golden lashes. "You know such men, Captain?"

"I do." He took a half step closer and lowered his voice. "And so do you."

For a moment she looked into his eyes, and hope flared. Might she relent? If he leaned forward, might she allow him to kiss her?

As if anticipating his intentions, she turned away. Or perhaps she had seen the groom approaching before Matthew did. Swallowing his disappointment, Matthew handed off the reins and followed her into the house.

❧

Still thinking about Miss Aubrey's tears and Crawford's guilty expression, Matthew sought out James Crawford the next afternoon. Finding him unoccupied on the back veranda while the rest of the party played ninepins, Matthew took advantage of the moment to speak to him alone. He waited until the man had helped himself to a drink from the cart and then approached.

"Mr. Crawford, might I have a private word?"

The man looked up at him, eyes narrowed. "I suppose. Though something tells me I shall not like it."

Matthew led the way down the veranda stairs and away from the keen ears of the attending footmen. Reaching the side yard, he said in a low voice, "Will you not do your duty by Miss Aubrey?"

"Duty?" Crawford echoed, incredulous. "Has she put you up to this?"

"Not at all. But the tale of your ill treatment has reached my ears."

"What has she said? I suppose she told you she and I had an understanding, but we did not. Not officially. Besides, my father would never have countenanced the match. She had to know that."

"Did she?" Matthew wondered what women found to admire in the man.

"I am fond of the girl, I admit. But she would not have suited then and certainly not now."

"What do you mean 'not now'? Now that you have destroyed her character?"

"A lady must guard her own character."

Matthew's hands fisted at his sides, angry at Crawford, yes, but also with Mariah. Why on earth had she trusted this man? "She no doubt believed you would wed her. So why not do your duty as a gentleman, marry her, and restore her reputation?"

Crawford's thin lip curled. "You would like that, would you not? Then you could have Miss Forsythe for yourself. Don't think I don't see your true motive. All your talk of duty. You would have me injure Miss Forsythe and my own status as a gentleman by breaking our engagement? Such things are not done, man, as you well know. Or would know, were you a gentleman yourself. But perhaps a man of your station does not know these things. All the fine clothes and fine estates in the world won't make you one of us. You think Belle would have you, when she rejected you once before? What—because you now have a few thousand pounds to throw around?"

Matthew spoke through clenched teeth. "No. She never sought to marry for money. That is *your* goal."

Crawford huffed. "You were beneath her then, and you are beneath her now."

"True," Matthew hissed. "But I, at least, would endeavor to deserve her. You never shall."

James Crawford landed the first punch, a stinging right to his jaw. Matthew's head reared back, but he managed to keep his feet. He returned the favor with a deep blow to the man's gut, and when Crawford doubled over, with a fist to his jaw. Crawford fell to the ground with a grunt and a curse.

The fight drew the attention of the ninepin players. Mr. Browne looked as though he might join the fray, but Mr. Hart stayed him by shoving his walking stick before him like a gate. The poet took one look at Hart's fierce expression and stepped back.

A lazy applause sounded from the veranda above them, and Matthew glanced up to see Ned Parker slowly clapping his hands, a smirk of amusement on his handsome face. "My, my, how diverting. Nothing in town to rival it."

Matthew turned and saw Isabella Forsythe staring at the fallen man, hand pressed to her mouth. Crawford groaned. With a fleeting look at his assailant, Isabella hurried past and knelt beside her intended. And in that bleak look, Matthew knew he had well and truly lost her.

Mariah opened the kitchen door, saw the blood trickling from Captain Bryant's lip, and gasped. "You are bleeding! Come in."

She ushered him inside, where he slumped into a kitchen chair with a loud exhale. She left him a moment to fetch a basin of water and a cloth, returning as quickly as she could.

"What happened?" she asked.

"I was a fool. That is what happened. I tried to talk sense to your Mr. Crawford."

She touched the cloth to his mouth and he winced. "That *was* foolish. And he isn't my anything."

"I was trying to remedy that."

Her hand paused in its ministrations. "Captain Bryant. You ought not to have done so."

"I know. The man is fond of you though. Admits it."

The cloth hovered midair. "Does he?"

"But he is determined to marry Miss Forsythe."

"Did you really think you could change his mind?"

He groaned. "I don't know what I thought. Probably didn't—that's the problem. Of course, he accused me of urging him to break things off with Isabella so I could have her myself. As if I could."

"Was that not your motivation?" It still saddened Mariah to see the lengths he would go to try to win back the woman who had spurned him.

"In part, of course. I have never made a secret of my intentions toward her. But I would help you if I could, Miss Aubrey."

"Don't, Captain. Please, let it be." She dabbed his mouth once more, inspected it, and then said with forced brightness, "There, the bleeding has stopped."

He looked at her closely. Too closely. "Has it? Has it truly stopped, Miss Aubrey?"

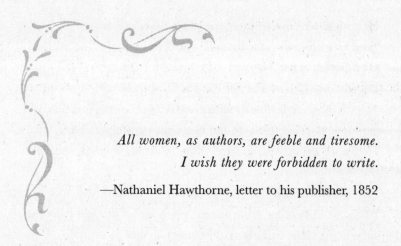

All women, as authors, are feeble and tiresome.
I wish they were forbidden to write.

—Nathaniel Hawthorne, letter to his publisher, 1852

chapter 31

week after Mr. Crosby's last visit and Martin's revelation, Mariah opened her door to Hugh Prin-Hallsey. His punctuality seemed a strong indication that her letter had well served its purpose.

"Hello, Hugh. Thank you for coming."

"Of course I came. Did you not send word that you had found something of your aunt's to interest me at last?"

"Indeed I did. Please come in." She gestured him into the drawing room.

There, he sat on the wing chair but leaned forward, clearly eager to learn why she had summoned him.

"Here is what I have found," she began. She placed *Euphemia's Return* on the low table before him, then stacked her aunt's journals and manuscripts beside it.

He frowned at the unfamiliar volumes. "What are these?"

"Journals my aunt kept from the time she was a girl."

He sputtered. "But you told me she left you nothing—"

"Nothing of yours," she interrupted. "Nothing of value. At least, not to an honest man."

He narrowed his eyes at her. "What do you mean?"

"I have finished *Euphemia's Return* and read my aunt's journals and writings as well. I find the style and language notably similar."

He leaned back. "And you are a literary expert now, are you, Miss Aubrey?"

"Even some of the settings and names are the same."

"That would not be so surprising, considering she and I lived in the same house. Knew many of the same people."

"Even the hand is the same."

For a moment he stilled, staring at her. Then he tapped the cover of *Euphemia's Return*. "You could not tell that from a printed book."

"No. But Crosby and Company kindly showed me the original manuscript from which the book was typeset and printed."

He studied her, measuring the threat she presented, she guessed, and formulating his response. He crossed one long leg over the other, apparently unconcerned. "I am not sure I believe you. But if you must know, Francesca kindly agreed to rewrite my pages in her own hand so that the publisher would credit the author feminine—a real Mrs. Wimble."

Mariah had expected this. Mr. Crosby had said the handwriting appeared decidedly feminine, and had guessed the same—that if Hugh were Mrs. Wimble, he had either hired a female scribe or had managed to imitate a feminine style of penmanship.

"My aunt, the woman you so openly despised, did this great favor for you?"

He shrugged. "She was not all bad, as I believe I said before. Perhaps she felt she owed me something for trying to usurp my mother's place . . . or for allowing her niece the gatehouse *gratis*."

"Mrs. Prin-Hallsey owed you nothing."

He grimaced, as he always did, upon hearing this appellation used for her aunt.

Mariah pressed, "Your stepmother would never have rewritten a book for you, for she was too busy writing her own."

His dark eyes sparked in anger. "She was *not* my stepmother, nor mother of any kind. She was a thorn in my side and a threat to the Prin-Hallsey name. She took and took from me, and if I did take something in return, I had every right to do so."

"I am surprised you would put your name on anything Francesca Prin-Hallsey wrote, when you admired her so little."

Hugh smirked. "Ah, but I did not put *my* name on it, did I?"

There it was, basically a confession. Mariah barely restrained herself from glancing toward the kitchen door, where Martin was supposed to be waiting. Had something happened to forestall him?

Hugh continued, his foot dangling and swaying over his crossed leg. "Wouldn't think of putting my name to such female tripe. Romantic drivel. Worthless in terms of literary value, but quite lucrative financially, I find. As heir, everything within the estate belongs to me. It was about time that woman turned out to be good for something."

Mariah straightened her shoulders. "No wonder she brought her other novels here after the first went missing. I shall show them to your publisher and he will know you did not write *Euphemia's Return*."

"Other novels?" he repeated, alert. "How many are there?"

"Two, but you shall never have them, unless you buy printed copies like everybody else."

"You mean to have them published?"

"Under her real name, yes."

He put both feet on the floor. "I don't believe I can allow you to do that."

Mariah met his glare with an icy one of her own. "I am afraid you have no choice."

"Don't I?" He leaned forward. "Do you think the publisher shall take your word over mine?"

Actually, Mr. Crosby had been slow to believe her. She and Martin had walked together to the Mill Inn to present her theory to Mr. Crosby, barely catching him before the Oxford coach departed. He'd finally agreed to take one of Francesca's manuscripts back to his offices to compare it to the original of *Euphemia's Return*.

Hugh sneered and added, "Why would Crosby and Company believe a woman with *your* reputation?"

At last, Martin pushed open the kitchen door and held it as Mr. Crosby strode into the room.

"Because Crosby and Company heard everything you just said."

Mariah winced. Mr. Crosby had heard everything. Oh yes, he had.

Matthew turned over in bed yet again. Illogical! That's what it was. Why should his thoughts be consumed with her now, when Isabella was under his very roof at last? This time it was not nightmares of war that disturbed his sleep, but thoughts of Mariah Aubrey.

Illogical!

The more Matthew learned about Miss Aubrey, the more he realized he should distance himself from her. So why did he find himself drawn to her? He could not allow himself to feel anything more than friendship for her. And even then, friendship from afar. Anything else would ruin his well-laid plans.

Overheated from tossing and turning, Matthew threw back his bedclothes, rose, and strode to the mantel clock. In a shaft of moonlight he saw that it had just gone midnight. He had awoken after less than an hour and doubted he would return to sleep anytime soon. Restless, he pulled on trousers, slipped a shirt over his head, and wrestled on his boots, which he preferred to the fancy buckled shoes, though shoes were easier to get on. Too warm to bother with a coat, he slipped from his room and passed silently through the house. From somewhere down the corridor he heard the faint sound of a female giggle but did not recognize the voice.

Stepping outside, he was at once cooled as the night breeze passed through the fine fabric of his shirt. His boots crunched over the gravel as he walked on, hoping to clear his head. And his heart. Above him the sky sparkled with stars as numerous as the diamonds he had once seen in a chest of confiscated African treasure.

"When I consider thy heavens, the work of thy fingers, the moon and the stars, which thou hast ordained . . ." He recalled reading that passage from the Psalms on more than one Sabbath in his role as spiritual leader, at least on Sundays, when the crew assembled for divine services after inspection. Often he had felt like a hypocrite, taking the thick black book—a rare gift from his father—in his hands and reading to the men as though he were worthy to do so.

He was not.

Matthew did believe in God. One could hardly sail the mighty seas and not believe in, revere, and stand in awe of his creator. And Jesus must have been powerful indeed, to calm the wind and the waves. Sometimes, however, Matthew could not believe that God knew a speck like him, or cared. Perhaps it was because his earthly father was cold and distant. Still, Matthew hoped he was wrong.

Matthew thought about another line from the Psalms, and recited it to himself as he walked. *"For thou art my rock and my fortress; therefore for thy name's sake lead me and guide me."*

Mariah sat at the kitchen table, enjoying the warmth of the dying embers in the cookstove as she sipped a late-night cup of tea. After the stressful events of the day, she felt too restless to sleep and instead sat rereading one of her aunt's novels by candlelight into the wee hours. Chaucer jumped up and sat on the chair beside her. He prodded her hand with his head, hoping to be petted. As she lifted her hand to oblige him, movement caught her eye through the kitchen window.

She rose. There in the moonlit back garden, Captain Bryant paced, side to side, not approaching her door, nor retreating. She watched him for several minutes, then went to the door and cracked it open.

"Tea?"

He stopped his pacing. For a moment he stared at her almost sullenly, as though he would refuse.

"Or warm milk, if you prefer?"

He exhaled deeply and slogged to the door.

Mariah laid aside the manuscript and set about filling the kettle. She placed it on the stove, bending to stir the embers. In his present state he likely wouldn't notice if the tea was tepid or weak.

He slumped into the seat, almost atop Chaucer, who meowed in indignation and bolted from the room. When Mariah sat in her chair, he reached out and caught her ink-stained hand in his.

He said nothing, only studied her fingers.

Nervously, Mariah began, "Martin has saved newspaper accounts of naval victories at sea, including your glorious triumphs."

Captain Bryant snorted softly. "Hardly glorious. I still have nightmares about all the bloodshed."

She gently tugged her hand, but he retained it, seemingly loath to let it go. "You did all those things to prove yourself to Miss Forsythe?"

He gave a brittle laugh. "I once thought so. I have come to realize she shares that privilege with my father."

She waited for him to explain. She was tempted to tell him about Hugh Prin-Hallsey, but refrained, realizing Captain Bryant had other things on his mind. She allowed him to keep hold of her hand, though she knew she should not.

He kept his gaze on her fingers. "No matter what I do, how much I achieve, it is never enough for him. Not being promoted to captain, not all the victories and prizes, not this estate. There is no rank high enough, no prize—or house—big enough to earn his esteem."

"Surely you needn't do all that to earn your father's affection. You are his son, after all."

"Then why is he never pleased with me?"

"I don't know. Perhaps—"

"I shall tell you why," Matthew interjected. "Because I am not my brother. Perfect Peter, who died at seventeen but who lives on in unadulterated perfection."

He rubbed his free hand over his eyes. "Peter was everything I wasn't. Studious, quiet, always reading some lofty tome I could make little sense of. He hoped to go into the church."

"Let me guess," Mariah said. "You were the mischievous one, always running about, making swords of sticks and getting into fisticuffs with boys twice your size."

He chuckled dryly. "I suppose that is why I thought the navy would suit me. It was everything I was good at—games of strategy, risk, fighting, swordplay. . . ."

His Adam's apple bobbed as he swallowed, paused, and swallowed again. "When Peter died, it was as if my parents died with him. All their joy gone. What little interest my father had shown in me dried up. No matter the good reports that came of me, all seemed to fall on deaf ears."

Mariah asked gently, "Did your father blame you for Peter's death?"

"Lord help me, I hope not," Matthew said ruefully. "I don't think I could bear that along with the rest. I don't see how he could, as I was already away at sea when Peter contracted lung fever. Always was rather sickly. Such a drafty, damp house. It's why I was so determined to bring my mother here. I fear she has the same weak constitution Peter had."

The kettle steamed, but Mariah stayed where she was, her hand in his.

They sat in silence for several minutes. Then Matthew shrugged. "At all events, I suppose that is why it was such a nettle to my soul when Mr. Forsythe pronounced me unsuitable. It was as if he was in league with my father. As if his judgment validated what I had grown to believe—I would never be good enough, no matter how hard I tried."

Mariah squeezed his hand. "Then perhaps it is time to stop trying."

He met her gaze, his eyes large and intense in the dim light. How tormented he looked, yet how appealing. She wished yet again that her secrets did not stand between them. Even if Isabella Forsythe did.

She said, "Miss Dixon tells me we are worth a great deal to God, just as we are."

He pursed his lips and blew a loud exhale. "That is difficult to believe sometimes."

"Yes," she whispered. "It is."

His mouth parted as though to say more, or as though to kiss her. Instead he stared at her a moment longer and then released her hand and rose.

"I should go. It is late. Thank you for tea."

"You have not had any."

"Right. Never mind. Good night." He bowed and turned, letting himself out and striding purposefully away.

Mariah checked the kettle. The fire had gone cold.

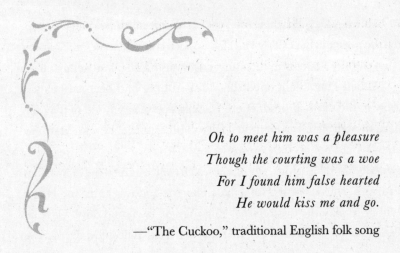

Oh to meet him was a pleasure
Though the courting was a woe
For I found him false hearted
He would kiss me and go.

—"The Cuckoo," traditional English folk song

chapter 32

uring the house party, Matthew had casually mentioned the theatrical he and Hart had taken part in. William had chimed in, describing the scripts, the sword fights, the props, with great animation. And how his face fairly shone whenever he mentioned the innocent dove portrayed so charmingly by Lizzy Barnes. As Matthew anticipated, several guests, especially of the female variety, enthused over the idea of putting on a theatrical of their own.

Matthew obliged them by obtaining the props and scripts from Miss Aubrey and distributing them to the ladies. Isabella and the Mabry girls quickly chose parts for themselves and debated which man among them was best suited for each role. Rehearsals soon began, and Matthew quickly realized this was going to be a far different experience, with finer costumes, an accomplished soprano singing the part of the nightingale, and real swords.

When asked, Matthew was reticent to describe the original performance in detail, but clearly Hart felt no such compunction, proclaiming Miss Aubrey's talents in directing, costume-making, and acting alike.

When Hart mentioned that Miss Aubrey had been cast as the crow in the original production, Isabella Forsythe refused to play the part, though a choice one, and it fell to Millicent Mabry, who Matthew knew would not do the part justice.

Miss Ann Hutchins, who eschewed frivolity, agreed only to participate as narrator, leaving Isabella to play the goddess Juno, and Helen Mabry to play the two nonspeaking roles of fawn and dove. Captain Parker claimed Matthew's former role as fox to Millicent Mabry's crow, as well as a role in "The Bear and the Lion" opposite Bartholomew Browne. Matthew had not realized his friend Parker was such a keen thespian.

Matthew himself was subjugated to a few minor roles. Isabella wished James Crawford to play Peacock to her Juno, but he was sullen and refused to participate, leaving Hart to fill that role once again.

During the first rehearsal, the hinge of the crow beak had come loose and several feathers of the peacock mask unfastened. Matthew took them to the gatehouse to ask Miss Aubrey what she might suggest. She offered to repair both if he could return for them the following day.

Matthew planned to return. Meant to return. But the ladies kept him so busy writing out extra copies of the script, rearranging the library for the performance, and painting a backdrop, that he quite forgot. And by the time he did remember, it was too late.

Disaster was already waiting in the wings.

૮૭

Mariah had mixed feelings about Captain Bryant's guests using the scripts and props she had created. On the one hand, she was glad to see them put to use. But on the other, she couldn't help but worry that her props and scripts would naturally make her a topic of conversation—an uncomfortable thought indeed.

But since she had never been able to resist a call for help, she repaired the beak and mask for Captain Bryant and awaited his return.

When he did not return the following day, or the day of the performance, Mariah wondered if there had been a miscommunication between them. Did he expect her to deliver the mask and headdress? As the appointed hour of the performance drew nigh, Mariah began to feel as forgotten as the props. Both Martin and Dixon had already gone to the Watfords for whist or she would have dispatched one of them. Reluctantly, she decided she must take the costumes to the great house herself.

Well, what is the worst that could happen? she bolstered herself. It appeared the entire party already knew of her presence and her part in the theatrical, so she had little to risk in going over. She would simply leave the headdress and mask at the door with a footman and ask that they be delivered into Captain Bryant's hands.

She slipped a long-sleeved spencer over her dusky blue gown and walked quickly through the pink-orange twilight to the great house. But as she lifted her hand to knock, the door opened, startling her. Captain Ned Parker appeared, a handsome man she knew only slightly. He had briefly flirted with her at his house party last summer, but she had been so focused on Mr. Crawford that she had given him no encouragement.

Captain Parker was on his way outside with a decanter of something golden, and a half-filled glass in his hands. "Miss Aubrey!" he exclaimed. "What a delight. I have not had the pleasure of meeting you the entire time I have been here. I do hope you are coming to join us for the theatrical?"

"I have only come to bring these." She lifted the props before her, like an admittance ticket at Almack's.

"Nonsense. You must stay. Hart and Bryant go on endlessly about what a wonderful performance you gave in 'The Fox and the Crow.' I am to play the fox, you know. How I would love for you to play opposite me. Then you might display your many talents for all to see."

Mariah was taken aback by his warm praise. Did he not know what had happened at his own house party? Surely he did. What balm to meet with someone who knew and yet still esteemed her.

She said, "I am certain the role is filled quite admirably by another lady."

"Millicent Mabry." He shuddered. "Silly thing. Giggled uncontrollably through the entire rehearsal."

Mariah allowed herself a small smile.

"Come, Miss Aubrey, don't desert us. You are likely the only clever female among us, unless you count Miss Hutchins, and I don't."

Ann Hutchins, Mariah guessed. "No, I shan't stay. I don't want to intrude."

Beneath a fringe of blond hair, his pale eyes gleamed. "And deny me the pleasure of your company because of a few simpleminded gossips? That hardly seems fair."

Yes, he definitely knew.

He leaned near. "Come, Miss Aubrey. If you prefer to stay out of sight, I will escort you to the smoking room off the library. There is an air vent there where gents used to spy on the ladies while they smoked their cigars in peace. No one shall see you, and you can watch our poor performance from there."

"I don't think that is a good idea, Captain."

"I should perform better, knowing you were there. Come, would you not like to see what this lot does with your script? Butcher it, no doubt, but are you not curious?"

She bit her lip. "I am curious, I own."

"Then it is settled." Tucking the decanter under his arm, he offered her his elbow and led her into the house. He escorted her across the hall and into the small secluded room. Then he excused himself, taking his decanter and glass with him.

Mariah stood alone in the smoking room, which bore only the faintest scent of tobacco. Rich leather chairs were clustered around, and at one end of the room was the vent he had mentioned, midway up the wall. She hoped no one was watching her through it. It took her several minutes to pluck up the courage to peek through—and when she did, she saw that the library beyond was empty.

Mariah had been relieved, if surprised, when Captain Parker left her. She feared what notions might arise in his brain had he been alone with her while continuing to empty that decanter. She recalled her old chaperone warning her to stay away from Ned Parker when he was drinking. But maybe she had been mistaken, for Captain Parker had seemed gentlemanly, even unexpectedly charming. Perhaps she had been wrong to discourage his interest last summer.

A shrill voice wheedled through the wall, and Mariah tiptoed to the vent once more. One of the Mabry girls—Helen, she thought—was trilling up and down the notes of the scale. And then, a beautiful fair-haired woman entered. Isabella Forsythe. Mariah had met her only briefly at the Parkers' party. How beautiful she was in her Grecian robes. Juno. Mariah felt a stab of resentment toward the striking blonde, who had once again come between her and love.

Another woman strode into the library—Ann Hutchins, whom Mariah had met once or twice before. Miss Hutchins was frowning and looked upset. Whatever news she imparted soon had Miss Forsythe and the Mabry girl looking greatly disappointed.

The door to the smoking room burst open behind her, and Mariah barely stifled a shriek. Turning, she saw it was only Captain Parker returning. He carried several objects in his arms, the crow headdress among them.

His handsome face was flushed, his eyes a bit bleary. The decanter was gone. Its contents gone . . . into him?

"It is fate, Miss Aubrey," he said. "Everyone is bitterly disappointed, and I am blessedly relieved. Millicent Mabry has suddenly taken ill.

Bad oysters. She will be fine by morning, but our theatrical is ruined, unless you save us."

Mariah's head had already begun shaking, refusing of its own accord.

The door opened again, this time more slowly. Mariah steeled herself, until she recognized Captain Bryant. He let himself in and closed the door behind him.

Parker gestured toward her, a smug grin on his face. "Here she is, Bryant."

"Miss Aubrey," the captain began. "Parker whispered to me that you were in here, but I confess I did not believe him."

"Can you think of anyone else to salvage the play at this late hour?" Parker asked.

"No, but we may simply reschedule."

"Not a bit of it. I am taking my leave tomorrow, or have you forgotten? And Browne goes with me."

Captain Bryant looked at him dully. "I had forgotten."

"Come, Miss Aubrey," Parker urged. "I thought you might wear Hart's mask as well as the beak contraption, if that makes you feel more secure. More incognito."

"You need not do this, Miss Aubrey," Captain Bryant said, eyes earnest.

"Oh, come, Captain," Parker scoffed. "She is perfectly safe, is she not? Surely you would not allow anyone to say a word against her in your own house."

"Of course not."

Parker handed Mariah the mask and crow headdress as though her participation were a *fait accompli*. Glancing significantly at Captain Bryant, he added, "And won't Miss Forsythe be grateful when you tell her the theatrical shall go on after all? What a hero you shall be in her eyes."

Mariah turned and once more looked through the vent at the assembled party, stewing and grumbling in the next room. She saw the young ladies and their chaperones and kind Mr. Hart. But no sign of James Crawford. Then she looked at Captain Bryant, knew how very much he wanted everything to go well, to please Miss Forsythe at any cost. Inwardly she sighed. She would do it for him.

"Very well. 'The Fox and the Crow,' and then I leave."

"Of course." Parker smiled, looking like a satisfied fox indeed.

Mariah stood at the back of the library, masked and wearing the headdress as Captain Bryant stepped to the front of the room and cleared his throat. "You will be glad to know that a substitute actress has been found and the theatrical will go on as planned. I know each of you will kindly welcome her to our humble stage and remember that she is here at our behest and not her own initiative. Understood?"

Heads swiveled toward the back of the room, and Mariah felt a flush creep up her neck. Hart smiled encouragingly, no doubt recognizing her instantly. Likely they all did. Helen Mabry smiled uncertainly, perhaps not remembering her. Miss Hutchins whispered something to Miss Forsythe, who blanched, then turned away. For the first time, Mariah felt oddly sorry for Isabella. How awkward this must be for her as well. For she and her friend clearly did remember her. No one, however, voiced a complaint.

Captain Bryant surveyed the room. "And as Parker seems to have gone missing, I shall reprise my role as the fox."

The library, where the guests had elected to hold their theatrical, held no stairway, but they had positioned a set of substantial library steps to elevate the crow. To this, Mariah walked forward as though to a gibbet, eyes straight ahead, feeling the stares of the others on her. As she climbed the steps, she glimpsed Mr. Browne and Mr. Crawford entering. The headdress and wooden wedge atop her head seemed suddenly to weigh several stones. The wheeled steps shifted slightly as she sat atop them, making Mariah feel dizzy and disoriented.

Why, oh, why did I agree to do this? Even wearing the peacock's feather mask over her eyes, she felt far too exposed. Vulnerable. *Just get through this,* she told herself. For Captain Bryant's sake. Even though he had not asked it of her.

Miss Hutchins took her place to the left of the staging area, where candelabra stood on the pianoforte to illumine her script. She read in precise, clipped tones that left Mariah actually appreciating Mrs. Pitt for her speaking voice—if nothing else.

She began, "A crow, having stolen a bit of cheese from a cottage window, perched herself high in a tree and held the choice morsel in her beak."

Mariah woodenly swiveled her beak from side to side. Mr. Browne grinned. Helen Mabry laughed. Miss Forsythe, she noticed, did not even smile. Sitting beside her, Mr. Crawford glanced at his intended's stony face, then away, expression inscrutable.

Captain Parker came into the room, late, setting his sword near the door and exchanging it for a glass of brandy, which he downed in one swallow.

Miss Hutchins continued, "A fox, seeing this, longed to possess the tasty morsel himself, and so devised a wily plan to acquire it. He would compliment the crow on her beauty."

Walking forward, Parker proclaimed, "That has certainly loosened the lips of many a gullible female throughout history. Has it not, Crawford?"

Strained looks were exchanged by several audience members. Miss Mabry lifted a hand to stifle a giggle.

Captain Bryant stepped forward, but Captain Parker pushed him aside, grabbing the tail from his waistband and swishing it in his hand like a lady's fan. He strode purposely toward the steps and stood beneath the "tree." He was tall enough that Mariah sat only a head or so above him.

"Parker," Bryant hissed. "Step aside. You are late and you are drunk. I relieve you of your—"

Parker cut him off. "I have not wasted five whole minutes learning my lines for you to usurp my role." He beamed up at Mariah. "I shan't miss my opportunity to flatter Miss . . . our mysterious Miss Crow."

Parker launched into his first line with great zeal, throwing out an arm with dramatic flair. "How handsome is the crow!"

He reached up and traced a finger over the deep blue fabric covering Mariah's legs. She started.

"I never observed it before, but your feathers are more delectable than ever I saw in my life."

Parker's fingers raked her shin. Mariah tried to move her leg aside, but there was nowhere to go. What was the man doing? How drunk was he?

"Parker!" Bryant hissed again.

"And what a fine shape and graceful body you have." Parker's eyes traveled over Mariah's figure, leg to neck and back again, and Mariah felt herself flush in shame.

Miss Hutchins took up her cue. "And so he flattered the crow, never meaning a word of it. The crow, tickled by his very civil language, nestled and preened, and hardly knew where she was."

Is that not precisely what had happened? Mariah thought. She had allowed herself to be tricked into this situation by his flattery. *Foolish, gullible girl!*

Captain Parker sighed dramatically. "If *only* you had a tolerable voice. And if only your character were as fair as your complexion."

Mariah's ears rang. *Had he really said that?* Her vision blurred. She was trapped before a hostile crowd at her own hanging, all those condemning eyes beaded on her. She couldn't even flee. Any sudden movement and she would fall from her perch.

Parker went on with his own version, clearly relishing her discomfort. "Oh, if only your purity were equal to your beauty, you would deservedly be considered the queen of birds."

Several in the audience began to murmur and squirm in their chairs, but Miss Hutchins, assumedly hearing only the gist of the line and finding its cadence matching the script, blithely opened her mouth to continue.

Before she could, Captain Bryant strode up on the stage. "That is enough, Parker."

Parker shrugged, untroubled. "Why should Crawford have all the fun? Why should you?"

"Parker. I am warning you." He grabbed the man's arm, but Parker shook it off.

While the two men argued, Mariah climbed stiffly down the steps. She could hardly see for the feathers and the tears. The headdress fell to the floor as she hurried blindly toward the door. Toward escape.

"Miss Aubrey," Mr. Hart's whisper met her at the door. "I am so sorry. I never imagined Parker was such a fiend."

She remembered she was wearing his peacock mask. She pulled it off, pressed it into his hands, and pushed past him into the hall. Her unsteady strides became a choppy running gait as she flew across the marble floor and out the front door.

Matthew stared at Captain Parker. This man he thought he knew. Even admired. What an unfeeling dog he really was. "Mr. Hart," he called. "Toss Captain Parker his sword."

"Matthew . . ." Hart protested.

He barked, "Now, Lieutenant."

Swearing under his breath, Hart picked up the sword from where it leaned near the door and lofted it toward Parker.

Parker caught it with practiced ease. "Time for 'The Lion and the Bear' already?" He smirked. "This time your opponent shall not be lame, Bryant. Are you certain you wish to risk real blades in place of wooden toys?"

In reply, Matthew drew his sword.

The clash of steel echoed through the room. The pantomime replaced by a very real drama.

"Gentlemen, please," Miss Hutchins said. "You will both regret this in the morning."

Hart muttered, "If they live that long."

"I am happy to fight, Bryant," Parker said glibly. "But I must know why you do. Have you bedded her as well?"

"No." *Clang.* Matthew struck hard. "I fight to stop your libelous tongue. Why should you want to hurt her? What has she ever done to you—ruined a stupid party?"

"It is what she has *not* done to me that raises my ire. The light-skirt had the nerve to rebuff me."

Bile seared Matthew's throat. "You vile snake. You are no gentleman, sir." He charged forward, but Parker dodged and parried.

Isabella threw up her hands. "You will fight over her? For her honor? When we all know she hasn't got any?"

Matthew clenched his jaw. But before he could speak, Crawford said, "Stay out of this, Belle, please."

She whirled on him. "Why should I? It affects me more than it does either of them. After all, it was my future husband she slept with."

Crawford leapt to his feet, throwing his chair back with such force that it careened into a table and sent a large vase shattering to the floor.

"Enough!" he shouted. It was such a raw, plaintive cry that all froze, shocked into silence.

"*I* went to Miss Aubrey's room that night. *I* told her I would make a huge, scandalous scene if she did not let me in. That is the only reason she consented. She trusted me, foolish girl! And I took advantage of that trust."

The confirming words hit Matthew like a punch in the gut, and he barely resisted the urge to deliver just such a blow to James Crawford.

Crawford paced the floor while the others looked on, mesmerized as though watching a Shakespearean tragedy, the fight forgotten.

"I told her I loved her, and she no doubt believed me. I certainly wanted her, like a child who wants what is forbidden him." He ran a hand through his hair. "For myself, I would have married her long ago. But my life is not my own. My father pulls the strings, and I dance to his will. He decreed I must marry Miss Forsythe."

Isabella's face hardened, but Crawford hastened to add, "And what should have been a sweet mandate was not enough for me. After I returned from the continent, I decided I had to see Miss Aubrey one more time. Alone. After all, I had allowed her to think I would marry her. I had written to her, many love letters. . . ."

Helen Mabry gasped. Everyone knew letters from a single man to a woman were tantamount to a proposal.

Crawford slapped his chest. "*I* am the scoundrel. Me. Not her! But that is not how *polite* society works, is it? The man can do as he pleases as long as he does not commit the unpardonable sin of breaking an engagement. Dashed unfair if you ask me, but nobody has. You were all too busy condemning her."

He turned a flinty face toward Matthew and squared his shoulders. "If you want to fight somebody, fight me. If you want to run me through with the sword, have ready. I deserve it for what I have done to her." Crawford spread his arms, exposing his chest and belly. Offering himself.

Matthew stood where he was, stymied by the strange, sickening scene. Parker too stood transfixed. Taking advantage of their indecision, Hart and Browne strode forward as one, each grasping one of Parker's arms. Hart jerked the sword from his hand.

Miss Forsythe's normally porcelain complexion was florid with mortification. Her steely indignation wilted, and she buried her face in her hands. Ann Hutchins hurried to her side while young Helen Mabry merely stared at them all, dumbfounded.

Matthew pressed his eyes closed. *Mariah*, he thought, and found himself running from the room after her, even though he knew it wasn't his place to do so. But if Crawford was just going to stand there like some maudlin martyr and the ingrate Parker make no move to apologize, then he would go after Mariah himself. Find her, try to console her, if such a thing were possible. To apologize for his own part in a charade gone terribly, terribly wrong.

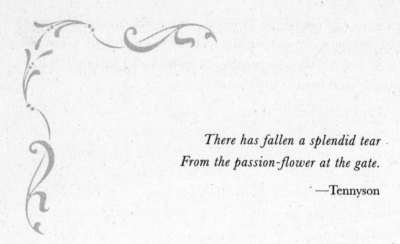

There has fallen a splendid tear
From the passion-flower at the gate.

—Tennyson

chapter 33

atthew sprinted down the drive and turned up the gatehouse lane. Seeing Mariah ahead of him, he called, "Miss Aubrey. Wait. Please."

She kept walking, weeping, voice shaking. "You said I would play my role and nothing would happen. There and gone."

He struggled to keep pace beside her, already out of breath from his run. "I know. I am very sorry. I never dreamed Parker would do such a thing."

"You said no one would say anything to me or about me. I would just perform the stupid play so your Miss Forsythe would be happy and that was all."

"I know, I know. I am an idiot. I never suspected Parker's plan."

"I should have." She shook her head. "I should have known. He was too kind, too flattering. It seems so obvious now. I am the most foolish girl alive."

He snagged her sleeve, halting her at last. "No, Parker is the imbecile. And Crawford, for that matter. You ran out before he delivered his dramatic monologue."

She covered her face with her hands. "I cannot stand to hear more."

He gently pried one of her hands away and clasped it in his. "This you will want to hear. He confessed everything. His ungentlemanlike behavior, his leading you to believe he would marry you, your innocence in arranging the unchaperoned meeting, since he—"

"I am not innocent." She shook her head, tears still falling. "I should never have opened my door. Never have trusted him. I should have resisted. . . ."

"Hush. None of us is perfectly innocent." He squeezed her hand. "I am not. We have all failed in one way or another. The point is, Crawford admitted he was to blame. Is that not good news?"

She held out her other hand, palm up, and belatedly he fished out and handed her his handkerchief. She wiped her eyes and nose. "It makes no real difference, but yes, I am relieved to hear it." She gave a ragged sigh, then added flatly, "I suppose this will clear the way for you and Miss Forsythe." Clearly, she did not relish the notion.

He had not thought of that. How strange that she should. "I don't know. Crawford seems determined to obey his father's wishes, and if Miss Forsythe will still have him . . ."

"Perhaps she won't. Perhaps she will now see him for what he really is. And what a superior man you are."

Was he? At the moment Matthew did not feel superior. He felt like a failure. Weak. It was on the tip of his tongue to say that Mariah was the superior woman, but he refrained. How muddled was his thinking. All he knew was that he wanted to take Mariah in his arms and kiss away her tears and send the rest of them packing. But after Crawford's treatment of her, that was the last thing he should do. And might Miss Aubrey be right? Might this not be the breakthrough he had been waiting for?

He cleared his throat. "Again, I apologize, Miss Aubrey. If there is anything I can do, you must let me know. In the meantime, I had better return to the house before my guests do more damage."

Damage, thought Mariah, watching the captain walk away, *is the perfect word for it.*

Dixon and Martin sat up with her, succoring her with hot tea, savory biscuits, and unconditional friendship. Dixon listened with tears and understanding as Mariah related the events of the evening— Martin, with mounting anger sparking in his normally placid eyes.

"Shall I avenge you, Miss Mariah? Find that scallywag and give him his due?"

"No, Martin, but thank you for the offer."

He patted her hand with his callused paw. "You know I would help you if I could."

She nodded. Tears tightened her throat, making it dangerous to speak. No wonder Aunt Fran had prized Jeremiah Martin. What stalwart, loyal friends he and Dixon were.

Mariah bid the two good-night, leaving them talking quietly in the kitchen.

Knowing she would not find sleep for several hours, Mariah settled herself in her bedchamber with paper and quill. She felt she needed to write, to purge from her mind the night's disaster—and the misdeeds at the root of it—on the scapegoat shoulders of Lydia Sorrow.

Even as he kissed and held her she knew she should protest, shove him away, sound the alarm.

But she did not.

And soon, it was too late. She had given in. Given all.

The door burst open. Not the adjoining door as she had feared, but the main door. Light from a candle lamp arced into the room. Lydia winced under its glare.

And the glare of the woman holding it.

"I wondered how long it would take you to sneak off to her."

"Shh . . . Cynthia, calm down."

"Calm down! When I find you in another woman's bed?"

"Lower your voice, madam."

"I will not. On the contrary. By morning the whole house shall hear of this. The whole county. I don't know which of us you have hurt more!"

With that the young woman turned and stormed from the room.

Lydia sat up, sweating and chilled, stunned and sickened by the scene. They had been discovered. She—compromised. Would the woman really tell everyone? If so, Lydia would be ruined in every sense of the word. Only a quick marriage would quiet the scandal and cruel gossip. And then, only in time.

Lydia recognized the woman and knew she had briefly met her, but in her state of mind could not recall her name. "Who is she?" she breathed.

A cold pall shrouded his features, turning down every plane, every line of his beloved face until she barely recognized him. His lip curled, and he refused to meet her gaze.

"My wife."

Mariah reread the last line. Then she changed it to read *My future wife.* The phrase was more fitting. At least for now.

There was no breakthrough with Miss Forsythe that night. She took to her room before Matthew returned to the house, sequestered with her bosom friend, Miss Hutchins. At least, Matthew consoled himself, she had closeted herself away from Crawford as well. He saw the man in the salon after midnight, head in his hands.

Matthew spent the night alternatively praying Isabella would come to him and wishing she would go.

In the morning he arose, dressed quickly, and took himself down to the breakfast room. But Isabella didn't appear. He learned from one of the footmen that she had requested breakfast sent up to her on a tray.

Captain Parker and Mr. Browne left early, and the others soon began packing up as well, instead of seeing the final week through as originally planned. Only Millicent Mabry, recovered from the oysters, seemed disappointed to see the party end.

Mrs. Parker, who had attended Millicent during her brief illness and had therefore missed the drama of the previous night, was clearly piqued with her son, but only, it seemed, because he had once again failed to take notice of Miss Hutchins as she'd hoped. Matthew felt sorry for the woman, disappointed as she was over her wastrel son. He thanked her warmly for her assistance and promised himself to visit his own mother at the first opportunity.

Matthew had just stepped back inside after seeing off the Miss Mabrys, when he heard raised voices upstairs and went up to see what the matter was. Midway along the corridor, he saw Crawford at the door of Isabella's bedchamber, hand on the latch, face pressed close, whining and cajoling. Matthew wondered if he was employing the same tactics he'd used to gain entry into Miss Aubrey's room. Miss Forsythe, it seemed, was more immune to his persuasion.

"Isabella, this is ridiculous!" he hissed. "Open the door so we can talk."

"No. Go away," came her muffled response.

Matthew was surprised that hearing Miss Forsythe rebuff the man was not more satisfying than it was. The raised voices grated on him, and he turned and loped down the stairs. He took himself back outside, to breathe in fresh air and solitude.

Several minutes later Mr. Crawford left the house. Alone. The sheepish man avoided his gaze as he passed and disappeared into the stable. Ten minutes or so later, the groom threw wide the door, and Crawford emerged on his horse and trotted away. His adversary was retreating. Matthew waited for the surge of elation to wash over him. It did not come.

Eleven o'clock. Noon. One. Still no sign of Miss Forsythe. Was she avoiding him as well? Likely she blamed him for the debacle, since he had allowed Miss Aubrey to participate. Or perhaps she was embarrassed and defensive over her connection with Crawford but was too proud to admit it. Whatever her feelings, it seemed she and Miss Hutchins planned to stay in her room until everyone else had gone.

Matthew was in the library, writing a letter to his mother, when a soft knock interrupted his train of thought. He glanced up to see the fair hair of Miss Forsythe as she poked her head inside the room.

"May I?"

"Of course. Come in." Matthew rose and stepped around the desk, his heart beating oddly, irregularly, in a strange combination of hope and dread.

She stopped a few yards from him and looked uncharacteristically timid—eyes furtive, hands clasped.

To break the silence, Matthew said, "Mr. Crawford has taken his leave."

"Yes, I know. I sent him away."

Matthew felt his brows rise in question and waited, holding his breath.

"I am through with him." She glided forward. "I know now it is you I want. You." Before he could respond, she threw her arms around his neck, pulled his head down, and kissed him fervently.

His body and brain reacted with a collision of desire and revulsion. He wrenched his mouth from hers. "Miss Forsythe, have you forgotten your intended so soon?"

Again she pressed her body to his, but this time instead of desire, pure irritation rose up within him. He grasped her elbows and thrust her from him. "Isabella, look. I know you were hurt, and you probably want to injure him in return. But not with me. It is too late for us."

She slowly shook her head, incredulous. "Did you not beg me to break my engagement with Crawford and marry you instead? I thought you and I had an understanding."

An understanding? Matthew's mind whirled and rebelled. Had they?

No! But if she had broken her engagement with Crawford because he had offered marriage . . .

Isabella's eyes glistened. "Will you betray me as well?"

Her pained words stilled Matthew, rendered him stunned, speechless. He loved Mariah, though he had fought it for some time. But *was* he duty-bound to Isabella? His mind rehearsed all the things he had said to her in trying to win her. Yes, any woman might reasonably assume . . . *Oh, dear God. What have I done? Forgive my foolish pride!*

He said gruffly, "You have broken your engagement?"

She squared her shoulders. "I am through with James Crawford. He's a fool. Why do you think I tarried so long in marrying him?"

"I don't know. I thought you had your doubts about the man."

She looked up at him expectantly. "Well then, was I not right to doubt?"

Matthew was filled with the dire angst he always felt after a bloody battle. What was wrong with him? This—she—was what he had wanted. Worked for. Why did he not take her in his arms and beg her to marry him? Why did he feel he should run far and fast and never look back?

"Miss Forsythe. Would you excuse me for a moment?"

Her eyes dimmed. "Of course. Is everything all right?"

He muttered, "Just, ah, give me a few minutes, please." He turned and walked from the room, leaving her standing there, clearly surprised and concerned by his reaction. In the hall, he strode toward the front door, as though his legs had already decided to make good on his impulse to flee.

Pausing, he ran a hand across his face and diverted to the front windows instead. There he stared out at the gardens of Windrush Court. He was so close. . . . Everything he'd thought he wanted was waiting in the palm of his hand. His nerves jangled. His stomach turned sour. He fisted his hands at his sides, whether to capture the dream or crush it, he was not certain.

Hoofbeats rumbled into his awareness. Through the wavy glass,

Matthew saw a horse and rider galloping up the drive, raising a cloud of dust. Matthew frowned and stepped outside. James Crawford rode up, horse heaving and lathered. Whip marks crisscrossed its hindquarters. Angered at the sight, Matthew strode toward the stable, calling for the groom.

Dismounting, Crawford snarled, "Where is she?"

"In the library. This poor animal looks half dead."

"I rode above twelve miles before turning back."

"With no thought to your horse?"

"I had someone more important on my mind." Without awaiting a reply, Crawford barreled across the drive and up the stairs to the house.

The young groom scurried out, and Matthew bid him to care for the ill-used creature. Then he followed Crawford inside.

When Matthew stepped into the library, Isabella pulled away from Crawford and stepped to Matthew's side, grasping his arm.

Crawford frowned. "Isabella. What are you doing?"

"I am returning to Captain Bryant, as you see."

Crawford's mouth was a hard line. "You and I are engaged to be married."

She narrowed her eyes. "An error I intend to redress."

"You would not dare. I have waited above a year for you—given you plenty of time to get over your pet about last summer. I'll not let you go now without a fight. Break our engagement and I will sue your father for breach of promise."

"It is all about the money for you, is it not? You don't really care about me. Never have."

"That is not true, Belle, and you know it. Yes, my father forced me in the beginning, but I have come to love you. Would I have waited all this time, passing up dozens of pretty, suitable girls, otherwise?"

She lifted her chin. "Go and marry one of your pretty, suitable girls. I don't care."

"You don't mean that. You are merely vexed. I know I acted stupidly, and I am sorry for it."

Listening to the lovers quarrel, the clouds parted in Matthew's brain and the truth dawned upon him in a wave of relief. He took a deep breath. "Miss Forsythe, I am relieved to hear you are still engaged to Mr. Crawford, for you see, I have become quite attached to Miss Aubrey."

She turned to him, mouth parted, eyes wide. "Miss Aubrey? After what she did? She is nothing but a—"

Matthew held up a warning hand. "Careful, Isabella. I will not hear a word against her. Do I make myself clear?"

Crawford's brows dipped low. "Bryant, I say. Must you—"

Matthew ignored him. "How would you like it, Miss Forsythe, if I told the world what you did upon greeting me a few minutes ago behind closed doors? And you an engaged woman?"

Her neck and cheeks suffused scarlet. Her face was far less pretty when wearing a deep frown. "You would not do such an ungentlemanly thing."

"Only if provoked. Only if I continue to hear whispers about Miss Aubrey."

"But . . . you tried to convince me . . . And I . . ."

"You have already wasted four years, *Belle*." Matthew spoke archly as relief began loosening his tongue. "Fortunately you were young then, and so you have not quite lost your bloom." He nodded toward Crawford. "But lose this one and have to start all over, with *your* reputation . . . ? I shudder to think of your chances of marrying well."

She slowly shook her head. "I was willing to defy my father to marry you. And bear the social taint of being called a jilt, and you have the nerve to throw it back in my face?"

He winced and said more formally, "I do apologize, Miss Forsythe. It was wrong of me to try to come between you and Crawford. But . . . you never even broke the engagement. I don't think you have any right to be offended."

Isabella's voice shook. "I wanted to be certain you meant what you said, but I see I was wrong to believe you a man of honor. Perhaps my father was right about you all along."

Matthew shrugged. "Perhaps he was. My wounded pride festered until I thought I would explode. I became fiercely determined to prove him and you, and everyone, wrong."

The image of Mariah's face filled his mind's eye. "It blinded me to my growing feelings for another—a generous, talented, and beautiful woman."

Isabella whispered, "You would choose her over me?"

Matthew nodded. "I am sorry if it hurts you, but yes. A thousand times over." To himself he added, *If she will have me.*

For a moment Miss Forsythe stared at him. Then she drew herself up and managed a tremulous smile. "Well then, Captain, I wish you happy." She turned on her heel. "Come, James. It is past time we took our leave."

Matthew looked on from the portico as Miss Forsythe, Miss Hutchins, and a sheepish Mr. Crawford rode away together in the Forsythe carriage, Crawford's horse tethered behind. He felt an empty lowness, but not the defeat he would have expected to feel even a fortnight ago.

He had been such a fool. Would Mariah even believe he loved *her* after he had so doggedly pursued another? He would need to wait; bide his time. Not launch from one proposal to the next. He would need to prove himself trustworthy, his intentions honorable. Especially after what she had gone through at the hands of another man. He shoved the thought—more painful than ever—to the back of his mind.

Hart appeared at his side, leaning against one of the portico columns as the carriage disappeared from view. He said nothing for a few moments, nothing to compete with the sounds of wheels and horse hooves. But when birdsong once again dominated the air, he asked, "Now what?"

Matthew sighed. "Now we relax and enjoy ourselves." He glanced at his friend. "Fancy a horse race?"

Hart's eyes searched his face, apparently relieved to find his spirits intact, and grinned like a lad. "Aye, aye, Captain!"

As they trudged toward the stables, Matthew realized he was glad it was over. He had prepared, entered battle, and fought hard. Victory had been in his sights and in his grasp, but he had read the warning signals and retreated just in time. He had not landed the prize, but at least there were few casualties, and he himself had survived remarkably unscathed.

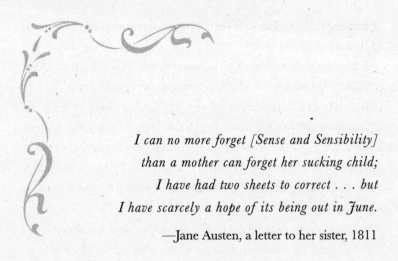

I can no more forget [Sense and Sensibility]
than a mother can forget her sucking child;
I have had two sheets to correct . . . but
I have scarcely a hope of its being out in June.

—Jane Austen, a letter to her sister, 1811

chapter 34

*S*itting in the drawing room, Dixon reviewed what Mariah had written so far in *The Tale of Lydia Sorrow.* Her finger traced each line as she silently read—Mariah had no wish to read this particular novel aloud. Anxious for her friend's reaction, Mariah paced behind the chair, too nervous to sit.

At one point Dixon turned to give Mariah a significant look over her spectacles. She then lifted her drawing pencil to cross something out. Mariah glanced over her shoulder as Dixon ran a line through:

His hand cupped her shoulder, then slowly slid down her arm,
grazing the side of her body, the swell of her, as he did so.

Mariah blushed, glad her brother Henry was not on hand for this reading.

Reaching the end, Dixon lowered the page, removed her spectacles, and rubbed her eyes.

Mariah gave an anticipatory wince. "What do you think?"

"Well . . ." Dixon paused. "It is certainly . . . painful to read."

Mariah huffed. "Try living it."

"Do you really want to go through with this?" Dixon's eyes were wide with concern. "I can certainly see that young women might find such a cautionary tale edifying, but . . ."

"I know." Mariah sighed. "I don't like it either. I grow weary of regret and misery."

"But did you not promise Mr. Crosby a third manuscript?"

"I did. And he assures me cautionary tales are all the crack in London. He named several that have sold quite briskly. *The Reformed Coquette, The Unfortunate Magdalen* . . ."

Dixon frowned. "Lydia Sorrow is not a Magdalen, and neither are you."

"I know. But I cannot help thinking that perhaps enough cautionary tales have already been written." She squeezed her eyes closed. "And why did I not heed a one of them?"

Dixon laid a hand on her arm, expression earnest. "Mariah. God is far more forgiving than people are, or than we are to ourselves. Society may never forgive and certainly never lets anyone forget. But God will forgive you if you ask Him. Better yet, He will forget it ever happened."

Mariah thought it sounded too good to be true. She certainly believed God forgave others. Why was it so hard to believe He would forgive her?

She and Dixon laid aside *Lydia Sorrow* for the time being and retired to the kitchen for tea.

Martin already had the table set and the tea steeping. As the ladies sat, he handed Mariah a letter.

"From Captain Bryant. He stopped by while you two were, em, occupied."

"We wouldn't have minded the interruption, Martin. Not for Captain Bryant."

"I offered to let you know he was here, but he said not to disturb you. Just asked me to give you the note."

That gave Mariah pause. Had Captain Bryant foreseen or even hoped he would not meet with her in person? She unfolded the letter. In the few hastily written lines, he explained that he was going to visit his parents and an old friend. Mariah wondered if the old friend was Miss Forsythe. But that was odd terminology to use for the woman he hoped to marry. Perhaps it was a fellow officer, she told herself, wishing he had specified.

She wondered if Captain Bryant had gotten the second chance with Miss Forsythe he so desired. He must have, she reasoned. Otherwise, would she not have seen him? She wondered, too, what might have happened between Matthew and herself had things gone differently.

He does admire me, she thought. Or at least he had, before he learned about Mr. Crawford. Even so, they were friends, and she was quite sure he found her attractive as well.

But they had known one another only a few months—one sunlit summer—whereas Matthew had pined for Isabella Forsythe for years. *She* would win, Mariah knew. She hoped Isabella truly loved him, would be good and faithful to him, endeavor to deserve him. Mariah wanted Matthew to be happy—truly she did. And now, it appeared he would be.

She was glad for him. She was. At the same time, she was perfectly miserable.

ॐ

Now that Windrush Court was free of "interlopers," as Martin described them, the inhabitants of the gatehouse, as well as Mr. and Mrs. Strong, Mr. Phelps, and no doubt the other servants, exhaled a unified sigh of relief. The grounds were once again theirs to roam and more leisure time theirs to enjoy, now that the extra work of entertaining a houseful of guests had abated.

But Mariah felt deflated. Like one of Dixon's bread loaves which had failed to rise. After all the highs and lows of the preceding months, now all was quiet. It was like the letdown after Epiphany, staring down the long dark throat of winter with nothing to look forward to, nothing on the horizon.

Her second book would be printed soon. That was something, she reminded herself. Henry had hand-delivered proof sheets of *Daughters of Brighton*, and Martin had offered to return them to Oxford as soon as she was finished with them. Certainly Mr. Crosby wouldn't cancel the printing so close to the book's release, not over one disparaging remark from a fraud like Hugh Prin-Hallsey. Besides, she and her publisher were protected by her *nom de plume*. As long as society did not know she was Lady A, her reputation should not affect the book. How could it? She did wonder whether he would want a third book from her. A third book she had yet to finish, in any case.

Most deflating of all, she admitted to herself, was the absence of Captain Bryant. Had he decided to sever ties with her after Mr. Crawford's confession?

Mariah was surprised to learn that Mr. Hart had not gone with him, until she recalled seeing Lizzy and Mr. Hart out walking several times recently, as well as Hart's wish to introduce Lizzy to his mother. Mariah wondered if he had proposed the journey yet. And if Mrs. Pitt would even allow Lizzy the time off to go with him.

At all events, Captain Bryant was gone, and she had not even told him about Hugh Prin-Hallsey's latest scheme to raise money. Even after the confrontation with Mr. Crosby, Hugh had remained adamant that he had every right to publish and profit from *Euphemia's Return*. Mr. Crosby said he would forgo legal action if Hugh would rescind all claim to the copyright and return the advance. Mariah imagined that money was long spent. How would Hugh repay it? Or would he refuse and risk legal trouble? She doubted Mr. Crosby would really take him to court and allow the public to learn that he had been fooled. Mariah did not know how it would turn out and was glad to leave it to the Crosby and Company solicitors.

Little Maggie sat perched on a stool at the worktable while Martin showed her how to make ginger biscuits. Maggie wore Mariah's apron and a smear of flour on her cheek and another on her chin. She looked utterly adorable, as did Martin as he doted on her.

Mariah sat at the kitchen table, correcting the proof sheets of *Daughters of Brighton*. In all truth, she was making very little progress, distracted as she was by the others. If she really wanted to be productive, she would take herself up to her solitary sitting room. But what her soul craved was the warm companionship of the kitchen.

Dixon sat at the table across from her, reading aloud from an old volume of *The Golden Prince Adventures*. Attempting it, at any rate.

"The young stowaway thought the ship would keel right over, so hard did the wind push at her sails. The deck took on the steep pitch of an icy sledding hill and was just as slippery. Would his life never be even-keeled again?

" 'Hard-a-starboard!' the one-armed captain bellowed to the quartermaster at the wheel. 'Steer small, blast you!'

"At the captain's signal, the second lieutenant shouted, 'Fire as you will, boys!'

"The ship shuddered, thundered, and pulsed as the nine-pounders went off, one after another blasting the looming pirate ship. Answering fire was returned—musket balls falling like deadly hail upon the deck until Tom was certain he was about to meet his Maker.

"Why had he thought life at sea would be all fun and adventure? Why had he found his father's workshop so stifling, so boring? What Tom would give to be home again.

"The bosun towering above him looked up as an eighteen-pounder arced down in their direction. He muttered, 'For what we are about to receive . . .' before he was—"

Dixon paused.

" '—blown to bloody bits.' "

She swallowed.

" 'As the mizzenmast behind him gave way, the captain scowled and shouted—' "

With a glance at innocent little Maggie, Dixon amended, " 'Oh, fiddlesticks!' "

Martin chuckled. "You needn't read it, Miss Susan. I realize it is not the customary fare of ladies."

Maggie grinned up at Dixon. "The first biscuits are ready. Will you taste one?"

Dixon set aside the book and rose. "I shall, though my appetite has suddenly deserted me for some reason." She gave Martin a telling look.

"Well, then leave off reading and help us cut the next batch." He smiled at her across the worktable. "Though I must say you have a lovely reading voice, Miss Susan. I could listen to you forever."

Dixon glanced up sharply, clearly stunned by the compliment. But Martin looked down, busily helping Maggie roll the biscuit dough. Was that a faint blush in the man's cheeks, or merely the heat from the oven?

Mariah bit back a grin. She asked, "Why did you stop writing, Martin?"

He shrugged. "I suppose I ran out of ideas. I had only that one voyage with Captain Prince, after all. Fran said I should write my own stories and I meant to, but for some reason, I found it difficult to write once she married Prin-Hallsey and we moved to Windrush Court. Oppressive place. Hammersmith always breathing down my neck. I lost the 'muse,' as they say. Not sure I shall ever find it again."

Wistfully, Mariah said, "I hope you shall."

A knock on the open kitchen door brought all their heads around. There stood Albert Phelps, bucket in hand.

"Oh . . . hello," Mr. Phelps began, taking in the homey scene, glancing from Dixon to Martin and back again. "Miss Dixon, I was come to help you pick your beans, but I see you are . . . otherwise engaged."

Mariah felt awkward tension rise on the fragrances of warm bread and ginger. Was, perhaps, the gardener aware for the first time of the competition he had in the form of Jeremiah Martin?

Two days later, after Martin had gone to Oxford and back with Mariah's proof sheets, Mr. Phelps returned to the gatehouse to claim Dixon for a stroll. Mariah took herself out onto the front lawn, to sit under her favorite tree and enjoy the fading warmth of the late August day.

Lizzy Barnes came striding across the road, flushed and agitated, a shabby valise in one hand and a twine-wrapped bundle in the other. "I have done it."

"Done what?"

"Told Mrs. Pitt I won't stay and work for her anymore—not when her son is threatening me."

"Threatening you?" Mariah stood and opened the door, shepherding Lizzy inside.

"Oh, he doesn't mean it. John's not violent, really. But he's seen me out walking with Mr. Hart, and he's devilish vexed. I tried to explain gentle-like that I like him as a friend and all, but not the way he likes me. And not the way I like Mr. Hart. But John wouldn't listen. He kept trying to kiss me, until I finally had no choice but to slap him. Hard." Lizzy sighed. "Poor John. He's jealous and desperate-sad and angry all at once. Mrs. Pitt is just plain angry."

"Oh, Lizzy. I am very sorry to hear it. You did the right thing though. I only wish I had a place for George too. Perhaps I could ask Captain Bryant if Windrush Court needs another groom or hall boy."

"Thank you, miss. George says he can take care of himself, but I do worry."

"Of course you do."

Several minutes later, she left Lizzy to settle herself in the narrow pantry off the kitchen that would be hers—she had refused the upstairs sitting room as too fine. But in a month or two, when the weather turned chill, Mariah would have to insist that Lizzy move abovestairs so Martin could have the pantry.

Dixon returned from her walk with Mr. Phelps just as Mariah set a teapot and four cups on the small table. "Lizzy has come at last," Mariah whispered, wondering if the girl had fallen asleep already, so quiet was her room.

But Dixon did not smile. In fact she looked quite troubled as she tied on her apron and began wiping down the worktable, although it was already perfectly clean.

Mariah watched her friend's distracted, jerky movements, then stepped to her side. Touching her arm, she asked quietly, "What is it?"

Dixon inhaled deeply and released a shuddering breath. "Albert Phelps has asked me to marry him."

Mariah should not have been surprised, but somehow she was. She had thought, perhaps, that Dixon had come to prefer Martin.

"He is a widower, you know," Dixon continued. "And from what Mrs. Strong says, the first Mrs. Phelps was a happy woman indeed. I don't doubt he would make a good husband, but . . ."

"But?"

"I . . . I don't want to leave you, Mariah."

"Dixon! We've talked about this. You mustn't forgo happiness on my account. You would be very near in the gardener's cottage, and we have Lizzy now, so we could make do. Though, of course, I should be loath to lose you. . . ." Mariah's words trailed off as she studied her friend's wan expression. "That is not the real reason you hesitate, is it?"

Susan Dixon shook her head.

A few moments later, Martin came into the kitchen, face grim. Dixon stiffened and began noisily rearranging pots and kettles.

Martin must have heard, Mariah realized. Perhaps Mr. Phelps had been too excited to keep the news to himself.

Mariah quickly excused herself. Martin's low, plaintive "Susan. Miss Dixon . . ." followed Mariah into the drawing room.

"You would be a fool to forgo a future with Albert Phelps, with his sunny cottage, secure post, and easygoing ways. If he were not a good man, I wouldn't say it, but he is. Much as I wish . . . Miss Dixon—"

The ting and clang of pots and pans finally ceased. Dixon objected, "You were to call me Susan."

"Perhaps the time for Christian names has passed," he said, resigned. "I have little to offer you. I haven't a proper job. Haven't a home. I haven't even two hands to offer you."

"I don't care about that."

"Well, I do. You deserve better."

Poor Martin, Mariah thought, taking herself upstairs. Stoic, noble Martin. What would Dixon do?

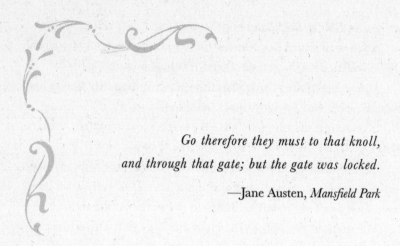

Go therefore they must to that knoll,
and through that gate; but the gate was locked.

—Jane Austen, *Mansfield Park*

chapter 35

hen they had not seen Maggie for three days in a row, Dixon became concerned. She had grown quite attached to the little girl over the past few months. And while laundry or kitchen duty sometimes kept Maggie away now and again, the girl always seemed to manage to come by every few days for a visit, a biscuit, or a brief flute lesson with Martin.

Dixon decided she would walk over to Honora House and check on the girl. Lizzy offered to accompany her, saying she knew all the places shy Maggie liked to hide and play. Mariah certainly hoped the little girl had not taken ill.

The thought of illness reminded her of Miss Amy, and Mariah asked the two to check on the Miss Merryweathers while they were there.

Half an hour later, Lizzy ran back through the front door of the gatehouse. Dixon came puffing across the road behind her, arm against her bosom. Mariah had never seen Susan Dixon run and certainly not in such an undignified manner.

"What is it?" Mariah asked Lizzy. "Is it Miss Amy?"

"No, miss." Lizzy leaned over and rested her hands on her knees, trying to catch her breath.

"Has Maggie taken ill?"

Lizzy shook her head.

Dixon trudged inside. Taking one look at her friend's ashen face, Mariah's voice rose in panic. "Dixon?"

Dixon bracketed her side with her hand. "It's Maggie. . . ." She panted. "Gone."

"Gone?" Mariah's heart lurched. "Not . . . dead."

Dixon shook her head, tears filling her prominent blue eyes. "They have sent her away."

"What? Where?"

Again Dixon shook her head, still breathing hard. "Mrs. Pitt won't say."

"I shall go and speak with her." Mariah turned and strode to the door.

Dixon caught her arm. "Don't. For all her patronizing smiles, she is vexed with you."

"Because I hired Lizzy away from her?"

"That and Captain Prince," Lizzy said. "She was terrible upset when they found that rope. I heard her say it must have been you and your friends what done it."

"You think she did this for revenge?" Mariah shook her head, and the realization coated her innards with dread. It was her fault. If only she had not stuck her nose into the welfare of the man on the roof. If only she had been satisfied to warn Lizzy.

"I am so sorry, Miss Dixon," Mariah said. "So terribly sorry."

"I don't blame you, Mariah. I blame that vile woman."

"Is there nothing to be done?"

A knock sounded on the front door, interrupting them. For a

moment no one moved—they simply stared wide-eyed at one another. Then, taking a deep breath, Mariah opened the door.

Her stomach dropped to see Mrs. Pitt standing there, hands folded primly before her, the plume of her hat swaying in the breeze.

"Mrs. Pitt." Mariah faltered, "We . . . were just speaking of you."

The matron gave a tightlipped smile. "So I divined through your open window."

Embarrassment and irritation warmed Mariah's neck, but Dixon laid a warning hand on her arm.

Mariah stepped back and Mrs. Pitt crossed the threshold. "I shall not stay. I simply came to make a few facts plain to you, Miss Aubrey. I have not been matron for twenty years without learning a few things about controlling the insolent and disobedient."

Mariah seethed. Only Dixon's staying hand kept her from lashing out and telling the woman exactly what she thought of her.

"If you had only stolen Miss Barnes, poisoned her against us, I might have overlooked your interference."

"I will come back, Mrs. Pitt," Lizzy said, voice high and plaintive. "Just return poor Maggie to us."

The woman silenced her with a forefinger and a glare. "And why should I want a disloyal chit like you?" She returned her cold eyes to Mariah. "But when you jeopardize my reputation as an effective matron, that I cannot ignore. Honora House is recompensed for the safekeeping of a certain unstable man. If he should have fallen to his death from that window during your friends' rope stunt, or be seen gallivanting about the parish or even in this particular gatehouse, the board of guardians might very well conclude that I was failing in my duty." She leaned forward, her gaunt face very near Mariah's. "And, Miss Aubrey, I *never* fail in my duty."

Mariah swallowed, barely resisting the urge to step back. "But Captain Prince returned of his own free will."

"Exactly." Mrs. Pitt's thin lips curled in a smug smile. "Which only demonstrates your disregard for the institution and the man's well-being. He knows what is good for him. There is no other place for a man like that. And should any further attempts be made to . . . disturb him, I am afraid I shall have no choice but to retaliate further."

A shiver went up Mariah's spine. "How? What will you do to him?"

"To him? Nothing, so long as the annual stipend is paid. But George Barnes might very well find himself sent to, shall we say, a less hospitable institution, regardless of my son's misguided affections for his sister. And I should hate to think what a cold winter in the workhouse would do to young George's cheery plump cheeks."

Lizzy's voice was hoarse with tears. "Don't, missus. Please, I beg of you."

She ignored Lizzy, her muddy eyes pinning Mariah with venom. "I do hope, Miss Aubrey, that I make myself perfectly clear?"

Not trusting her voice, Mariah merely nodded.

Mrs. Pitt turned on her heel and strode out of the gatehouse.

As soon as Dixon closed the door behind her, Lizzy gave a keening wail, pressing her temples as though to keep her head intact. "Did I not tell you the Pitts were not to be crossed?"

"I am sorry, Lizzy."

"Why did I listen to you? I should have stayed. Put up with John Pitt's rovin' eyes and hands. I must go back. Beg John to persuade her. I'll do anything to protect George. Anything."

"Lizzy, don't. You mustn't sacrifice yourself. We'll think of another way."

Dixon said, "Perhaps someone of influence, like Mr. Prin-Hallsey, might persuade her to tell us where Maggie is."

Mariah shook her head. "Do you think Hugh Prin-Hallsey would help me after I exposed him as a fraud?"

Dixon frowned in thought. "Perhaps the vicar?"

"You are better acquainted with him than I, but I was under the impression he and Mrs. Pitt were closely allied."

Dixon blinked rapidly, trying unsuccessfully to keep tears from rolling down her cheeks. "That poor angel. She has already lost so much, everybody who ever loved her. And now to be abandoned again . . . How lonely and confused she must feel."

Tentatively, Mariah put her hands on her friend's shoulders and, when Dixon didn't stiffen, embraced her gently. By now tears were falling down Mariah's cheeks as well, and Lizzy was sniffling like a child.

Martin shuffled in from plucking their dinner, wiping his hands on a cloth. He looked from one tear-streaked face to another. "What's all this, then?"

Mariah looked at him over Dixon's shoulder. "It's Maggie. They've sent her away."

"What?" His face clouded in shock and grief.

"She may have been sent to another poorhouse," Lizzy said. "Or worse, a workhouse."

"She wouldn't!" Dixon exclaimed, pulling away from Mariah. "Not a defenseless little girl like that."

Lizzy nodded grimly. "She would."

"Which workhouse? Did she say?" Martin asked.

"No." Dixon threw up her hands. "And she refuses to tell us!"

Mariah knew better than to assure Dixon all would be well. For everyone knew what a dire fate the workhouse was. Not only were they hard dismal places more like a prison than a poorhouse, but workhouses were infamous for selling children to textile mills as "pauper apprentices"—cheap labor that basically enslaved a child until she was twenty-one years old. If she lived that long.

Martin strode forward and somehow managed to catch both of Dixon's flailing hands in his single grasp. "Susan, listen to me. We shall find her. Somehow we shall. Do you hear me?"

Dixon looked at him through her tears, her chin trembling. There were answering tears in his eyes as well. "But how?"

❧

After visiting his parents and his old friend Captain McCulloch, Matthew returned to Windrush Court. He felt like a new man, released from the driving quest to prove himself to Miss Forsythe, her father, his father, and society at large. He had an inkling that Mariah Aubrey thought him worthy just as he was and was eager to see her again. He'd had enough of biding his time.

After a bath and a change of clothes, he went directly to the gatehouse. Mariah met him at the kitchen door, tears streaming down her face. His pulse raced in alarm. How forlorn, how tortured she looked. Instinctively, he opened his arms as he might to his sister. Mariah flew into them, like an exhausted bird coming home to roost, and buried her face against his chest.

He wrapped his arms around her trembling body and held her close. "Mariah, what is it? What has happened?"

She lifted her face. "It's Maggie. Mrs. Pitt has sent her away, and it is all my fault."

Matthew started. "But why?"

"Because of Lizzy, and Captain Prince."

Matthew reeled. The woman had sent away that little girl to punish Mariah? Unthinkable! "Did she say as much?"

Mariah nodded and buried her face once more. Gently, he took her shoulders and held her a little from him so he could look at her. Tears pooled in her amber eyes and coursed down her cheeks. His chest ached to see it. He raised his arms and cradled her face in his hands. His thumbs wiped the tears from her cheeks, but they were quickly replaced.

"Dixon cried herself to sleep. You've never heard such a desolate sound. My heart broke to hear it. Why did I have to interfere? Why did I not guess what Mrs. Pitt might do? Even Martin wept to hear the news. Martin!"

Matthew knew the man was fond of the child but had not realized how deep the attachment ran. "It is not your fault, Mariah. If anyone is to blame for that stunt, it is my comrades and me. We were the ones who left that rope as evidence for the woman to find."

"But none of you would ever have known about Captain Prince if I hadn't seen him, hadn't told you and Martin, hadn't asked Mrs. Pitt about him. . . ."

"Nonsense, Mariah. Eventually someone else would have seen him had you not. You were only trying to help."

"No, I was trying to satisfy my horrid curiosity. Solve a mystery. I am so selfish!"

"Mariah. Hush. You are not to blame. We are all in this together now, and I shall do whatever I can to help."

"Will you?"

"Of course," he soothed, though he had no idea what he could do. He smoothed strands of hair from her face, damp with tears, and gently pushed them behind her ears. He leaned forward and placed a chaste kiss on her forehead. And when she did not protest, another on her right temple, then her left, very near the little beauty mark beside her eyebrow.

She leaned into him, placing her hands against his chest, and he was lost. He wrapped one arm around her once more, and with the other hand stroked her face. He lowered his mouth and kissed her upturned nose as he had long been tempted to do, then her damp cheek, tasting the salty sweetness of her skin.

Cradling her chin, he angled her face and lowered his mouth until his lips were very near hers. Dare he? Everything within him longed to kiss her deeply and passionately. But would it be right with her so upset? He knew he ought not take advantage of her emotional state, her need for comfort.

He pulled his hand away in a clenched fist, needing every ounce of self-control to keep from pressing his mouth to hers. Drawing a ragged breath, he forced himself to take a step back. He grasped her hand and led her to her customary seat at the kitchen table. Matthew sat on the other side, not trusting himself to sit beside her just yet. He did not release her hand, however, allowing himself that physical connection across the small table, his fingers holding hers, his thumb stroking the back of her hand.

"Start at the beginning and tell me everything."

Mariah took a deep breath and told him all that happened and all that Mrs. Pitt had said.

At one point, he muttered something unflattering about the matron under his breath, which somehow mollified Mariah, as if it justified her own uncharitable feelings toward the woman.

"In the morning, I shall go and speak with the vicar," Captain Bryant said. "Who else is on the board of guardians?"

"I imagine Hugh Prin-Hallsey, in his father's stead, but he is likely only a member in absentia. Then there is the undersheriff."

"Who is more likely to arrest us than help us, if Mrs. Pitt is so vexed over the old captain's so-called 'escape.' "

Mariah nodded her agreement.

He would start with the vicar.

But late the next morning, Captain Bryant returned from his call at the vicarage, dejected. "He said the matron has every right to expel inmates who are causing problems for other residents, or the institution at large. He said he could ask for a review of her records or even an appeal of her decision by the board, but the next meeting isn't for three weeks."

"That is forever to a child!"

He nodded grimly. "And even then, there is no guarantee the board will rule against their matron over the word of a few meddling neighbors."

"How bleak it sounds."

He pressed her hand. "Don't lose heart. I have not given up. Neither has Martin."

You say the book is indecent. You say I am immodest.
But Sir in the depiction of love, modesty is the
fullness of truth; and decency frankness; and so I must
also be frank with you, and ask that you remove my name
from the title page in all future printings;
"A lady" will do well enough.

—Jane Austen, letter to publisher about *Pride & Prejudice*

chapter 36

When a knock came to the gatehouse door in early September,
Mariah opened it to find George Barnes and a stranger—
a man with a messenger bag slung across one shoulder and behind
him, a lathered horse.

"This is her," George announced proudly. "He couldn't find you,
but I told him I'd show him where you lived." George leaned close
to her and whispered, "Captain Prince says hello. I told him about
Maggie. Devilish vexed he was to hear it too."

The courier eyed the direction printed on the parcel in his hand.
"Miss M. Aubrey?"

"Yes."

"Delivery for you."

"One moment, please." She turned to find her purse, but Dixon appeared at her elbow and handed the young man his due. In turn the courier flipped George a shilling for his trouble.

"Thank you, sir." George beamed.

Mariah thanked the courier and waved good-bye to George. Her pleasure over receiving what must be her second book was dampened by confusion. "This is strange," she said, brow puckering. "Last time Mr. Crosby gave the book to my brother, who in turn delivered it to me in person."

"Well," Dixon said, "I suppose a second book isn't quite the event the first one is."

"True. Still, he has never sent a messenger before."

Mariah took the parcel to the drawing-room table and cut the strings with her penknife. While Dixon hovered beside her, Mariah peeled back the paper. The book within was bound in blue paper-covered boards. The spine bore a white label, which was lettered with the title only. *Daughters of Brighton.* Perfect. Then Mariah lifted the cover.

And froze.

For a moment, Mariah simply stared, shock pulsing through her veins, sweat trickling down her hairline and dampening her palms. She shut the book.

"What is it?" Dixon asked over Mariah's shoulder. "They misspell something?"

Mariah blinked, unconsciously hoping to clear her vision, and looked again. It was still there.

There on the title page for the whole world to see.

Daughters of Brighton
by
Miss Mariah Aubrey
Author of A Winter in Bath

Not by Lady A. *Not* by any other *nom de plume*. But by her, Mariah Aubrey, laid bare.

This had not been on the proofs she'd checked!

Dixon nudged her hand away so she could see. That same hand flew to her mouth to cover a gasp.

Emotions dueled for preeminence within Mariah. Betrayal—how could he when he knew how much she wished to remain anonymous? Sick dread—how would her parents react? And what of Captain Bryant?

Was Mr. Crosby really so convinced it would increase sales that he had gone against her wishes? If so he might very soon regret that decision when those who knew of her fall refused to buy anything she wrote.

What could she do? She could write to Henry. Ask him to confront Mr. Crosby on her behalf and demand a reprint.

She thought of her new manuscript, *The Tale of Lydia Sorrow*. Fear washed over her—fear tinged with a hint of ugly revenge. If she published it, now that people would know who she was, readers might very well guess James Crawford's identity and know what he had done. But no. Any small revenge she might achieve would be far outweighed by the greater pain it would cause her family. Not only because she had published, but because of *what* she had published.

Yet staring at the title page before her, Mariah realized that even if she never finished another book, it was only a matter of time until repercussions from her publisher, her family, perhaps even from Captain Bryant, made themselves felt.

After conferring with Martin and Dixon, Mariah decided they would travel down to Oxford the following day, in case there was still time to recall the books before they were distributed to booksellers. But before they could go anywhere, Mr. Crosby arrived in a private carriage hired for the occasion. Seeing him from the window, Mariah's blood began to pound in her ears.

Then Henry descended from the equipage behind him. Had Crosby brought her brother along to protect himself from a scene? Mariah wondered why he had bothered to send the first volume ahead if he planned to come in person. Was it to allow her to vent the worst of her anger in private, and spare himself the first crush of her wrath or the embarrassment of her tears?

Dixon looked heavenward, shaking her head. Martin opened the door and stepped aside. Nerves quaking, Mariah stood in the threshold to await her guests.

Henry rushed forward and grasped her hands. His concerned eyes probed hers. "How are you, Rye?"

"In a panic," she said. "How should I be?"

Behind them, Mr. Crosby cleared his throat. Henry released her, and she stepped back, gesturing the men inside.

"Miss Aubrey," Mr. Crosby began, hat in hand. "I know you must be angry, but please grant me a fair hearing." He glanced at Martin and Dixon. "In private."

Mariah took a deep breath. "Very well."

She nodded to her friends and they left the room. Mariah sat down and Henry stood behind her chair. With a glance at Mr. Crosby, she jerked her hand toward the settee.

He sat awkwardly, arranging his coattails while she clasped her hands in her lap.

"I promise you I had no part in it," Mr. Crosby began. "The printer swears I sent a man with express written orders to add your name to the title page. Even produced an order written on Crosby and Company stationery. Someone must have filched it from my office."

Mariah doubted him. Guessed he was lying to appease her by laying the blame on some hapless printer's door, or some nameless, faceless messenger. How could she credit either, when he had long made it clear he would prefer to use her real name?

He studied her warily. "I see in your eyes what you are thinking, Miss Aubrey, but I tell you I did not knowingly do this. Even though I had wished it and must seem suspect, I would never so break the trust of any Crosby and Company author. I promise you—on the grave of my father, Anthony King Crosby Senior—I am telling you the truth."

His voice shook with such veracity that Mariah had no choice but to believe him sincere. She forced a stiff nod.

Henry stepped forward and, sounding very like the solicitor he was, asked, "May I see the order?"

Mr. Crosby extracted a letter from his pocket and began to unfold and smooth it. "I really cannot blame the printer," he said. "Nor hold him financially responsible. He's never had reason to doubt any instructions that have been given him before."

He handed Henry the paper. Grimly her brother read it, then passed it to Mariah.

"But . . . " Even before the question *Who would do such a thing?* had fully formed in her mind, Mariah knew the answer.

Hugh Prin-Hallsey.

She glanced at the proffered note on the engraved Crosby and Company stationery:

> *The authoress, faced with a dying parent, has decided to give said parent the pleasure of seeing his daughter's name in print before he dies. Therefore, please set in type the author's name, so that the title page reads:*
>
> *[title]*
> *by*
> *Miss Mariah Aubrey*
> *Author of A Winter in Bath*

Mariah realized stationery was not the only thing Hugh had filched from Mr. Crosby's office. Apparently he had taken the opportunity to verify his suspicions about Lady A's identity as well.

Mr. Crosby asked tentatively, "I hope that bit about your parent is not true?"

Henry shook his head, answering for them both. But Mariah wondered what this would do to their father. For by this stroke, Hugh had not only revealed Mariah as the author of this book, but of her first novel as well.

Hugh had done to her what she had done to him. Unmasked the real author and the fraud all in one blow. Mariah felt the irony wash over her. *He should be the one penning books about regret and revenge,* she thought. He had bested her.

"Can you not reprint?" Henry asked.

Mr. Crosby grimaced. "In all truth, I cannot afford to do so. I must sell this inventory or end in bankruptcy."

"But I thought Crosby and Company very successful," Mariah said.

"Things are running a bit tight at present, but I hope the situation will soon improve." He smiled bravely. "Look on the bright side, Miss Aubrey. Have I not said all along that sales would be helped by the use of your name? Frances Burney published her first novel anonymously without the knowledge or permission of her father. But she then switched to her real name, with no detriment to her person. And I think you may rest assured that no catastrophic fate shall befall you either."

Had he not overheard Hugh's "woman with *your* reputation" comment after all? Or did he truly not care?

Mariah could only pray he was right.

Matthew spent several days visiting poorhouses and workhouses in neighboring parishes, as well as the house of industry in Oxford. All were adamant that they had not admitted any new inmates matching Maggie's description. He would have to widen his search. But first he returned to Windrush Court.

Though he had no further answers about the missing girl, still Matthew longed to see Mariah again. How clear everything seemed to him now. He had loved her for some time and wished to tell her so. If he was not mistaken, she was fond of him as well.

At the back of his mind buzzed nagging questions about Crawford and Mariah, but he pushed them away. He would try to somehow forget it ever happened. He could not bear to think of the two of them together. Not when he hoped, once this crisis with Maggie had passed, that he might court Mariah himself.

But Mariah greeted him at the gatehouse door with none of the sweet smiles he had hoped for. Only a somber reserve. Had he misread her feelings?

She led him into the drawing room and pulled a chair from the table. She said formally, "Please sit down."

Matthew sat, but snagged her hand as he did so. "Mariah . . ."

"Shh. Say nothing you may wish back after I show you what I need to show you."

"That sounds dire." He playfully brushed the toe of his boot against her dress hem. "Have you a peg leg under there?"

Her bleak expression sobered him and he pressed her fingers. "No more bad news about Maggie, I trust?"

She pulled her hand away. Turned to retrieve something from the bookshelf. "I didn't want you to see or hear of it elsewhere."

This does not sound good, Matthew thought, and braced himself for impact.

Mariah laid the book before him and opened it to the title page. Then she stepped back, holding her breath, and waited.

He stared for several moments but said nothing.

Driven to fill the tense silence, she said, "I never planned to use my real name, but there was a last-minute change and the publisher refuses to reprint." She decided it would be futile to blame Hugh. She could not prove it, and even if she could, *how* the truth came out was really not the salient point.

"I cannot believe it," he finally said.

Her stomach dropped. "Is it so bad?" she asked, hating the tremor in her voice.

He did not meet her gaze. "This from the woman who declared words were so important to her. I see how they might be, as you pay your rent by them. And when I think of how you let me go on, criticizing *A Winter in Bath*. I thought you were only defensive on behalf of your sex, or of novels in general, never dreaming . . ." He shook his head, and when he finally looked at her, hurt and irritation dulled his eyes. "You said you weighed and measured words. I thought that meant honesty was important to you. When all along you were not honest with me."

He rose and pushed back his chair, his face grey and stiff. "First I discover one dark secret about you and now this. Another lie."

Mariah's voice shook. "That is not fair. I did not intend to lie. Only to keep it private. You know people consider it unladylike. My father would be furious."

"You were never going to tell me, were you? Just as you would never have told me about Crawford. You only tell me now because your hand has been forced yet again."

She winced. "Am I obligated to tell everyone? To disgorge my guilt on both counts at first meeting? Like a leper calling out 'Unclean, unclean' to all who approach? As my landlord had you some right to know?"

He turned fiery eyes on her. "Landlord be hanged. I thought we were friends." He thrust a hand through his hair. "Have I even heard the worst of it? What other secrets are you keeping? Was there a child?"

She gasped. "No!"

"But you . . . you are not a maid?"

When she made no reply, his jaw clenched, and he averted his gaze as though he could not stand to look at her. "I knew as much, and yet . . . Now I see that what I have learned by painful experience is true after all. Women are forever casting an appealing image they cannot live up to."

Daggers of remorse plunged deeper than ever before, puncturing

Mariah's chest until she could not speak or breathe. Tears pricked her eyes, but she blinked them back furiously. She had never heard him speak in so cutting a tone, or with such injury in his eyes. His words hurt all the more because they were true.

From across the billiards table, William Hart glared at him, dumbfounded and angry. "You said what?"

"Are you not shocked?"

"About which part? Crawford being an imbecile, or you?"

"What have I done but been felled by an unexpected blow? First I learn her character is not all it should be, and now I learn she has a secret life she has been keeping from us."

Even as he said the words, Matthew knew he had overreacted. He had known, or at least suspected, the truth about Mariah and Crawford for some time but had refused to face it. After all, there had been no reason to take it to heart when he had planned to marry Isabella. But this reasoning had not kept him from storing up disappointment and even resentment over Mariah having been with another man. News of her clandestine novel writing had only served to spark the powder horn already smoldering within him.

Hart scowled. "As far as her indiscretion with Crawford, she has paid a high price already. What would you have her do? Drag it about like an anchor all her days?"

"No. But I don't like being made a fool of."

"You are making *yourself* a fool. Is your past any better than hers?"

Anger sparked. "You forget yourself, Lieutenant."

"No. You forget yourself, Captain. For I was there. I was there when you ignored the signal flag and took the ship anyway, for one more capture, one more prize, though it would not affect the outcome of the war. I was there when you held your head in your hands over those young men who might still be alive had you not done so. I was there in port too. And well I remember that pretty Spanish girl with eyes only for the rich *capitan*."

"Don't." Matthew pressed a hand to his eyes to block out Hart's words, and the wounded expression on Mariah's face when he'd lashed out at her.

"Why not? You would have Miss Aubrey display her secrets, but I cannot breathe a word about yours?"

Could Hart not understand his struggle? Even though Matthew had given up his quest to prove himself to society, any man would be upset to have his fears confirmed—to learn that the woman he loved was not a maid. Did it make him an archaic sapskull to wish she were? Her reputation would not be helped by this latest revelation, once news of her novel writing circulated.

But with what had befallen his own dear sister—and with all God had forgiven him—how could he join those condemning her?

He could not.

"Dash it, Hart." Matthew rubbed the back of his neck and sighed. "Must you always be right?"

What a hypocrite he had been, Matthew realized, to judge Miss Aubrey for her deeds, when his own huge failings ever loomed before him. *Forgive me*, he breathed. *Forgive me*. He directed that silent plea both to the woman he loved and to the God who loved him.

Overwhelmed with remorse, Matthew resisted the urge to run directly to the gatehouse and plead his case. Instead he sat at the library desk to ponder the best way to communicate his sincerest apologies and hopes to Miss Mariah Aubrey, authoress.

Hitting on an idea, he took up paper, quill, and ink. With a prayer for smooth sailing on his lips, he began to write.

My dear Miss Aubrey,

Since you are a person who values words, I have decided to write you a story. A poor attempt, no doubt, but here is my version of an Aesopian fable I call "The Foolish Fox and the Two Birds. . . ."

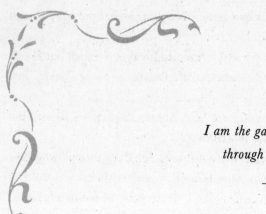

I am the gate; whoever enters
through me will be saved.

—Jesus Christ (NIV)

chapter 37

orried when she saw neither of the Miss Merryweathers outside, Mariah stepped cautiously into the poorhouse. There, Agnes crossed the entry hall, hot-water bottle in her hands.

"Miss Merryweather," Mariah whispered. "How is Miss Amy?"

Colorless lips tight, Agnes grimly shook her head. "Not good. But she'll want to see you. Come along."

Mariah fell into step with the slight woman, glancing back nervously over her shoulder, fearing Mrs. Pitt might see her and order her from the premises.

"They've got her in the infirmary now. Right through here."

Mariah followed Agnes past the office used by the visiting apothecary and the occasional surgeon, past the glass-plated and locked cupboard where the day-to-day remedies were stored, and past a series of small sickrooms. At the last door in the passageway, Agnes gestured Mariah in before her.

"I've brought you a visitor, Amy. But don't let her tire you," Agnes said.

"Can't get any more tired," Amy said with a weak grin. "Hello, Miss Mariah."

She and Mariah exchanged tender smiles.

Agnes bustled over and tucked the hot-water bottle under the bedclothes. "There, that should stop your shivering."

For though the room was perfectly warm, Amy was covered in blankets and even wore a red muffler around her neck.

Amy fingered the muffler and said wistfully, "I never made you one, Miss Mariah."

How small, how frail the dear woman looked. Mariah blinked back tears just to see so little of her remaining. "Never mind, Miss Amy. I don't. You are all loveliness with that splash of red round your neck."

Amy tugged ineffectually at the muffler. "You take it."

"No, I couldn't."

"Why not?" Amy gave a wisp of a chuckle. "I shall not need it where I am bound. No damp rooms in my Father's house."

Agnes mumbled something under her breath that sounded like *father indeed.*

Mariah said, "Perhaps Agnes would like it."

Amy gave a dismissive flutter of her hand. "Oh, I made her a red one long ago. She refuses to wear it. This one should be yours."

Agnes thought red a color for a Jezebel, Mariah recalled. She could understand the woman wanting no reminder of a life anyone would wish to forget.

She glanced at Agnes, and the woman nodded her approval. "Then I will treasure it. Thank you."

Mariah helped Amy unwind the soft muffler from around her neck.

With bent, trembling fingers, Amy pressed it into Mariah's hands. "You wear it, my dear. And you remember."

Mariah's throat tightened. "I shall never forget you."

Amy gave a little snort. "*Pfff.* Forget me all you like, but don't forget what it means." Amy kept hold of Mariah's hand, expression earnest. "None of us gets through this life without a tangle or two. Accept His mercy and move forward. Don't hold on to the knots and forget the life ahead."

Tears blurring her vision, Mariah gently squeezed Amy's hand and whispered, "Thank you."

She would remember.

Mariah glanced across the bed, and her heart clenched to see tears streaming down the weathered cheeks of stoic Agnes Merryweather.

Agnes took her sister's other hand. "Please don't leave me, Amy. Not again."

"Promise me you'll follow after me, Aggie. Promise me you'll pass through the gate."

The gate? Mariah wondered.

Miss Amy must have seen Mariah's confusion, for she pointed one finger straight up. "Not *your* gate, my dear. His gate."

The door creaked open behind them, and there stood Captain Prince. He looked upon Amy Merryweather, diminished by time and illness, and his face seemed to cave in on itself. "Oh, my dear girl. My old friend."

Amy smiled, lovely still. "Captain. How good of you to come."

He stumbled to her bed. Kneeling beside it, he grasped one of her small bird-claw hands in his and wept.

"There, there," Miss Amy soothed. "It is not farewell, my dear captain, but *au revoir*. Until we meet again."

Mariah and Agnes silently moved to the door to allow the two to share a rare, and likely final, moment alone.

In the corridor, Agnes Merryweather looked weary and shaken. Lost. Mariah took her hand gingerly, anticipating it being thrown off.

Instead, Agnes gripped hard, the metal of her thin ring biting into Mariah's flesh.

She did not complain.

"How close they seem," Mariah said. "But can they really know one another so well, when he has been kept isolated?"

Agnes allowed Mariah to lead her down the passage to two chairs. "Oh, Amy would sneak up to his room whenever she could. Poor dear could hardly walk, but she would pull herself up those long stairs. Wore her out, but nothing I said would stop her going. For all his failings, John Pitt is a bit of a romantic. He would sometimes slip away so the two could talk privately through the door."

"Still, never really together . . ."

"Oh, they knew each other long before the poorhouse."

That's right, Mariah recalled. What had Captain Prince said? Something about remembering Miss Amy awaiting him back in England?

Agnes's eyes remained misty, focused on some distant point across the dark passageway, across the years, across the memories.

"It is because of him she is alive today, though not for many more hours, I fear. . . ." Her thin shoulders shook, and she lifted a handkerchief to her narrow, lined face.

Mariah put an arm around the quaking woman. After Agnes recovered herself, Mariah asked gently, "How did they meet?"

Agnes nodded. "It was when Amy was . . . when my father sent her away. Vile man. Needed money for drink, so he sold his very own flesh and blood."

Shock jarred Mariah. *What!* It could not be. Agnes must be confused. Mariah had assumed the bitter Agnes was the sister Mrs. Pitt had meant, the one who had lived through such ignominy. Could she have been so utterly mistaken? Or had Agnes transferred her own story to her sister to distance herself from the memories, to make it possible to revisit those bleak days?

"She was forced to work in a bawdy house in Bristol," Agnes continued. "A port town, you know. I understand the captain looked up and saw her sitting in the window, staring up at the stars. Somehow he recognized her. I guess he had seen her years before in Whitmore, where we lived. Knew who she was by appearance, if not by name. Knew enough of my father to guess the rest.

"He went inside and demanded to see the woman in the window. The hateful proprietor brought her down like so many oranges to be squeezed and sniffed to extract the highest price. Amy said the captain, in full dress uniform, stared at her, almost angrily she thought, and she was fearful of him. She'd had more than enough experience with angry, cruel men. But there was something about his eyes, his bearing, that made her realize he was not angry with *her*. He asked, 'How much for the girl?' A price was given. But he said, 'No, not for an hour, not for a night. Forever. For her freedom.'

"A ridiculously high figure was named, the peddler of flesh clearly having no wish to part with his profitable acquisition. In fact, the amount was far higher than the sum Father had received for her. But without a word, without taking his eyes from Amy's, Captain Prince reached into his coat pocket and withdrew a heavy purse of gold and tossed it at the man. Then he said to Amy, 'Get your things. We are leaving.' "

"What a story!" Mariah breathed, mind reeling. Had cheerful, godly Amy really been a . . . She could not even think the word in the same sentence with Amy's name. How had she survived, her spirits intact?

Agnes nodded. "The captain placed Amy in a boardinghouse with a God-fearing family he knew. They were loath to take her in, for she looked the part she'd been forced to play. But they did, for his sake. They had a few lovely days together, Amy told me later, and he was a perfect gentleman. He encouraged her to write to me, and she did so—to my great relief, as she had not been allowed to do so before. The captain's ship was leaving port, and he said he would be gone many months but promised he would visit her first thing upon his return."

Agnes leaned her head back against the wall behind their chairs.

"Amy believed he would marry her. I did not. Kind as he was, she was too far beneath him, even before her fall at my father's hand. But I had not the heart to caution her. And so we waited. Six or seven months later, news came that his ship had sunk, and most of the men, the captain included, had lost their lives."

"How dreadful." The sadness of it struck Mariah anew, although she had heard the story of the shipwreck before, from Captain Prince's point of view.

"It was dreadful, for Amy. As for me, I got my sister back. Only then was she willing to quit the place where she'd kept vigil for him and return to Whitmore. Our father died leaving debts, and eventually we had to sell our family home. We took a small pair of rooms together and got on quite well. Those were happy years for us both. Though Amy never quite got over her loss and her health began to decline."

"How astounded she must have been to find him here. In the last place she wanted to be, no doubt!"

Agnes sniffed. "Astounded indeed. It salved the pain of having to come here—though of course Amy credited God. But it was several months before the other inmates trusted us enough to tell us about the man on the roof. It was longer yet until she recognized his voice. For a long while she thought she must be imagining things—for Captain Prince was dead, was he not?"

Mariah said, "He told us about his head injury, the memory loss, the years as a castaway. . . ."

Agnes nodded her familiarity with those events and wiped her sharp nose with the worn handkerchief.

"Still," Mariah continued. "How surprising that he should end up here in this little-known poorhouse beside Windrush Court."

Agnes looked at her pointedly. "Not surprising at all, really, considering we were all born and raised in this very parish." Tears swamped her eyes again. "How glad I am he *is* here. For poor Amy's sake."

But somehow Mariah felt less sorry for Amy than she did for poor Agnes, the sister being left behind.

❧

Restless, her mind whirling with worry over Miss Amy, Maggie, and an angry Captain Bryant, sleep eluded Mariah that night. She left her candle burning on her bedside table, hoping the light might fend off the worst of the dark dread filling her, especially when she thought of the hardships Maggie might be exposed to at that very moment. Remembering Miss Amy's—as well as Dixon's—admonition, Mariah prayed, contritely asking God to forgive not only her offenses, but for wavering in her devotion. She also asked God to watch over Maggie and Miss Amy, and to heal the rift between her and Matthew. She felt more peaceful afterwards but still could not sleep.

Giving up, Mariah pulled out one of her aunt's journals and began reading. She decided it would be the very remedy for her sleeplessness, especially after enduring a number of tedious pages describing Francesca's plans to renovate the rose salon and her own bedchamber after her marriage to Frederick Prin-Hallsey, complete with lists of tapestries, upholstery, and furniture to buy, friezes to be commissioned, et cetera.

Mariah skipped ahead several pages and read with more, if morbid, interest of Francesca's feelings about her second husband's failing health, as well as the mounting tension between her and Hugh.

But then something quite different caught her eye.

The Prin-Hallseys never fail to surprise me. I have learned something rather shocking. In all truth, I am not certain I should write it down. For could not my own fate be tied up in, or unraveled, should the truth come out?

I have learned that Honora Prin-Hallsey's reasons for granting the funds and land for the poorhouse were not selfless after all. She was not motivated by Christian charity in the least, or certainly not as primary aim.

Perhaps that is not entirely fair. I suppose they could have conjured some other means of keeping Windrush Court for themselves. Some ruthless workhouse in the north, or some asylum in London. Or a convenient shooting accident, fall, or overdose of laudanum. So perhaps I judge them too harshly. After all, here I sit, knowing what I know, and doing nothing to change the situation. Mine, or his.

Dare I tell Hugh? A part of me revels at the thrill of revenge that would be mine to savor as bearer of such devastating news. To see the proud, demeaning young man lose all. But then that old sense of self-preservation rears its stabilizing head and cautions me to consider the consequences.

I wondered if he was the man I had glimpsed about the place when I was a girl. Was he the elder son, the one who disappeared as I once overheard Mrs. Prin-Hallsey confide to my mother?

I stumbled across a framed painting when I was refurbishing the house. It was wrapped in paper and stored at the back of a cupboard. The man in the portrait appeared to be in his late twenties and seemed mildly familiar. It might have been the same man I had seen years ago, but I could not be certain. I knew the eldest son had gone against his parents' wishes in joining the navy, but was that such a breach that they would remove his portrait from the hall—especially once he was missing and assumed dead? I asked Frederick about it, and at first he attempted to pass off the young man as an ancestor, but the style of clothes and of the painting itself seemed too modern to me. When I persisted, he finally confided the truth, though he was careful to assure me his brother was not in his right mind, and it was out of kindness that he did not have him institutionalized elsewhere.

Kindness? I found that unlikely. Self-interest? That I would believe.

As would I, Mariah thought, staring off into the flickering shadows as the sputtering candle stub guttered and smoked. She closed the journal. Was it true? Was Captain Prince really a Prin-Hallsey? *The* Prin-Hallsey?

Reading from her aunt's journal had certainly distracted her from her worries, but now her mind whirled over an entirely different set of circumstances . . . and what the startling truth might mean for them all.

Then out spake brave Horatius,
The Captain of the Gate:
To every man upon this earth
Death cometh soon or late.

—Thomas Babington

chapter 38

*T*hough she had not slept well, *Mariah arose* early in the morning, while the house was still quiet. Even Lizzy and early riser Dixon were still abed. Tiptoeing into the kitchen to start the fire, she was surprised to see a sealed letter on the floor, just inside the back door.

The letter was marked with her name—*Miss Aubrey*—in a masculine hand. Her pulse quickened. Fire forgotten, she sat down and with eager fingers broke the seal and unfolded the single sheet. Reading Matthew's introduction, her heart thumped. As she read "The Foolish Fox and the Two Birds," she alternately chuckled and pressed a hand to her heart.

Once there was a foolish, determined fox, who came into a far
country, determined to catch one of the rare yellow songbirds that

sojourned there. For many days he pursued the bewitching songbird, but she scorned him, flitting about from branch to branch, high above him.

Another bird perched in a modest nest near the fox's den. She was a beautiful bird as well, but not, perhaps, as showy as the yellow songbird. Nor could she sing. Her feathers were dark, her eyes golden and wise. She befriended the fox, called out warnings when danger came near, or when he was about to step into a trap. Blithely he thanked her and went on his way, chasing after the fickle songbird.

How foolish was the fox. How blind. To not see, not value the friendship, the affection, the trust the brown bird offered him.

One day he caught the songbird, only to realize he did not want her after all.

He ran to the humble nest of the brown bird and called up to her, but she would not answer him.

Was he too late, or might she yet forgive him?

Mariah blinked back tears. No, it was not too late. And yes, she would forgive him.

Eager to tell him so, and to confide the discoveries from her aunt's journals, Mariah quickly dressed and walked through a cool mist to Windrush Court. But instead of Matthew, she saw Hugh Prin-Hallsey jogging down the front steps. She hesitated, fighting the urge to duck behind a shaped hedge and retreat unseen, but she steeled her resolve and strode forward.

"Well, if it isn't Lady A," he said, and actually smiled at her. Revenge certainly agreed with him.

"I suppose I need not ask why you did it, Hugh," Mariah said, surprised the man was up and about so early. "But I am still struggling to reconcile the act with the man I thought you were. I had never considered you vengeful."

Hugh nodded. "By nature I am more of a live-and-let-live sort of fellow. But I take it very ill when someone gets between me and my next guinea. Or persists in referring to a certain vexing woman as Mrs. Prin-Hallsey."

Mariah sighed. "It was her name, Hugh."

He slanted her a sly grin. "And *Lady A* was your name, but I managed to end that farce, did I not?"

Mariah was unexpectedly grieved by this chasm between them. Perhaps it had always been there, but she had not realized its depth, distracted as she had been at first by his charming bravado, his affable façade.

"Yes," she said quietly. "You have ended it."

She studied Hugh's implacable expression. Should she tell him what she had discovered in the poorhouse and confirmed in her aunt's journals? Just as Francesca had been, Mariah was tempted to have her own revenge against this man. Moreover, she wanted to see Captain Prince—or Prin-Hallsey, if that was his real name—freed and restored to his rightful place. But would Hugh even believe her? Yes, he would, she realized, even if he would not admit it. For Hugh had recognized the man on the roof that day—she was sure of it.

She took a deep breath. "I have met your uncle."

One dark brow rose. "My uncle?"

"Yes, you remember. The old man on the poorhouse roof? The man you recognized? He is your father's *elder* brother."

Hugh met her gaze unflinchingly. He did not gape or rail as she had expected him to. Instead he merely smirked, his dark eyes glinting. "Poor Bryant."

She frowned. "No. The captain can always find another house, but you stand to lose everything."

He shrugged. "It is time I left the old place in any case and struck out on my own."

"You are leaving?" Mariah asked. "For good this time?"

"For good?" He pulled a face. "When have I ever done that?"

Mariah stared at him, disconcerted by his unruffled, knowing smirk. Would he somehow manage to destroy the evidence before the authorities or solicitors could verify Captain Prince's claim? Worse, had she endangered the old captain by placing him between Hugh and "his next guinea"?

A chill ran down her spine at the thought.

"Miss! Miss Mariah!"

Mariah turned. There was Lizzy, standing at the end of the gatehouse lane in her nightdress and shawl, gesturing urgently. "Come quickly!"

Foreboding seized Mariah at the sight. Hugh forgotten, Mariah hurried back to the gatehouse.

As she ran, Mariah's stomach twisted in dread. No good news came to call so early. She anticipated George or someone else from the poorhouse bringing news of Miss Amy's death. But she did not expect Captain Prince himself.

Yet there he stood in the drawing room, slouch hat in hand, fully dressed but in stocking feet. His crumpled face told her the rest.

Mariah ached for him. "Captain Prince, do sit down."

Dixon tiptoed down the stairs, dressed, but her hair still hanging in its long plait. She looked from Mariah to Captain Prince, and instead of complaining of the early hour, she nodded grim understanding. "I'll make tea," she said softly, before scuttling through to the kitchen.

She must have taken herself out to the stable and roused Martin as well, for several minutes later, both he and Dixon came in bearing tea things. Mariah invited them all to sit down together at the table, then repeated the news Captain Prince had indeed come to impart. Amy Merryweather had died in her sleep during the night. At peace and ready to meet her Maker.

Captain Prince's eyes shone with tears, and his voice was haggard. "She was a good friend to me. My light and warmth in that dreary place."

A thick silence followed.

After a time, Lizzy excused herself to dress, and Mariah asked tentatively, "Captain, will you now tell us what happened when you returned to England?"

The man nodded, his expression downcast.

"I am afraid I have no figgy dowdy to offer you, Captain," Martin said.

He waved the apology away as a gnat, his eyes focused inward.

"The proprietor of the boardinghouse believed the Miss Merryweathers had returned to their home village, though she did not recall its name. I did remember, for I had grown up nearby. I stayed in Bristol for a short time doing odd jobs until I could earn enough money for coach fare. When I arrived in Whitmore, I went first to the old Merryweather house, but strangers were living there. How they looked at me—as though I were a beggar or worse. I lost the courage to ask after Amy Merryweather then, afraid she was no longer in the village, afraid that if she were, she would not be happy to see me. And certainly no one would have been happy to see me as I was. Shabby, salt-stained clothes, skin and bones, brown as a nut. I truly hoped Miss Amy had married some kind, decent man during my long absence, even as I knew how very unlikely that was.

"I decided to return home first, assuming the place was still standing and my brother would allow me in. I remembered him, though I doubted he would recognize me. I planned to have a bath and shave and borrow some decent clothes before I began seeking Miss Amy in earnest.

"What a row! At first Frederick refused to believe me. He said, *'My brother is dead. Long dead. And you, sir, are an imposter.'* Later, I realized that he and his wife had heard rumors that I was still alive—sightings of me on the island and aboard the trader's ship, whispered by sailors and passed from ship to ship, from crews to their families, and finally to the populace at large."

Martin nodded. "I myself heard the rumors and very much wanted to believe them."

The captain dipped his head. "Thank you. My brother and his wife did not share your sentiments, however. They had not sat idle while the rumors began circulating, for lo and behold, if they didn't have a place prepared for me when I returned. Had me declared a lunatic too, so Frederick would inherit the estate. I cannot blame them, not fully. For I was off in my attic then, and I am not quite right yet. Doubt I ever will be, this side of heaven."

Mariah shook her head. "Your brother may have planned to take legal steps to make himself heir, but I don't believe he actually did so. Perhaps he only told you that to keep you from leaving Honora House. If you thought you had nowhere else to go . . ." Mariah let the words drift away. She rose, lifting a forefinger. "Wait one moment."

She dashed upstairs and returned with Fran's journal. She found the section she had been reading the night before. "Listen to what my aunt wrote."

Mariah paused to catch her breath, then read, " 'I suppose Hugh could go through lengthy and expensive legal proceedings to have the man declared incompetent, but I can find no evidence of Frederick and Honora having done this. Too public, I suppose. Too scandalous. Too risky. Besides, why should they bother? For while searching through my husband's desk, I did find one legal document. A certificate declaring Percival Prin-Hallsey dead, having been missing for more than seven years. Frederick and Honora never acknowledged his return. Instead they hid the inconvenient truth humanely away in order to retain their home and control of the purse strings.' "

Mariah took a deep breath and continued, " 'For here is the truth. Windrush Court does not legally belong to Hugh Prin-Hallsey. Yes, he is Frederick's heir, but Frederick never legally owned it either. It rightfully belongs to Frederick's elder brother. Not dead as assumed and hoped and legally declared. But secretly living in the poorhouse across the road.' "

Mariah glanced up from the journal. Martin and Dixon sat, stunned and frowning.

Finally, Martin asked, "But . . . if you are a Prin-Hallsey, how did you come by the name Prince?"

The captain intertwined his long fingers. "My parents wanted me to be a gentleman, you see. When I was seventeen, they sent me to Oxford to be educated. But that was not the life I wanted for myself. So I ran off and joined up as a volunteer seaman. I could not sign on under my real name, could I? Not with my father likely to track me down and haul me home before the ship had even left port."

Here, the captain chuckled dryly. "Even had I not wished to evade my father, I would have been loath to use my real name. A high-falutin' name like Percival Prin-Hallsey would have earned me endless taunts from rough-and-rowdy seamen and extra lashes from the bosun. No thank you, sir."

Martin, brows high, nodded his agreement.

"Three years later, a captain appointed me midshipman," Captain Prince continued. "I think he knew who I really was, but he never said a word. Perhaps he had a disapproving father as well, I don't know. Three or four years after that, I passed the lieutenant's examination. I liked everything about the navy, and the navy liked me."

He raised his glass in salute, and Martin raised a teacup in reply.

"I had no plans to stay away forever, and no plans to go home. I was living day by day, promotion by promotion, and loving every minute of it."

Mariah said, "My aunt mentioned finding a portrait of a man in his late twenties, and guessed it might be you. But how could that be, if you left home at seventeen?"

Captain Prince looked up, searching his memory. "When I was about eight and twenty, I learned my father had died. That old captain slipped me a newspaper clipping and granted me leave. While I never got on with my father, I loved my mother and decided I would go to her, give what comfort I could, and assure her I was well. It was then that I saw the Merryweather twins in the village. I had heard of their father—he was a notorious drunkard. But his daughters had become young women while I was away. I did not know their Christian names at the time, but one does not forget a pair of such lovely girls."

Mariah bit her lip. He was right. One did not forget them.

The captain inhaled deeply before continuing. "I arrived at Windrush Court to find my mother in poor health, but she was happy and relieved to see me. I was glad I went when I did, for she did not live many years longer. My brother was away in London at the time, and I never saw him the entire fortnight I was home. My mother wrote to him, but he did not deem my return worth missing the social season. While I was home, my mother commissioned an artist to paint my portrait. Dreadful man wanted me to sit still for hours on end, and I could not abide it. In the end, he drew my face in detail and said he would finish the rest later from sketches and memory. Probably turned out badly, for all I know."

"I wonder where it is now," Mariah murmured, hoping Hugh had not sold it.

"I don't know." The man shrugged. "I returned to sea and progressed in my career. Finally, I received my first commission as captain. I found Amy just a few days before I sailed away, expecting great things. . . ."

Percival Prin-Hallsey's eyes filled anew, and Mariah reached out and laid a hand on his arm.

"What will you do now, Captain?"

He shook his head, apparently bewildered.

Martin said, "We will help you gain your permanent release from the poorhouse. You are neither dead nor incompetent. Windrush Court is rightfully yours."

"Captain Bryant has another few weeks left in his lease," Mariah added. "But I don't think he will mind relinquishing it. To think of all you have been through, all the hardships. I am certain he will be as glad as we all would be to see you back where you belong."

Captain Prince shook his head. "The hardships I experienced were nothing to Miss Amy's. Nothing!"

Mariah patted his arm. "But she had your friendship, Captain, don't forget. And a beloved sister by her side."

He wiped his eyes. "I never understood how she managed it." Slowly he shook his head. "To remain so full of faith and joy despite it all."

Mariah remembered the single knot and the line of red wool stretching over the rise and out of sight.

And understood.

Let other pens dwell on guilt and misery.

—Jane Austen

chapter 39

After Captain Prince left, returning to the poorhouse to offer Agnes Merryweather what comfort he could, Mariah sat down and flipped through the neglected pages of *Lydia Sorrow*. She felt as though the tale had been written—and lived—by another person. One whom she remembered, was vaguely acquainted with, but whose pain and regret and desire for revenge were no longer her own.

Lizzy knocked on the open sitting-room door, her young face alight with barely contained excitement.

"Mr. Hart wants me to meet his mother. May I go, miss? May I?"

Mariah's chest rose and fell in waves of wistful happiness. "Of course you may."

"William says I may bring George as chaperone, so Mrs. Pitt is not tempted to send him away while I'm gone. He knows how I worry about him. Is that not good news?"

"Very good news."

Mariah offered to lend a larger valise, and gave Lizzy two of her own gowns for the trip. The girl was delighted and embraced

Mariah warmly. "Oh, thank you, miss. I shouldn't want to embarrass William."

"You would never do that. He thinks the world of you."

Dimples appeared on Lizzy's flushed cheeks. "Yes, he does."

This is how love should be, Mariah thought. Two honest people, forthright in their intentions, loving and protecting one another.

Thinking of Lizzy and Mr. Hart, as well as Miss Amy and Captain Prince, and even Dixon and her suitors, Mariah rose and stood before the hearth, where a fire had been laid against the misty chill of a damp September day. One by one, she began feeding pages of *Lydia Sorrow* to the flames. She would start afresh. She no longer desired revenge or to be avenged. She desired only forgiveness. And, God willing, a second chance.

"Let other pens dwell on guilt and misery," she remembered hearing a friend of a friend say, and found it resonated with her own soul.

She would write an uplifting tale of mercy and true love, she decided. One with a happy ending.

Well . . . she could dream, couldn't she?

Leaving the gatehouse a short while later, Mariah came across Captain Bryant and Martin sitting on the garden bench. She overheard Martin relating the tale of Captain Prince's origins and identity.

"Can you believe it? Now we know why the authorities could not trace the missing captain to a Prince family. So you see, we were both right."

Captain Bryant nodded, but Mariah thought he looked rather dazed by the news.

"Where is he now?" he asked.

"Gone back to the poorhouse to comfort Miss Amy's sister, he said."

Martin saw her and quickly rose. Captain Bryant followed suit.

"Miss Mariah here can tell you the rest," Martin said abruptly and disappeared into the house. It was done without subtlety, but even so, she appreciated Martin's thoughtfulness. She longed to speak to Captain Bryant alone.

He was regarding her warily, she realized, and no wonder after their last meeting.

She stepped nearer and began, "I am in receipt of your letter and your . . . tale."

He nodded, eyes cautious.

"And I think it fair to say you could easily have a second career in . . . shipbuilding." She smiled mischievously, and his reserve dissolved into a welcoming grin.

"Just as you might have a second career as an opera singer," he teased.

She held his gaze as their smiles faded into something else, something deeper and more serious. "I forgive you," she whispered. "Will you forgive me?"

He reached over and took her hand in his. "It is done."

Her pulse quickened at his touch. With his free hand, he gestured toward the bench, and she sat down.

"I had hoped to find you earlier to tell you about Captain Prince," she said. "But with Miss Amy's death and everything . . ." She let her words trail off and instead asked, "Are you not glad now Hugh refused to sell you Windrush Court?"

Sitting beside her, Captain Bryant looked skyward and inhaled deeply. He made no answer.

Mariah's heart began beating dully. "He did refuse, did he not?"

"Initially, yes."

She studied his flat expression, realization dawning. "Oh no. . . ."

He sighed. "Oh yes. I have already given Hugh Prin-Hallsey a sizeable sum in good faith on the place. Now only to find that not one brick was his to sell, or mine to buy."

Mariah shook her head, mind whirling. "Then we shall have to find him and demand repayment."

He gave her a wry look. "Mariah. What do you suppose is the likelihood of my getting one farthing back from Hugh Prin-Hallsey?"

She stared into his bleak brown eyes but found she could utter no false assurances. "Was it a great deal of money?" she asked softly.

Not meeting her gaze, he nodded.

"Oh, Captain, I am so sorry. You have lost your fortune."

Slowly he shook his head. Looking into her eyes, he squeezed her hand. "*Here* is my fortune."

But Mariah's guilt kept her from fully hearing and acknowledging his words. "I feel so responsible. Hugh was a sort of cousin, after all."

One side of his mouth rose. "How you do take on the weight of the world, Mariah. Whereas I feel as if I have finally shed an anchor." He exhaled and straightened. "I have some money left but will need to find employment soon. Seek another commission."

"But, Matthew—the bloodshed, the nightmares . . ."

"I know. And now with Napoleon exiled, there are ten captains vying for every ship the navy will maintain. Still, there are other options. The West Africa Squadron is working to suppress the Atlantic slave trade, but that is a thankless task, I understand. The squadron's few frigates are mere water spiders in a vast ocean, and the slavers continue to sail around undeterred. Yet, I might go, if not for you, Mariah."

If not for me . . . ? Mariah found she could hardly breathe.

When she made no reply, he added, "That small fleet has insufficient quarters for a captain, let alone a captain's . . ." He hesitated. "For a woman."

Mariah nodded her vague understanding, but her thoughts were spinning and her heart beating so loudly she was not certain she heard correctly.

Matthew continued, "I visited an old friend of mine recently, a Captain McCulloch. He is spearheading the creation of a new fleet he calls the Coast Blockade Service. I believe he would give me a post. It would not pay very handsomely, nor be impressive or romantic."

"Is that so important?"

He gave her a sidelong glance. "In novels, the heroes are always captains or lords, are they not?"

He attempted a grin to lighten the moment, but she regarded him soberly.

"A woman who truly loved you would not care if you were a baker, a chandler, or a captain. I should not."

He stilled, looked at her fondly, and stroked her cheek—a cheek suddenly very warm as she realized what she had said.

"My sister said something very like that not long ago," Matthew whispered. "And predicted I would find a woman who thought and felt as you do." He leaned near, his whispered words a caress on her cheek. "Meddlesome creature was right again."

He leaned nearer yet, until Mariah knew—hoped—he would kiss her.

Someone behind them cleared his throat. Matthew squeezed his eyes closed in exasperation and somehow managed to bite his tongue. *Now what?* He turned and saw Martin standing on the other side of the gate, gesturing him over.

"Captain. Sorry to disturb. I tried to wait until you two were finished . . . em, talking. But it's urgent."

Martin waved a piece of paper, as though Matthew should know what it signified. Sighing, Matthew smiled apologetically at Mariah and gave her hand a parting squeeze. Then he rose and strode over to the gate.

Martin spoke in an agitated whisper through the bars. "We've got it. We know where they sent Maggie." He unfolded the torn piece of paper.

"How?" Matthew asked. "Did Mrs. Pitt relent?"

"No, sir. It was Captain Prince. Prin-Hallsey. What have you. He snuck into the office and went through her files. Found an entry in her registry, explaining the transfer, or falsifying excuses, if you ask me. Young George just brought over this note." He thrust the paper through the bars into Matthew's hand. "She sent her to Westhill House."

"Westhill House?" Matthew read the scrawl to confirm the news. "I know the place. It is the workhouse in Highworth."

He turned to share the news with Mariah but saw that she had already retreated into the house, allowing the two men to speak in private.

Martin touched his arm through the bars. "I wasn't certain I should tell Miss Mariah or Miss Susan. Didn't want to get their hopes up, in case Maggie has been apprenticed to one of the mills." He winced. "I figured you might know what to do. Besides," he added sheepishly, "you are the only one of us who has a horse."

Matthew nodded, thoughts racing.

Martin continued, "I could go myself, but I doubt they would release a little girl to the likes of me. Don't know that they would to you either, no offense, but we've got to try." His voice thickened. "I cannot abide the thought of the poor little mite alone amongst strangers. She no doubt thinks we have all forgotten her."

Matthew placed a hand on Martin's shoulder. "I shall go straight away and see what can be done." He hesitated. "Perhaps you were right not to tell the ladies—not yet. We don't want to arouse their hopes only to dash them. But I leave that decision to you." He hesitated. "Martin, do me a favor. Tell Miss Aubrey I have had to leave . . . on business. But be sure and tell her that we will finish our conversation as soon as I return. Understood?"

Martin nodded. "Right. Gone on business. Will finish chat forthwith."

What has happened? Why all the secrecy? Mariah tried to concentrate on peeling apples, and instead nicked her finger. *Fiddle!*

Martin came into the kitchen a few minutes later. "There you are, Miss Mariah. Captain Bryant charged me to tell you something."

"Oh?" she said casually, trying to mask her emotions.

"He's gone off on business and will speak to you when he returns."

"What manner of business?" she asked, her voice quavering.

"I . . . I couldn't rightly say, miss. But Captain Bryant is gone to Highworth, he has—that much I can tell you."

Highworth. That was where the Forsythes had their country estate. Where Mr. Forsythe lived, even though Isabella spent much of her time with an aunt in London. Mariah wondered if Martin had brought a message from Miss Forsythe. That would explain the secrecy. But surely Matthew had not gone to see Isabella or her father. Not after the conversation the two of them had just had. True, Matthew had not asked for her hand, but he had hinted at a future together. Or had she imagined the implications of his words, because she so desired them to exist? *Just as I did with Mr. Crawford?*

Doubts and sinking dread filled her, even as she told herself she was being foolish. "I see," she said, feeling as if she did indeed see all too well.

An hour later, Mariah went outside to dump the apple peels. She saw Susan Dixon and Albert Phelps standing in the gatehouse lane. Hat in his hands, Mr. Phelps hung his head as he listened to whatever Dixon was telling him. From the look of his slumped shoulders and crestfallen expression, Mariah guessed she was turning down his offer of marriage.

Poor man, Mariah thought, heart squeezing in empathy. She went inside and busied herself in the drawing room to give the two privacy.

When the back door opened several minutes later, Mariah stepped tentatively into the kitchen to see how Dixon was feeling. She thought her old friend looked drawn and weary.

"Everything all right?" Mariah asked softly.

Miss Dixon's eyes were damp. "Hated to do it." She sniffed. "But it had to be done."

Mariah nodded. "How did he take it?"

Dixon paused to consider. "Better than I feared. He harbors no grudge. Says he's already known the 'bliss of wedlock' and wishes me happy."

Mariah had underestimated the man. She squeezed Dixon's hand and left her. She hoped her friend would not regret her decision, for as far as Mariah knew, Martin had never offered marriage. Might there forever be two spinsters in the gatehouse?

On Martin's birthday a few days later, the three of them sat at the kitchen table together, a paper-wrapped parcel between them. Mariah and Dixon watched nervously as Martin peeled back the paper with both hand and hook. Mariah hoped he wouldn't be offended by Dixon's gift.

Dixon said, "You need not use it if you don't want to. I thought you might like to wear it to church, perhaps, like a Sunday suit of clothes."

He glanced up from his unwrapping. "A new neckcloth, is it?"

Dixon shook her head, looking quite anxious.

He opened the box and stared. Mariah craned her neck to see as well. For she had only heard about, but not yet seen, the object Dixon had ordered all the way from London.

Within a layer of tissue lay an artificial hand, with a leather socket and tubular frame to attach it beneath the elbow.

"I am not saying you *need* it," Dixon stressed. "Honestly, I don't mind the hook at all. I am accustomed to it. I just thought you might like it. If you don't, you needn't wear it. You can . . . hang your hat on it or something."

The hand, fingers gently curved inward, wore a black leather glove, with the glove's twin loose in the box beside it, so that both hands would match in appearance. Curious, Martin peeled off the glove. The palm and fingers were realistically shaped, though obviously wrought of metal.

"Where did you get this?" Martin asked, eyes still on the hand, expression inscrutable.

Dixon swallowed, clearly concerned she had caused offense. "From a blacksmith whose forefathers were armorers to knights."

Her large eyes were wide and vulnerable as she awaited his reaction.

Finally, Martin laid his hand over hers and regarded her fondly. "Thank you, Susan. It is the most unusual gift I have ever received. And the most thoughtful."

Mariah was touched, amused, and simultaneously saddened by the sweet scene. How she wished Maggie were there to see it. How she wished Matthew were there as well.

But Captain Bryant had been gone for three days without a single word. She told herself it was foolish to worry about Isabella Forsythe. But what else could be keeping him away? *Merciful Father, help me not to fear. I know you have forgiven me and Matthew has forgiven me. Help me to forgive myself. I am certain there must be a reasonable explanation for his absence. Please grant me peace until he returns or I shall go mad!*

Mr. Hart, Lizzy, and George were gone as well. Gone to the coast to meet Mr. Hart's mother. She wished them well.

And all the while she prayed for Maggie, wherever she was.

My friends are my estate.

—Emily Dickinson

chapter 40

They had planned to wait until Captain Bryant's return, thinking his authority might sway Mrs. Pitt more than the small influence any of them might wield. But when a week had passed with no word from him, they decided to wait no longer to speak with her about Captain Prince.

Considering Mrs. Pitt's dislike of Mariah, Jeremiah Martin strapped on his new hand and commissioned himself to confront the poorhouse matron. Dixon, Mariah noticed, watched him go with possessive pride gleaming in her blue eyes.

He returned three quarters of an hour later, alone, his face flushed from the exertion of the walk, or the encounter, or both.

"Well?" Dixon asked as Martin joined the two anxious ladies at the kitchen table.

"I shall tell you everything," Martin said, and delivered a detailed account worthy of an Aubrey theatrical.

"I walked in and announced in my most officious manner, 'I am Jeremiah Martin, secretary to the late Francesca Prin-Hallsey.' "

Secretary? Mariah thought. She supposed *manservant* would not sound as official.

Martin continued, "I said, 'It has come to my attention that you are holding one Percival Prin-Hallsey, known as Captain Prince, who is heir and rightful master of Windrush Court. I am here to demand his immediate release.' "

"You didn't. . . ." Dixon breathed.

Mariah was impressed by his courage. Or audacity.

Martin nodded. "She merely stared at me, so I said, 'I can produce all the proof you—or the undersheriff—might like. Including records of the annual sum paid you to keep the man against his will.'

" 'Against his will?' the imperious woman said. 'The man you refer to comes and goes as he pleases and always has. If he is who you say he is, why has he not bothered to take himself across the road and demand his rightful place, as you call it, before now?'

"It was a fair question. I explained that Frederick Prin-Hallsey had told his brother he'd been declared legally incompetent to inherit, so he thought he had nowhere else to go.

"Mrs. Pitt insisted that he *is* incompetent, but I said, 'I think not. Confused and forgetful, perhaps, but no worse than the average man his age. At all events, there is no record of him being declared anything but dead, and that charge, madam, we shall have no trouble refuting. I can involve the undersheriff and solicitors, if you prefer . . . ?'

"She glared but did not challenge me. Instead she said, 'If he leaves here, he will not be welcomed back should he—or anyone else—change his mind. Do I make myself clear? Even when you realize he is not fit to be master of anything, and in need of a place to live, he will not be allowed to return. Not as long as I am matron.'

"It gave me pause, I own. For the captain is not the man he once was. But I held my ground, thinking if he needed care or even supervision, I, or another caretaker, might be hired to do so, allowing him to live in the comfort of his family home."

"Very true," Dixon said, nodding her approval.

"I likely should not have said what I said next. But hearing her deride noble Captain Prince so coldly, her wafer-thin lip curled, I could not help myself. I said, 'Perhaps, madam, you shall not be matron here very much longer, should the board of guardians, or the newspapers, hear of your part in this.' "

Mariah gasped.

"You didn't. . . ." Dixon breathed again.

He shrugged. "She did not seem particularly troubled by it. She said, 'I had no part in *this*, as you say. Any arrangements made between the Prin-Hallsey family and Honora House were made with my late husband. I was not privy to the details and only kept the man as instructed.' "

"I wonder if it was wise to threaten that woman," Dixon said, "considering her power. Considering what she did to poor little Maggie." Her chin trembled.

Martin reached over and covered her hand with his own. There had been quite a lot of that of late, Mariah realized. She wondered if Martin had finally proposed.

Forcing her gaze away from the clasped hands, Mariah asked, "Did she agree to release him?"

"I did not ask." Martin's tone was matter-of-fact. "I told her we would be back in the morning to collect him."

"Oh dear," Dixon said. "What if he disappears before then? Is sent away, like Maggie?"

It was a possibility none of them wished to contemplate.

Early the next morning, Mariah accompanied Martin back to Honora House to find Captain Prince. Before they even reached the poorhouse, they saw him sitting outside on the bench with Agnes Merryweather. Relief filled Mariah at the sight. Clearly, he was no longer being confined to his room. Nor had he been sent away. It was an auspicious beginning.

But as they talked with him, the man was less than enthusiastic about quitting the place. He twisted his hands and said, "Do you think, Mr. Martin, it is wise for me to leave? I have been here so long. It is really all I know. The only home I remember clearly, save for those years with the Malagasy."

"I shall help you, Captain," Martin offered. "Be your right hand, if you like, until you are settled. There's naught to fear."

"But I know nothing of running an estate."

"There is a steward, a Mr. Hammersmith, to tend to that, sir."

The captain rubbed the scar at his temple. "I don't know. . . ."

Agnes, sitting ramrod straight, turned her stern gaze upon him. "Oh come, Percy," she all but scolded. "You were master and commander of the *Largos* and a crew of hundreds. What is one house and a gaggle of servants to a great man like you?"

In the end, Agnes and Martin were able to convince Captain Prince to at least walk over and see Windrush Court. While not ready to commit to leaving Honora House for good, he did agree to a brief call, *if* Miss Merryweather would go with him. Agnes said she would be honored to accompany the captain on his first visit to Windrush Court in nearly twenty years.

They informed the matron that they were only going for a stroll, not leaving per se, fearing the woman might do away with all of Captain Prince's possessions before they returned. Mrs. Pitt seethed but said nothing as they took their leave.

Agnes stepped out of Honora House dressed in hat and gloves for the outing. And though it was a mild mid-September day, she wore a bright red muffler around her neck—the one Amy had made for her long ago. Seeing it, Mariah's heart squeezed.

The captain offered his arm, but Agnes hesitated. She said briskly, "I am not an invalid, Captain, but thank you just the same."

They walked away from the poorhouse and across the road. Captain Prince eyed the gate as they headed toward the front door of the gatehouse. "Why can we not go through the gate, Miss Aubrey, instead of tramping through your house?"

"The gate has been locked for years, Captain," she said.

He lifted his chin. "Ah. Let me guess, ever since the old gatekeeper saw me on the roof. Probably reported it to my brother."

"Is that why?" Martin asked.

"I doubt such a thing could be a coincidence. Don't you?"

Martin nodded. "Indeed."

Passing through the gatehouse, they walked up the lane and along the curved drive to Windrush Court. Agnes, Mariah saw, was not frail as her sister had been, and kept up with the captain's smart stride with apparent ease.

"There it is, Agnes," Captain Prince said, gesturing toward the great house. "What do you think?"

"I have seen it before, a long time ago. But it is much grander than I recall."

"Do you think so? It is smaller than I recall." He winked at her, Mariah noticed, and Agnes's lip tightened.

Mariah feared Agnes might be offended, but when they reached the front steps of Windrush Court, Captain Prince again offered his arm, and this time Agnes took it without comment.

Dixon, Martin, and Mariah followed them as far as the portico. But before they could enter the house, hooves sounded in the distance. Mariah turned to see a pair of riders on horseback trotting in from the main gate, followed by a horse and carriage. She steeled herself. Captain Bryant had returned at last. Whom had he brought with him? Surely not Isabella Forsythe. Had his parents finally agreed to come? Or was he bringing another party of guests?

But as the figures drew closer, Mariah's chest tightened and her mouth grew slack.

Dixon appeared at her elbow. "Are you all right, Mariah?"

Mariah lifted her hand and pointed. Dixon followed her gaze and gasped, covering her mouth with her hand. Then she reached out and gripped Martin's arm with her free hand.

"What is it?" he asked, warmth and tender concern in his expression as his eyes roamed Susan Dixon's face.

She, too, pointed.

But Martin did not share their shocked silence. Instead he raised his hands—both of them—in triumph. He exclaimed, "It's Maggie! He's found her!" And jogged down the stairs.

For there, coming up the drive, were Captain Bryant on Storm, and little Maggie riding sidesaddle on a bay that reminded Mariah of her own beloved horse back home.

"Maggie!" Dixon ran down the stairs and across the verge so fast, she passed Martin. Seeing her, the little girl beamed and all but leapt off the horse and into Susan Dixon's waiting arms.

Martin reached them, lifting a hand to pat Maggie's shoulder. Maggie leaned toward him and wrapped her arms around Martin's neck even as Dixon held her, joining the three in a tangle of limbs and love.

Tears filled Mariah's eyes at the sight. *Thank you*, she breathed.

When Dixon set Maggie down, the little girl took Martin's new hand in hers, regarding it with smiles of surprise and delight.

Martin teased, "I asked for Miss Dixon's hand, and instead she gave me this one."

Dixon shook her head, tears sparkling in her eyes. "Oh, go on with you."

Mariah could feel Captain Bryant's eyes on her but, doubts and insecurities rising, avoided his gaze. She was afraid of what she might see in his dear brown eyes. Would there be cool distance there, where once had been warm intimacy? She had experienced such a startling reversal once before. But Captain Bryant was not James Crawford, she reminded herself.

The carriage pulled up, and Lizzy, George, and Mr. Hart waved to her from its window. How surprising that they should return at the same time as Captain Bryant.

As the three stepped down from the carriage, Mariah walked over and hugged Lizzy and asked about their trip. From Lizzy's blushing, happy face, it appeared the visit to Mrs. Hart had gone very well, a fact Mr. Hart was quick to confirm.

"Mother adores her."

"And I her." Lizzy glowed. "She's such a dear."

Captain Bryant walked over to join them, but Mariah excused herself to welcome Maggie home. She squeezed the little girl's hand and smiled into her cherubic face, hoping the few weeks of loneliness and deprivation would not leave their mark.

Behind Maggie, the horse she had ridden bent its head to nibble at the lawn. Startled, Mariah stared. The bay mare, her lithe chestnut body marked with black mane, tail, ears, and socks, was not only similar to Mariah's horse, it *was* her horse. Mariah's own beloved Lady. *How in the world . . . ?* Lady, released from her rider, ambled across the drive in search of taller grass or freedom.

Mariah followed her, calling softly and stretching out her hand.

The mare's ears tipped back, cautious, wary. Had she forgotten Mariah's voice after a year's absence? But then the graceful neck turned and the big long-lashed eyes regarded her. She snorted and sniffed as Mariah walked slowly forward, speaking in quiet, gentle tones. "Hello, my dear girl. How I have missed you. Will you come to me?"

Lady whinnied and tossed her head. She took a few steps toward Mariah, and Mariah's heart lifted in satisfaction. When the velvety whiskered muzzle whispered into her palm, Mariah smiled. With her other hand, she began stroking the sleek reddish-brown neck.

Matthew appeared on the other side of the horse, his eyes bright yet watchful, studying her reaction.

Mariah was glad to have Lady as a buffer between them. "How did you come by her?"

"Maggie, or your horse?" He gave a small grin.

"Both. I am overcome with curiosity."

"Martin discovered Maggie had been sent to the workhouse in Highworth."

"How did he learn that?"

Captain Bryant stroked the mare's forelock. "Captain Prince helped himself to Mrs. Pitt's records, I understand. We thought it best not to tell you and Miss Dixon in case nothing could be done."

She was too relieved to have Maggie back to argue this point. "They just gave her to you?"

"No, not initially. But my sister's husband, you see, is curate in Highworth. He is friendly with several members of that institution's board of governors. He arranged Maggie's release. Still, he warned it would take time. Meanwhile, I visited my parents and wrote to Hart, thinking if Miss Barnes joined us, Maggie might feel more at ease."

Their returning together had been no accident. "Very wise. But what must your parents have thought of all that coming and going?"

He nodded thoughtfully. "It is ironic. Nothing I have done or accomplished in my career has impressed my father. But for some reason, my mission to find and restore one little girl has." His voice thickened. "Even told me he was proud of me."

Mariah pressed a hand to her chest, wishing she might lay a hand on his arm instead. "Oh, Matthew. How wonderful."

Holding her gaze, he stepped around the horse. "As happy as I was to help Maggie, and of course Martin and Miss Dixon, I confess I did it for you."

Mariah drew in a painful breath.

He continued. "While I was waiting for Hart and Miss Barnes to join me, I traveled to Milton to see if I might purchase your horse."

"My father sold her to you?"

"Gave her."

Joy and incredulity warred within her. "I cannot believe it. Father agreed?"

"Yes, he gave his permission."

Permission. The word reminded her of Captain Bryant's long quest. "Did you . . . happen to call on the Forsythes while you were in Highworth?"

Tilting his head, he regarded her cautiously. "No, why should I?" He grimaced. "Did not Martin give you my message?"

"Yes, but only that you were gone on some manner of business to Highworth. Where the Forsythes' estate lies."

"Mariah, you did not think . . . ?"

"I tried not to. I was even successful at it. Most of the time."

He took Mariah's hand in both of his. "I went to Highworth only to find and return Maggie. The only lady's father I consulted was your own. His, the only permission I sought." He lifted her hand and pressed warm lips to her fingers. "And not only permission to restore Lady to you."

Mariah's heart bumped hard against her breast.

"Ahoy there, Captain Bryant!" Captain Prince hailed, waving from the portico.

Mariah felt awkward, realizing they had been about to visit the house Captain Bryant was still paying for and without his permission. She explained quickly, "Captain Prince hoped to tour the house after so many years away, but—"

"Of course," Matthew said easily.

"You do not mind?"

"Not at all."

Captain Prince came trotting down the steps, and the two men shook hands. "Captain Bryant. Never fear. Mr. Martin has told me of your lease. I will, of course, honor it. The place is yours until, what, the end of September?"

Mariah and Matthew exchanged a poignant, knowing look. They would have to tell the man about his scoundrel of a nephew. But not today.

After Hart and Lizzy stepped forward to greet the captain and

Miss Merryweather, Matthew suggested genially, "Why do we not all tour the house together?"

Everyone agreed.

They strolled through the soaring entry hall, little Maggie and George gazing up in wonder at the ornate ceiling and glittering chandelier. At the bottom of the grand staircase, Agnes Merryweather looked up and gasped, stopping where she stood. The others followed her gaze.

Mariah felt her own mouth gape. There at the first landing, where once had hung two portraits of Prin-Hallsey men, now hung three: Frederick, Hugh, and Percival.

She glanced at Martin, who gave her a knowing wink.

Silently, Agnes gripped the railing and slowly mounted the stairs. Standing on the landing, she studied the portrait of Captain Prince as a younger man. "Amy spoke often of how handsome you were," she said. "She was right."

The captain stepped up and stood beside her, while the others stayed below. He said, "I am very sorry Amy did not live to see this day. We might have all shared this occasion, even this house, had you liked."

Agnes dragged her gaze from the portrait. "Take no offense, Captain. But Amy has a far finer mansion now."

"I believe you are right." He smiled at her, his attention snagged by her red scarf. "I say, I like that muffler. Is it not very like the ones Miss Amy made?"

Agnes looked down at Mariah and their eyes locked. "Yes. Very like."

The captain offered Agnes his arm once more, and they companionably mounted the remaining stairs. With Lizzy, Mr. Hart, Martin, Dixon, and George, plus Maggie skipping alongside, they toured the boyhood and future home of Percival "Prince" Prin-Hallsey.

Mariah and Matthew brought up the rear of the party. They walked side by side, arms behind their respective backs, listening to the exclamations of Captain Prince as he extolled favorite rooms and recollected boyhood pranks within them.

Mariah tilted her head nearer Captain Bryant and whispered, "It was very kind of you, but I cannot accept Lady. I cannot afford to keep a horse."

He gave her a sidelong glance. "I can still manage that expense."

"But I cannot allow you to do so."

"Can you not consider it a wedding present?"

She stopped where she was and stared up at him, throat tight.

Glancing ahead at the others, Matthew took her arm and propelled her into the empty salon. "I love you, Mariah," he whispered. "Surely you know that."

A sprig of hope blossomed within her, but she remained silent. She waited as Matthew paused, thinking carefully before speaking. Outside, thunder grumbled. Rain began to *peck-peck* against the windowpanes.

He said, "My pursuit of Miss Forsythe did blind me for a time to my growing feelings for you. But my rogue heart decided you were the one it loved, despite my mind's best efforts to stay the course."

Gazing at her, his warm brown eyes lingered on her mouth. His voice took on the gentle urging tone Mariah had used with Lady. "How I have missed you, my dear girl. Will you forgive me for being such a fool?"

Throat too tight to speak, Mariah merely nodded.

The shadow left his face. The corners of his eyes crinkled. " 'I came here to win one woman, and instead am lost to another,' " he said, quoting a line from Simon Wells's play. "I . . ." He hesitated, lips pursed. "Will you . . ." He broke off with a wince and a huff. "Not here. Come with me."

He grasped her hand and pulled her to the door. Peeking out and seeing the touring party stepping into another chamber, Matthew tugged her arm.

"Matthew! What are you doing?" Mariah protested, but the truth was, she didn't care. She would follow him anywhere.

Together they skimmed down the stairs, across the hall, and out the front door. Heedless of the steady rain now falling, they raced down the curved drive. Mariah laughed, running hard to match his longer strides, already guessing his intention.

He did not stop until they reached the gatehouse, dashed through it, and flung open the front door. There, finally, he stopped. Holding on to one another's forearms, they stood, gasping, chests heaving, and tried to catch their breaths.

"I love you, Mariah Aubrey," Matthew said between pants. He cradled her face in his hands, eyes roving her features with a fiery possessiveness that thrilled her. His breath tickled her upper lip, and then his mouth touched hers with a feathery kiss. "I wanted to ask you here, where we first met. Will you marry me? Stay with me, wherever I go?"

He angled his head and pressed his lips to hers, kissing her firmly, deeply, passionately. Her heart ached with pleasure. Her knees threatened to give way. He released her only long enough to wrap both arms around her and hold her tightly to his chest. "Say you will."

For one uncertain moment, Mariah recalled her failures, and felt unworthy of such love. But then she thought once more of dear Amy Merryweather, fallen, yet redeemed at a great price by her "prince." Is that not what God had done for her? He had given all He had; had forgiven and loved her. And He was waiting for her to love Him in return.

Tears once more filled her eyes. Mariah's lip trembled, but she managed a wavering smile and breathless reply.

"I will."

epilogue

Captain Matthew Bryant and Miss Mariah Aubrey were married on a crisp late-October morning in the Whitmore village church.

After the service, they rode back to Windrush Court in an open, ribbon-festooned barouche, while the guests followed on foot, walking back to the estate for the wedding breakfast.

Reaching the gatehouse first, Matthew hopped down from the carriage and threw wide the gate. Captain Prince, in his first act as master of Windrush Court, had already dispatched the lock. Then Matthew climbed up once more, urged the horse into motion, and he and Mariah passed through the gate. There, so near where they had first met, Captain and Mrs. Bryant shared a lingering kiss while they awaited their guests.

A few minutes later, the first of them appeared. At the beginning of the procession were residents of the poorhouse, who best knew the way, led by George and Sam. Tears stung Mariah's eyes as she gazed in wonder at the cheerful parade. For each person from the poorhouse wore a bright red muffler—their sober church-going clothes transformed into cheerful garments by the colorful wraiths floating about their necks, made over the years by Amy Merryweather's hands, and reminiscent of her spirit.

Matthew looked at her and their gazes caught and held. Mariah's vision blurred with happy tears, but she blinked them away, not wanting to miss a single sight, a single face.

After a clutch of jovial poorhouse residents came two couples arm in arm—Lizzy and Mr. Hart, and Agnes Merryweather with Captain Prince. After them came John and Helen Bryant, followed by Mr. and Mrs. Strong, Mr. Phelps, and the vicar. And finally, Martin, Dixon, Maggie, and Mariah's brother, Henry. What delight to see so many dear, smiling faces pass through the gate. Matthew's sister and her husband had been prevented from coming because their child was due any day. Mariah would have loved for her own sister and parents to be there as well, but she refused to let their absence spoil her joy.

They feasted at long tables beneath autumn-red maples, laughed, told stories, and shared bittersweet memories of loved ones not present that day.

After the fine meal, of which even Martin approved, local musicians played, and at one point Martin and Maggie joined in—him on his three-fingered flute and Maggie raising her pure, stirring voice in song.

Then three people Mariah had not expected to see came through the gate, and her heart raced. Her mother, father, and Julia. Beside Mariah, Matthew gripped her trembling fingers and smiled reassurance.

Keeping a tight hold of his hand, Mariah walked with her new husband to greet her family after a separation of more than a year.

Julia rushed forward. "Mariah! I am so sorry we missed the wedding. The carriage lost a wheel, and the men took forever in repairing it."

Mariah pressed her hand. "That is all right. How pleased I am to see you now."

Julia's eyes sparkled. "I shall soon be a married woman too. Father has consented. Is that not good news?"

"Very good news."

Julia embraced her tightly and whispered near her ear. "Mother and I read both of your novels. We are so proud of you."

When Julia released her, their mother stepped forward, tears brightening her hazel eyes. "How beautiful you look, my dear." She leaned near and kissed Mariah's cheek. "I am very happy for you."

Fearfully, Mariah glanced next at her father, but he was looking at Matthew.

Mariah swallowed. "Father, I believe you have met Captain Matthew Bryant, my husband."

Sir Thomas nodded. "Yes. He came to see me not long ago, to ask my permission to marry you and to . . . make his opinion plain on several subjects."

"Thank you for coming, sir." Matthew held out his hand, and after a pause, Sir Thomas Aubrey shook it.

He then turned to his eldest daughter. "Mariah, I regret not only missing your wedding, but this last year of your life as well. I have treated you unfairly and hope you will forgive me."

Amy Merryweather's voice flitted through Mariah's mind. *"Whoever said life was fair?"* It gave her the courage to smile and say, "Of course I do."

Her father awkwardly patted her shoulder, the most affection Mariah could recall receiving from him, and she could not speak further for the hot tightness in her throat.

Theirs was not the only wedding that autumn.

William Hart and Lizzy married not long after Matthew and Mariah did. Sooner, perhaps, than they had planned, as their appointment depended on their being man and wife. The Harts had been chosen by the board of guardians as the new master and matron of Honora House. Mrs. Pitt had stepped down, whether to avoid recrimination over the Prince Prin-Hallsey affair or to accept an offer of marriage from the undersheriff, or both, no one knew for certain.

Captain P. Prin-Hallsey had settled into his role as long-overdue master of Windrush Court. He petitioned the navy for back pay, and in the meantime—not encumbered by gambling debts as was his wayward nephew—lived modestly but comfortably off the income from the estate.

When Captain Prince learned how his nephew had defrauded Matthew, he insisted on making recompense. He sold the London townhouse as a first step toward repaying the debt. Further, he drafted a will declaring Matthew Bryant his heir and the future owner of Windrush Court. Hugh, they later learned, was believed to be lodging in a shabby Cheapside inn.

Judging by the captain's many visits back to the poorhouse, it seemed clear he was intent on convincing Agnes Merryweather to marry him and share the manor house with him, to spend her remaining years in the comfort and companionship she deserved. So far, Agnes had refused his offer, though she did accept the captain's invitations to take a meal with him, or share an evening of tales and whist. Mariah had never seen the woman look so happy and hoped the captain would prevail.

That year's final wedding, a Christmas wedding, was that of Jeremiah Martin and Susan Dixon. Maggie and Mariah attended the bride, the dearest and most beautiful bride Mariah had ever seen. Martin, too, looked dapper. He wore a new suit and renewed confidence now that he was writing again, thanks to Mr. Crosby's—and Dixon's—persuasion. Soon, the *Golden Prince* would set sail once more.

After that last wedding, Captain and Mrs. Bryant took their leave of Windrush Court. As they drove away, Mariah looked back and saw little Maggie Martin standing before the gatehouse, waving a fond farewell. Despite the season, she wore a youthful springtime hat that had lain in the attic long enough. Martin and Dixon requested to raise the girl as their own, and both Maggie and the governors heartily agreed. How glad Mariah was to know that there would be a girl in the gatehouse for years to come.

Matthew and Mariah were bound for a delayed wedding trip to Italy, and who knew what adventures beyond—for she could write anywhere, could she not? This was only the beginning.

author's note

Jane Austen fans will recognize her influence in this book. For example, one of my favorite Austen heroes, Captain Wentworth of *Persuasion*, inspired the background of my Captain Bryant—along with a dash of Forester's Horatio Hornblower. More significantly, I was moved by Austen's Maria Bertram, who "destroyed her own character" and was sent away with a sole companion to "an establishment being formed for them in another country—remote and private."

Of course in *Mansfield Park*, we do not admire vain and adulterous Maria Bertram, and most readers likely feel she earned her just deserts. But what if Maria (pronounced "Mariah" in Jane Austen's day) were a character we actually cared about? Would we be content to leave her in her lonely exile? As someone who has made her share of mistakes in life, I am thankful for forgiveness and second chances. And I enjoyed giving Mariah Aubrey hers as well.

Mariah is a secret author, as Jane Austen was during her lifetime. Many authors (female and male alike) published anonymously or under pseudonyms in the eighteenth and nineteenth centuries. Jane Austen published her novels "by a lady" or "by the author of" one of her previous novels. In some cases, the identity of anonymous authors remains unknown.

In chapters 8 and 12, I have borrowed two brief excerpts from one of these novels, entitled, *The Corinna of England, and a Heroine in the Shade: a Modern Romance,* by the Author of *The Winter in Bath*. It was published anonymously in two volumes in 1809 by London-based B. Crosby and Co. The identity of the author is still being debated. (Source: Chawton

House Library.) Except, of course, for *Aesop's Fables*, all other excerpts and journal entries are of my own creation.

Also, in chapter 21, I sprinkled in a few actual reviews of Jane Austen's novels from the time of their release. It ought to make writers everywhere feel better to know that even Miss Austen received the occasional snide review.

I enjoyed researching the lives of early women authors like Maria Edgeworth, Charlotte Lennox, Fanny Burney, and of course Jane Austen. There are many sources available should you want to read more. I also enjoyed learning a bit about publishing in the early nineteenth century. In reality, typesetting, printing, and binding books was a lengthy process before computers and modern printing presses. But for the sake of the story, I compressed these timelines.

On a maritime research note, I should mention two things. First, the war was not actually over, as my characters believed. Napoleon escaped his first exile in early 1815, and the war resumed. After Napoleon's defeat at Waterloo, he was again exiled, and the war officially ended later that year. Second, Captain Joseph McCulloch did not propose the Coast Blockade Service until 1815, the year after this story concludes. The service came into being the following year. I hope history buffs will forgive the liberties I took to include it in the story.

The gatehouse pictured on the cover is the very one I had in mind while writing this novel. In reality, it is located at Deene Park, Northamptonshire, once the country residence of Lord Cardigan, the "Homicidal Earl" who led the Charge of the Light Brigade. My sincere thanks to designer Jennifer Parker for another beautiful cover.

As always, I would like to acknowledge the help and encouragement of my family, church family, friends, co-workers, first reader Cari Weber, and my editor Karen Schurrer. Many thanks to Jeff Beech-Garwood, Matthew Camp, Bill Kelley, and author Laurie Alice Eakes for helping with historical (and cricket!) details. Also to Cheri Hanson for help with the Malagasy language. Lastly, warm gratitude goes to my readers, who send the most uplifting e-mails. I appreciate you all.

discussion questions

1. Had you known that Jane Austen's name never appeared in her books during her lifetime? Did it surprise you that novel writing was considered (at least by some) improper and unladylike? In what ways might those attitudes continue today?

2. Mariah's situation (sent away after an indiscretion to live in relative isolation) was loosely based on the fate of one of Jane Austen's characters in *Mansfield Park* (although Maria Bertram was a married woman who had an affair). Did you think Mariah Aubrey's father treated her unfairly? How have attitudes toward "virtue and vice" changed since the early 1800s?

3. Did you learn anything new from the historical quotes at the beginning of each chapter? What quote in particular did you like? Why?

4. Did you figure out the mystery of Captain Prince early on? What about the "treasure" of the gatehouse? Did you spot any red herrings (false clues) that led you to believe there might be real treasure (say, jewels or gold) in the gatehouse?

5. Captain Bryant spent many years trying to gain his father's approval. Can you relate? How so? What makes father/child relationships so important?

6. Did you find yourself growing fond of any character that you did not care for at the outset? Which character was your favorite? Why?

7. What was your reaction to Amy Merryweather's red yarn as a symbol of our life to come? (As a reminder, she said, "Don't hold on to the knots and forget the life ahead.") Have you had to get past knots in your own life?

8. Mariah did not blame God for her problems, but she no longer felt worthy of His love. Have you or someone you've known had difficulty embracing forgiveness? How did that affect your relationships and/or self-esteem?

9. Go back and read the first two words and the last two words of the book. Any thoughts on why the author may have chosen them?

10. If you could ask the author one question, what would it be? (Note: Feel free to e-mail any such questions to *julie@julieklassen.com* and she will do her best to answer them.)

about the author

JULIE KLASSEN loves all things Jane—*Jane Eyre* and Jane Austen. She is a fiction editor and novelist. Her book *The Silent Governess* won a 2010 Christy Award and was also a finalist in the Minnesota Book Awards, *ForeWord Reviews* Book of the Year Awards, and the RITA Awards. Julie is a graduate of the University of Illinois. She and her husband have two sons and live in St. Paul, Minnesota.

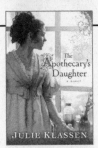